SIN OF SILENCE

Sinner's Empire Book 1

NIKITA SLATER

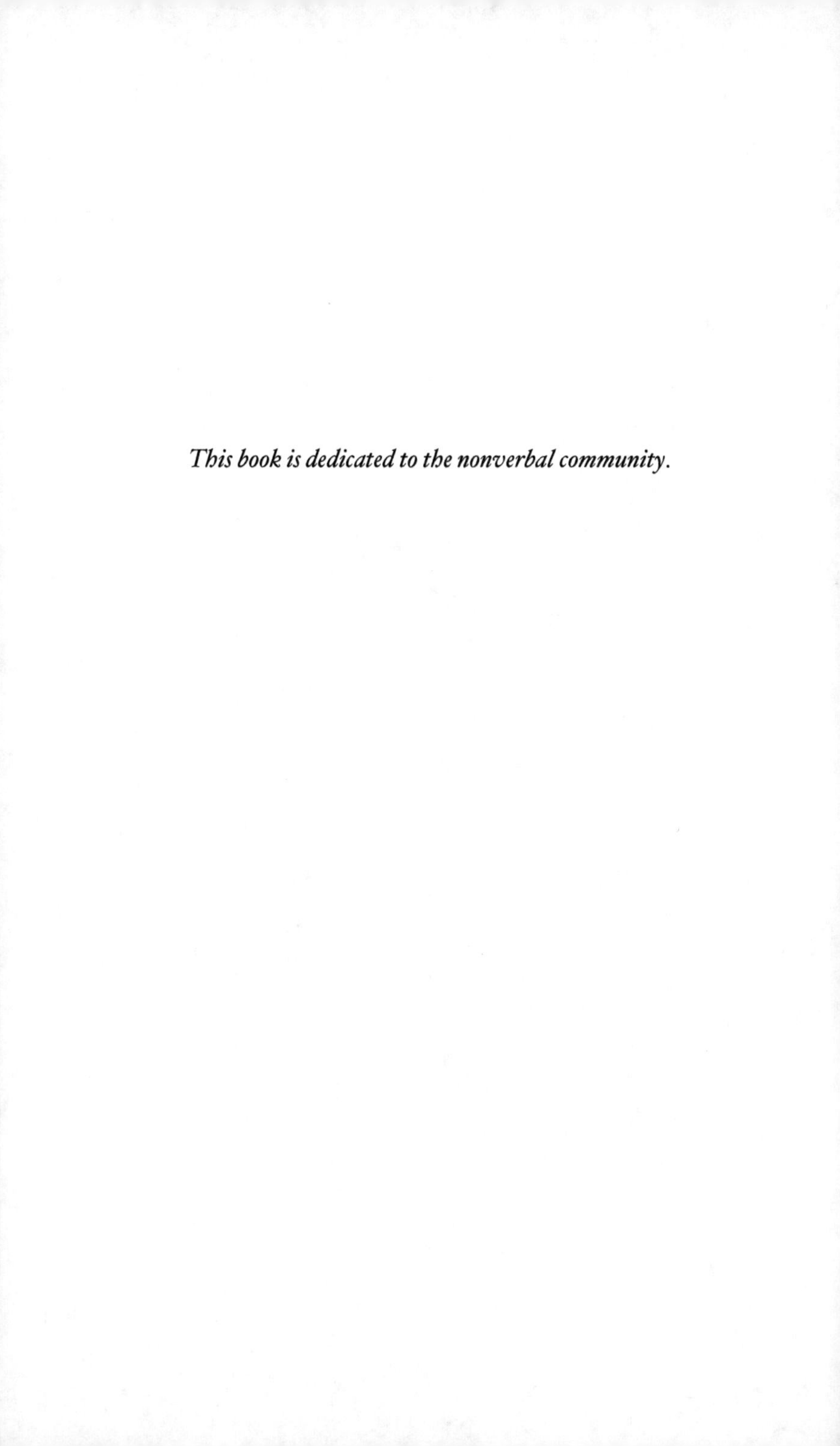

This book is dedicated to the nonverbal community.

AUTHOR'S NOTE

Dear readers,

Sin of Silence is the first book in the Sinner's Empire trilogy, which follows the romance of Shaun and Jozef. The second book will release on February 27th, 2021, and the third book will release in Spring 2021.

In Sin of Silence there is a character who is non-verbal and uses sign language to communicate. Over the course of a year, I researched methods of non-verbal communication, specifically sign languages. As sign language doesn't mirror spoken language, my intent was to be as authentic as possible. However, I quickly discovered that translating sign language onto the page is very difficult, especially for someone without a background in signing. The word order can be confusing, and the grammar is different from spoken language. I made the decision to go with flow over a straight translation, which is why the signed conversations in this book resemble spoken conversations.

There are many wonderful aspects to sign language that I would love to share with you, but that would be an entire book in itself (and probably is!). Instead, I will leave you with this; there are different sign languages throughout the world, and many are incomprehensible to each other. Our heroine, Shaun, is from Quebec, Canada where Quebec Sign Language, known in French as Langue dis signes québécoise (LSQ), is the predominant sign language used in francophone Canada. Jozef, our hero/antihero, lives in the Czech Republic where French Sign Language (FSL) is the official sign language. LSQ is related to FSL, so Shaun and Jozef would be able to understand one another. For ease of storytelling I refer mainly to FSL.

I hope you enjoy Sin of Silence!
Sincerely,
Nikita Slater

CHAPTER ONE

Jozef marked the woman for pickup, pointing to where she stood. Alone, vulnerable, and fragile against a backdrop of ruined concrete and military tents.

Havel's eyes followed. Once he caught sight of her, a frown wrinkled his thick brows. He wasn't comfortable with what they were about to do. It bothered him. Though it shouldn't. He'd snatched plenty of people in his time, cut them up too, and shot some of them. Why this one woman should bother him was beyond Jozef.

"You sure?" Havel asked quietly, his eyes following her as she finished her break, stood up and stretched, arching her back and tipping her head from side to side, loosening tight muscles. Then she reentered the tent building she'd exited ten minutes before.

Jozef grunted an affirmative.

He wanted to follow her, to watch her while she worked. Those elegant fingers, touching her patients, healing them. She was a goddess. Striking and beautiful in a sea of ugly. Amidst the ruins of what used to be a permanent hospital, now a bombed-out shell, she was a thing of true beauty. Since the area was still considered central to the war efforts, the military had decided they would rebuild a makeshift hospital on top of the old one. She was foreign, she didn't belong in Ukraine. She was providing medical assistance to those caught up in the war. It was almost a shame to mark her.

She was the best he could find. Unlikely to have family or friends in the area, no one to miss her. She would disappear as quietly as she arrived. Others would assume she went home, back to wherever she came from. Her family back home would believe she'd keen killed here. It wasn't a perfect plan, but it would work for as long as they needed her.

Jozef would force her to help them, to heal the man who had information about his uncle's abduction. Jozef's uncle, Krystoff Koba, head of the Czech Koba crime family, had been taken from his vehicle in downtown Kiev by armed mobsters while visiting a family friend. The kidnappers were demanding a token ransom, but Jozef suspected deeper motives. His uncle ran a vast and complex crime syndicate; he was king of his empire. A hard man to deal with for everyone except his close family members. Once out of favour, always out of favour, and the man who took Krystoff had fallen from favour years ago. The war in Ukraine further complicated an already strained relationship.

Revenge was not the motive or Krystoff would've been killed in the street in a brutal and bloody statement of might. No, the person responsible for Krystoff's abduction wanted something else, something valuable. Jozef needed to know the motive, needed to play the game carefully. He didn't need the kidnapper getting jumpy and murdering his uncle. He also didn't want the other Vory finding out. Jozef needed to get his uncle back and figure out what the fuck was going on, especially since the only person who could possibly gain from Krystoff's death was Jozef, and Jozef sure as fuck hadn't taken the old man.

While Jozef and his team made plans to infiltrate their enemy's territory, Jozef's brutally intelligent aunt, Krystoff's wife, was distracting the kidnappers with promises of wealth and trade deals. Dasha would dangle them on the line until Jozef was ready to make his move. With any other woman, Jozef might worry about her giving away the game. But not Aunt Dasha. She would hold onto her icy poise even as the rival family mailed pieces of her husband's body to her.

So far, they had only mailed a finger, the small one, cut at the knuckle. It was a clean cut and had obviously bled, indicating Krystoff was alive when the finger was removed. After a brief discussion with his aunt, Jozef had made his way into Ukraine, close to the front lines of the war on the Russian border. He hunted until he found the weasel who'd sent the package to Aunt Dasha; a shopkeeper by the name of Gustav, who had a good side hustle mailing objects of a sensitive nature.

Unfortunately, Gustav had collapsed under interrogation before giving up any information he might have had on the person who hired him to send the finger. Now the man was in a basement, in an abandoned village outside the city of Luhansk. Terek was with him, making sure he wouldn't slip away while Jozef and Havel picked up a doctor. The man was refusing to speak. If he died, they would lose their only lead to finding Krystoff.

Jozef stared at the door she went through. He needed a doctor. A woman would be easier to capture. No family on that continent, easier to get rid of when they were done with her. She was the one Jozef wanted.

CHAPTER TWO

"Mom, I'm fine, really."

Shaun took a long thirsty gulp of water before hurriedly wiping her mouth and putting the bottle back in the fridge. She flexed her shoulder blades, wincing a little at the crackling sound and the tight, pinched feeling in her neck. She was on day three of a four-day twelve-hour rotation. She shook her head. It wasn't like she stuck to her working hours. She worked when there was work to be done, and she went back to her tiny boarding room when she could no longer stand up and keep her eyes open.

"I read in the news that there was a bombing close to the hospital last night. Did you hear it?" Fatima asked anxiously over the phone.

Shaun frowned in concentration. She tried to get her tired brain to remember if anything had happened the evening before. Usually after long shifts she would go home and eat a quick, cold meal, take a lukewarm shower with appalling water pressure then pass out until her next shift began.

Still, she had to reassure her mother. It was the only way to keep Fatima sane while her daughter willingly ventured into the hearts of war zones. "No, Mom, it was nowhere near here. Trust me, I'd have noticed if a bomb went off near the hospital. We're not all that close to the front lines, and the town is no longer being targeted."

Shaun was telling the truth. Partly. It was true that the hospital wasn't a target, but it was located closer to the front lines than Shaun knew her mother would be comfortable with. Luhansk, or Luhansk People's Republic, was rebel-held, which automatically made the area more dangerous. The government couldn't step in to provide law and order in the now lawless, rebel-held no-man's-land.

"I hate that you aren't safe at home."

"I know, and I'm sorry, but this is what I need to be doing." They'd had the same conversation dozens of times, almost without deviation. It was pointless, but Shaun understood her mother's need to express her fear. "How's your garden doing? Are the sunflowers taller than you yet?"

Fatima perked up and chatted about her garden for a few minutes, giving Shaun a chance to eat her snack of almonds and fruit before she got back to her rounds.

Doctors were scarce in that part of Ukraine, having been killed in the fighting or fleeing to safer areas as the war advanced, taking down entire cities in the process. Doctors Without Borders came in to help manage the humanitarian crisis on the front lines. Shaun, a neurosurgeon, had been called in from her home city of Montréal, Quebec, Canada, along with two American nurses and a Brazilian radiologist. They worked alongside the skeleton crew of hospital staff who had elected to stay behind.

The hours were long, the accommodations were awful, and the future was uncertain, but being part of the Doctors Without Borders team was one of the most fulfilling things Shaun had done with her life. She'd put herself through med school, she'd put her time in at the bottom of the pond in order to pay off student loans, and now she was free to pursue her passion: providing medical care to people in need – people in desperate situations. Additionally, Doctors Without Borders was a chance to immerse herself in another country, culture and language. It was fulfilling on so many levels.

Shaun listened to her mother for a few more minutes, most of the conversation happening on Fatima's side.

"Mom, I have to get back to work. Give Fitzy a kiss for me."

Fatima laughed. "Only if I want my throat cut. That cat lives for you alone."

Shaun smiled as she thought of her giant ornery orange tabby.

"Thanks for taking him for me." Shaun blinked away tears as a wave of homesickness hit her. "Love you both."

"Love you too," Fatima said before hanging up.

Shaun had barely tucked her phone away when the door flung open. She jumped and turned as it banged into the wall.

"Doctor Patterson, oh thank goodness." A harassed looking Janet, an American nurse, rushed into the break room. Her blond hair, which had been in a tight ponytail that morning, was now frizzing around her head. Her eyes were red-rimmed from fatigue. She'd only been in the camp for a few weeks, but she would get used to the long brutal hours. Shaun was on her fourth month.

Shaun straightened her shoulders, shaking off her exhaustion and putting on her professional face. "What do you need?"

"Asthma attack in emergency, bed four. 10-year-old male presenting with shallow breathing, coughing and wheezing. He's not getting enough oxygen. He's starting to turn blue."

Shaun strode out of the room, Janet running to keep up with her.

"How long has the attack been going on for?" Shaun asked.

"It started about an hour before he arrived, according to his mother. It's been 20 minutes since he was first examined."

"Where is Doctor Zelensky?" One of the local doctors was supposed to be covering emergency.

Janet shrugged and pressed her arm against a door, flipping it open so they could walk through. "Yolanda thinks he went to do a house call. Someone who can't be moved."

"Okay," Shaun said. "I'll have a quick look, but we may have to intubate. Is the mother calm?"

"No." Janet shook her head. "Almost as hysterical as I felt when I couldn't find you."

Shaun smiled grimly. "I'll need you to get her out of the exam room and have someone join me for the procedure. Danilo is on desk, so send him in. The patient may need to be held, depending on his level of alertness."

It turned out the child was no longer responsive when they arrived. Janet rushed the mother out of the room and Danilo, one of the local nurses, stayed to help. Shaun carefully intubated the boy and then gradually filled his lungs with air, essentially breathing for him through a plastic tube.

"Pulse returning to normal," Danilo said from where he stood across from her.

She nodded and began to relax. The boy would live. His mother should move him out of the city. Too much dust and debris floating in the air from the bombings. This wasn't the only case of acute and severe asthma Shaun had seen. In fact, it was becoming more and more common for people to wander in complaining of breathing problems, whether they were asthmatic or not.

"Please get a box of the Prednisone," she told Danilo. "I'll watch him for a few minutes, then we can invite his mom to come back in and show her how to administer the steroid."

He nodded and left while Shaun turned back to the table. Scared blue eyes looked up at her, surprisingly sharp considering the ordeal he'd gone through. He must be utterly exhausted. She smiled big for him, forcing her lips to stretch into a grin. Even if she wasn't feeling it on the inside, she would pretend for his sake. He deserved a smile until he could see his mom again.

"You're doing great... kiddo," she said in stumbling Ukrainian, realizing she had no idea what his name was. Usually the nurse told her when giving her a rundown of the symptoms. They'd forgotten in their rush to get him breathing again.

The boy blinked up at her.

She continued to smile and dropped her hand to squeeze his shoulder.

Then his eyes moved past her to settle on something behind her.

Shaun turned her head slowly, intuition lifting the hairs on her neck, telling her to drop to the ground, to run, to scream. Something in the child's expression told Shaun that there was a threat standing right behind her.

Sure enough, when she turned her head, she found herself staring down the barrel of a gun. A loud gasp flew from her lips. Her eyes followed the length of the gun to the gloved hand holding it. A man's hand, a leather glove. Pale skin, tattoos between the edge of his glove and the cuff of his leather jacket. They reappeared from beneath the collar of his shirt and wound their way up his neck. They were both barbaric and beautiful, completely out of place in the hospital.

The man had dark hair, cut close to his scalp. He wore sunglasses so she couldn't see his eyes, but the set of his face told her everything. Prominent cheekbones, sharp wide jawline, and thin, cruel lips with a scar slashing right through the middle, as though someone had tried to cut his mouth.

She was going to die.

She closed her eyes, deciding to take a moment to come to peace with her destiny. She was okay with dying, even expected it to some extent, given the places she chose to work, but she was sad about the child. Wished she could shield him, from both the danger of a gunman in the hospital and the trauma of seeing her killed.

Pain burst through her cheek and her eyes flew open, her hand automatically coming up to touch her face where he hit her with the gun. She winced. It hurt, but nothing was broken and there was no blood. Tears filled her eyes and she stared at the man who was threatening her. The gun was still trained on her, the sunglasses staring blankly down at her. He was tall. So was Shaun, at almost six feet, she could stand toe to toe with most men. Not this this guy; he was three or four inches taller.

"What do you want?" she asked, her voice shaky.

He jerked his head to the door. Her eyes followed, and he nodded, waving the gun, indicating she should walk out ahead of him. Comprehension hit and she shook her head. "No," she said, stepping back. She wouldn't leave with him. She wasn't that stupid.

He stiffened, then shifted his arm, his shoulder flexing beneath the supple leather of his coat. He trained the gun on the bed, on the boy. Shaun moved to stand between the child and the gun. He'd have to shoot her to get to the boy. He lowered the gun a few inches and waved it at the door again.

What was he trying to say, and why didn't he just tell her what he wanted?

He took a threatening step toward her and impatiently reached up to drag the sunglasses off his face. She stared, her heart pounding in terror. Without them, he should look more human, but he didn't. His eyes were a startling deep blue, so dark they looked almost black, like the bottom of a frozen lake. He shoved his sunglasses in his jacket pocket and took hold of her arm in a painful grip. He gave her a shake and waved the gun, first at the boy, then back toward the door.

"You want me to go with you?" she asked breathlessly.

His eyes seemed to darken and he nodded, jerking his head again. She really didn't want to leave the room with him, but she couldn't allow him to shoot the child either. Maybe if she went with him, she could reason with him once they were away from other people.

"Okay," she whispered. "Let's go."

"I couldn't find the prednisone, but we have..." Danilo walked into the room holding a bottle in his hand. When he caught sight of the man and the gun he stopped, his back against the door as it swung shut behind him. "Doctor Patterson?"

Her name was the last thing he said as a bullet went through his right eye, killing him on the spot. His body was still falling when the gunman dragged Shaun forward, forcing her to step over her dead colleague and out into the hallway. She twisted around to look behind her, catching the wide, terrified eyes of the boy, now sitting up in his bed and staring after them.

"You killed him!" Shaun yelled, yanking on the arm he was holding tightly.

He swung her into a wall, which shook ominously when her weight hit it. The whole structure was nearly as thin as carboard, meant to come down and go up quickly and easily. She would be a lot more than winded if he'd just thrown her into a real wall. He was much bigger than her and he was using his strength to force her compliance.

"Shaun – "

Shaun looked over, her head moving against the wall.

Janet was rushing down the hall toward them, heedless of the gun coming up toward her. Shaun threw herself against his arm, knocking his aim to the side. A bullet slammed through the opposite wall; the bullet meant for Janet. He shoved Shaun away from him and brought his arm back up, but Janet had flung herself into one of the exam rooms. Instead of going after her, he took Shaun's arm again and hauled her against his side, running with her down the hall.

He was after her specifically it would seem. He could have grabbed someone from the reception area if he wanted any medical professional. Instead he'd gone to the trouble of searching her out in the hospital, putting himself and everyone else at risk. They rounded a corner where a patient was standing in the hallway.

"Get back!" Shaun screamed, not wanting him to get shot.

The man took one look and ducked out of the way.

They hurtled through the hospital at such a dizzying pace that Shaun lost track of where she was until they were standing outside, the sky a bright blur above them. She tried to look around, figure out what was happening, but her captor wrapped an arm around her middle, picked her up off the ground and flung her toward a white paneled van. Someone else grabbed her and dragged her inside.

She managed to let out one more scream before the gunman jumped in the back of the van, slammed the door shut and brought his hand down on the driver's shoulder. The driver nodded his acknowledgment and the van started moving. The gunman turned back to look at her. She curled her legs protectively underneath herself and pressed her spine against the metal panel. The look on his face was a weird mix of satisfaction and despair.

CHAPTER THREE

Oh god, they weren't blindfolding her or anything, which meant they didn't care if she saw where they were driving. They didn't care if she saw their faces. Which probably meant that they weren't planning on letting her live.

Despair, fear and anger rushed through her. She didn't want to die. She was only thirty-four; she'd finally managed to claw her way out from under a mountain of student loan debt. She was widely considered one of the world's most up and coming neurosurgeons, at the head of her field in successfully using cutting-edge technology during surgery. She wasn't ready to lose all that.

"Where are you taking me?" she asked, trying and failing to keep the fear from her voice.

Her captor glanced at her, his cold gaze sweeping her briefly before turning away. He was sitting on a bench across from her, his elbows on his knees, his body tilted toward the men in the seats at the front. He looked completely composed, as though murdering a nurse and kidnapping a doctor from a hospital was an everyday event for him.

"Please," she tried again. "Talk to me. Tell me why you did

this? Are you looking for ransom? Is someone hurt? Do you need a doctor?"

Nothing in his face indicated he was listening.

She tried appealing to the men up front, inching her way toward them, glancing over their shoulders to get a better look at her kidnappers. She hadn't been able to see much during the hectic moments when she was dragged into the van. Her heart sank as she peeked at them. They looked almost as scary as the man who had taken her... the man who shot Danilo in the face.

A wave of nausea hit her and she pressed her hand against her stomach to keep it from climbing up her throat and spewing out of her mouth. She felt grief for Danilo, a young man killed in the prime of his life, and a nearly overwhelming fear for herself. The man who'd grabbed her was not afraid to kill, and he seemed to be in charge. Whatever they were kidnapping her for, once her usefulness ended, she would die.

"Please help me," she begged, her eyes on the man who'd grabbed her, but her appeal aimed at the men in the front seat.

The passenger twisted around and shot her a glare. "Shut up and sit back."

He spoke English with a thick accent she couldn't place, but she didn't think it was local. She'd been surrounded by Ukrainians for months; this man was different. From some other Eastern European country.

"Please, I don't know why I was taken," Shaun pleaded. "I think you have the wrong person."

"You a doctor?" he demanded, his cool brown eyes on her. This man was also tattooed, all over his neck, hands and face.

"Yes." There was no point in keeping it from them. She was wearing scrubs and a name tag that gave away her identity as Dr. Shaun Patterson, attending physician. She had been in the hospital in the middle of a procedure. All she needed was a stethoscope around her neck to finish the picture.

"Then we got the right person," he grunted, turning back around, dismissing her.

So, they were definitely after a doctor. She didn't know if this information made her position better or worse. She could maybe use their need for a doctor as leverage, but she'd have to figure out what the situation was first. Maybe they had another captive they needed her to care for, or maybe one of their own was shot. That seemed pretty likely, given the brief glimpse she already had into their lives.

Shaun fell silent as the men drove. There wasn't much she could say. She knew enough to recognize that these men were likely organized crime. They didn't look like regular thugs. At least, not the guy who grabbed her from the hospital. He had a regal air about him. He held his head up and his shoulders back. The way he walked and the hardness in his face spoke of pride and arrogance. He was dressed meticulously, and he was quick, in his actions and thoughts. He wasn't stupid.

The van took so many twists and turns that she couldn't keep track of where they were going. It sped along at a fast clip despite the debris that littered the city streets from a series of rockets that had been launched into the city months ago, making it close to uninhabitable. When the bumpy road grew smoother, she started to wonder if they were leaving the city.

She tried to crawl up onto her knees to look through the windshield. The man sitting across from her moved so swiftly, she didn't have a chance to do more than flinch when he reached for her. He gripped her shoulder, his long, gloved fingers digging into her delicate bones. Pain radiated through her and she gasped, trying to lurch away from him.

He continued to hold her, staring down at her with those eerie lake-blue eyes. It was like he was speaking to her without speaking to her, telling her to sit down and shut up. To not move. When he lifted his arm and pointed at the back of the van, she followed his wordless order without question. She crawled away from him, badly wanting to escape his presence.

She sat on the floor near a piece of rug and some boxes, dragged her knees up and rested her arms on top of them. She refused to look at him again, though she could see him settle back down out of her periphery. She wanted to scream and demand to know where she was going but she was too scared. These men were responsible for one death and a kidnapping that she knew of, and she didn't want to provoke them.

They drove for about twenty more minutes before coming to a bumpy stop. Shaun tensed and watched the men as they opened doors and slid from the van. The boss thug gestured at her to come forward. She shook her head and slid as far back as she could. Oh god, were they going to kill her here? Were they making some kind of political statement by snatching a foreign doctor and killing her?

"No, please," she begged, cringing against the door.

He growled something incomprehensible and lunged toward her, catching her wrist and dragging her toward the door. He didn't give Shaun a chance to find her footing, so she stumbled and landed hard on her knees in the van. He yanked her viciously out the door and let go of her wrist, allowing her to fall to the ground. She stared up at her tormentor, but he reached down, grabbed her arm and pulled her to her feet, then yanked her toward an old house.

She frantically looked around, searching for help, trying to figure out where she was. There were only a couple of buildings visible in her field of vision, otherwise just a bunch of hills and empty fields. She opened her mouth to scream out, to call for help, but quickly found herself facing the barrel of a gun. She slammed her lips together and tried to breathe through the terror as her vision narrowed to that one point.

She tried to reassure herself as she was pulled into the dank, windowless stone house. He didn't need to bring her all this way just to kill her. He could've killed her at the hospital, like he'd killed Danilo. They obviously needed a doctor. She just needed to play along until she found a chance to get away from them.

She was rushed through a corridor, then down a flight of old wooden stairs to the basement. The air became noticeably cooler, and she shivered and blinked after stepping into a large, empty room, attempting to see in the gloom. She turned to her captor, her heart pounding. Was this place going to become her prison? Her grave? Why would they bring her here?

He snapped his fingers and pointed impatiently past her shoulder. She glanced back, and realized they weren't alone. There was a human-shaped bundle of rags on the ground. She stared at it for a few seconds, then took a tentative step forward, the doctor in her both curious and worried. If there was an injured person there, she would have no choice but to try to help them.

The stench of urine became strong as she approached warily. She dropped to her knees next to the bundle, realizing right away that she was correct, there was a person underneath the dirt, blood and torn clothes. She glared up at her captor before turning her attention to the man on the floor. She did her best to assess his injuries both visually and with her hands. He was still breathing, though his breaths were shallow. His pulse was weak but erratic and there was a blue tinge to his lips.

"You want me to attend this man?" she asked without looking up, her fingers flying over his injuries, while her brain assessed what she would need to heal him. She checked his circulation, airway and breathing. "It looks like he might be suffering from cardiac arrest, but I can't know for sure without the proper equipment. He's going to need the hospital. We need to transport him right away."

Her captor grabbed hold of her head and wrenched it around until she was forced to look at him, his fingers biting painfully into her chin. She tried to scramble backwards, but his grip was so painfully tight that she had no choice but to sit still. He pointed at her, pointing two fingers to indicate her eyes, then he pointed at himself.

He let her chin go and stepped back.

"Y-you want me to watch you?" Was it possible that he was non-verbal? She'd been so terrified that she hadn't questioned why he hadn't said a single word during the kidnapping.

He lifted his hands and began making rapid signs. Her heart sank. Sign language. That was why she'd been chosen, of all the hospital personnel. She understood sign language, both Quebec sign language and French sign language, the latter being the version he was using. Shaun could sign back if needed, though she was rusty. She'd learned as a child, so she could communicate easily with her cousin, Monique, who was hearing impaired.

You fix him, he signed to her.

"Of course," she readily agreed, then she hesitated. "But what will you do with me after? W-will you let me go?"

He stared down at her, and her heart sank even further. Of course he wouldn't let her go. At least he wasn't outright lying to her. He seemed to understand her though, so either he could read lips or he wasn't hearing impaired.

"Are you going to kill me?" she asked bluntly.

He pointed at her, then toward the man on the ground, then signed, *fix him.*

"He needs a hospital!" she snapped.

No hospital.

"Then I can't fix him, I don't have what I need. I think he's had a heart attack and there's no way to treat that kind of illness without the proper medical equipment." She sat back on her haunches and lifted her hands helplessly. The man was going to die in that dirty basement, and she was likely going to die alongside him.

Her captor pulled his gun from the holster underneath his leather jacket and pointed it at her head. She flinched back but held his gaze. If she had to die, then she preferred to see it coming. Preferred to look her executioner in the eyes. He held his hand steady and stared down at her, speaking with his stony expression. Either she fixed the man, or she died.

"Okay," she whispered. "I'll do what I can."

He reholstered his gun and signed to her, *what supplies do you need?*

She stared helplessly down at the guy. She'd been truthful when she told her captor that she didn't have what she needed to fix the man. If he was indeed suffering from a heart attack, his pulmonary artery was blocked. Likely from the stress of the beating. She would have to do the best she could.

"Okay, get me some aspirin and a spoon." She would try to crush the aspirin and administer it orally. It would work faster intravenously, but again, she didn't have the equipment. Hopefully she could thin his blood enough to partially unblock the artery and buy him some time. Glancing over his other injuries, she added, "I'll also need some bandages, antibiotic ointment, clean water, and a splint, I think, for his arm." She would have to make do with a quick field fix and then hope that her captors would eventually allow her to get the man to a hospital.

"He won't survive long without a hospital though... if your

intention is that he should live." She eyed the man towering over her skeptically. "If I'm correct, then he's had a massive cardiac event and will likely need open heart surgery, which can't be done in a dirty basement with no equipment."

He didn't answer, instead turning to stride away, going back up the stairs to the floor above, she assumed to find the supplies she'd requested. Shaun climbed to her feet and took a quick inventory of the basement. Dirt floor, stone walls, two windows, both tiny with bars covering them, no other doors besides the one at the top of the stairs. She reached over her head to try the bars on the window anyway. If she could pull the grate off, she might be able to crawl through the window. It was small, but Shaun was thin. Small breasts, no hips, nothing to get in the way. For once, Shaun was happy with her less than curvy figure.

The grate proved impossible to move though, and all she managed to do was knock a pile of dust from the sill into her face. She coughed and stepped away from the wall, waving at the dust in the air. She ran to the other window and tried again. She pulled as hard as she could, hard enough that her fingers ached with the effort, but nothing moved. She stepped back, shaking her head in despair. She had to get out; her life depended on it.

A groan drew her attention and she turned around to see her patient stirring. He moaned pitiably and moved his unbroken arm. Shaun went to his side and sank down on the floor next to him.

"I'm a doctor," she said clearly, trying to keep the tremor of fear from her voice. "I'm going to help you."

He made another sound but didn't turn his head at her voice. She couldn't tell how alert he was. "Can you tell me where it hurts the most?" she asked, placing a reassuring hand on his shoulder.

She wasn't sure if or how he would answer, but after a

moment he raised his good arm off the floor and slid it into the front of his torn suit jacket, placing it over his chest. She slid her hand on top of his and felt around his ribcage. Broken ribs. Those would hurt like a bitch and make each breath he took feel like he was swallowing fire.

"Okay, I think you have a few broken ribs, but they don't seem to have punctured your lungs. Which is good news, even if it hurts like a son-of-a-bitch." He blinked one eye open and tried to focus on her face. The other was swollen shut. "It's a good sign that you can hear me," she assured him.

She examined him slowly, one section of his body at a time, cataloguing injuries. What she came up with was a horrifying map of vicious intent. He had a broken arm, several contusions to the head, abrasions to his face and most of his body. A broken nose, four broken fingers, a few broken ribs. Nothing life threatening unless he had an internal injury. It must be his heart. Probably couldn't take the sustained beating it looked like he was given.

The blue tint to his face and lips, along with his shallow, pained breaths worried her. If he didn't get immediate help, he was going to die. Given the extent of injuries, she was surprised he'd lived this long. There was no bleeding outside the body, which was helping him stay alive. The people who had done this to him knew exactly what they were doing, where to hit him without killing him. Too bad they hadn't counted on a weak heart.

A bucket hit the ground next to her, making her jump. Water sloshed out the side, splashing her. There was a big foot in a leather boot next to the bucket. She followed it up, past denim-clad legs, to a belt, and a leather coat. His hands were hanging down, one close enough to her face that she could see the detailed tattoos covering the back of it. There were words on each finger, but she didn't know what they said, and a web with a spider on the back of his hand, a dagger and a rose with blood drops on his wrist. Through the ink she could see the veins popping out on his skin and winding up his wrist. She shivered and looked away. Those were the hands of a killer.

She forced her gaze up to his face and pleaded with him, "This man will not survive if he doesn't get to a surgery in the next hour."

He dropped what he was holding in his other hand: some cloths, a bottle of aspirin, a spoon and what looked like a bottle of peroxide. He snatched her by the back of the head, digging his fingers into her hair and shaking her. Shaun let out a pained yelp and reached up to clasp his wrist, trying to lessen the pressure on her scalp. It felt like he was about to rip her hair out at the roots. He let her go so suddenly that she fell back on her ass.

He crouched next to her, signing, *if he dies, you die.*

She looked at him in despair, searching for an ounce of mercy in his cold gaze. There was none. "Then I guess I die, because I can't fix this man down here, with only these supplies. He needs a hospital, period."

He glared at her; his frustration evident. *Wake him up, now.*

She narrowed her eyes at him and shuffled slightly closer to the man on the floor. "Did you do this to him?"

He made a growling sound under his breath, and signed, *make him able to talk.*

She gave him a penetrating stare and thought hard about her fragile position. The gun was just under his arm. It would only take one quick move and he could shoot her. She had a five percent chance of surviving a shot to the head. She took a deep breath, thought about the consequences of what she was doing, and decided five percent was better than breaking her oath to her profession.

Shaun shook her head. "I won't wake him up just so you can torture him some more."

He growled and grabbed hold of her head again, shaking her. Her teeth rattled and it felt like he was about to twist her head off. She shoved him, but it was like trying to move a boulder.

"Stop it!" she yelled.

CHAPTER FOUR

"I won't fix him!" she shouted as clearly as she could through the thundering in her head, caused by his tight grip on her head and the crazy pattering of her heart.

He threw her away from him in frustration. Shaun fell sideways, but quickly crawled back to the man on the floor. Every instinct in her body was screaming at her to do something, to start working on him. To find a way to get him to the hospital where he could get the medical attention he needed. Instead, she was forced to watch him die a slow and painful death because she refused to help him if her captor was just going to question him and kill him.

She eyed the tattoos on her pacing kidnapper's hands and neck and wondered how deep in the mafia he was. The part of Ukraine that she worked in had become lawless due to the removal of most forms of authority except military, who were concentrated on fighting the rebellion. For the most part, the hospital and its occupants were left alone.

Unless someone needed a doctor, a person who couldn't use normal channels. Reality hit her like a punch to the gut, bringing with it a good dose of nausea. They needed her to fix the guy, so the guy could talk, then both she and the guy would become disposable.

The lack of law enforcement in the area would ensure that no one was available to actively look for Shaun. Or, to look for her body, if it came to that.

He pulled the gun from his holster and, kneeling next to her, pressed the muzzle against the side of her head. She stared up at him, her dark gaze clashing with his blue eyes. She couldn't find anything in that empty gaze, nothing to help her out of this situation. She summoned as much bravery as she could manage.

"I will not help you."

He cocked the pistol, the clicking sound loud in her ear.

She continued to stare at him, desperately trying to keep a straight face, to keep the fear out of her expression. If she was going to die right here, right now, in this dirty little basement, then she was going to do it with whatever dignity she had. She would do it with professional pride, knowing that she was doing the right thing.

"No," she said simply.

He pulled the gun back, and her eyes drifted automatically closed as she felt death rush toward her. An explosion burst through her head, followed by bright flashes behind her eyelids, and for a split second she thought she was dead. As pain razed through her skull, she realized he hadn't actually shot her, but hit her instead.

Anger rushed through her and she balled up her fists. She opened her eyes and glared up at him. "Next time you hit me, you may as well kill me, because I will kick your fucking ass."

She saw a flash of surprise in the clear depths of his eyes, and there was a slight lift of his lips into a smirk. He was amused by her words. Probably wasn't used to someone like her fighting back. He probably preferred his victims docile until he killed them. Well, he wasn't going to get that with Shaun.

She was a fighter.

He sat on his haunches and contemplated his captive. Then he leaned over, brushing her arm with his, making her jerk back, and pressed the gun to the head of his other victim. The man he'd most likely beaten until his heart had given out. Though the gun was pressed to the skull of the man lying on the floor, her captor still stared at her, speaking with his face and eyes.

Despair rushed through her. What should she do? She couldn't actually let the man be murdered right in front of her, could she? Not if there was something she could do. She'd made an oath to do no harm. Yet, would she be doing more harm by helping? Patching him up just enough that he could be awake for his own death?

She glanced over the man and reassessed his injuries. The main issue was a suspected coronary. She couldn't know for certain what was going on inside him, but her best estimate was that this man had no more than a few hours left without intervention. A lot could happen in two hours. Maybe by some miracle, the hospital had managed to alert the military to her abduction, and maybe they were casting a net in hopes of finding her. It sucked that she wasn't within the city limits anymore but had been driven out to the countryside. Maybe someone saw the van and reported it. Maybe, just maybe the military was on its way.

She couldn't let the patient die if there was even the glimmer of a chance that she could save him. She sighed deeply and nodded. "Okay, I'll do what I can. But I don't know if it'll be enough for you to talk to him. He's pretty far gone."

She hoped if the man on the floor was listening at all, that he was capable of understanding the conversation taking place over his prone body. Shaun thought it would be best for him to stay unconscious, even if that meant he had to pretend. The longer he was unresponsive, the longer he and Shaun would stay alive.

Her kidnapper tucked his gun back into the holster and stood. He took a few steps away and leaned against a stone wall, his arms crossed in front of him in a negligent pose. Shaun suspected he could be across the room and on top of her within seconds if she made any wrong moves. He made his position very clear, in both his posture and the hard stare that never wavered from Shaun; he wasn't budging until he got what he wanted.

She worked silently for several minutes, crushing up a handful of aspirins and mixing the white powder with some water before slowly trickling the liquid into her patient's mouth. She used her finger to rub the extra mixture from the spoon onto his gums, where the skin was thin and the blood vessels were close to the surface, allowing the medication to reach his bloodstream faster. He didn't swallow, which meant he was unconscious again. She checked his pulse. It was worryingly faint.

There wasn't much more she could do about his heart.

She turned to the rest of him, tugging on clothes, and inventorying and treating injuries, until the basement faded away and it was just her and her patient. His body, his injuries spoke to her, even while he could not. She had enough experience from her time spent working in the Montréal General Hospital that she could tell what had made the marks and how much pressure had been applied. If she had to guess, she would say that he took several punches to the face, chest and abdomen, kicks to all of his limbs, probably when he'd fallen to the ground. His hands and fingers had been stomped on, as were his feet. The intent had been to cause extreme pain without doing life threatening damage.

Shaun had no way of dealing with a cardiac arrest beyond thinning his blood with aspirin, and without a hospital, it would ultimately be what killed him. After she finished cleaning and dressing the injuries that she could actually treat, she sat back on her heels and surveyed the man. It was no use – he was going to die, and he was going to do it soon. His breathing was shallow and his skin was grey and clammy.

"That's all I can do," she said, feeling helpless and afraid.

She lifted her eyes to meet the unsympathetic ones of the man across the room. He hadn't moved while she worked, just watched. He now shifted his eyes down to her patient, his victim. He took a long look, then signed to her, *wake him up*.

She didn't know how to make him understand that she couldn't just wake the patient. She sighed and rubbed at the headache hovering over her left eyebrow. A stress headache that came along once in a while when she found herself in an impossible situation.

"What's your name?" She decided on a new tactic; try to form some kind of bond with her captor so he might trust her.

He pushed away from the wall, straightened and rolled his shoulders back as though releasing tension. Finally, he signed the letters - J - O - Z - E - F.

She nodded, and said softly, "Jozef."

He looked at her, his eyes dropping down to her mouth, a strange expression flitting across his hawk-like features.

"Jozef." She deliberately repeated his name. "You have to understand, this isn't a matter of just 'wake him up' or 'don't wake him up'. You, or whoever did this to him, beat him until his heart gave out. On top of his other injuries, he probably has a concussion at best and a skull fracture at worst. He may never wake up."

Jozef growled and began pacing the basement, his big booted feet kicking up dust from the floor. He was such a terrifying and imposing figure. If she had to guess, she would put him in his mid-thirties, same as her. He was probably a professional criminal with a good dose of street thug. He was the type of person that mamas and small children would cross the street to avoid.

Throughout her career, Shaun refused to avoid anyone, to be intimidated by people like Jozef. In her profession, she'd learned that anyone was capable of anything. Sweet little old ladies could be serial killers and the biggest, noisiest, scariest looking men could be teddy bears who cried over a few stitches. She'd seen it all and knew better than to judge. Unfortunately, Jozef was proving himself to be the former, rather than the latter. He'd already killed one person and she was terribly afraid there were two more on his list.

After another minute of pacing, he turned on his heel and strode out of the basement. The moment he was gone, Shaun hovered over top of her patient and shook his shoulder.

"Hey, wake up. Can you hear me?"

There was no response, so she tried harder, tried to wake him up without jarring his injuries too much. She checked his breathing and his pulse again and realized it was a lost cause. This man was going to die very soon, and he was going to do it without helping her escape.

Before she could come up with something else, she heard the clatter of feet on the rickety wooden steps. She glanced up in fear as Jozef returned with another person, one of the men from the van. Jozef walked toward her, his steps so rapid, she lurched back. He didn't reach for her though, instead picking up the bucket of now dirty water and throwing it in the face of the man on the ground.

Shaun gasped and grabbed hold of his wrist, trying to pull him back. As soon as her fingers touched Jozef's arm, he gave her a look of such loathing that she instantly dropped her hand and scuttled backwards on the dirt floor. He switched his focus from her to the injured man, who was sputtering water and groaning in pain.

Jozef grabbed hold of his collar with both hands and lifted him off the ground, his legs swinging uselessly underneath him. Shaun wanted to scream out, to tell him to leave the man alone, that he was in too much pain to be of any use. It didn't seem to matter though, she was the only one cared about his state beyond getting him to tell them whatever they needed.

The man who had come downstairs with Jozef, the one who spoke with her in the van, stepped up to them and snarled, "Tell us where Krystoff is."

The injured man blinked several times as if trying to remove a fog, then groaned loudly, bringing his unbroken arm up to shield himself. It was no use though, as Jozef dropped one arm, using his other hand to hold the guy up off the floor. Shaun was amazed at the strength it would take to do that. She could usually tell how much a person weighed by looking at them, a hazard of her profession, and she suspected Jozef was holding a two-hundred-pound man as if he weighed no more than a sack of groceries.

Jozef pulled his fist back and sent it flying into the other guy's gut. Hitting him in the belly, then continuing to punch him, getting him in the face, arms and stomach. The hits would be unbearable over top of his other wounds and the squeezing pain in his chest, but they weren't lethal. Jozef seemed to know what he was doing; like a surgeon, he was precise.

Shaun bit her lip so hard that it bled into her mouth. She wanted to scream. She wanted to leap to her feet and defend her patient, but she knew it was a lost cause. They were going to kill this guy and then her. Maybe if she kept her silence, they would forget about her. At least for now. She'd seen too much death in her career, which had prepared her for the inevitability of dying, but now, every precious second seemed to count. She wanted as many as she could get, even if those seconds came along with the horror of watching someone else beaten to death.

She was about to cry out that the man was dying, that he couldn't talk to them, when his groans turned to words. The words were garbled gibberish, pushed through a mouth full of blood and broken teeth. Shaun didn't understand what he was saying, then she realized that he wasn't speaking English, but Ukrainian. She'd managed to pick up enough to interact with her patients on a basic level, but she hadn't been in the country long enough to speak fluently, or understand it well, especially when the words were being spoken with rapid desperation.

Finally, the words ended, and Jozef nodded. He dropped the man, who fell backward with a crash, his head hitting the floor so hard it bounced. Shaun winced and started to crawl toward him. Maybe if they were done the interrogation they would leave and she could tend to the man, at least make his passing a little more comfortable.

Before she could reach him, Jozef pulled his gun again, trained it on the man and put a bullet through his head. It was a clean shot. The head remained intact, the only sign of a fatal injury a couple of drops of blood seeping from the wound. Shaun let out a scream of horror and scrambled away, crawling back until she was pressed against a wall.

Her heart thundered, and she looked up at Jozef, expecting the gun to swing around toward her. She was going to die in that dirty basement, next to the stranger she'd failed to protect. She didn't know what to expect. She thought maybe her mind would flood with images of her family, or maybe a bright light. Instead, there was nothing but blank terror. Every instinct within her was screaming at her to run away, to try her hardest to escape the fate that was rushing at her, but her limbs were locked, and she could do nothing but watch the gun swing toward her.

She stared up at Jozef defiantly, tried to tell him silently that he didn't scare her, that she was prepared for death. None of it was true, but he didn't need to know that. She watched as his finger tightened on the trigger, just the way it had seconds earlier. His fingers were so starkly beautiful, with the intricate ink painting them. She wondered if he played an instrument; his hands would look beautiful flying over chords as he made music.

Then she thought of her parents and prepared to die.

CHAPTER FIVE

Shaun was expecting to feel a raw ripping pain tear through her, followed closely by death. She wasn't expecting to have someone grip her arm and wrench her up to her feet. The move was so fast, so sudden, that she felt instantly dizzy. When her vision cleared, she was confronted with the intense stunning blue eyes of her captor. His forehead was wrinkled in a frown.

"What are you doing?" the other man demanded. "We got what we need. Finish the job so we can get on with it."

She felt sick, genuinely nauseous to the point that she would've doubled over and gripped her knees if she could have. By 'finish the job,' he meant kill her. She was a loose end, a witness to a murder. They had no choice, she had to go. Jozef glared at the other man, and then turned and dragged her toward the stairs.

Shaun was dizzy, hyperventilating, floaty. She was disassociating from what was happening. Multiple times in the space of an hour or so, she'd been positive she was going to die, then, when the real thing finally came, when she was certain he intended to pull the trigger, something had held him back.

She didn't know what, couldn't explain it. She couldn't even really be grateful that she was still alive. She couldn't possibly guess what was going to happen to her now.

Jozef pulled her up the stairs and through the house. She glanced around and saw dusty unused furniture. There were still drop clothes on some of the items. She suspected the family that had lived there fled the war, closing up the house and moving somewhere safer. These guys were probably seizing on an opportunity to use it while it was empty. It was in a remote area outside of the city, ideal for criminal activity. At least, she hoped her hypothesis was true. What if they'd killed the family and were using the house as a base for their operations?

Jozef hauled her toward the van, opened the passenger door and flung her at it. She caught the edge of the frame and glanced back in time to see his leather jacket filling her vision. He didn't wait for her to climb in but shoved her until she was halfway laying across the seat and gripping the dashboard for balance. He stuffed her legs inside and slammed the door shut. She righted herself and turned to watch as he confronted the man who stormed out of the house behind him. They embarked on an angry conversation, the thug guy yelling at Jozef, and Jozef responding with rapid, angry hand gestures.

Shaun had no idea what they were saying, the conversation was too fast, too angry, and Jozef's back was to her so she couldn't see his hands. Finally, the guy gave a sharp nod and turned his malevolent gaze on her, staring at her through the passenger window. He pulled the van keys from his pocket and tossed them at Jozef, then he turned on his heel and strode back into the house.

Jozef watched the house for a few seconds, seeming to gather himself, then came around the front of the van and opened the door, climbing into the driver's seat. He ignored her, sliding the keys into the ignition and turning. As the engine flared to life, hope filled her chest. He hadn't killed her in the basement along with that other man, and he was taking her somewhere else, maybe back to the hospital. Hell, she didn't care if he ditched her in the middle of nowhere, she was just happy to be alive.

Shaun's relief was short-lived when Jozef turned off the main road and started following a bumpy dirt road into a sparsely wooded area. Her alarm grew as they continued to drive with no houses or signs of civilization. Her heart began to pound and her palms grew clammy.

"Where are we going?" she asked, then shook her head at herself.

Of course, he couldn't answer while he was driving. He wouldn't even look at her, giving her absolutely no reassurance.

"Are you... are you... going to kill me?" she had some trouble forcing the words past a throat constricting with panic.

She gripped the door latch so tightly she thought it might leave a permanent mark in her hand. Not that it would matter if he was about to kill her shortly. Surreptitiously she tried the door, but it was child locked. She couldn't get out unless he let her out.

She tried to take long even breaths, rather than shallow gasps. She thought back to the single class she'd taken on hostage situations. She'd travelled to war zones, often in places where terrorism was a real threat. It had seemed smart at the time to take a class on hostage negotiation in case she ever found herself in a situation that would demand that kind of skill. Between her panic and the fact that she'd taken the class about five years ago, she couldn't recall all the steps, but a few filtered through the terror.

Talk to the person holding you, humanize yourself in their eyes.

"I'm thirty-four." She looked directly at him as she spoke. Again, not so much as a twitch gave away that he was listening, but she was going to try anyway. "I'm a neurosurgeon in Montréal, Canada, but sometimes I work with Doctors Without Borders. We travel to other countries to help bolster the health-care system during times of crisis. I have a cat named Fitzwilliam Darcy, but we call him Fitzy. He lives with my mom when I'm not at home. He's a really good boy, he always eats all of his food, and he uses his litter box. Sometimes he gets out and causes havoc in the neighborhood. He's a big guy and he likes to hunt so he's brought home some pretty big birds."

Shaun was babbling, but she didn't know what else to do. She tried to clear her thoughts and start over. Jozef wouldn't care about her twenty-pound beast of an orange tabby. She had to somehow convince him that she was more valuable alive than dead. She needed to give him something of value, something he could relate to.

"I'm the only person my mom has left. My dad passed away a few years ago of pancreatic cancer. There was nothing we could do but watch him deteriorate." She closed her eyes and summoned a picture of her father in her mind. He was a big man, much bigger than either Shaun or her mother. He wore glasses, almost always had a serious expression that covered a playful nature. He taught neuroscience at the University. His funeral had been massive with mourners from all the different communities he'd been part of including faculty and students from the university, colleagues from the hospital, and volunteers from various charitable organizations. He was so well loved. She needed that unconditional love and support right now, to get through whatever was coming her way. "My mom was devastated when he died, it took a lot to get her on her feet again. She needs me. She hates that I travel into war zones, she's terrified something will happen to me. Without me, she won't have anyone."

Despair pierced her as she realized not a single word was getting through. He continued to drive, though he was slowing down. If she was going to convince him, she had to do it now, before they got to their destination. She frantically searched for something, anything, that could sway him. Then she landed on it, their rare form of communication.

"You knew that I knew sign language, didn't you?"

His eyes slid to her for a second, then flicked forward.

"I've been trying to figure out how you knew to target me," she continued. "You knew that I could understand FSL; that's why you picked me, isn't it? But how did you know?" When he didn't answer, she continued, "You saw me with that kid, didn't you?"

Shaun had stumbled over a child, around ten years old, begging for food vouchers outside of a shop. She'd kneeled on the ground next to him and tried to talk to him, but he'd shaken his head and pointed at his ears. Sadly, it wasn't uncommon for either temporary or permanent hearing loss to occur from the concussive force of a bomb.

Shaun had used sign language with the boy. He'd tried to follow her hand movements, and she realized that he was just learning sign language. She convinced him to come with her to the hospital for a quick check up and to learn more sign language.

He'd run home to ask permission from his mom and had been coming to the hospital every day since. That had been about a week ago. She supposed Jozef could have seen her using it in the hospital, with her little protege following her around, but she doubted it. Someone as terrifying and imposing as Jozef would stand out.

Jozef looked at her and gave a brief nod. He refocused on

his driving, turning the wheel and pulling the vehicle off the road. She felt dizzy with panic and lack of air. She continued to grip the door handle.

"You knew that I knew how to understand you before you realized you needed me. That man was injured sometime today." Her words came out in a jumble, but she hoped he understood. "Did you follow me back to the hospital that day? Were you curious about me? Because the only people who can understand you are probably in your inner circle." She was guessing, but maybe if she got close enough to the truth, she could connect with him.

He stopped the van and turned the ignition off. They were in a section of trees, not too thick, but remote enough to hide a dead body. Her body. No one would find her out here. Not for a long, long time. Shaun's mother would never know. Her daughter would disappear without a word. Dead in a warzone, but not because of the war.

Jozef turned to look at her, his forehead creased into a troubled frown.

Shaun stared back at him, and then did the only thing she could think of to get through to him. She signed, *please don't kill me. I don't want to die.*

He gave no indication that he either saw or understood. His face smoothed back into indifference and he reached for his door. As soon as it opened, her door unlocked too. Shaun gripped the latch and yanked, then shoved the door open. She hadn't been wearing a seatbelt, so she was able to fling herself unhindered from the vehicle and start running.

Shaun was not a runner, but she kept herself in decent physical shape. Long hours on her feet at the hospital required that she take good care of herself. Eat good foods, exercise whenever she could spare a few minutes. She thought she might have a decent chance of evading her captor. He was tall and bulky with muscle. How fast could a thug really run?

He probably spent most of his time committing crimes instead of jogging.

He was on top of her in under a minute.

She could hear him crashing through the brush behind her. Before she had a chance to look over her shoulder, he grabbed her around the waist and shoved her to the ground.

Shaun hit hard, the side of her face striking a branch as she landed. She felt searing pain through her cheek as the branch scraped her. She rolled onto her back and stared up at him. Jozef towered over her, his legs on either side of hers. They stared at each other for a long time, tension laden emotion flowing between them, like lightning strikes.

She felt him, felt his gaze, his gut-wrenching intention. His determination to do what he had to. His despair, his hatred, his desire. He had to kill her, but it was tearing him up inside. Not like when he'd killed Danilo and the man in the basement: stone cold, emotionless. She suspected this was the real Jozef, deep inside, his heart on his sleeve. He didn't want to kill Shaun.

She'd never felt quite the connection with another human being the way she did now. She was stunned by it. Is that what happened to people before they died? They connected with those around them as they returned to the earth? She'd never believed in anything like that before, she was too logical. But, as she faced her own death, she needed to latch onto something, or someone, so she wouldn't feel so alone. Even if it was the person who was about to end her life.

Jozef reached down and gripped her shoulder, wrenching her to her knees. Pain shot through her arm. She cried out and grabbed her shoulder. He moved his hand away and reached into his leather jacket, pulling out the same gun he'd used to kill Danilo and the other man. Shaun stared at it, sick dread now replacing the almost euphoric feeling she'd experienced seconds earlier. This was it, the moment of her death.

He turned the pistol on her, pressing it to her head. Her eyes started to drift shut, but then she changed her mind and opened them. She would look at her murderer as he killed her. If she had to die, then she would gaze upon Jozef. The man who couldn't talk. The man who had a duty to perform. One that came above his humanity.

"Please find a way to tell my mom where my body is. Her name is Fatima Patterson of Montréal, Canada."

Her eyes locked with his and he gave only the slightest nod, indicating he'd heard her. Determination and despair clashed in his beautiful velvet blue eyes. She wondered, as she looked at him, what he saw in her eyes? Fear, hatred, anger? Or acceptance and regret?

His finger tightened on the trigger.

CHAPTER SIX

Each breath seemed to linger in her chest for much longer than usual before puffing out through her mouth. Was this what death felt like? Time slowed down to a crawl and each sense hyper-engaged all at the same time. But then, Jozef jerked the gun away from her head and time sped back up. The warm sunshine filtered through the leaves high above their heads. The flutter of a bird's wings sounded as it took flight.

Jozef stalked away from her, his shoes rustling in the dead leaves and grass. He grasped his head as indecision warred in his brain. Shaun stayed crouched on the ground, watching warily. Then he turned and grabbed her again, yanking her to her feet. Shaun swayed and thought she would go back down until he steadied her, sliding his gun hand around her back. She gasped and jerked in his arms as she felt the metal press against her spine.

He growled in frustration and set her away from him. As she stumbled back, he put his gun underneath his jacket and back into its holster. The air left Shaun's lungs in a whoosh, and her knees started to give out. Once more, he lunged toward her as she fell. This time when he caught her, she allowed his touch. It was either that or fall in a painful heap to the ground.

He held her upright, looking down at her with a frown. He waited for a few minutes as she filled her lungs slowly with air and breathed out, over and over until her heart wasn't racing and her panic began to subside. Their eyes locked and a kind of energy seemed to pass between them, as though he was giving her some of his strength while she sorted herself out. They breathed together, in and out, until she was calmer. Finally, when she was in control of herself, he righted her and, gripping her arm, walked her back to the van.

As they walked, the full impact of what almost happened hit her and Shaun began shaking uncontrollably. She had come within seconds of losing her life. Maybe it was her decision to keep her eyes open that saved her. Or maybe it was her plea that he find a way to tell her mother where to find her body. Whatever it was, it might only be temporary. She would have to try and find out what he planned on doing with her, since it looked like shooting her in the head and leaving her body in the woods was no longer on the table.

When they reached the van, Shaun grabbed the door handle, about to open it, but Jozef's hand came down on her shoulder. He turned her around to face him and then took a step back. She looked at him in confusion, her adrenalin starting to rise again. Had he changed his mind? Did he want to make sure to kill her outside of the van so he wouldn't have to worry about bloodstains inside it?

Most people who used sign language used a combination of facial cues, body language and hand signs to express themselves. Facial expressions were often vital in order to communicate mood and intent. Jozef was completely different. His facial expressions were mostly closed, and his body language was stiff and uncompromising, which left her with only hand signals for communication.

He lifted his hands and began signing, *I'm not going to kill you.*

Relief slammed into her with the intensity of a freight train, stealing her breath for a moment. He wasn't going to kill her!

"Thank you," she said quickly.

I can't let you go; you're a witness.

"I promise I won't say anything."

He shook his head. *You're a liability now. You must stay with me. Permanently.*

"But how can I do that? Eventually I have to go home." She understood what he was saying, but she wanted to deny it.

If she wanted to live, then she would have to become his captive. Forever. But how could she possibly do that? Never see her mother again? Never go back to her surgery at the hospital? What kind of life was that? She couldn't wrap her mind around it.

He reached out and shook her arm, regaining her attention. *Choose now, dead witness, or stay with me and stay alive.*

She was still shaking her head, but reality was sinking in. She wasn't going to choose death. So she would have to choose life... as his captive. Or at least until she could either convince him to let her go or escape. She stopped shaking her head and bowed it instead.

"Okay, I'll stay with you," she whispered.

He tipped her chin up and signed, *you must marry me.*

Dread swept through her. She shook her head. "No."

Yes, you will become my wife.

"Or die?" she demanded.

Yes.

She pressed herself back against the van. It was too much. He could keep her with him, he didn't have to marry her. To make it so... official. Shaun had never given marriage much consideration. She'd dated a little, but never anything serious. Work consumed her every waking moment until the men just drifted away and she forgot they were ever there. Somehow, she couldn't imagine Jozef ever drifting out of her line of notice. He was too commanding, too electric and powerful.

"Why do I have to marry you?" she asked, clinging desperately to the hope that she could convince him otherwise. She wasn't ready to commit herself to him, a man she suspected was mob affiliated.

He narrowed his eyes at her, his gaze flicking down her body. She was wearing her basic sky-blue scrubs, nothing enticing. He seemed to be debating with himself on what to say to her, or maybe how much to say to her. Then he gave a sharp nod. *My uncle will not allow you to live. You are a witness and witnesses don't stay alive.*

"Your uncle makes decisions like that?" Her throat was dry, and she had to swallow. She was definitely dealing with the mob, which took things to an even scarier level.

Jozef nodded, *my uncle is head of the family.*

If the head of the family was Jozef's uncle, then Jozef was probably his enforcer. The muscle behind the man at the top. Though Jozef seemed high up in the organization, his uncle would have final say. Including over her life. If the old man gave the word, her life would end, and probably by Jozef's hands. But if she were Jozef's wife, then maybe the uncle would allow her to live.

Jozef watched her as she worked it out in her head. She was going to have to marry the man who'd kidnapped her, threatened and hit her, and then almost shot her. The man who went against every ethical belief she held as a doctor. She would essentially become his property. Nausea nearly sent her back to her knees. She gripped the doorframe.

He slapped her arm again, and when she looked at him, he signed, *answer*.

She shivered and whispered, "Okay, I'll marry you."

CHAPTER SEVEN

Kiev, Ukraine: One day later

Jozef didn't have a lot of time to plan the rescue of his uncle. Gustav, the man they had beaten for information, had told them where to find the kidnapped head of the Koba family and who was holding him. A rival mafia family located in Kiev, headed by Vasiliy Stanovich, were holding the Koba patriarch in their family estate, located in Kiev.

Once Jozef had identified Krystoff's kidnappers, he was able to quickly research the family. Ferret out their weaknesses and a likely reason behind the abduction. The current global economy hadn't been kind to the Stanovich family, as they hadn't updated technology and techniques to move with the changing times. They were living in the past, hoping to make bank off the old ways; drug sales and extortion. As their family gradually sank into the lower ranks of the Vory, the head of the family had gone to Krystoff three years ago for help and had been refused. Jozef suspected the family took Krystoff for either revenge or to force his hand.

Jozef found a significant weakness in the Stanovich's armour. A drug-addicted son who liked to brag about his family's exploits when he was drinking. Havel had gotten the kid drunk and questioned him, in the guise of friendly curiosity, while pumping up the kid's ego. Pavel had spilled everything, including the fact that Krystoff was soon to be moved. Apparently, Vasiliy had grown impatient with Aunt Dasha's hedging.

Jozef needed to launch the rescue before Krystoff was moved again or killed. He increased the map size on his laptop and tapped his fingertip against the screen. Havel nodded and scratched his chin. "Never been inside the place, but knowing Vasiliy, we can expect some kind of security detail."

This was consistent with the information they'd gotten out of Pavel. The kid was being held in a separate room, sleeping off a vicious hangover. It was possible he wouldn't figure out that he was being held hostage until Jozef's uncle was returned to the family.

The kid was useless though. Vasiliy didn't care about his son and would probably thank them for doing him the favour of murdering the kid, who was an embarrassment to his organization. Only the mother seemed to like him, and her voice only counted for so much. But they could use Pavel as a message if they had to, even if it was a weak one.

First, they would attempt to get Krystoff out of the building, and if that didn't work, they'd go to plan B: mail pieces of Pavel to his mother until she badgered her husband into saving the kid.

Jozef opened another photograph and blew up a picture of the Vasiliy family home. He turned to Havel and gave him a rundown on his plan so far. Together the two men worked on their team strategy, Jozef signing to Havel, while Havel spoke out loud. Havel understood sign language, having worked with Jozef since he was old enough to take on the role of family enforcer, but Havel was more comfortable with spoken language.

Jozef thought of Doctor Shaun Patterson. Thirty-four years old, with a cat and a mother. She would be comfortable using only sign language with him, the way she had when he'd seen her on the street with the boy. It was something he hadn't realized he craved until that moment in the van when she'd turned to him and signed, *please don't kill me*.

After their confrontation in the woods, he'd handcuffed her in the van and driven back to the house to pick up the others. They'd made the long eight-hour drive to where Krystoff was being held and then spent twelve hours holed up with a loyal contact in Kiev as they prepared to hit the Stanovich estate. Shaun was locked in another room, alone, except for the occasional check-in by their host's sister, Mara. According to Mara, Shaun had barely spoken, except to ask for her freedom, and, when that failed, to ask where Jozef was.

He tried to extinguish the spark that fired inside him when she asked after him. She didn't care about him. She'd seen him kill twice; she was terrified of him. What she knew of him was that he was the man who had decided to keep her alive. He was her only chance at salvation, which was why she was asking after him. She wanted to make sure he hadn't abandoned her to a bunch of lethal strangers who might kill her the moment he was gone. He needed to remember that Shaun didn't care and couldn't care about him. He was lonely and using their tenuous connection to imagine deeper feelings.

Feelings weren't allowed in the mafia. At least not when it came to outsiders. Feelings were reserved for family, for those who Jozef was loyal to. Not for a doctor he'd been forced to pick up. She was nothing. She didn't matter, and neither did the flicker of hope he felt every time he looked at her. His desire when she looked at him from beneath her strikingly long black lashes. The feeling in his chest every time she, an outsider, understood what he was saying.

Once they were married, she would no longer be an outsider. She would be his. To hold, to explore these feelings with, to talk to until he was satisfied.

As if echoing his thoughts, Havel said quietly, "Your uncle won't like that you kept the woman alive."

Jozef didn't respond at first, giving his second-in-command a cold look. Then he signed, *she will become my wife.*

"You think Krystoff won't have your wife killed if he thinks she might risk the family business?"

Jozef growled but didn't contradict Havel. His man was right. Krystoff would put the organization first, before himself, before his love for his nephew.

She will be part of this family, Jozef insisted.

Havel shrugged. "I just want you to think about this, before you make any decisions. Once you free the old man, he will be responsible for making the big decisions once more, including what happens to your girl."

Jozef looked at Havel sharply. Was he suggesting they not rescue Krystoff? But that would be impossible, it would be disloyal. As far as Jozef knew, Havel was fiercely loyal to the Koba organization.

Then Havel veered away from Jozef's suspicions.

"If you go ahead and marry the girl without Krystoff's permission, you'll risk being exiled from the family and you're too powerful to be left alive. If you decided to split, you could easily take half the organization with you."

Ah, Havel was worried on Jozef's behalf. He wasn't proposing disloyalty to the head of the family, but caution. Jozef stood and squeezed Havel's shoulder, then dropped his hand. *I will not do anything to jeopardize my position. I will gain my uncle's permission before I marry the woman.*

"And if he denies you?"

It was a very likely possibility.

He will not.

Rescuing Krystoff Koba went as smoothly as Jozef could have hoped, and he had his team to thank for that. Jozef and his men, Havel, Terek, Halil and Nikolay had worked together as a unit for years and operated like a well-oiled machine. They didn't need words to complete an operation. Their uncanny bond and unfailing work ethic made them nearly invincible. Krystoff would frequently hire them out as a team to do mercenary work in neighboring countries. They had become known as the fiercest mobsters in Eastern Europe.

He nodded to Halil who took the signal, shooting the man guarding the rear garden gate. The man fell noiselessly to the ground and the team moved past him and into the house before he took his last breath. Unless they ran into trouble, the door man would be the only person to die during the operation. They didn't want to go to war with this family. Not until they had Krystoff and were given the official order.

Jozef needed to understand why his uncle was taken before he would decimate the organization that had made such a bold move.

They swarmed soundlessly through the mansion, not once encountering a single member of security. This wasn't because they were heading into a trap, or at least Jozef hoped not. It was because his team knew the exact rotation of the guards and knew how to move as though they were ghosts. Halil and Terek went ahead of Jozef, checking that his path to the cellar room Krystoff was being held in was empty.

It took some time to get the cellar door open. It was locked with a state-of-the-art dual handprint and coded lock. Nikolay was specialized in electronics and worked on the lock for fifteen tense minutes while Jozef and his team covered him. Finally, the lock clicked, and the door swung open.

Jozef allowed Halil to go ahead of him and then followed. The others would maintain guard on the door, holding their position if they had to. It didn't take Jozef long to find his uncle as he was the only prisoner being held in the cellar. He was in a clean room with a door, locked from the outside with a basic bolt.

"Jozef?" Krystoff sat up on his cot and squinted toward the men in the doorway, his gaze on the silenced pistol in Jozef's hand.

Jozef strode to his uncle and, turning on the light on his phone, searched him for injuries. There seemed to be nothing, except a bandage around his hand where his finger had been cut off. Krystoff moved without stiffness, indicating he probably hadn't been beaten.

"You came." The statement sounded almost like a question, as though he'd doubted Jozef.

Jozef grunted. This was one of those rare moments that he wished he could speak, could reassure his uncle. Krystoff had learned sign language when Jozef was young so they would be able to converse with ease, but there wasn't enough light in the room for Jozef's hands to be visible, and he didn't want to put his weapon down.

Instead, Jozef took his uncle by the arm and tugged him, indicating he should stand. When he did, Krystoff surprised Jozef by hugging him close, his arms clasping around the younger man. Jozef wasn't used to being touched by anyone, let alone his coolly professional uncle. Sometimes his Aunt Dasha would hug him, and even rarer, his two female cousins. He got the feeling that, though the family cared about him, they didn't know how to act around their *vztekl'y pes*, the rabid dog of the Koba family.

Jozef stepped away from his uncle and indicated he should

precede Jozef out the door. Jozef and Nikolay made their way swiftly back up the stairs and out of the cellar with Krystoff sandwiched between them, Jozef's hand on his shoulder in case he needed to shove the older man to the ground and cover him. Krystoff didn't balk at the precautions; he knew to trust Jozef's team with his safety.

Their exit was as swift and silent as their entrance, with no more casualties. They bundled the head of the Koba family into the back of their van and drove away from the area at a leisurely pace, not wanting to bring more attention to themselves than they needed to. Not until they cleared the area controlled by Vasiliy did everyone in the van sigh in relief. Havel clapped Krystoff on the back, and the old man gave him a tired smile and nodded his gratitude across the back of the van to Jozef.

Thank you, my son, he signed, his hands barely visible in the dim lighting.

Shaun was cold, shivering in the dark on a bare mattress in a bare room. She was hungry and she had to urinate. She hadn't gotten the sense from her captors that they intended for her to be miserable. It was more likely that they were too busy to think about her. Still, she was starting to worry that if they forgot for much longer, she would have to start shouting.

She'd been attempting to sleep, the sun having long since gone down and the only light now a dim streetlight down the road from where her room was facing. She'd tried the window, but it was bolted shut. She wondered if this room was actually meant for prisoners, given how solid the door and lock were, and her inability to open the window. She closed her eyes, drifting in and out of consciousness. She had no way to tell time, but she suspected she wasn't sleeping for more than a few minutes at a time.

It was during one of these brief periods when she was snatching a few minutes of sleep that her door banged open. She opened her eyes and sat up on the mattress, pushing hair off her forehead. She'd taken her hair out of its tight bun and it was now a wild mass of tight curls in a halo around her head. Normally she'd work them into braids for easy maintenance while she was working, but even that basic hair care had fallen to the wayside during her long shifts in the Luhansk hospital. The mass was nearly shoulder length, although when she had it chemically relaxed it would go halfway down her back.

She blinked into the gloom and then squinted her displeasure as the overhead light was flicked on. After a moment of blindness, she was able to focus on the intruder.

Jozef.

Her heart picked up and fear began pumping through her veins as she recognized him. Despite his words that he didn't plan on killing her anymore, she couldn't help but see the gun and feel the press of the steel muzzle against her temple every time she looked at him.

He jerked his head toward the door, indicating she should come with him.

"I have to go to the bathroom," she said quickly, scooting to the edge of the bed. When he frowned, she added, "Please, Jozef. I've been in here for hours with no relief." She hoped adding his name would help humanize her in his eyes, make it harder for him to deprive her of basic needs.

He jerked his head in a nod and once more indicated she should follow him. She stood and approached the door cautiously. He backed up so she could pass and waved his hand out the door. She walked into the hallway, holding her breath as she brushed past him. He walked closely behind her. About halfway down the hall he grabbed her arm to stop her. Shaun jumped at his touch and glanced at him.

He dropped his hand and pointed at a door. Shaun approached slowly, peaking inside and then saw the outline of a tub, sink and toilet. She sighed her relief and rushed through the door, turning to close it behind her. He gripped the edge of the door, stopping her from closing it completely. She glanced over at him, but decided it wasn't worth the fight. She didn't know where she stood with him yet and wasn't willing to push her luck.

She reached for the light, but he pushed her hand away and pointed at the toilet, then he turned his back, pulling the door partly shut. She stared at him, or more accurately, his back. It looked like she was going to pee in the dark with an audience. Not that it mattered, there was enough light coming in through the small window that she could at least make her way to the toilet and feel around. She'd certainly had urinated in worse conditions than this. There hadn't been any flush toilets where she'd been stationed in Sri Lanka.

Once she finished, she washed her hands. He turned toward her, took her arm, and pulled her back out into the hallway. She walked with him down a set of stairs to the main floor. They followed another darkened hallway into a room filled with people.

Shaun balked, catching sight of the man who'd argued with Jozef about killing her in the basement. She'd learned his name was Havel and, judging from the way he spoke to Jozef, he was some kind of enforcer or second-in-command.

Havel glanced at her then swiftly turned away, a cigarette clenched between his teeth. Jozef walked into her back when she stopped suddenly. His hands landed on her hips, steadying her as she was jolted forward. She glanced back at him, but his gaze went past hers and landed on someone else.

Shaun followed his line of sight.

An older man, his hair and beard grey and unwashed, was sitting slumped in a chair next to a fireplace. The light from the fire cast shadows over his body. He was big, probably quite imposing when standing. He was holding a hand to his face, and his other hand, which was bandaged, rested in his lap. The bandage concerned Shaun. Did they want her to help yet another prisoner? Was she about to go through the same scenario as the basement? Patching up a man just so this motley crew could torture and kill him.

She didn't think that was what was happening here. The man was in a deferential spot, near the fire with a blanket on his lap, sitting in a leather armchair. He seemed to be an important man. Perhaps the uncle Jozef had mentioned in the forest.

When Shaun and Jozef entered the room, the man looked up at them with a kind of tired curiosity reflected in his gaze. He had sharp blue eyes, the same shade as Jozef's. As they passed over Shaun, they narrowed in speculation.

She thought she understood. Not only did she stand out as a stranger and a foreigner in what she suspected was a tight-knit group, but she was black. Her skin colour set her apart from every person in the room, and most people in Ukraine. She wasn't usually self-conscious, either about her skin colour or anything else, but when every eye in the room landed on her, she felt her cheeks burn in response.

She shifted slightly to lean back against Jozef. In this room filled with criminals, he was the only one she knew for sure wasn't prepared to shoot her. Everyone else had varying expressions of skeptical, impatient and downright nasty. She really, really didn't want to be the focus of attention anymore. Jozef, whose hand was still on her hip, gave her a gentle squeeze, which surprised her. So far in all of her dealings with him, he hadn't shown a gentle bone in his body. Yet, he seemed to be trying to reassure her, which had the opposite effect. She now knew that she should be very afraid of the man sitting by the fire.

It was the older man who finally broke the silence. "You're a doctor?" He spoke English, but his accent was thick, as though he didn't do it often.

"Yes," she said, a little hesitantly. Obviously, he meant her since there wasn't anyone else in the room wearing scrubs.

"I think my nephew wishes for you to look me over before we leave for our next destination." His gaze flickered past her shoulder to land on Jozef. "Complete nonsense, but the boy is stubborn. Won't leave until I've been properly inspected."

Jozef being likened to a boy felt completely incongruous. There was nothing young and cute about him. He was all man with a good dose of terrifying. The older gentleman was looking at Jozef through the lens of family. So he *was* the uncle that Jozef had told her about when he told her that they would have to be married.

"Well, don't just stand there," he barked, losing patience. "Let's get this over with. Everyone out. Jozef and the girl can stay."

Shaun hated being called a 'girl'. It was demeaning and completely inappropriate for a woman of her education and profession. Ordinarily, she would correct him by telling him she preferred her name, or if he must use a noun, then woman. She kept her silence though, not ready to antagonize him.

Jozef pushed Shaun farther into the room, making space by the door for the others to leave. The woman who had brought food and water to Shaun earlier in the day glanced at her as she passed. Her expression was pitying, which made Shaun wonder what exactly she was in for. She stiffened her spine. It didn't matter. She was a medical professional, and she would treat Jozef's uncle as she would any other patient. What happened to her after was irrelevant.

She was a doctor; her job was to heal.

Once everyone had left and the door was closed, she walked to the fireplace. She glanced around and, spotting a stool, pulled it closer. As she sank down, seating herself in front of him, she asked softly, "What's your name?"

He stared at her; his sharp gaze somewhat malevolent. She hoped this was his default expression and that he wasn't using it on her in particular. Because if he really felt toward her the way his expression was leaning, then she wouldn't survive the night.

"You do not need to know my name to look at my wound, *divka*." His voice was deep and guttural as he stumbled over his English.

She shrugged, and said in slow, halting Ukrainian, "I ask the names of all my patients." She reached for his hand, going for his obvious injury first. "It makes it easier to ask them how they feel, where it hurts, how they were injured."

He didn't pull away as she unraveled the gauze bandage, pulling it first away from his hand, then his finger. She sank her teeth into her lip to stop the gasp that tried to fly out when she saw the damage inflicted on him. She lifted her gaze to meet his and was awed by the blank look he was giving her in return. They could have been at a tea party for all the indication of pain he was giving. He did not have the look of a man who had been tortured within the last several days.

"You are very brave," he said mockingly, switching to Ukrainian. "You speak Ukrainian badly and are not shy to put me in my place. You must be very sure of yourself."

"I'm completely terrified, actually, but as you are now my patient, I want you to be comfortable while I treat your injury. I thought you would be more comfortable speaking Ukrainian."

He inclined his head toward her, his deep blue gaze taking on a thoughtful look.

She tugged his hand further away from his body, resting it

on her knees, and inspected it in the firelight. She twisted around and said to Jozef, "I need more light, please."

Jozef nodded and reached behind himself to flick on the light. He strode to the window to draw the heavy curtains across, blocking any view of them from the street. The wound on her patient's finger was straight and even, as though it had been cut with scissors or hedge clippers. The cut was infected though and most likely quite painful. Puss oozed from the stump and the skin around the wound was white instead of a healthy pink. The instrument that had taken the finger had probably been dirty and the wound most likely hadn't been sterilized after.

"Your wound is closing, but it's infected. You need antibiotic ointment, a fresh bandage and a round of strong antibiotics."

Shaun jumped as a bag landed next to her on the floor. She leaned over and opened it, immediately recognizing an array of medical aides. She glanced up at Jozef, who stood behind her chair, his arms crossed over his chest. He'd taken his leather coat off. She could now see the tattoos that ran all the way up his corded arms. The sleeves of his T-shirt were stretched taut across the muscles of his arms. She'd seen first-hand the strength those arms carried when he lifted the man from the basement off the floor.

She refocused on her patient, opening the first-aid kit wider and inspecting the contents. She pulled out a tube of antibiotic ointment, a gauze bandage, some tape and a pair of gloves. Pulling the gloves on, she set about tending to her patient. She was careful and methodical, making sure the man who might hold her life in his hands would have no complaint about her care of him. At first, the room was silent while she worked. After a few minutes she felt his gaze lift from the top of her bent head to Jozef, who was still standing behind her.

"You intend that we leave tonight?"

She felt the air stir behind her as Jozef answered the question. She desperately wanted to turn and look, to watch the graceful movements his strong hands were making, but she stayed concentrated on her job. Judging from the older man's next words, Jozef's response had been an affirmative.

"All of us, or will you leave anyone in the city to keep an eye on Vasiliy?"

Again, she felt, rather than saw, Jozef communicate with his uncle.

"Ah, yes, Havel is a good choice. Trustworthy and measured. He will make sure things here are settled. Have him follow us home in a few days. By then we should have prepared a response to this action taken by my enemy."

Shaun glanced up at her patient and he looked down at her. She didn't like that they were talking business in front of her. She was supposed to be a bystander – just a stranger who'd gotten caught up in their drama. If they weren't afraid to discuss important matters in front of her, then that meant she was either family, or collateral damage. And she certainly wasn't family yet.

"You will tell our hosts to lay low until the dust settles. We can't be positive that Vasiliy won't come after anyone who helped with my rescue, though I am still unsure of his motives. If he wanted me dead, then he would have done it while he had me under his control. He had to know that you would come for me." Her patient spoke almost as if he was speaking to himself. His gaze seemed far away, and she didn't think Jozef was responding, though she couldn't be positive since she couldn't see him from her position.

"Perhaps he wanted you to die a slower death," she muttered.

The older man didn't pretend not to hear her. "Why do you say that, girl?"

"My name is Doctor Shaun Patterson, not girl," she said

crisply and straightened her spine as she looked up at him. "And if this infection was left for even one more day, you would be looking at gangrene and blood poisoning. An extremely painful way to die."

He waved his good hand through the air negligently. "These people do not think this way. If they were to have me killed, they would do it quickly, and yes painfully. They did not intend for me to die, even if that was the outcome of their stupidity. No, they intended to hold me only and threaten my family."

Jozef made a short growling sound that made Shaun turn around to glance at him. He was signing at his uncle with movements that were so rapid she was having trouble catching them all.

"Don't talk that way, boy," the other man said sharply. "I trust all members of my family, especially you. I never once doubted your loyalty while I spent a week locked in that cell. In fact, I simply counted the hours until you arrived. There was no doubt in my mind that you would come for me."

She glanced back down, finishing the bandage and securing it with medical tape. Had Jozef just implicated himself? But why? Especially when it was clear he had nothing to do with his uncle's abduction. She stayed silent, watching their exchange, trying to pick up as much as she could from the strange one-sided conversation.

"This is not a path we will go down, my boy. We are a solid family and I will not doubt a single member. Vasiliy must have another motive for making such a stupid move. You will find out the truth and we will move forward with his punishment." He paused, watching as Jozef bowed his head in acquiesce. Then his gaze moved to Shaun. "What about this girl, what is her purpose for being here?"

Jozef explained to his uncle that she had been needed to

patch up their detainee so Jozef and his team could ascertain his Uncle's whereabouts. Shaun was grateful when she realized Jozef wasn't telling his uncle that she'd failed to revive the man in the basement.

When Jozef finished speaking, his uncle looked at her for a long time. When his gaze turned from thoughtful to regretful, Shaun realized which side of collateral damage she was about to land on. It was what she feared would happen. She was a loose end that needed tying up. She dropped her head, tears rushing to her eyes.

"You have helped me, and I am grateful," he said to her, leaning back in his chair and resting his bandaged hand on his lap. "Jozef will make it quick."

At least he didn't do her the disservice of pretending he wasn't ordering her execution. Shaun lifted angry eyes to his. "You'll excuse me if I don't thank you, I'm not quite ready to die."

The older man tipped his head and gave her a cool half smile. "You wouldn't be human if you didn't have the instinct to live."

Shaun opened her mouth to tell him he could go fuck himself, when Jozef's hand dropped heavily onto her shoulder, pinning her in place. She glanced back at him, but he wasn't looking at her. He was looking at his uncle, and, though he wasn't speaking, or even signing, whatever he was communicating to the other man seemed to be eloquent enough that words weren't required.

"You wish to keep this woman?" he asked, surprise lingering in his voice.

He looked at Shaun, his eyes running from the top of her wild curls, down her body to her sneaker-clad feet. She shuffled them under her stool, feeling almost naked after that heavy perusal.

"You've never asked me for anything." The words had an edge of wonder. "Not once in all these years."

Finally, after several more seconds passed, he reached out and picked up Shaun's hand, holding it briefly in his good hand, and squeezing. "Welcome to the family, Ms. Patterson, I am Krystoff Koba."

CHAPTER NINE

"Your aunt will want to plan the wedding."

Jozef's uncle looked over at him, the glint in his eye somewhere between serious and teasing. Jozef's aunt was well known for her love of parties. She would insist on planning every detail of the wedding right down to the brand of toilet paper rolls in the guest washrooms.

Jozef glanced down at his fiancé of only a few hours. She was sound asleep, occupying the seat between Jozef and his uncle. Her head was resting on Jozef's shoulder, the tiny huffs of breath escaping her lips skittering across his skin and the puff of hair on top of her head tickling his neck. He wanted to touch the tiny black curls, see what they felt like, what the skin of her cheek felt like, but he couldn't. Attachment was weakness. If Jozef showed tenderness toward this woman, others might decide she could be used as a weapon.

Jozef might love and admire his uncle, but he knew better than to trust the head of the Koba family.

"Your women friends will hate her," Krystoff commented, pushing his tired body down in his seat and closing his eyes. "They will be jealous of the foreigner who has managed to capture your attention. Your work will be cut out for you with this one."

He was referring to Jozef's various lovers. As the enforcer for the Koba family, Jozef came into his fair share of feminine attention. He was not one to say no to a quick fuck, but he didn't particularly care for any of them. Never enough to fuck more than a handful of times. His last lover had lasted longer than the others but had ultimately bored him. Giselle had been a fun distraction, but he'd cut her loose months ago.

Krystoff turned his head to look at Shaun, his gaze trailing her features in the dim lighting of the back of their car. Though it was the middle of the night, they were driving back to Prague. The patriarch of the Koba family had been away from his post for long enough.

Krystoff, Jozef and Shaun rode in the back of the spacious car while Terek and Halil rode in the front. The rest of their men were in the car behind them. Havel stayed in Kiev to ensure no one came after the family that'd harboured them.

"I hope you know what you're doing with this one." Krystoff's voice was thoughtful, his gaze still on the slumbering woman. Jozef wished Krystoff would stop looking at her with such intensity. "She could be a threat to everything we've worked for. Yes, she's very beautiful and the idea of killing an innocent and a doctor is not an easy one. But in this business, we must put family first."

Jozef understood what his uncle was saying. He should have killed her in the clearing. He hadn't been able to pull the trigger, and he wasn't sure why exactly. Something about her was different. As his uncle pointed out, she was beautiful, but Jozef had met beautiful women before and even killed them when it was warranted. Gender and beauty meant nothing to him when it came to family, loyalty and business.

Perhaps it was because she was a doctor. She had devoted her life to studying medicine and helping others. That kind of unselfish personality was non-existent in the mob. Jozef couldn't bring himself to destroy a person like that. At least not until he understood her draw.

He didn't try to sign his thoughts, but he gave his uncle an eloquent look.

Krystoff shook his head and chuckled. "Smart move declaring that she would become your wife. Make her part of the family so we can't outright kill her."

Though it had been a smart move, deciding Shaun would become his wife, Jozef didn't actually need to marry her. He could've driven her back to the hospital and then disappeared from her life. He could have forced her promise of silence. No, his desire to marry her was purely selfish. He was fascinated by her. He wanted her and couldn't come up with a better way of having her. Marriage would bind them together and keep her safe from his family.

As if echoing his thoughts, Krystoff said, "Be sure, boy. This marriage will be for life. There is only one way out of the family."

Krystoff's words didn't faze Jozef. He wanted to tie Shaun to him, keep her by his side. Those brief moments they'd spent together in the woods had cemented a bond that transcended the very different lives they led. Though he knew Shaun felt it too, Jozef was not a naïve man; there would be many hardships in their path forward, but his desire for the woman was not one of those difficulties.

He traced her features with his eyes. She had smooth, flawless brown skin. The colour was lighter than her springy black hair but darker than her pretty golden irises. A long straight nose, eyes that tilted slightly inward at the corners and lips that he longed to see curved in a smile. Though she was tall, she was quite thin, as though she'd missed too many meals. She had slight curves packed into ugly scrubs.

Jozef enjoyed women; it was one of the perks of his posi-

tion. When he went out to the clubs the bounty was plenti-
ful. He could pick up any woman available to him. Despite his
lack of voice, his scarred, tattooed skin and abrupt manners,
women flocked to the power and mystery surrounding him.

Yet, Doctor Shaun Patterson put the model-like beautiful
women he was used to fucking to shame. It wasn't her looks,
though she was indeed just as beautiful as them. It was something more. It was her altruism that made her different. That
made her shine like a beacon of goodness in the night.
Despite her fear, she'd still attempted to help the dying man
in the basement. She'd also helped Krystoff knowing that he
could easily order her death.

Maybe that was it – she was new and shiny. He wanted to
touch her goodness and see what it felt like to a man who had
known only violence and crime. When his fascination waned,
as it inevitably would, he might be more ready to let her go.

Despite this last thought, he couldn't tear his eyes from
her. Somehow, deep down, he knew that he would never want
to let her go. There was something about her that told him
she was his for life.

"She won't adjust easily to our lifestyle," Krystoff mused,
reading Jozef's thoughts. "A woman like her, someone who
chooses to work in a war zone out of the goodness of her
heart will not settle into a life of crime easily."

Though the car was dim, Jozef signed to his uncle, *she will
not commit any crimes.*

Krystoff caught enough to understand his nephew. He
shook his head, a grim smile hovering about his lips. "Don't
be stupid, nephew. She may not be committing the crimes,
but you certainly will. If you think that she will condone her
husband's activities, I can tell you now that you are wrong."

Josef's signs were swift and decisive. *She will settle into a
new life. There is no need for further discussion.*

Krystoff raised an eyebrow and chuckled. "You are touchy

with your new woman. A good sign for a good marriage, I hope."

Jozef didn't say anything, but settled into his seat, pulling the slumbering woman closer against him. His uncle might be head of the Koba crime family, but Jozef was a power unto himself. Everyone revolved around him, including his uncle. They had no choice. Jozef was the power, the muscle, the brains behind the crown. Though Krystoff's words held weight, if he wanted to keep his seat of power, he would align himself with Jozef's desires.

Jozef closed his eyes and prepared to sleep. They were still a few hours away from Prague. He curved his hand over her leg, resting it there, a sign of his possession. Shaun belonged to him and any man who tried to remove her would die a swift and painful death.

"I never saw Vasiliy himself while enjoying his hospitality, but one of his men spoke to me when I was in the cellar." Krystoff's tired voice filtered through the darkness.

Jozef tilted his head to look at his uncle, showing he was listening.

"He let slip that the *Prizrak* was responsible for my abduction. Perhaps a nickname for Vasiliy, since he is not often seen in public."

Prizrak... or phantom.

Jozef frowned as a thought tickled his memory. A recent shipment intercepted. He'd lost a man and then the authorities had descended, picking up the rest, as though they'd been tipped off. When Jozef had gone to meet his guy on the inside, after the dust had settled, he'd said they were ambushed in a coordinated attack. Then he'd muttered the word 'prizrak' before being taken back to his cell.

Jozef had shrugged it off as a strange turn of phrase. Now he wondered if the two incidents were connected.

CHAPTER TEN

"Krystoff!" Dasha's shout echoed through the front hall of the mansion as she rushed down the huge double staircase toward them.

Jozef stood next to his uncle with a hand on his arm to steady him. Krystoff was pale with fatigue and the pain of his injury, but he managed a smile for his wife.

Shaun stood behind Jozef with two bodyguards at her back. The bodyguards would remain with Krystoff until Jozef could unravel the reason why Vasiliy had taken the head of the Koba family. Jozef wanted to be reasonably sure they wouldn't attack again.

Aunt Dasha threw herself into Krystoff's arms. He grunted, wincing as his exhausted and injured body took the brunt of her weight. She burst into tears and sobbed out her anger and fear into his lapel.

It was well known that Krystoff and Dasha hadn't been a love match when their families made the alliance thirty years ago. The two had fought as only two bloodthirsty members of mafia royalty could. It wasn't until Dasha had nearly died giving birth to their second child that Krystoff had realized he had feelings for his wife. They reconciled and became one of the most powerful couples in Europe.

Jozef touched his aunt's head, attempting to gain her attention. Krystoff was swaying on his feet, dirty, injured and exhausted. He needed to find a shower and a bed as soon as possible. Dasha needed to calm down and take care of her husband.

Dasha looked over at Jozef and, as he was in the middle of signing his request to her, she flung herself at him. Unable to finish his sentence, he caught her and held her as she cried out her gratitude.

Jozef smiled in grim humour. Aunt Dasha was a force to be reckoned with. She had actively negotiated for her husband's release, but now that he was safe, she was turning into a hysterical wife.

"Th-thank you for bringing my Krysto back to me," she sobbed against Jozef who patted her back awkwardly.

Krystoff stepped in to peel her away and as she moved back from Jozef her eyes landed on their newcomer. She stiffened and frowned, her hand dropping to her robe pocket where Jozef was positive she kept a pistol.

"Who is this?" Dasha asked coolly, all trace of tears now gone.

Dasha was a regal woman. She held herself with an air of confidence and superiority at all times. She would soften around family, but never around a stranger, as her malevolent gaze made clear. A person was either family or an outsider. An outsider in the mansion, unless they were having an event, was not acceptable.

Jozef didn't answer her question since she wasn't looking at him. The bane of his life was attempting to communicate with people who seemed determined to look in the wrong direction.

"This is Dr. Shaun Patterson." Krystoff made the introduction. "She helped save my life." He pulled Dasha around to greet Shaun. "Dr. Patterson, this is my wife, Mrs. Dasha Koba."

Dasha automatically put her hand out, eyeing the stranger in her home with curiosity. Shaun hesitated for a split second and then took the hand offered to her, squeezing it lightly before dropping it. Jozef took a hard look at Shaun. Despite her dusky skin, she looked pale and exhausted. She wasn't supposed to be alive, so he hadn't taken any pains to see to her comfort. Now he felt guilty. When was the last time she ate? Slept? She'd had to beg him to use the washroom earlier.

Jozef was used to being a solitary figure, even among the family. He was the guard dog. Brutal, loyal, dangerous. Characteristics that had served him well until now. He would have to make an effort to soften himself around Shaun, remember he had a woman now. Someone to take care of.

"Thank you for saving my husband's life. I will be eternally grateful for this," Dasha said with a modicum of warmth, her eyes surveying their tired guest. "I apologize for being curious, but can you please tell me how you came to be involved in our situation?"

Dasha was a sharp woman and Jozef searched his brain for a way to explain the day's events in a way that would appease his aunt, who was even more fierce when it came to family than her husband. He didn't need to bother, Shaun jumped in with the truth, perhaps in an attempt to gain his aunt's sympathies.

"Your nephew kidnapped me from a hospital and forced me to help save a man who he ended up shooting anyway." She sounded more offended than terrified, which Jozef took as a good sign. "Then he took me out to the woods, put a gun to my head and nearly killed me, too. We agreed that marriage was better than death. I patched up your husband after he was rescued, and now I'm here."

The look on Dasha's face was approaching comical. Though she could certainly be as vicious as any of their elite enforcers, she still lived to a certain standard. One did not talk business in the foyer of the mansion. Of course, Shaun wasn't just any business, she was about to become the newest member of their family.

Dasha stepped forward, away from her husband and took hold of Shaun's arms. "Oh, my dear, what a terrible story. It must have been such a shock to see that poor man die, and so suddenly."

Jozef had a silent chuckle as his aunt skipped right over the kidnapping part of the story, making it sound like the man had spontaneously died and Shaun just happened to witness the entire thing. Shaun looked dazed as Dasha hurried her into the house.

"You must be exhausted after all that," Dasha clucked. "I'll have Stasia, my personal maid, set up a room for you and the cook will bring up a snack. You'll want to get some rest after your ordeal."

Jozef took hold of Shaun's shoulder and tugged her back to his side, breaking Dasha's hold. His aunt frowned at him, but Jozef rapidly signed that Shaun would be staying with him in his suite. He wasn't about to let Shaun out of his sight. Not while she was so new to the house and the situation.

Dasha shook her head and frowned at Jozef. "She needs time to adjust, *drahoušek*. She should not stay in your suite until after the wedding."

Jozef gave her a hard stare. He didn't sign his thoughts. He didn't need to. His family had become experts at deciphering his body language and facial expressions, rare as they were. He wouldn't release Shaun to the care of his aunt. The doctor would be staying with him, married or not.

Dasha sighed and shrugged her shoulders, her concerned gaze on Shaun. Though Dasha was tough as nails, she did have a heart. She loved her nephew, but knew how brutal he could be. It was unlikely that Shaun would fall easily into marriage with the Koba's second-in-command. Once she got some rest, she would very likely fight her fate and it would be Jozef's job to make her see that her options were limited.

Still, Dasha knew better than to contradict him. After Krystoff, Jozef was next in line for head of the family.

"I'll send some food up for the two of you." Dasha's gaze settled on Shaun once more and she seemed to hesitate before asking, "Would… could you please look at Krystoff in the morning? I want to be sure he's one hundred percent after his ordeal."

Shaun nodded and gave Dasha as much of a smile as she could, given her current situation. "Of course. I need to rebandage his hand anyway."

"Excellent," Dasha said briskly, taking her husband's arm and pulling him toward the stairs. Over her shoulder she added, "We have a room we use as a makeshift infirmary. You are welcome to work in there while you're with us."

Jozef wanted to correct his aunt, remind her that Shaun's placement was permanent. He didn't want his doctor to think she might be able to one day leave them. Dasha was already climbing the stairs though, her back to them. Jozef gritted his teeth and pulled Shaun to the left, toward his suite of rooms. Another pet peeve of his, when people closed out conversations with him by turning away. Unless he punched them in the head to regain their attention and then force them to look at his hands while he signed, he was shit out of luck for ever getting the last word.

"I want my own room." Shaun's voice was slightly more strident as she made the demand, clearly feeling bolstered by his aunt's seeming support.

He wanted to tell her that his aunt would be the first to put a gun to Shaun's head if she were to become a threat to the family. Instead, he pulled her through the first floor of the mansion to his suite, slamming the door shut and locking it once they were inside. His suite consisted of a main room with his TV, couch and dining set, a washroom, an office, his room and a separate bedroom he'd converted into a gym.

Shaun yanked her arm from his grip and immediately tried the door. She reached for the lock, but Jozef took her hand and squeezed tightly. She gasped and tried to pull away, but he refused to release her. He dragged her further into the room and pushed her toward the couch.

She landed on it heavily and half fell sideways. "Stop pushing me around!" she snapped, gripping the back of the couch and righting herself. She glared up at him. "I don't like being locked up, I don't like being pushed and I don't think I'm being unreasonable to expect my own room."

Jozef was exhausted after a fucking long week with little to no sleep. He didn't need attitude from this woman, even if she had a good reason to be mad. He needed her to settle down and accept her situation so they could get on with it. Namely, sleep.

Jozef did the only thing he knew how to do when confronted with a person who wasn't listening to him. He pulled his gun from the holster under his leather jacket and pressed the barrel against her forehead, a reminder of her precarious situation. He did it automatically, without thinking. The gun had become such an extension of him that he saw it as more of an extra limb than a weapon.

Shaun clearly thought of it as a weapon. Her eyes widened with fear, tears giving them a shine as she stared up at him. Her entire body froze as though she thought he would pull the trigger if she so much as breathed.

Jozef regretted his action, since he'd told her he wouldn't kill her and now she thought he would go back on that promise. He put the gun away.

She collapsed back onto the couch and let out a hiccoughing sob. She dropped her head into her hands and cried. Her shoulders shook and tears dripped from between her fingers.

He wasn't sure what to do. The only women he'd ever had to comfort were his cousins when they were young. Both had grown into adults with the same backbone as their mother. They rarely cried anymore, at least not around him.

Jozef didn't like Shaun's tears, especially because he was the cause. He wanted to tell her to stop, to reassure her that he wasn't going to kill her, but she wasn't looking at him. He dropped to his haunches in front of her and touched her hair. She jerked back and lifted her head to look at him fearfully. Tears marked her stricken face. He hated that look, wanted to erase it from her face.

But he couldn't. It was more than likely he would have to continue terrorizing her until she was forced to settle into her new existence. She was a saint among thieves, and he was head of the thieves. She didn't belong in his world. In the long run she might end up wishing he'd killed her in that clearing.

The weight of his responsibility toward this woman settled heavily on him. She was a human and unless he intended to turn her into a mindless slave, he would have to find a balance between making sure she understood her place and preserving her core personality. For some reason, it was important to him that who she was remained intact while under his care. He'd made the decision not to kill her and now she belonged to him.

"I've never seen a real gun before... except for police officers." Her voice was quiet and strained. She didn't look him in the eye as she spoke but kept her gaze on her clasped hands. "I've never had a gun pointed at me and I've never seen someone die violently."

Jozef reached out slowly so she could see his hand. He touched her knee with his knuckle, but nothing more. He didn't want her to feel threatened again. He lifted his hand and tilted her chin until her eyes were on him.

You are safe.

She shook her head and a tear dripped down her face, creating a wet trail. "You put a gun to my head five times in the past two days. I don't feel safe, Jozef."

Jozef loved the way she said his name, soft and sweet, even though she spoke of her fear of him. He nodded thoughtfully. *I will never again put a gun to your head.*

She stared at him for several long seconds. "Can you make that promise?" she whispered.

Jozef lifted a hand to his chest and tapped over his heart. *You have my word.*

"Okay." She let out a long sigh, the tension releasing from her shoulders. Once she was able to gather her composure, she looked around the room, curious for the first time. "I'm exhausted. Where can I sleep?"

She wasn't going to like the answer. She wasn't looking at him, so he was saved from having to answer. Instead, Jozef stood and held a hand out to her. She looked at it and then hesitantly placed her hand in his palm.

Jozef curled his fingers around hers, liking the feel of her delicate bones shifting beneath her skin. If he chose to close his hand into a fist, he could crush her.

He stood and drew her to her feet next to him. He waved his hand toward the door to his bedroom. Their bedroom.

CHAPTER ELEVEN

Jozef opened the door and indicated that Shaun should step through. She did as he asked and quickly stepped away from him. She opened her mouth to thank him for showing her to the guest room, but he stepped in with her, then closed and locked the door behind them. She turned warily as he strode across the room, dragging his leather jacket from his shoulders as he walked.

He tossed the jacket on a chair and reached for the buttons on his shirt. It was becoming rapidly clear that they were not in a guest room, as she had thought, but in Jozef's room. A king-size bed occupied the space in front of a large stone fireplace, which was glowing brightly in the cool evening air. Someone had lit a fire in anticipation of Jozef's arrival.

There was also a large battered leather chair, a small plush couch, a chest of drawers and a wardrobe in the room. Against the wall was a bookshelf, stuffed full, with several books tossed haphazardly on top. Though the room itself was large, it had a cozy feel. It was sparsely furnished, but the few furnishings he had were meant for comfort.

Shaun backed up and reached for the door, intent on going back out to the living room. Jozef was across the room so fast she was left gasping as he whirled her around and shoved her against the door.

He didn't try to use sign language but allowed his stern gaze to speak for him. He had one hand on Shaun's arm and the other on the door next to her head. His scent, a combination of masculine sweat and leather, made her head spin.

"Please don't make me sleep with you," she begged him, her gaze darting past him to the bed.

He growled in frustration and let her go, taking a step back and shoving a hand through his dark hair, making it stand on end. *I won't touch you, but you sleep in here.*

She shook her head. "Why do we have to sleep together?"

This is not negotiable, he signed, his hands moving quickly as he conveyed his annoyance. *Either you get in the bed or you take the couch. I don't care which one. I'm tired. I'm going to sleep.*

Shaun's head spun as she tried to keep up with his rapid hand movements. Before she finished absorbing the last sentence, he turned away from her, strode back to the fireplace and continued unbuttoning his shirt. He pulled it from his shoulders and tossed it on top of his leather jacket on the chair next to the fireplace.

Shaun's eyes were immediately drawn to the chiseled musculature of his back. It was as brutal as the rest of him, clearly defined muscles shifting as he moved. He had a black phoenix rising up his inked back, its wings stretched out across each of his shoulders, its beak pointing down. Her gaze strayed to the small round marks at the bottom of his back, near his spine. Bullet holes.

It hit her exactly how far out of her depth she was. Shaun had always thought of herself as a street savvy woman. She'd grown up with affluent parents and the perks of their jobs, but she hadn't been sheltered. As a black woman, living in a predominantly Caucasian city, she'd experienced some racism in school. At the hospital she'd worked on all kinds of different wounds and illnesses. In her work with Doctors Without Borders, she'd seen and treated horrific injuries. But none of that had prepared her for what she'd experienced at Jozef's hands.

Jozef finished undressing, unbuckling his pants and sliding them down his strong thighs. He stepped out of them and tossed them over the same chair. He touched the waistband of his boxer briefs, paused and glanced at Shaun, then dropped his hands, leaving them on.

Though Shaun had seen many naked bodies in her work as a doctor, this one was different. This one was dangerous. His flesh was marked with knife and bullet wounds. She traced them with her eyes, wondering how he came by each scar. One particular puckered bullet wound drew her attention and she slowly walked toward him, her eyes glued to his back.

He turned, looking at her suspiciously as she approached him. She hadn't willingly gone to him once since he kidnapped her. But this was different; this was something she knew. Something she understood.

She tentatively touched his shoulder and tried to turn him around. He resisted, but eventually half-turned and moved his head so that he could keep his gaze on her. She brushed her finger across the middle of his back, just over the wound, tracing it, feeling it. Gooseflesh raised across his skin where she touched. It was a brutal scar, one that probably took months to heal.

"How did you survive?" Shaun asked quietly. "This is right over your heart. It should've killed you instantly or driven a shattered rib into the organ."

He turned from her, pulling away from her touch. He sat down on the edge of the bed and rubbed a hand over his tired face. She thought maybe he wouldn't answer, but he finally looked up at her, his piercing blue eyes meeting hers.

The bullet entered my back from the side rather than straight in. It glanced off my rib, exited through my side and entered here, lodging in my arm.

He lifted his arm and pointed at the skin on the underside of his bicep. For a few brief seconds, Shaun was distracted by the bulge of his muscles – sweet Jesus this man was ripped – but then she saw the small entry wound in his arm.

"You were very lucky," she murmured, stepping away from him, suddenly realizing her proximity to the killer.

He shook his head. *I didn't feel lucky.*

Shaun gave him a tired smile. "I imagine you probably didn't."

They looked at each other for an uncomfortable minute. Captor and captive. Shaun knew that she must never relax her guard. She was quite literally residing in a den of thieves.

"I'll sleep on the couch." She inserted a colder note into her voice and turned swiftly away from Jozef. Before she could walk away from him though, he reached out and snatched her hand, pulling her back.

Shaun glanced at him fearfully, afraid he'd changed his mind about sharing a bed with her. Instead, he released her hand and reached behind him, gathering up a blanket and pillow, pushing them into her arms. He pointed at the couch, which was sitting to the right of the fireplace at the end of the bed. It would make for a cozy warm place to sleep. Shaun had slept in worse places; she wasn't going to complain.

Shaun held the bedding against her and walked to the couch, sinking into the cushions. It was comfortable enough, though not very long. She would have to sleep on her side with her legs curled up. Hopefully, it wouldn't take long for her to get out of there. She had absolutely no intention of actually marrying the mobster, which left her two options: escape or be rescued.

She heard Jozef rustling around, then the light went out and minutes later his deep snores filled the room. She was amazed that he was able to actually fall asleep with a person he barely knew in the same room. Not just any person, but a surgeon who knew dozens of ways to make him die before he could ever touch her. Either he was ridiculously unflappable, or he was just that tired.

Shaun stared at the door, then back at Jozef's form on the bed. He was bathed in shadows and flickering firelight. She could leave. Just walk out the door and try to leave the premises. She gripped the edge of the couch as she thought about it, then shook her head and forced her body to relax. She was physically and mentally exhausted, in no shape to launch an escape attempt. She was confident she wouldn't make it out the front door. Jozef seemed like an extremely vigilant man, and there would be security all over the place. No, what she needed to do was sleep, regain her strength and mental faculties. Then she'd think her way out of this situation.

Shaun set the pillow on the end of the couch, curled onto her side and dragged the blanket over her body. She stared at the glowing embers of the fireplace until her eyelids grew heavy and sleep claimed her.

CHAPTER TWELVE

Dasha fussed relentlessly until Krystoff finally gathered her against his chest. "Stop, Wife," he murmured against her rich chestnut hair. "I promise, I won't disappear if you stop touching me."

Rather than feeling comforted, Dasha burst into tears and sobbed into his shirt while he held her, running his hand over her smooth hair. "I know!" she wailed. "But they cut off your finger, Krysto!"

She pushed away from him and paced the length of their bedroom, tears streaming down her face, hands thrown up in the air as she talked and walked.

Krystoff took her momentary distraction to sink tiredly onto the mattress of their bed. He nearly groaned out loud at the pleasure of being in his own bed again. A hard, lumpy single mattress on a wooden plank with no pillow or blanket had been the extent of his accommodation for a week.

"It could have been much worse, Dasha."

"No, it wouldn't have been," she snapped, going from despair to anger in a flash as she paced the room in front of him, giving him an excellent view of her shapely legs as they peeked from beneath her robe.

Dasha was fifty-one years old and still as fine as the day he'd married her. In fact, he thought she looked even better. Age and experience suited his wife. "Vasiliy doesn't have the balls to do more than cut off one small finger."

Krystoff shook his head at her phrasing. She'd gone from wailing over the loss of his precious finger to dismissing it as trivial, in almost the same breath.

"Vasiliy may be ineffectual, but he could be dangerous in his stupidity." Krystoff snatched her hand as she walked past him. He dragged her toward him until she was standing between his spread legs, looking down at him with solemn brown eyes. "Until I understand his motives, we must be vigilant."

"You think he will try again?" Dasha asked skeptically.

Krystoff shrugged. "As I've said, we don't know what he will do."

"Why don't you just kill him?" Dasha asked, as though murder was as simple as breathing. His bloodthirsty wife was used to having an entire hit squad at her fingertips.

"You know it's not as easy as that," Krystoff chided. "Vasiliy has established himself deep in Europe's underground. He cozies up to those who can further his business aspirations. Your own father had alliances with the man, including a marriage to your half-sister. He may be inept but he's not completely stupid. He has somehow managed to involve himself in as many aspects of Koba business as he can. I suspect it is because he hasn't managed to successfully insinuate himself directly into our lives, where he would have the might of the Kobas at his back, despite marrying your sister."

"She is *no* sister of mine," Dasha hissed in annoyance.

Krystoff suppressed a smile. Over thirty years had passed, but Dasha was still bitter toward her younger half-sister. The girl had thrown herself at a drunk Krystoff after a night of celebration with his friends. She'd tried to seduce him and convince him to marry her instead of Dasha.

Krystoff hadn't wanted anything to do with a single member of the family. There was no honour among her birth family. They would do business with a man one day and shoot him in the back the next. The only reason Krystoff had agreed to marriage with the elder daughter was because his father had an unpaid blood debt to the family.

Eventually, after a decade of vicious fighting, Dasha and Krystoff had discovered an unexpected love. It helped that she hated her family as much as he did. When Vasiliy married into the family circle, Krystoff had cut ties with both Vasiliy and Dasha's family, much to Vasiliy's chagrin.

Dasha rolled her eyes. "This whole thing is ridiculous. Vasiliy has been a thorn in our side for years. It's time to be done with him."

Krystoff yanked on Dasha's arm, dragging her off her feet and tumbling her onto the bed next to him. He rolled onto his side, looking down at her and sliding his hand into the front of her robe, seeking the smooth skin beneath. She smiled up at him, her shoulders relaxing into the bed. She reached up to touch his face, smoothing her fingers over his brow, then his mustache and beard.

"I will remove Vasiliy when it's time, but for now he must remain alive." Krystoff's voice held a note of finality. "Now, tell me what you think of our nephew's soon-to-be bride."

Dasha's eyes lit up with the special light she got only when there was a wedding on the horizon. One that she got to plan. "I think she's perfect," Dasha announced excitedly, rolling against her husband and speaking animatedly, her nose inches from his. "She's beautiful, but serious and smart. Jozef has never brought a woman home before. She must really be something special. She'll look absolutely stunning in the dress I'm envisioning for her."

Krystoff frowned. He hadn't considered that Jozef might actually have feelings for the doctor. They'd only met two days ago; they couldn't possibly have formed a bond. Then again, Shaun had gone through a traumatic event with Jozef at her side, possibly igniting his protective instincts. The ones usually reserved for his family.

Jozef had earned the nickname *divoký pes*, feral dog, because he was so viciously protective of his family. He hired other men who were nearly as rabid to serve as the first line of defense between the Kobas and the rest of the world. Jozef's loyalty was not something Krystoff would ever question.

Yet, there was something about the way Jozef looked at the doctor. Something that went deeper than simple lust or curiosity.

When Jozef had announced his intentions to marry Shaun, Krystoff had decided to allow him the fantasy until he lost interest and she could be quietly removed. Now, he was less certain this would happen, which concerned him. The Kobas married within their own circles. They didn't choose outsiders, people who wouldn't understand their way of life.

"Don't get too attached to the girl," Krystoff said quietly.

Dasha pushed herself up on one elbow, her dark hair swirling around her shoulders. She propped her chin up on her hand. "Whyever not?"

Krystoff didn't answer, but he didn't need to. Dasha would know what her husband was thinking.

She smiled at him. "Nonsense, she'll fit in just fine." At Krystoff's raised brow, she explained, "I think she'll be good for us. We get so involved in this lifestyle, so caught up in our own circles, that sometimes we don't see what goes on in the world outside. I think Shaun will bring a fresh breath of the outside world to our family. New perspectives."

Krystoff shook his head. "She is a highly intelligent foreigner from overseas, where freedom is prized above all else, including family. She will not settle easily."

Dasha refused to back down. "Regardless, she'll be a good match for Jozef. He needs some good in his life."

"He has his family," Krystoff said stubbornly.

"He needs more." Dasha sealed her words with a kiss.

Krystoff could never resist her kisses. He gripped the back of her head and deepened the kiss, uncaring of his wound. He rolled her beneath him, dragging her bathrobe open. He wanted nothing more than to lose himself in his wife.

CHAPTER THIRTEEN

Shaun stretched, luxuriating in the feel of soft blankets and silky sheets. She rolled onto her side and curled up, rubbing her cheek against the smooth fabric of the pillow. A delicious scent teased her nose. It was familiar but she couldn't place it. She buried her head in the pillow and breathed in. It was a masculine scent, like natural body odour mixed with something spicy and leather. It was nice.

She frowned. Had she brought a guy home the night before?

Her eyes flew open and she sat up with a gasp, staring around in consternation. The light filtering through the curtain-covered windows was dim and it took her a moment to realize where she was. She was not in her small room with her lumpy bed in Luhansk.

The events of the day before rushed at her in flashes. She pressed her spine against the headboard and covered her face with her hands. What had she gotten herself into?

Her mother warned her that something might happen if she continued to work with Doctors Without Borders. Shaun had shrugged off her mother's concern and done her best to reassure Fatima, but the reality was her job could be danger-ous. She worked in war zones, felt the vibrations in the ground as bombs went off nearby. She often treated infectious diseases that were nonexistent in Canada. She could've been killed at any moment. In fact, she'd had colleagues killed at similar camps.

But nothing she'd ever done had prepared her for this. To be kidnapped by a mafia family and dragged into the Czech Republic, where she was told she would soon be married to the scariest member of the family. Her situation defied imagi-nation. It was like a movie, and everyone knew how mafia movies usually ended.

One thing was for certain, Shaun would have to find a way out. But before she could figure out a plan that wouldn't get her shot, she was going to have to find a bathroom. Her morning bladder was screaming at her to get her ass out of bed and moving.

As she was shoving the blankets off her legs, she realized she was in the bed and not on the couch. This thought made her freeze all over again as she contemplated how this was possible. Jozef must've moved her. She wasn't entirely surprised that she hadn't woken up through the process of him lifting her off the couch and placing her on the bed. Shaun had slept in some pretty unsavory conditions and had grown used to sleeping through just about anything.

She pushed herself out of the bed and stood, looking around. Besides the door leading out into the main room, which she suspected was locked, there was another door. She headed in that direction, hoping for a bathroom.

She was pleased to find that she was correct and quickly did her business, flushing the toilet and washing her hands. Once this was finished, she looked around the spacious bath-room, noting the opulent features. She hadn't seen much of the Koba family mansion yet, but what she had seen was an interesting mix of modern convenience and old-fashioned luxury.

Everything was made out of heavy, good quality woods and marbles. The bathroom itself had both a deep tub and a shower, both spotless. The large vanity stretched from one end of the bathroom to the other with two sinks in it. Off to the side was a display of fresh lovely smelling orchids. She would bet her freedom Jozef had nothing to do with their presence. Which meant there were maids coming in, probably daily, to clean and leave freshly cut flowers.

Perhaps this could be an avenue of escape for her. If she managed to convince one of the staff to help her, she might be able to get out of the mansion unscathed. The staff would know every entrance and exit and how much security was in place.

Shaun decided to risk taking a shower. She hadn't bathed in three days and was ready to feel clean again. She was pleased to find a lock on the bathroom door and flipped the latch. It made her feel safer as she stripped off her scrubs, wrinkling her nose at the smell. She'd been kidnapped in those scrubs, forced to work on a dying man, run for her life through the woods, and slept in them twice. She had no issues if she never saw them again.

Shaun heated the water and stepped under the spray, moaning in gratitude as hot water rushed over her naked body. Many of the places she travelled to didn't have hot water unless it was boiled. Her tiny apartment in Luhansk had a tiny heater for the whole building, which meant she hadn't had a truly hot shower in four months.

She took her time, carefully scrubbing each part of her skin and checking out the products available. They were all masculine and none were particularly fancy. A tiny part of her was gratified that there didn't seem to be the presence of another woman in Jozef's bathroom. Not that she was jealous, but if the man was talking about marrying her, the fact that there didn't seem to be any hint of a girlfriend made her feel marginally better about the whole situation.

She finished her shower and reached for a towel, realizing that there was only one nearby. Probably Jozef's. She pulled it off the rack and held it up to her body, sniffing it. A wave of his scent hit her so hard it took her by surprise. She gasped and nearly dropped the towel as her body reacted instinctively, flooding with desire.

She did not need that, not at all. She was getting the hell out of here at the first opportunity and no part of her was going to be attracted to her captor. She quickly dried off and tossed the towel back on the rack, not bothering to tidy it properly. She didn't particularly want to put on her dirty scrubs, but she didn't have anything else to wear.

She pulled her shirt over her head and dragged the pants over her legs but stuffed her dirty panties in her pocket. She absolutely refused to put dirty panties on. She had to draw the line somewhere.

She opened the door to the bathroom and froze when she spotted Jozef in the bedroom. He was sitting on the bed, his arms slung over his knees and his gaze on the phone in his hand. He looked up when she entered, his blue eyes roving over her body.

They stared at each other for so long the moments began to stretch and get awkward. Shaun wondered if he did it on purpose. Used his lack of voice to disconcert others. Well, it wasn't going to work on her. In her profession she met every kind of person under the sun. She'd had more than her fair share of awkward conversations.

"I would like to talk to my mother please," she said, trying for a tone of confident and deferential at the same time. She could get angry later if she had to, but she figured being on her best behaviour would probably get her further.

Jozef shook his head.

Shaun frowned at him. "No, I can't call my mother?"

He shook his head again and this time Shaun had to shove her annoyance down, reminding herself she was talking to a killer.

"My mom will be worried, Jozef." Shaun kept her voice conciliatory. "She'll be devastated when she hears that I was taken from the hospital." She bit her lip to stop the rush of tears. "She probably already knows and is freaking out."

Jozef continued to stare at her, his eyes taking on a glacial look. He didn't respond and Shaun guessed he didn't need to. He'd told her 'no' twice. Nothing she said was going to change his mind. Still, she had to try.

"I'm the only person my mother has left. If she thinks I'm dead, it'll devastate her."

He remained unmoving and Shaun's shoulders slumped. He wasn't going to allow her to contact her mother. Jozef may have preserved Shaun's life, but that didn't mean he owed her anything, including a phone call. She blinked back her tears.

Jozef pointed to something at the bottom of the bed and she realized it was a bundle of clothes. She approached cautiously, but was eager for something else to wear, so reached for the clothing, despite their proximity to Jozef. Knowing that he could reach out and grab her as quick as a snake frightened her. She'd seen him kill two people, felt the cold press of steel against her head as he came seconds away from murdering her.

Until she found a way out of this place, she wasn't going to do anything that might piss off her captor. Or at least she was going to try her best not to upset him. She would wear his clothes, eat his food and sleep on the couch. She would play 'good captive' until she found a way out.

The clothes were far richer than she was used to. She could tell just by touching them. The soft fabric slid through her fingers like a silken waterfall. She held up a blouse, pink with white flowers. A pink flowing skirt matched the blouse perfectly. A bra and panty set were tucked beneath the items of clothes. She blushed but picked them up, hoping they fit. As she turned to walk away, she spotted a pair of high heels in a pretty cream colour.

Shaun shook her head and wondered if she could get away with just putting her running shoes back on. She could count on one hand the number of times she'd worn high heels in her life. Heels did not fit into a doctor's lifestyle. She was also nearly six feet tall. When she wore heels, she tended to tower over her dates.

Somehow she didn't think Jozef would care if she was taller than him. He was a man very much in control of himself. She couldn't imagine him being threatened by a tall career woman.

Shaun reentered the bathroom, changed quickly and presented herself back in the bedroom. Jozef got up from the bed and stretched, giving Shaun a good view of him. Her heart beat a little faster as she imagined the slabs of muscle beneath the suit he now wore. It was unfortunate that she knew what this man looked like naked, because dressed there was very little hint of the bulging muscles beneath.

He wore a wine-coloured shirt, unbuttoned at the throat, tucked into a pair of dress pants with a thick leather belt. The patent leather shoes on his feet looked expensive and Shaun bet they cost about as much as her monthly salary.

She looked around for her running shoes but didn't see them. "Where are my shoes?"

Put those on. Jozef pointed at the high heels.

Shaun grimaced. It didn't look like she would have a choice. Someone had taken her shoes and she wasn't willing to argue with Jozef, which meant she wasn't going to have access to them. If she didn't find a good pair of running shoes, escaping the mansion was going to be tough business. She could easily picture herself foiling her own escape plan as she tripped and broke a limb on her way out.

We're eating breakfast with my family. Jozef gestured at the door, indicating they would leave together.

Was she ready to meet the Koba crime family of the Czech Republic? Absolutely not. Did she have a choice? Probably not.

In line with her desire to show Jozef that she was a compliant captive, Shaun merely nodded her head and agreed to go to breakfast. Her heart pounded in fear and her palms grew damp as they walked through the opulent hallways of the sprawling mansion to the dining room. Shaun tried to remember which way they went and how they got there, but she quickly lost track as they passed room after room.

Her heart sank as she realized leaving the mansion would be incredibly difficult. Not only was it massive and twisty, but they passed at least half a dozen security personnel on their way to the dining room. She suspected there were more outside the house, keeping watch for potential threats. They would've all been briefed on the new house resident, which meant they would also probably know to watch for her if she tried to run.

Shaun was truly beginning to worry about how deep into enemy territory she'd landed herself. If she couldn't figure this situation out, she might actually end up married to a ruthless thug, eating her morning meal with his entire crime family on a regular basis.

She couldn't hold in her gasp as they entered a room so grand that she wondered how it wasn't in a museum. The walls were filled with mirrors, gilded-framed paintings and other items she instinctively knew were very old and valuable. In the middle of the room was a massive table that looked big enough to easily seat thirty people.

At the far end of the table, next to a large window facing a well-manicured lawn, was a group of well-dressed people who all turned as Jozef entered the room with Shaun. She stopped abruptly, her stomach swirling in trepidation, making her feel nauseous. All eyes were on her.

Jozef placed a broad hand at the small of her back, giving her a modicum of comfort as he urged her forward. The length of the room until they made their way to the head of the table felt like the longest walk she had ever taken.

Shaun was used to standing out in a crowd. Though she was far from the only black woman in Montréal, most of the places she frequented were predominantly Caucasian. She had been the only black health care worker with Doctors Without Borders in Ukraine, which didn't help her blend in. It was probably partially due to the way she looked that she caught Jozef's attention that day he saw her using sign language with the child. She stood out like a beacon on the streets of Luhansk.

Dasha stood as they approached the table, a gracious smile stretching her lips. "Shaun, welcome. Come meet the family."

CHAPTER FOURTEEN

Jozef urged Shaun forward with a hand on her back. Her timidness with his family was calling to the protector in him. Together they walked the length of the room toward two empty chairs at the table. Jozef's seat was on the right-hand side of Krystoff and Shaun's chair was beside Jozef's.

As Shaun sat, Jozef pushed her seat in. She clutched the sides of her chair as he pushed and looked up at him, her golden eyes wide and concerned. He took his hands off her seat and took his place beside her. She reached out quickly to pick up the water glass in front of her and took a hasty sip. Jozef noted that her hand was shaking, though she covered it by replacing the glass on the table quickly.

He regretted that she was nervous around him, around his entire family, but he didn't blame her. She'd gone through a traumatic few days, something that an innocent woman should never have experienced. But she was handling the situation beautifully, far better than Jozef would've thought. She wasn't hysterical, she wasn't begging him to let her go and she wasn't throwing a tantrum. He wouldn't have blamed her for any of those reactions.

"I hope you don't mind, Shaun, I've had our cook make a feast for us in honour of your arrival. Normally, we eat our morning meals separately." Aunt Dasha was the first to break the tense silence, her smile filled with warmth as she waved her hand to indicate the bounty in front of her.

Shaun didn't say anything for a few seconds and Jozef wondered what she was thinking. She was so silent most of the time, absorbing her surroundings. He suspected her intelligent brain was constantly thinking, trying to figure out a way out of the situation.

She wasn't going anywhere though. Unfortunately, she had seen too much. Besides that, there was something about her that made Jozef long to explore the connection between them. She was foreign, different. Not just the way she looked, or the country she came from, but everything about her. The way she thought, her desire to heal. The way she moved: precise, confident, elegant.

He could easily see her in an operating room, her fingers dancing expertly through someone's body. But it wasn't just her beauty and grace that attracted him, it was her existence. She was so different from him and his family. Jozef lived violence, but this woman was the opposite. She healed. Her profession was giving the gift of life to those who were critically ill. She intrigued him.

"I'm actually very hungry," Shaun said, giving Aunt Dasha a small smile. "Thank you for your hospitality."

Though her words were stiff, they were also polite. Jozef adored his aunt, even though she could be an absolute bitch when she wanted to be. She had heart. When Jozef's parents died, she'd taken him under her wing as though he was one of her own children. She'd raised him, learned sign language along with her husband, and insisted her children learn as well so they could communicate with him. Jozef owed Dasha a debt of gratitude that he could never repay. Any future wife of his would have to get along with his aunt and he appreciated that his aunt was putting in effort to make Shaun feel welcome.

It was a bizarre situation for all of them. Having a strange woman in their midst, one who was there under duress, was unprecedented. Captives went to the shed, then they went into the ground. Shaun was the only exception in the history of their organization. Aunt Dasha and Shaun were both dealing with the situation as best they could.

"Where are you from?" This question came from Jozef's cousin, Saskia. Her tone was bordering on rude.

"I'm from Montréal, Canada," Shaun answered, her own tone guarded.

"What are you doing here?" Saskia demanded, ignoring her mother's sharp admonishment to be polite.

"I work with an organization called Doctors Without Borders, or Médecins Sans Frontières." Her accent as she spoke the words was so perfect, Jozef wanted to ask her to say it again, then something else in French. "For the past four months, I have been working in a hospital in Ukraine, close to the front lines."

Shaun glanced at Jozef, her brain clearly flashing back to the moment he'd taken her from the hospital, the moment he murdered her colleague. The haunted look in her eyes was unmistakable.

Once again, a feeling of regret arose in Jozef. It was unusual for him to regret anything. Everything he did in life was thought out and methodical, including kidnapping Dr. Shaun Patterson. He'd needed a doctor and he preferred to have one that he could communicate with. Finding her was like finding hidden treasure in the soundless murky depths of an ocean.

While he enjoyed the idea of keeping her, looked forward to being married to the intelligent, beautiful doctor, he didn't like that he'd been the one to terrorize her. The thought of causing her harm cut deep, an uncomfortable sensation for a man who dealt death with the same casualness he used to order a meal.

Had they met somewhere else, under different circumstances, he would've approached her, showed her that they shared a language, an uncommon one. She would've smiled at him, the way she'd smiled at the boy on the street. She would have used her graceful hand movements to greet him. Eventually, he might've asked her out. He could've taken her to the club that his family owned, or on a walk through the streets of Prague, shown her the Old Square. Instead, she was his captive and he was her tormentor.

"I know who Doctors Without Borders are. I'm not stupid," Saskia snapped. "What I want to know is what you were doing there. Are you some kind of do-gooder? You're willing to sacrifice your life for the dregs of society left on the front lines?"

Jozef's face heated as anger surged through him. He slapped the table with his palm to draw his cousin's attention and swiftly signed to her, *keep a civil tongue in your head.*

"We don't bring strangers into our home," Saskia said coldly, not afraid to stand up to their feral dog. "I've been told from the day I was born, no strangers, and I've followed this house rule to the letter. Now Jozef is allowed to drag a foreigner home?"

Jozef glanced down at Shaun, worried that she would be upset by his hotheaded cousin. Instead, she gazed at the girl calmly, an expression of understanding on her face. Jozef wished that she would look at him that way.

Before Jozef could continue arguing with his cousin, his uncle stepped in to decisively shut her down. "Shaun is Jozef's fiancé. She is not a stranger to us. She will live in this home, and you will be polite to her. End of argument."

"I doubt it," Leeza piped up from beside her sister.

Leeza was the older sister, more levelheaded. Next to Leeza was her husband, Adam. There was an empty spot next to Adam for the couple's son, Kristoph. The child missed many of their family meals though, as he was autistic and often unable to attend, depending on his state of mind that day.

"I apologize for my sister's behaviour. You are of course welcome here," Leeza said, her accent thick. She'd never been able to pick up English as well as her sister and mother. They spoke almost flawlessly, with little accent, while Leeza and Krystoff retained heavy accents.

Leeza stood and leaned across the crystal glasses and porcelain plates, sticking her hand out to Shaun. Shaun looked startled. The table was so massive Leeza's hand only came halfway across. Jozef bit back a smile and shook his head.

Shaun stood as well and shook the proffered hand, squeezing before letting go. When she relaxed back into her seat, Jozef could feel some of the tension draining from her. Despite their chosen profession, the Kobas generally were not bad people. Unfortunately, Shaun was an innocent caught up in their drama. Ordinarily, as enforcer, it would be Jozef's job to keep innocents out of the family business.

As Leeza settled back into her seat, she pinned Jozef with a look. "My understanding is that she was taken from Luhansk rather quickly. Does she have any clothes besides the ones I provided this morning? Does she have toiletries, or feminine products?"

Jozef shook his head.

"Then that's our first order of business today," Leeza said

brightly, with a smile. "I will take Shaun shopping and we'll purchase all of the necessities she'll need."

"No, thank you..." Shaun tried to protest, but Jozef reached out and squeezed her hand, looking over at her and shaking his head as he caught her eye.

Jozef signed to his cousin. *You may take her shopping, but under no circumstances is she to be out of your sight. You will take bodyguards and you will remain with her at all times.*

He reached into his pocket and took out his wallet, digging out his credit card and tossing it across the table toward his cousin. She snatched it up, a mischievous grin spreading across her face.

"I'm coming too," Saskia chimed in, her annoyance forgotten over the thought of a shopping spree. "It's been ages since I've managed to get to the Gucci store."

Leeza rolled her eyes as she pocketed the credit card. "You and your famous designer houses. You should try someone local, support our shopkeepers."

"And end up looking like you," Saskia said sarcastically, eyeing her sister with mock horror. "No, thank you."

The sisters were almost polar opposite in their clothing choices; Leeza was conservative while Saskia preferred edgier clothes. Despite their differences, the one thing the two women could agree on was how much they enjoyed a shopping trip. Especially if someone else was picking up the bill. Jozef hoped Shaun wouldn't feel too hopelessly out of her depth with his two shopaholic cousins.

"Girls, we have a guest present, please don't argue," Aunt Dasha chided gently.

The rest of the meal went well, with conversation flowing easily around the table. Unless spoken to directly, Shaun remained silent. She ate the food placed in front of her and watched the family as they chatted with each other, her gaze remaining slightly concerned and haunted but occasionally amused at the gentle ribbing. That was the look Jozef hoped he could grow. He hoped that one day she would forget their beginning and settle into some semblance of a relationship with him. It didn't even need to be happy, just real. Because a real marriage would bind her to him, erase the danger of her knowing too much. And it would place in his grasp a good woman, a person who would have been far out of his reach only a week ago.

He looked down at her as she bent her head to fork a bite of eggs into her mouth. Meeting her had been a stroke of luck and Jozef wasn't stupid enough to let go of his lady luck.

CHAPTER FIFTEEN

Shaun stood quietly and watched while preparations were made for the shopping trip. She was surprised at how long it took and how much was involved in the planning. Jozef had lined up the five guards who would be accompanying the women and was lecturing them, his hand signals rapid and smooth. Once again, she marvelled at his lack of expression. It was so unusual to see someone use sign language without involving facial expressions.

At first, Shaun tried to follow what he was saying. He was instructing them on things like checking the vehicles before entering, making sure all exits were covered, and making sure each woman was accompanied by at least one guard, with three guards for Shaun. She was not allowed out of their sight for any reason, except to go into a change room without an exit.

His movements were so rapid that she quickly grew tired of watching. The group was standing in the lobby of the mansion, next to the large double doors. Dasha was talking quietly with her daughters while Jozef instructed his guards. Shaun's gaze lingered on everyone and everything as she attempted to retain as much information as she could, which was a lot. Shaun had learned many tricks in medical school for memorizing information so she could pass her exams.

Each of the guards had at least one weapon visible, though she suspected they probably had more beneath jackets, and strapped to hips or ankles. Even Saskia was checking a small pistol, opening the chamber and squinting at it before snapping it shut and shoving it in her purse.

It was the sort of scene Shaun might expect to see in a movie. She was the only one shocked by the extravagance, the security, the weapons, everything. She felt like she was living some kind of dream, or more accurately, a nightmare. It was so difficult to wrap her head around the things she was seeing and experiencing.

Leeza reached out to touch Shaun's arm. "Everything okay?"

Shaun thought about the question. Was everything okay? Not really. At that very moment she was supposed to be in a field hospital, preparing for surgery on a soldier who been struck in the chest with shrapnel. She'd been waiting for the swelling to go down, for him to gain strength so that he could survive the surgery. Now, he would be left in the hands of a less skilled surgeon.

Shaun didn't know how to feel about that. She should be angry that she'd been dragged from her extremely important work and forced to come here, to this mansion, to be married off to a member of the Koba crime family. But she wasn't angry. She didn't feel scared or sad, either. Any of those emotions would've been appropriate, even welcome.

Instead... she felt numb. If she were to self-diagnose, she would say that she was likely experiencing prolonged shock. A physiological response to her kidnapping; a response meant to protect her. But the shock was slowing her down, making her brain feel sluggish. She needed to snap out of it, come up with a plan.

"Hey... we can plan a shopping trip for another day if you're not ready." Leeza's concerned gaze was on Shaun's face.

Shaun blinked and shook her head. The last thing she wanted was to miss a chance to go into the city. There were far more opportunities for escape there than at the heavily guarded mansion.

"Sorry," she murmured and attempted a smile. "I drifted away for a moment. I'm fine, all set to go."

Leeza looked relieved while Saskia let out a short cackle of laughter. Dasha frowned at her youngest daughter.

"She said sorry and she's Canadian," Saskia giggled. "I've always wanted to hear a Canadian say that. She had the accent and everything, it was perfect."

Leeza laughed too but reached out to swat her sister's arm. "You're so immature; be polite to our guest."

Shaun's lips curled up at the exchange and she surprised herself by wanting to laugh with the sisters. It was so strange to watch the Koba family interact. They seemed so... normal. Not what she would've expected from a ruthless mafia family, though she didn't know exactly what she expected. Maybe guns at the dinner table, snide comments, backstabbing, a graveyard in the garden. She certainly hadn't expected the warmth and caring she was experiencing from them.

Shaun jumped when someone touched her arm and she looked down at the strong fingers wrapping around her. Jozef tugged her to the side, away from everyone else. Her gaze travelled up his fingers to his veined hands, past the tattoos to the rolled-up sleeves of his dress shirt and finally to his face.

His deep blue eyes were solemn as he looked down at her, the scar across his lips a stark reminder of the violence surrounding these people. Everything about him was tense and serious. Shaun hadn't actually seen him in any other mood yet. He always looked grim, as though he expected the worst. Maybe he had to be that way in order to be an effective enforcer. If he prepared for the worst, then he would always be ready for whatever came at him. Shaun had personal experience with the terrible decisions this man had to make.

She thought about how deftly he'd handled his uncle's kidnapping. How he'd found the one woman in that area of Ukraine who was both a doctor and could understand sign language. The way he'd gotten the information he needed out of his hostage, despite the setback of his victim having a heart attack, and then proceeded to release his uncle from imprisonment. Like clockwork, everything he did was smooth and well-planned.

Everything except her. He hadn't planned on keeping her alive.

He gave her a little shake and Shaun realized he was trying to communicate with her, but she'd been gazing blankly at his face. She blinked rapidly and dropped her eyes to his hands, interpreting what he was telling her. He slowed his movements so she could easily follow.

You will not try to escape while you are in the city. Purchase anything you need or want, regardless of cost. You will listen to your bodyguards and follow my cousins' lead.

Shaun nodded. She wanted to ask what would happen if she did try to run or if she refused to listen to her bodyguards, but they were surrounded by people, both family and security. She didn't want to hint that she was going to do her level best to figure out a way to get away from her escort.

Perhaps he could read her mind, or maybe her intentions were written on her face. Either way Jozef gripped her chin and tilted her face up to his. His eyes darkened and he frowned down at her, warning her without a word what would happen if she tried to escape. She shivered under his fierce glare and took a step back, her gaze fixed on his scarred throat.

Jozef guided her back to his men and introduced her to one of them. *This is K-A-R-L, he's in charge of family security. He will act as your personal bodyguard.*

Shaun shook Karl's hand and wondered if he was in charge of making sure she didn't escape or in charge of keeping her safe. She wondered if he was being permanently assigned to her or if it was just for the day, and how he felt about having to protect a foreign captive. She didn't ask any of her questions though. Karl had a large bulge under his jacket that could only be a gun and his face was carved from a boulder.

After the preparations were made, the three women were escorted to the vehicles. Leeza chose to ride in the dark SUV with Shaun while two bodyguards occupied the front seats. Saskia chose to take the vehicle behind theirs, with the other three guards.

Shaun was about to climb inside the SUV when Jozef caught her arm and swung her around, pulling her into his chest. He shoved his fingers into her hair, pinching her scalp. He tipped her head back and placed a quick, stinging kiss on her lips.

Before Shaun could react, he was pushing her into the vehicle and slamming the door shut. She stared at him through the window as the car fired to life under the hands of their driver. A small smile creased his scarred lips as she lifted her fingers to her mouth.

As they travelled into Prague, Leeza chattered happily about all the shops they would visit and where they might eat lunch.

Shaun's gaze remained out the window, though she murmured her agreement whenever Leeza fell silent, seeming to expect an answer from her companion. It was telling that

Jozef was okay with Shaun leaving the property without a blindfold or anything. The mansion was on the edge of Prague, on its own sprawling piece of land. The drive into downtown took about forty minutes, but Shaun was able to memorize every twist and turn.

Jozef must be really serious about marrying her if he was buying her a new wardrobe and was okay with her knowing her way to and from the mansion. If she were somehow to escape, she could easily send the authorities after the Koba family. They must be very confident in their ability to contain Shaun.

Leeza let out a trill of laughter that drew Shaun's attention. The other woman looked carefree and happy, which gave Shaun a pang as she realized that Leeza would likely be arrested too if Shaun accused the family of kidnapping. She was an accessory. Shaun wasn't naïve enough to believe that any single member of the family didn't know the circumstances surrounding her engagement to Jozef.

She wondered if they were okay with it though. Shaun couldn't imagine any circumstance under which she would be okay with the illegal imprisonment of another woman. Maybe this was life as usual for them, but since she hadn't seen any other captive women in the mansion, she somehow doubted that this was a normal circumstance.

Shaun was growing tired of pretending that she wasn't a kidnap victim, of going along with the Koba family who thought nothing of stealing a person and handing her over the marriage.

"Why are you being nice to me?" Shaun asked bluntly.

Leeza looked taken aback. A shutter dropped over her face and her expression smoothed into blankness. Shaun felt guilty that she was ruining what was likely a rare day in the city for Leeza. At breakfast she'd indicated that her son was a handful and she spent most of her time with him.

"I just... you know why I'm here, right?" Shaun's voice was hushed so that they wouldn't be overheard by the men in the front of the car.

Leeza stared at her for a moment as though gathering her thoughts. When she spoke, her voice was slow and cool. "Tell me, why are you here?"

Shaun frowned. Maybe the eldest Koba daughter didn't know about her situation. "Jozef abducted me out of the hospital in Luhansk while I was mid-procedure. He pointed his gun at a child and then killed one of the RN's in front of me." When Leeza's expression remained the same, Shaun continued, her voice low and urgent, her eyes darting to the front seat, "He wanted me to save someone's life just so he could kill them. Now, he's forcing me to marry him. You can't be okay with that."

Shaun stared at the other woman pleadingly, hoping maybe she would be shocked by what Shaun was saying, maybe help her escape. Leeza's next words confirmed Shaun's earlier assumption, the entire family knew what was going on.

"My cousin is saving your life," Leeza said coldly. "If I were you, I would accept his gift and never again speak of your reason for becoming a part of our family. You will live a longer, happier life if you forget your reasons for marrying Jozef."

Shaun turned in her seat to face Leeza, speaking with a desperate passion, attracting a glance in the rearview mirror from Karl, who was sitting in the front passenger seat. "You don't understand, I didn't choose this. A choice between life and death isn't really a choice, is it?"

Leeza let out a sharp laugh. "If you believe that, then you've never been hurt so bad that you wished you could die."

Shaun was taken aback by the other woman's words. Had Leeza experienced something so terrible she wished to die? Or was she talking about someone else?

"You're right, I haven't," Shaun said quietly, acknowledging that there were things in the world worse than death. "But I'm a surgeon, a good one too. I worked hard to get to where I am, I can't just give that up. My life has meaning."

Leeza stiffened, her gaze becoming even more glacial. She glanced out the window on her side of the car, her jaw tense. After a few minutes, the tension ebbed and when she looked at Shaun her face was once again bright and smiley. She reached out to squeeze Shaun's hand.

"And so your life will continue to have meaning. It might just be another kind of meaning than you planned on." Her words were warm, though her gaze was vaguely threatening. "You'll be fine, you just need to dig deep and find a way to accept your new life."

"And if I don't?" Shaun's voice was barely above a whisper.

Leeza shook her head, her gaze softening as she stared at Shaun. "You don't want to know."

CHAPTER SIXTEEN

"Do you think burlap will be in again next season?" Saskia asked, running her hand over a row of silk scarves.

"I don't think burlap has ever been in." Leeza picked up a scarf with a price tag that made Shaun feel a little faint and slung it around her neck, turning to pose in the nearest mirror.

"That's because you get your fashion sense from drugstore catalogues," Saskia said tartly, snatching a dress off a rack and stalking to the change rooms.

As the day progressed, Shaun became more and more convinced that the Koba crime family was trying to break her will through shopping. They wouldn't have to kill her if she killed herself just to escape the tediousness of going to multiple stores and listening to the two sisters bicker constantly.

At each store they visited, the bodyguards insisted on sweeping the premises before posting a man at every exit. Not a single one of them cracked a smile during the entire shopping trip.

The process was tedious, and Shaun was becoming progressively more tired. She fulfilled Jozef's wish by purchasing enough items to fill a wardrobe. She also picked up some toiletries and accessories. After each tour through a new store, one of the bodyguards was sent back to a vehicle, his arms laden with packages.

Though constantly vigilant for an opportunity to escape, Shaun hadn't once come up with a reasonable way to ditch her escort. The guards were always near. Even when she was in a change room, she could see the polished shoes of a man on the other side of the curtain.

Leeza constantly hovered near her, never entering the change rooms herself. It was as though she thought the moment she turned her back, Shaun would bolt. Shaun was going to give the other woman the benefit of the doubt though and say that she was hovering out of concern rather than a desire to keep an eye on Shaun.

"It's almost five." Leeza looked down at the time on her phone. "We'll have to hustle back to the house so we can get ready for our evening meal."

"Does the entire family eat all together, like this morning?"

It was Saskia who spoke from the other side of the curtain, where she was changing out of a burlap inspired dress. "Every single evening. Daddy insists. Though we don't usually do breakfast together. Today was a special occasion just for you." The last part was spoken in a snarky tone.

Leeza rolled her eyes toward Shaun, but Shaun shook her head. It didn't matter if Saskia was slow to warm up to her. She wasn't going to be around for long anyway.

If they were headed back to the mansion after the shop, this was her last chance to act. She glanced around and snatched up the first item she saw, then reached out for a pair of shoes.

"I think I'll try these on," she said quickly. Too quickly. Dammit.

Leeza gave her a penetrating look but then smiled and nodded. "Come out when you're done so we can see what it looks like."

"Judging from what she's already bought today, I can tell you what it'll look like," Saskia piped up from the other side of the curtain.

"Okay, brat, not all of us want to look like homeless tramps." Leeza shook her head and stepped to the side as Shaun walked around her toward the changing room.

Shaun chose one on the end, but she knew she wasn't going to be able to escape from it. There were people everywhere and even though the change rooms were off to the side, the whole row of cubicles were in the main part of the store.

She frantically looked around the tiny room, trying desperately to come up with a plan. She could smash the glass mirror and cause a distraction, maybe enough of one to run past everyone. But she knew that wouldn't work. Even if she managed to distract a few people, not all of the guards would react slowly. They acted as security for an elite crime family for a reason. Their reflexes would be fast and they likely never let their guard down.

She quickly changed out of her borrowed skirt and shirt and tugged on the dress she'd grabbed off the rack. She didn't even look in the mirror, she was so frantic to find a way to escape.

Shaun snatched up her purse, one that she'd bought earlier in the day, and grabbed a tube of red lipstick, purchased at a pharmacy. She tried to be as quiet as she could while taking off the cellophane wrapper. Then she dug through her purse for anything she could use for notepaper. She came up with nothing.

She bit her lip and stared at the curtain, wondering how long she could stay in there before they came looking for her. No doubt Leeza would be concerned in less than a minute. She was the one who'd stayed closest to Shaun throughout the day, either out of a sense of loyalty to her family or concern for Shaun.

An idea hit her as she was staring blankly at the white curtain. She jumped to her feet, took the edge of the curtain and gently peeled it back, pressing it against the wall beside the opening. Hopefully the guard on the other side wouldn't notice the rustling of fabric. She took the tube of red lipstick and quickly wrote a message along the seam of the curtain. When she allowed it to fall back into place, the lipstick smears were barely visible.

Her heart was racing and her palms were sweaty. She'd never done anything like this. Then again, she'd never been kidnapped before. The whole scenario was all new to her.

She shoved the items back in her purse and stepped out of the cubicle.

A long low whistle greeted her, snapping Shaun out of her momentary panic over being caught. She stared at Saskia uncomprehending.

"Damn, girl," Saskia said excitedly, her eyes roving over Shaun's body. "I take it back; your fashion sense doesn't suck as bad as I thought. Holy shit, I've never seen anything so gorgeous."

Shaun was startled. Considering this compliment came from Saskia, the dress really must be something. She glanced down at herself and saw a waterfall of clinging silver fabric. Leeza took her by the shoulder and turned her toward the floor length mirror beside the dressing rooms.

Shaun gasped and took a tentative step closer to the mirror. Saskia hadn't been kidding. Shaun had never looked so good. Nor she had she ever been transformed so completely by a single item of clothing. The silver fabric had different shades to it which worked to trick the eye into believing that the dress came to life, flowing across her body every time she moved. It was a bias cut at the thigh, with the slit high enough that if she wore low-cut panties everyone would see. On the other side the fabric draped to her feet. The top was practically nonexistent, plunging in a cowl neck to her bellybutton with spaghetti straps going over her shoulders and ending midway down her back.

"Wow," Shaun whispered.

"Wow," Leeza said from beside her.

"I wouldn't kick you out of my bed if you were wearing that dress," Saskia joined in.

Leeza looked over at Saskia with exasperation. Saskia shrugged, scooped up her purchases and headed toward the hovering salesclerk, who happily took them from her, ringing them up and bagging them.

"I'll just change out of this." Shaun moved reluctantly away from the mirror. While she had no desire to remain a captive, she couldn't pretend it wasn't fun to use Jozef's credit card on some pretty extravagant purchases.

She reached for the changing room curtain, but a salesclerk got there before her.

"Please, allow me." He peeled the curtain back, exposing the bright red lipstick to everyone in the room.

The message was out in the open for everyone to read: I've been kidnapped by Jozef Koba. Contact the authorities.

Shaun squeezed her eyes shut as Leeza let out a gasp.

"What it this?" The clerk looked confused as he stretched the message out.

Shaun opened her eyes in time to see two of the guards bent over the message. Saskia was staring at her from the front desk, her gaze speculative. Two guards stood at the entrance of the store, their arms crossed, cold gazes fixed in front of them and the last guard was just outside the store window talking on his cell phone.

Shaun realized the guard who had been at the back door of the shop was no longer there. It was a long shot. A really, really long shot, but she didn't have a choice. She wasn't wearing shoes and her dress wasn't exactly meant for running, but now was her only chance. She had to go.

With a final glance at Saskia, who was closest to her, she bolted, running as fast as she could toward the back door of the shop. Maybe if she could fling it open and throw herself into the crowded market alley, she might be able to lose herself. Maybe duck into another shop. She was banking on the element of surprise.

She could hear the guards crashing around behind her and decided to knock over as many displays as she could on her way through the shop, hoping to slow them down. She leapt over a rack and knocked over a pile of sweaters. As the guards stumbled after her, she heard Saskia shouting instructions to them.

The blood was pumping through Shaun's veins as she hurtled down the hallway, past the staff room, toward where she thought the back door might be. She rounded a corner, her arms outstretched to reach for the door when she caught sight of Leeza.

Leeza was standing in the middle of the hallway, her legs spread, and her arms stretched in front of her, a gun in her right hand while her left hand was holding it steady. Shaun stopped so abruptly that she ended up tripping over her own feet, slamming into a wall and collapsing to the floor on her hands and knees.

She looked up and found herself once again facing down the barrel of a gun. The fight drained out of her and she pushed herself back onto her ass, leaned against the wall and dropped her face into her hands. She gave into the urge to cry, allowing the tears to fall freely.

She figured she was entitled to a good cry.

Shaun had seen death rushing at her through the barrel of a gun too many times that week. She was over it. She was more than over it. If one more person pointed a gun at her, she was going to call their bluff.

Shaun felt the air move around her and glanced up to see Leeza crouched in front of her, her gun nowhere in sight. Shaun assumed she must've tucked it back into her purse or a holster somewhere on her body. Two of the guards were standing in the hallway, looking grim. One of them was on the phone with who she assumed must be Jozef.

"I'm in trouble," Shaun whispered, swiping at the tears on her cheeks.

Leeza reached out and squeezed her knee. "Yeah, you are. But you're not dead and that's something."

CHAPTER SEVENTEEN

"Saty is here," Krystoff said, flicking the ash from his cigar into an ashtray. Technically the club was non-smoking, but the rules didn't apply to the club owners. "I truly despise that little weasel."

Jozef followed Krystoff's line of sight, his own gaze settling on a short, stocky man who was speaking to a muscular bouncer. Saty looked around, caught sight of Jozef, Krystoff, and Havel in the VIP section and began making his way to the back of the club.

Jozef stiffened as the man approached.

"Krystoff, my friend." Saty greeted the men heartily. "Good to see you alive and well."

There was a pregnant pause before Krystoff drawled, "Is there a reason you should not be seeing me alive and well?"

Saty looked uncomfortable and glanced around, likely taking stock of Krystoff's manpower if it came down to a fight. Though there were few people on the floor of the club, as it was only early afternoon, Krystoff had men at every entrance. His usual precaution, which is why it was so concerning that Vasiliy had managed to get to him. Saty's eyes lingered on Jozef, clearly assessing the younger Koba as the real threat.

"No, no, I just mean you look to be in good health."

"Again," Krystoff drawled coldly, deliberately picking up his whiskey with his mutilated hand, and taking a sip before continuing, "Is there a reason I should not be in good health?"

"Uh... heard a rumour... clearly not true." Saty glanced over his shoulder once more as if he regretted approaching the Koba patriarch. "If you'll excuse me, I need to say hello to a good friend."

"Jozef will be in touch about payment for your last shipment," Krystoff drawled.

Saty's eyes landed on Jozef and he visibly shuddered. He owed the Kobas a significant amount of money. He liked to pretend he was playing the mafia game, but he was as ineffectual as he was weak. The Kobas were happy to take his money, but otherwise wanted nothing to do with him. Saty saw them as a way into higher society. He was wrong.

Jozef merely sat, watching the comings and goings of the club with a bored expression. It was a facade. Jozef was always alert when it came to business, especially in the club, which was a cauldron of people moving and mixing. The club was where they did most of their business. It was public, it belonged to the Koba family and it was considered neutral territory for all the local crime families, of which the Kobas were royalty.

Meeting in the club made their associates feel safe, though it was a false sense of security. Jozef could cut off a man's head in the middle of the club on a Friday night without repercussions. They owned everything and everyone in the club as well as a good portion of the Prague police force.

Jozef's job consisted of many parts. He was Krystoff's

second-in-command and the Koba enforcer. He led a group of men who made sure all missions went smoothly, payments were collected, and no one overreached in their territory. He had to be alert and ready for anything. Attempts on both Krystoff's and his lives were not unheard of. Jozef had lost his voice in one such attack that killed his parents when he was a boy. The killer hadn't managed to finish him before Jozef was able to kill the man with the knife he'd left sticking out of Jozef's throat. Or so he'd been told; Jozef had no memory of the incident.

It was that spunk he'd shown as a child that'd elevated him in the eyes of Krystoff Koba, eldest brother of the Koba siblings. Krystoff had adopted him and raised him as his own son. Jozef had spent his life making sure Krystoff would never have a moment's regret. He was vicious and bloodthirsty so his uncle could be congenial and respectful with his allies. Jozef was the guard dog for the family; the *vztekl´y pes*.

"It is good that you are seen," Havel announced to Krystoff once Saty had retreated from their table. Havel had rejoined the family after making sure the fallout from Krystoff's kidnapping was minimized.

Krystoff grunted. "My hand fucking hurts."

Havel smirked. "Get the pretty doctor to look at it again. She looks like she has a soft touch."

Jozef let out a growl and narrowed his eyes at his second-in-command. His stiff posture indicated he would like nothing more than to tear Havel's heart out, despite their many years of friendship. Havel's expression immediately shifted to contrition and he uttered a quick apology.

Jozef ignored him, picked up his glass of ice water and drained it.

Krystoff's sharp gaze was on his nephew. "Don't get attached, son."

Jozef lifted cold eyes to his uncle and set his glass down before signing, *are you threatening my woman, uncle?*

Krystoff looked suddenly weary. "You know as well as I do that some people aren't meant for this life. She's a doctor, a decent person, not one to condone our lifestyle. If I'm any judge of character, I can tell you right now, she won't settle into this life."

I'm keeping her, Jozef insisted.

Krystoff bobbed his head in a nod. "By all means, son. Keep the woman, enjoy her. God knows you've earned a little fun. But don't get attached. She may have to be put down eventually."

Jozef let out a ferocious growl and glared at his uncle, not something he'd done before. He showed Krystoff respect on all occasions, especially in front of witnesses. It was part of the reason the Koba family was able to operate as effectively as they did in Prague. Krystoff was the patriarch, the face and personality of the business. Jozef was in charge of operations. The shadowy presence who ensured Krystoff's will in all things. Jozef's men supported the two, and the family gave them a place to go home to.

You will not harm Shaun under any circumstance, Jozef hands flew, his signing faster than normal, giving away his anger. *You agreed to the marriage.*

Rather than take offence at Jozef's attitude, Krystoff sipped his drink thoughtfully, taking a few moments before he answered. "This woman has come to mean something to you already. I wasn't sure marriage would be the best way to go, but if you truly want to make her part of the family, then we will welcome her." Krystoff's dark gaze searched Jozef's granite face. "You have my word that she will not be harmed. She's yours, no interference."

Jozef continued to stare, but his posture gradually eased.

"You'll have to keep her contained. Find a way to keep your woman without crushing her spirit."

Jozef ignored the comment, nodding his head toward the front of the club where three men piled in, looking around nervously. Krystoff straightened in his seat, his expression growing hard. Jozef and Havel followed suit.

Jozef recognized the lead man. They belonged to Vasiliy. Jozef lifted an eyebrow in surprise as the men approached the table. It took balls to not only walk into the enemy's territory, but to walk right up to him as if embarking on a friendly chat session. They were seriously underestimating Jozef if they thought a public venue would keep them alive. Jozef stood as they approached, crossing his arms and making his biceps bulge. Havel did the same and they took position on either side of Krystoff.

The leader of the trio urged them forward, his cool gaze on Krystoff, who set his injured hand on the table. It was a calculated move. The loss of the finger could be seen as a weakness. The enemy had managed to grab him and make him suffer, but he'd been rescued and was now resuming his place. By showing his hand, he was saying that his injury was insignificant, and he hadn't forgotten what they'd done to him.

"I recognize you," Krystoff said bluntly, his gaze landing on the leader. "You were running point when I was grabbed. You held me while another cut my finger off."

The man dipped his head in acknowledgment. "I hope you know I was only following orders. It was nothing personal."

Krystoff stared at the man, his gaze glacial. "Life is personal, and you took several days of mine." He let that sink in before continuing, "What are you doing here?"

The man shuffled his feet and glanced sideways at Jozef, who was the most intimidating of the Koba syndicate.

Everyone had heard of the Koba guard dog. "Mr. Stanovich is deeply regretful over your recent misunderstanding. He would like to make amends by opening discussions with you regarding a truce and perhaps some trade options."

Krystoff laughed, his voice a deep boom throughout the club. Anyone who knew him, knew they should retreat rapidly from that sound. It usually preceded violence. Krystoff moved his gaze to Jozef and nodded. Jozef strode past the three men, who watched him warily as he dragged a velvet curtain around the VIP area they were sitting in, closing them off from view of the club. It was the Koba family private club with an extremely limited and vetted guest list. Anyone who entered knew the price if they repeated anything that went down at the club. Still, they didn't need to be direct witnesses to what was about to happen.

"So... Vasiliy wants to do business with me after attempting to use me as leverage," Krystoff mused. "He thinks to force my hand by mutilating my hand." His cold gaze rose to the men lined up in front of him. "He has underestimated me."

The leader looked decidedly nervous and glanced repeatedly at the closed velvet curtain and Jozef who now stood behind them, his arms loose at his sides. While the men talked, Jozef took his leather gloves from his jacket pocket and tugged them on.

"H-he wants to express his condolences and hopes that you might consider doing business with him in the future. Perhaps we can offer reparations for your suffering," the man spoke quickly, his hand straying to his jacket. His gun would have been checked in by club security, but Jozef knew men like this probably carried hidden weapons. His razor-sharp gaze followed their every movement.

"Business is certainly out of the question," Krystoff said

coldly. "I do not do business with men who breach my trust. But reparations... yes, we can put those on the table."

The guy swallowed nervously and tried to shuffle back but ran into Jozef who stood behind him, unmoving. Jozef's gaze met his uncle's, but Krystoff gave a slight shake to his head.

"You can give me one thing," Krystoff drawled.

"Anything." Vasiliy's man agreed desperately, seizing on the opportunity to curry favour with the crime boss.

"Tell me who the Phantom is."

Jozef frowned, remembering his uncle saying the word after he was rescued. He hadn't given it another thought, but it clearly weighed on Krystoff's mind.

"He's no one," the guy said quickly. "One of Vasiliy's contacts."

Krystoff tapped the fingers of his good hand against the table. "One of you idiots mentioned he was responsible for my abduction, which makes sense, since Vasiliy didn't seem to know what to do with me. I'm thinking my kidnapping was a botched a job for a third party, yeah?"

The guy looked distinctly green as he withstood Krystoff's glare. Jozef and Havel glanced at each other. Who was the Phantom? If they were a player in the European or Russian Underworlds, shouldn't one of them have heard of him?

"I... I don't know what you're talking about." His eyes darted around the room as he sweated profusely. "Vasiliy orchestrated the kidnapping so he could negotiate a relationship with your organization, that's all."

"You see," Krystoff drawled. "This makes no sense to me. In what scenario would any sane person think that kidnapping and torturing a rival is the key to forging an alliance?" When the man didn't answer, Krystoff continued, "The answer is, no one would think that. Which leads me to another conclusion.

Either Vasiliy wanted me for some other unknown reason, or he was working under another's orders. Someone who doesn't have the resources to take me into custody."

Krystoff leaned against the table, giving the sweating man a level look. "You have one chance to tell me who the Phantom is. Give me a name and you will walk out of this club."

The guy swallowed, a bead of sweat trailing down his hairline. "There is no name. He goes by the name Phantom, but we've never – "

Krystoff nodded at Jozef who moved so fast, none of the three men had time to react. Jozef took the leader by the neck, rammed his elbow into the man's spine and slammed his face into the table. His nose shattered with a sickening crunch and he screamed in pain, struggling against Jozef's hold.

When it looked like the other two men were attempting to reach ankle holsters, Jozef pulled his own gun and placed it against the back of the man's head. Krystoff moved slowly, unfolding his big body until he rose to his full height. He bent over the table and looked into the eyes of the man Jozef was holding.

"I will take my reparations another way and send a message to your boss at the same time."

The man spat out a stream of blood and saliva onto the table. "What do you want? He'll pay it. He'll pay anything!"

Krystoff let out another bone chilling laugh. "Look around you, what do I want with more money?"

"Then what?" he asked desperately.

"Let's start with your head." Krystoff nodded to Jozef who pulled the trigger.

Horrified at seeing their comrade's skull blown out on a table, the other two men scrambled toward the curtain. Havel cut them off, a gun in each hand pointed at the two men, his expression deadly.

Jozef allowed the body to slide off the table and thump to the floor. He lifted glittering blue eyes to his uncle.

"Send my message." Krystoff picked up his drink and drained it, as though he didn't have a single care. He dropped the empty glass on the table next to a pool of blood slowly spreading across the varnished surface. "Find out if you can get more information on this Phantom."

Krystoff straightened his suit jacket and excused himself from the VIP area so Jozef could do his job. Krystoff never stayed for the bloody part. He certainly knew how to use a weapon and he'd spent his fair share of time terrorizing his way to the top of Czechia's crime scene, but he'd moved past those days and preferred to stay away from the blood and gore.

Havel held the two men down while Jozef took their fingers. He didn't stop at two. He figured the message would be clearer the more fingers he took.

Their screams echoed through the club as the music pumped louder through the speakers and a woman laughed at something her partner whispered to her. As Jozef was instructing a waitress to grab a takeout box for the severed fingers his phone rang. He answered, hitting the tone to tell the person on the other side he was listening.

CHAPTER EIGHTEEN

Dasha met Shaun, Leeza and Saskia in the mansion foyer. She was wearing a pink silk bathrobe over matching pajamas, as though she'd prepared for a lazy day at home. The four-inch heels and full makeup were completely incongruent with her outfit. Shaun watched in bemusement as the older woman rushed toward her and took her by the arm, pulling her inside.

"Girls," Dasha said over her shoulder to her daughters. "Make sure her bags are brought in and taken to Jozef's suite."

Without waiting for a response, Dasha rushed Shaun through the mansion. Shaun was impressed with how fast the older woman could walk, considering her choice of footwear. Shaun was still barefoot from when she'd kicked off her shoes in the dressing room before attempting to run through the shop. The two women walked at such a dizzying pace through the first floor of the mansion, Shaun had no idea where they were going until they arrived at Jozef's suite.

Dasha pulled a set of keys from her pocket, unlocked the door and shoved it open, pushing Shaun inside. She followed and held the door as several servants followed with Shaun's bags. Shaun was stunned by how fast everyone was moving. Dasha pointed toward the bedroom and the two women waited silently while the servants piled everything onto and next to the couch.

"Do you need anything else, ma'am?" a butler asked Dasha.

She shook her head. "That's all for now, but please stay close. Alert us when Jozef is in the house."

Shaun's heart picked up speed in anticipation and terror at hearing Jozef's name. What was he going to do once he found out about Shaun's escape attempt?

As though reading her mind, Dasha said in a serious voice, "He knows and he's on his way."

The bodyguard had likely called Jozef the second she was safely tucked in the car. Shaun figured Leeza had called to alert her mother, which is how she'd known to meet them at the door so quickly. Dasha was rifling through Shaun's packages, tossing the occasional item on the bed.

"Is he going to be angry?" Shaun asked tentatively. For all she knew, Dasha was angry too. After seeing Leeza with a gun, Shaun was starting to realize that the women of this family were just as deadly as the men.

Dasha straightened and turned to look at Shaun, her expression grim. It was that look that made Shaun viscerally aware of how vulnerable she was. She was inside the mansion of a crime family. They could do anything to her and not a damn person would stop them. She'd been a complete idiot to enact a half-formed plan that was doomed to fail from the start. She should have waited, lulled them into thinking she was reconciled to her situation and then found a fool-proof way of leaving. Instead, she'd acted on impulse and fear.

"Jozef doesn't get angry." Dasha continued to empty shopping bags. "He uses cool logic in everything he does. If he decides to put a bullet in your head, he'll do it calmly."

Shaun's mouth went dry and it took real effort to stiffen her spine so she wouldn't collapse to the floor. She couldn't handle the constant adrenalin rushes razing through her body. They were making her slow and sluggish. She needed to stay as calm as possible so she could think on her feet.

"I've seen him angry," she told Dasha, reaching out to fold a shirt from the pile of clothes gradually growing bigger.

Dasha stopped and looked at Shaun, a frown creasing her perfectly plucked and coloured eyebrows. "I've never seen Jozef get angry, or much of anything else. Not even when Krystoff was taken. I've long suspected his ability to feel emotion has been damaged. The day Jozef's parents were murdered, his heart froze along with any feelings he had."

Dasha was wrong. Shaun had seen a variety of emotions in Jozef. It seemed odd to her that she could pick out the emotions of a man she barely knew, and his own family couldn't.

Shaun pulled the stretchy fabric of a skirt between her fingers. "But he loves you and the rest of the family. I could tell by sharing one meal with you."

Dasha shrugged. "Sure, he loves us, but he doesn't express it. No love, no fear, no anger, no feelings."

"When we were... when he..." she paused, trying to find a delicate way of telling the man's aunt that he'd shot someone point blank in the head and then turned the gun on Shaun. Dasha waved her hand impatiently as if to tell Shaun to get on with it. "When he was trying to get me to patch someone up, he seemed really angry when I refused."

Dasha stared at her with speculative eyes. "What do you mean by angry?"

"Uh..." Though she didn't want to, Shaun forced herself to remember the interaction. "He pushed me down and got right in my face. He was frowning and signing so fast I couldn't follow what he was trying to say, but I got enough that I understood he was angry with me for refusing. Then, after he'd... killed the person, he seemed angry again when he put the gun to my head."

"You can speak sign language?" Dasha asked sharply, her expression melting from concern to understanding.

Shaun nodded, surprised Dasha didn't know. She tried to remember if she'd used sign language in front of Krystoff and realized she hadn't. The aunt and uncle had no idea that Shaun could easily communicate with their nephew when most other people couldn't.

Dasha seemed to absorb what Shaun was saying, before turning back to the pile of clothes, shoes and toiletries on the bed. She picked out a few items and handed them to Shaun. "Change into this."

As Shaun changed, Dasha rushed around the room, tucking Shaun's new clothes and toiletries away. Shaun thought it was a strange activity to engage in at a moment that felt very dire. The outfit Dasha chose was comfortable and flattering, but then, all of Shaun's new clothes were flattering. She pulled on a pair of bright flower-patterned leggings and a black silk shirt that fit loosely but had a low enough neckline to show hints of Shaun's cleavage.

"And these." Dasha tossed a pair of nude ballet flats onto the floor next to Shaun.

Shaun slid them onto her feet, completely confused as to why she needed to change in such a hurry but unwilling to cause a fuss. She was also quite grateful to be able to slip out of the skimpy silver dress that she'd still been wearing. She assumed someone had paid for the expensive gown before they left the shop in such a rush.

A sharp knock on the door made both women look up. Dasha rushed to the door and opened it a crack.

"He's in the driveway," the butler told Dasha.

"Thank you, now please go back to your duties," Dasha said briskly, already closing the door in his face.

She looked at Shaun, pulling her lower lip between her teeth. Finally, she seemed to come to some kind of conclusion. She strode over to Shaun, took her hand and indicated they should sit together on the bed. Dasha retained a tight hold on Shaun's hand, sitting it on her lap.

"Listen carefully and do everything I say." Her words spilled out in a rush and her eyes were glued to the door. "You do everything he tells you promptly and without argument. Don't bother to apologize for trying to run away, he won't accept it. In our world, apologies are about as good as rats. If you have to apologize for something, then you shouldn't have done it in the first place."

"I wasn't planning on apologizing," Shaun said quietly. "I'm not sorry I tried to run away."

Dasha nodded her approval. "Good girl, he'll respect you more for that attitude. But keep it to yourself. Keep it all to yourself. He'll do whatever he's planning to do anyway."

Shaun wasn't so sure. After all, he'd pulled back after fully intending to shoot her in the head. She nodded her understanding anyway. "I'll do as you say."

Dasha squeezed her hand. "It's for the best. My nephew has developed an attachment to you and I've never seen him care about anyone other than family. I dearly hope whatever feelings he's developing will keep you safe."

"Why do you care?" Shaun asked, trying to understand what Dasha could gain from helping her.

Dasha's answer was simple. "We were asked to welcome you into our family. As our family is a small one that doesn't grow often, I take that order seriously. You are one of us and I will try my best to protect you as I would any other member of this family."

Shaun was floored by Dasha's words, especially since she'd only known the woman for two days. "Thank you," she said humbly, wishing she could do more to earn the loyalty Dasha was showing her. It shouldn't matter to Shaun; Dasha was complicit in her abduction. Yet for some reason, she couldn't think of the older woman as a kidnapper.

Dasha took Shaun's chin in her hand and looked at her closely, then nodded her head. "You're attractive, you're smart and you can communicate with him. These are all points in your favour. Let's hope it's enough."

Shaun's mouth went dry. The way Dasha was speaking it almost sounded as though her life were in danger. Would Jozef really kill her for trying to escape? He had to know she'd try.

Dasha let go of Shaun and stood, stepping away from the bed. The door opened and Jozef strode inside, his eyes immediately zeroing in on Shaun. She stood, using the bed to keep her legs steady because she was shaking like a leaf under his stern stare. Dasha walked toward him, but his gaze didn't waver from Shaun. Dasha stopped and touched his arm.

"Go easy," she told him. "You knew she would try to run."

Dasha left the room, taking all the warmth with her.

Shaun tried desperately to remember everything Dasha had told her, but it all fled as she raised terrified eyes to the mobster who was slowly crossing the room toward her. Shaun wanted to back away from him but there was nowhere to go unless she crawled across the bed. She stood frozen, even as he approached her until he was standing so close, she could smell the spicy scent of his aftershave.

The scent was very appealing to Shaun. She never wore any kind of perfume, body spray or even scented deodorant. It was against hospital rules. She was so used to the smell of disinfectant cleaning solutions and antibacterial soaps that when she found a scent appealing it really drew her. Despite the danger of the situation she wanted to close the distance between them, press herself against his body and bask in his scent.

She'd felt a connection to him from the very beginning. They'd gone through several emotionally charged moments together and now they were bound to each other. It was a strange feeling. She was still terrified of him, still hyperaware of the danger of her situation, but a part of her wanted to be there, with him. Shaun was so used to taking control in the operating room that having it taken from her was a strange feeling, but not wholly unappealing.

He was standing very still, staring down at her, his expression smooth and inscrutable.

She lifted her chin. "I'm not sorry I did it."

She wasn't exactly going against Dasha's advice. She wasn't apologizing.

Jozef stiffened and his hand dropped to the holster at his waist. He wasn't wearing a jacket so his holster was visible.

Shaun saw a splatter of blood on the cuff of his shirt. She didn't think the blood was his, which meant he'd hurt someone since she saw him that morning. The idea made her shudder. She was so far out of her element with these people. Her entire world was geared toward preserving life, and now she found herself in the midst of a group of people who thought nothing of murder.

As his hand landed on the butt of his gun, Shaun lifted accusing eyes to meet his. "You promised you wouldn't point a gun at me again."

He didn't move.

"If you shoot me, you'll always know you broke your promise."

He growled; a ferocious sound torn from deep in his throat. His hand snapped out so fast she didn't have time to move out of the way. He gripped her by the throat and shoved her backwards onto the bed. She landed with a bounce, pinned to the mattress by his hand at her neck. She gripped his wrist with both of her hands as he kneeled on either side of her hips.

He squeezed until she could barely breathe and tears jumped to her eyes. She choked on a cough and struggled beneath him for a few useless seconds before forcing herself to calm down. She tried to breathe, slow and even, taking in as much air as she could.

His cold gaze didn't leave her face. She could feel his struggle as he held her. The same struggle he'd had in the forest. Kill her, as he would kill any other witness, or allow her to live. Make her disappear or keep her locked up and force her to marry him.

She had to help him make the right choice.

Shaun took her hands away from his wrists and did her best to sign to him in the tiny space between them, using short, quick signals.

Please, I don't want to die.

CHAPTER NINETEEN

Jozef stared down at her, blinking until he was able to focus on her hands. She was saying, *I don't want to die,* over and over. He'd had tunnel vision when he'd entered the room. From the moment Karl had told him of her escape attempt, all he'd been able to think about was getting to her, setting eyes on her. He didn't know why, but he needed to make sure she was real and still under his care.

Once he saw that she was safe, the fury had set in. Like an inferno raging through his body, he hadn't been able to douse the flames of his anger. He wanted to take hold of her, shake her, demand she tell him why she wanted to escape.

He knew exactly why she would want to leave. He'd be deeply surprised if she actually wanted to stay. She was everything he was not. Her life was so different from his that they never would have met in the normal course of things. Yet, Jozef had found her and taken her; now she belonged to him.

He wasn't going to kill her. After that moment in the forest when he hadn't been able to pull the trigger, he knew that he would never be able to follow through with killing her. She was safe from him. If he was being honest, she was safe from any other harm, too. He couldn't stomach the thought of anything happening to her, but she did need a reminder of his possession.

He had to impress upon her that escape was impossible. She could harm herself in the attempt, and if she somehow succeeded, he could lose her. She was a highly intelligent woman who was used to thinking on her feet. After she'd mentioned Doctors Without Borders at the breakfast table, Jozef had googled the organization and discovered they worked all over the world in all kinds of conditions. Which meant she was more than capable of taking care of herself.

If he didn't find a way to convince her to stay, he had no doubt that eventually she would figure out a way to leave that was far more effective than a dash through a dress shop.

He stood, dragging her off the mattress. She tried to sign something else to him, but he ignored her. He didn't want to be swayed by her pleas. She needed to find out what could happen to her if she tried to escape again, which meant he had to come up with a punishment. He moved his grip from her neck to her arm as he thought about it.

The shed.

It was harsh, not meant for a woman, especially an innocent. The shed was an on-property prison where they took people for interrogation and execution. It was cold, dark and empty, but it wasn't permanent. It wouldn't hurt or kill her. Jozef could use the prison to show her what her alternative was if she refused to settle down.

He hoped it wouldn't break her, but he had to do something. If she continued acting up, his uncle would pressure Jozef to get rid of her. As much as Krystoff loved his nephew, he wouldn't allow Jozef to keep a woman who could bring down the family with the information she had on them. If

Krystoff demanded Jozef take the girl out, then Jozef would have to make some tough decisions. No part of him wanted to go head-to-head with his family, but he couldn't allow them to harm Shaun. She had to learn to behave, to follow their code.

He walked swiftly through the mansion, his grip on her tight enough to cause pain. She was no longer attempting to use sign language; now she was talking rapidly, her voice edged with hysteria as he dragged her.

"Please tell me where you're taking me," she begged him. "You promised not to kill me. Jozef, please!"

She tripped and almost fell. Using her arm, he swung her back up, but he didn't break stride. She was going to have bruises up and down her arm tomorrow. He almost wished he could tell her it would be okay, that she needed to slow her breathing and relax, but he also needed her to be terrified. It was an impossible situation, not one he'd ever been in before. He hated treating Shaun badly.

Jozef dragged her through the kitchen and out the back door, startling the cook and his assistant. Shaun tripped over the steps and this time he allowed her to fall in the dirt. She lay on her side in a bed of crushed flowers, sobbing and curling into herself. Jozef knelt next to her, getting right in her face where she had no choice but to watch his hands.

Get up now.

The tears continued to fall while her breaths came out in frantic rushes. She was shaking so hard it was a miracle she didn't collapse completely. Her pupils were dilated and unfocused. She wasn't reading his hand motions but retreating into herself. She was having a panic attack. He hesitated to continue, worried about her mental state. He had no choice though; she had to learn what could happen if she tried to escape again.

He lifted her in his arms, cradling her against his body as he continued to walk with her through the perfectly manicured gardens. She curled into his chest, still crying, unable to focus on anything besides her own terror.

Jozef hardened his heart as he walked. This was the only way. The life of an organized crime family was a brutal one, and if Jozef wanted Shaun to be part of his world, he needed to toughen her up. Force her to fall in line.

They called the property's prison 'the shed' because it looked like a large version of an old building where an estate gardener might keep his tools. The shed housed four cells: each a concrete room with a wooden pallet, a toilet, a sink and a thick metal door with a grate in it. Jozef hated the idea of taking Shaun to this building, but he carried on with his plan. He strode through the shed to one of the back rooms, one that he knew was cleaner and less drafty than the rest.

She clung to him as he attempted to set her down on the wooden pallet against the wall. It made his heart thump the way her fingers grasped hold of his shirt, the way she pressed her face against him, wetting the fabric with her tears. His dick responded automatically, leaping to attention. This was a woman he'd been attracted to from the moment he set eyes on her. He never intended to take advantage of that attraction, but her long elegant fingers scrabbling against his skin and his shirt was doing things to him.

He took hold of her wrists, shackling them with his fingers and pulling her hands away from him. He crouched in front of her, trying to make eye contact. Tears flooded her beautiful golden-brown eyes, making them look bigger, almost luminescent. He transferred both of her wrists to one of his hands and used his thumb to try to wipe the tears from beneath her eyes. They were quickly replaced by more tears.

Finally, when he thought she was calm enough to listen, he dropped her hands and lifted his own.

You will stay here for the night, he signed to her.

She sniffed loudly and turned her head to the side to wipe her nose against the sleeve of her shirt. Her eyes drifted around the room as if only now realizing she was inside a building. Gradually, as her brain caught up with her eyes and she realized where she was, what the room was used for, terror replaced curiosity.

"Please don't leave me here," she begged him, reaching out for him again.

Jozef jerked to his feet and stepped away from her. If those soft hands landed on his skin one more time, he would be putty in her hands. He wouldn't be able to resist the lure of giving her whatever she asked for. Her sweet voice, her goodness, everything about her was the opposite of him. He wanted her so badly he was tempted to take her right there on the wooden pallet.

But that wouldn't be fair to her. That would be a brutal and abrupt introduction to his world, one that she might not be able to forgive. He needed to keep his head, give her time to adjust and teach her how to acclimate to the Koba empire.

He turned and walked away from her, away from her sobs and away from her begging. It was one of the hardest things Jozef had ever done in his life.

Jozef slammed the door shut to her cell and locked it. He made it five steps away from the door, away from the hysteria he could hear rising in her wails. His heart felt crushed beneath her grief. He had driven her to this. A doctor, a professional woman, crumbling in on herself in despair. Jozef almost wished he'd put a bullet in her head when he had the chance, given her the dignified death she deserved, rather than a life she feared and despised.

He couldn't leave her like this, yet she needed to learn a lesson. Unable to walk away from her broken-hearted cries, Jozef retraced his steps back to the prison, leaned against the door and slid to the ground. He would be her guardian for the night. He would be here for her, even if she didn't know it.

He slung his arms over his upraised knees, leaned his head back against the door and listened, his heart crying with her.

CHAPTER TWENTY

It took a long time for Shaun to calm down. She cried for herself, for her mom, for Danilo, her dead colleague. Her sobs gradually become soft hiccups until she was finally able to look around and take stock of her situation.

She was ashamed of herself. Since coming into Jozef's life she'd done nothing but fall apart. She had gone from a self-possessed, cool, collected surgeon to a woman who couldn't keep her shit together. Shaun was the type of doctor who could stand in an emergency room and calmly direct other medical personnel during a flood of patients. At a glance, she could easily assess injuries and severity, and know which way to send them based on need. She'd conducted surgeries while listening to gunfire outside of a hospital. Nothing had rattled her calm professionalism.

Yet, when it came to her own situation, she simply wasn't able to cope. She'd lived in war zones, yet she had never experienced war herself. She was being faced with a situation that a week ago would have seemed so fantastical she would've asked if it was the plot to a movie. It was no wonder she had no idea how to react to everything happening.

Shaun pushed herself off the hard, wooden pallet and stood on shaking legs. She walked unsteadily to the sink and turned the cold water tap on. She splashed her face and then cupped her hands and drank some of the water. She used her wet hands to smooth her hair back.

Feeling better, she went back to the pallet and sat down, curling her legs underneath her and leaning against the concrete wall. She took a good look around and shuddered.

The room was a square concrete box, approximately 10' x 10'. She was sure it was meant to hold prisoners. There were no windows except for the one in the door, which had bars in it. There was a single dull lightbulb swinging from the high ceiling. Too high for her to reach.

Shaun tried the door but found it locked. She decided she wasn't brave enough to call out and see if there were any guards on the other side of the door. She didn't know who would answer and the possibilities frightened her. What if Jozef was on the other side and she called him back? What if he finally put a bullet in her head this time? What if one of his cronies was on the other side? She was vulnerable, easily hurt. She didn't even know how to defend herself if she had to. She only knew how to run and so far, even that hadn't worked for her.

Far from being able to think of another plan to get herself out of the situation, Shaun was exhausted. Her long shopping trip, her sprint for freedom, her tense wait for Jozef with his aunt, being dragged down to this prison: it had all worked together to sap every ounce of energy from her. She lay on her side on the pallet and closed her eyes. She didn't think she would fall asleep, but at least she could rest.

Shaun counted her breaths, four beats in and seven out. She'd learned the technique in a mindfulness class that she had taken online. It actually helped her calm down. To release the stress from her body.

After several minutes of counting, Shaun drifted into sleep. When she woke again, she was confused and disoriented. She shoved herself up on the hard pallet, flinching from the stiffness in her joints. She squinted into the semi-darkness and it finally dawned on her where she was. A prison.

A hand touched her shoulder and Shaun jumped, twisting around, bringing her hands up in defense. Lying next to her was Jozef.

"Wh – what are you doing here?" she stammered.

Her eyes travelled down his body where he was sprawled out, his hands tucked behind his head. He was alert and he didn't look tired. Shaun suspected that he came in to lie down with her but hadn't fallen asleep yet. Perhaps the jostling had woken her.

Rather than answer, he reached up, took hold of her arm and tugged her back down to his side. Shaun tried not to overthink it as she sank against Jozef, pressing her face to his hard chest and tucking her hands against him. The pallet was so narrow that she was forced to push herself flush against him. He didn't seem to mind.

Shaun lay in tense silence as his arm came around her body and his hand wrapped over her shoulder. When he made no other move to touch her, she allowed her eyes to droop. She began breathing and counting again, drawing his scent in through her nose and breathing it out through her mouth.

Her body flooded with tingles as she breathed him in. She tried to tell herself that there was no way she was attracted to her captor, but Shaun knew it was bullshit. She was a doctor; she was well aware of what her physiological responses to Jozef meant. Her body didn't care what her mind knew. Her body didn't care that she could die at any moment. It wanted Jozef.

Shaun drifted back into sleep, the warmth of Jozef's reassuring presence lulling her. When she woke up in the morning, he was still there, his arm around her shoulder and his gaze on her face. She smothered a yawn and wondered if he'd stayed awake or if he'd fallen asleep with her.

She pushed away from him and sat up. This time, instead of tugging her back down, he sat up with her, flexing his hands against the edge of the pallet and rolling his shoulders back until they cracked. He tipped his head to one side and then the other, cracking his neck.

Shaun had always hated the sounds of cracking bones and muscles. They reminded her too much of breaks and strains. Personally, she avoided the chiropractor like the plague, preferring to go to a massage therapist. She rolled her own shoulders back and winced as they cracked. Sleeping on a wooden pallet was not comfortable.

"You stayed with me," she ventured, glancing sideways at him where he was sitting next to her.

He didn't turn to look at her when he lifted his hands to make quick signs. *You were shivering in your sleep and there are no blankets in here.*

"You were worried I was cold?" she asked tentatively.

He didn't answer her question, but stood and signed, *we should get back to the house.*

Shaun's heart sank. She wanted to talk about what'd happened, find out what it meant. Why would he try to comfort her? Why put her in a cell at all if he hadn't really intended to punish her? It hadn't been much of a punishment, since he'd provided her with everything she needed, including his own body heat. She was starting to think a night on a wooden pallet was a fair trade for an escape attempt. She'd probably do it again. She was positive this was not the point Jozef had been trying to make with her.

Shaun stood as well, but a wave of dizziness hit her. She

had missed supper the evening before and slept deeply, using Jozef's warmth as a blanket. Now, her body was having trouble adjusting. Jozef reached out to steady her, his long fingers wrapping around her bicep.

"I'm okay," she murmured.

He nodded but slid his arm around her waist to escort her from the building. She allowed the familiarity, finding comfort in it.

As they made their way out to the garden, the intensely bright sun blinded her and she tripped over the threshold of the prison, nearly hitting the tiles on the other side. Jozef caught her and cradled her protectively in his arms. Shaun looked up at him and their gazes caught.

Everything about this man called to her. If only she'd met him in a normal way, maybe on the street... maybe if she'd come to Prague for a visit before going back home to Canada, she would've agreed to a date if he'd asked her. Maybe she would've asked him. She didn't know, but she knew that their connection was real and unshakable. She didn't think it was just the intense life-threatening moments that they'd shared, but something deeper. Like their souls met and knew each other, even if their earthly minds didn't understand the connection.

Jozef swung her up into his arms and held her close against his chest. Shaun clutched his shoulders and murmured a weak protest, telling him that she was okay to walk, that the sun had only blinded her for a few seconds. He ignored her though, continuing to stride through the garden and into the house. Shaun decided to relax and accept the ride.

Truth be told she was exhausted, both physically and mentally. Even after a long night of sleep, she still felt drained. A result of her time working on the front lines of the

Ukrainian conflict, and of her kidnapping. Such heightened anxiety would definitely take a toll on the body. Though she was a doctor, she was no stranger to anxiety. She felt it every time she worked with Doctors without Borders. She believed in their mandate, believed in her work with them, but that belief didn't stop the fear every time she travelled to a war zone. Every time she risked her life to treat others.

Jozef had unfortunately proved all of her concerns to be true. She had been in a war zone when she found herself being violently kidnapped. She wouldn't have been in a position to be abducted if she'd been safe at home in Canada, working in the Montréal hospital where she'd taken her residency.

"Jozef." His name rang sharply through the lobby of the mansion as they were passing through to Jozef's private quarters.

Jozef paused to look over his shoulder as Dasha approached them. She looked annoyed at Jozef, but her gaze shifted to concern when she glanced down at Shaun in Jozef's arms.

"Is she hurt?" Dasha's accusing gaze pierced her nephew.

Jozef shook his head at the same time as Shaun replied, "I'm okay. I don't even really know why he's carrying me. I tripped in the garden...."

Dasha reached out to pat Shaun's arm. "It's fine, dear. I'm more concerned that you spent the night in the shed." Her accusing gaze lifted to her nephew. "Family does not stay in the shed."

Shaun turned her face against Jozef to hide the smile that was stretching her lips. Really, it was one of the first things she had to smile about since entering the mansion and she was grateful. Dasha was standing up for her. Giving her nephew shit for locking Shaun in "the shed". Shaun felt elated that anyone in the mansion cared enough about her well-being to inquire. They all knew about Shaun's escape attempt yesterday. Dasha had even warned her about Jozef's reaction, had attempted to give Shaun advice. Shaun was beginning to look at the other woman as a kind of mother figure; a very deadly one, but still occasionally warm and most definitely effective.

Jozef turned away from his aunt and took a step toward his apartment, but Dasha caught hold of his arm and hurried around to face them.

"People are starting to talk," she said quickly, her concerned gaze now on her nephew. "They know you brought a woman home with you and her unique..." Dasha's eyes lingered on Shaun's face, as she continued, "complexion means there'll be questions if she's linked to the missing doctor in Ukraine. We need to announce the engagement right away if we're going to quell these rumours."

Shaun wanted to laugh at Dasha's way of saying Shaun was a black woman, which made her stand out in that part of the world. Jozef gave another sharp nod that Shaun interpreted as his permission. Apparently, Dasha interpreted it the same way.

"Good. I'll make an announcement to the papers. We'll have the engagement party here at the mansion." She pulled her phone out of the clutch purse attached to her wrist and tapped on the calendar app. "I think next Saturday should work. It's short notice, but we're extremely rich, people are used to eccentricity from the rich."

Shaun couldn't help herself, she giggled at Dasha's nonchalant comment. Dasha's face softened and she addressed Shaun directly. "I hope you don't mind if I plan it for you, dear. You've barely been here a minute and you won't know how things operate yet. I'll order the flowers, decorations and orchestra, and I'll prepare a guest list. I'll have it brought to Jozef's suite within the day for your approval."

Shaun didn't know what to say. She had so many questions, so many thoughts. Who was going to be on the guest list? Was it a real engagement party or a fake one? And since they were technically engaged, or about to become so, was Jozef's suite now hers as well?

Jozef shifted Shaun in his arms. She glanced up at him and caught a scowl directed at his aunt. He was becoming impatient.

"Okay, you two get going. I'm sure you could use a rest in a real bed after spending the night in the shed." Dasha's words were pointed as she sent a glare to her nephew and patted Shaun's arm again. As Jozef strode away from his aunt, she added, "Take Shaun to the club tonight. At least make an appearance with her before the engagement party. People can get used to seeing her face before it becomes official."

Jozef didn't say anything, not that he could with his arms full of Shaun. He ignored his aunt's demand and continued through the stone hallways toward his own set of rooms. Shaun wondered if each family member had a suite like Jozef's. It was like an apartment inside of the great big mansion. It made sense. Each grown-up family member could be independent while still living close to the family.

Jozef set Shaun back on her feet once they reached the door to his suite. He unlocked the door and pushed it open, waving Shaun inside. She took a few steps into the room but didn't get far before Jozef wrapped his hand around her arm and swung her back toward him.

"You don't need to carry me anymore – " Shaun started, but her words were crushed under a kiss.

Shaun gasped in surprise and Jozef took advantage, wrapping his arms tightly around her and pressing his tongue into her mouth, kissing her with a passion she hadn't expected. He hadn't made a single romantic move toward her other than to declare that they would be married and one quick peck on the lips before her ill-fated shopping trip.

Shaun was shocked, she was disturbed... and she was excited. The world faded as his lips danced with hers.

CHAPTER TWENTY-ONE

After a quick shower and a change in his walk-in closet, Jozef left Shaun alone in his room. The first thing she did was try the door. As she suspected, there was a man standing on the other side. He was pretty rough looking, his head shaved, tattoos covering his body including his neck and head. He wore a suit though, similar to what Jozef wore, but less expensive she guessed.

"Can I help you, ma'am?" His words were slow and heavily accented, as though he was new to English.

"Dr. Patterson," she corrected him automatically.

"Dr. Pay... der...son," he said respectfully, struggling to wrap his tongue around her name, the syllables halting with his heavy guttural accent.

Shaun bit back a laugh at his attempt to say her name. She said it again, this time slower. He repeated it perfectly, finishing with a smile. Shaun had noticed that the family spoke flawless English, as though they'd been born to it. Yet most of the staff around the mansion, including the security, spoke heavily accented broken English.

Shaun wondered what Jozef's accent would sound like, if he could speak. He did make sounds, like grunts, growls and sighs. She suspected he would have a deep voice, rough, not smooth. Like whiskey, not wine.

She shook her head at the guard. "No, thank you, I don't need anything." She turned to step back into the room and close the door, but then remembered she still hadn't eaten. "Actually, can you, or someone else, please get me something to eat?"

"Of course." He snapped his fingers and another man materialized as though out of thin air. "Alert the kitchen that Dr. Patterson would like a tray." The guard looked at her with a quick grin and she gave him an answering smile. He turned back to the other man. "Please ensure that lunch is sent to Mr. Jozef Koba's room right away."

Shaun was surprised at how formally the man spoke, as though he'd been trained as a butler, but worked as a thug for his side job.

"Thank you," she murmured and retreated, closing the door.

She looked at the lock for a moment and toyed with the idea of flipping it but decided it would make no difference. The door was thick enough, but she suspected the man on the other side, as well as Jozef and perhaps a few other people in the mansion had keys. She was probably the only one without a key.

Besides, though she knew better, the man on the other side seemed harmless. Or at least like he didn't plan on hurting Shaun any time soon.

She glanced around the room, wondering what she should do with herself. She was still a little tired from her night spent on a wooden pallet, but not tired enough to lie down and go back to sleep. The apartment was already tidy, so there was no point in indulging her obsessive need to make sure that any area she inhabited was uncluttered. People teased her about having OCD, but she knew it came from her years spent as a surgeon. She had to know where each and every tool was before she cut into a person. She had to know that those tools were sterilized and in perfect condition. Those impulses bled into her regular life.

Shaun wasn't used to being idle and knew she would grow quickly bored in the mansion if she had no job to do. And at the moment, there wasn't a single thing she could think of to do in Jozef's suite, except rest and relax.

She wandered over to a shelf and picked up a book, glancing through the pages. The words were foreign to her and she wondered what language it was in. In her time with Doctors Without Borders she'd learned that households across the world, but especially in Eastern Europe, tended to have books in multiple languages. In fact, most people tended to speak more than one language.

Coming from Canada, Shaun could relate to some extent. She spoke English and Québec French and understood two types of sign language, and that was more than many Canadians. People in Eastern Europe, and she suspected Western Europe as well, tended to speak many languages.

Unable to read the books, Shaun settled herself on the couch in front of the TV. She picked up the remote and began flipping through channels. Even if she couldn't understand what the characters were saying, at least she would get some amusement from the action. She finally settled on an American drama that had been dubbed in another language.

Half an hour later there was a knock on the door. Shaun barely had time to twist around on the couch before the door was being pushed open and a tray carried through. She got to her feet and stood awkwardly as a young woman carried the tray in.

"Saskia," she said in surprise as she recognized Jozef's younger cousin, the one who hadn't warmed up to her. Although, after yesterday's debacle, the older cousin, Leeza, might hate her now too. The memory of the other woman holding a gun on Shaun made her shudder.

Saskia dropped the tray on a table behind the couch, making the cutlery rattle. The girl stepped back and looked around as though she'd never been in Jozef's suite before. For all Shaun knew, she hadn't. Jozef seemed like a private man, not a person who entertained in his private suite.

"Pretty sweet place," Saskia drawled, running her hand over the back of the plush leather couch.

"Never been here before?" Shaun asked dryly, picking up a plate of buttered toast and carrying it back to the couch where she sat down again.

Saskia shrugged. "Jozef doesn't entertain much."

"What are you doing here?" Shaun asked bluntly. "I didn't take you for someone who appreciated serving duties."

Saskia wrinkled her nose and dropped onto the couch beside Shaun. She reached out and snatched a half piece of toast from Shaun's plate. Shaun raised an eyebrow. She hadn't realized they were at the food-sharing stage of their relationship yet. Though Jozef was considered the feral dog of the family, his younger cousin certainly knew how to act like one too.

"I wanted to see how you're doing," she said casually. "I heard you spent the night out in the shed. That's pretty badass. You know how many people spend the night in the shed and come out alive?"

Shaun shook her head. "How many?"

Saskia swallowed the last of her toast and licked her fingers. "I don't actually know, but I would guess not many. I've definitely never seen a woman taken out to the shed."

"I guess I'm lucky then." Shaun was having trouble keeping the sarcasm from her voice.

"You are lucky," Saskia insisted earnestly. "After the move you pulled in the store yesterday, I thought for sure my dad would make Jozef get rid of you."

Both women fell silent as they contemplated what 'getting rid of' meant.

"It was a pretty badass move trying to run from the guards." Saskia glanced slyly at Shaun. "Didn't think you had it in you. You're so quiet, so compliant. I honestly thought you were just gonna settle into things and go with the flow. You proved us wrong."

"Don't sound so happy," Shaun said sarcastically, eating another piece of toast.

Saskia twisted around and reached over the back of the couch, digging through Shaun's lunch. She turned back around with a piece of bacon clutched in her hand. "I am happy. Life can be pretty boring around here, but I suspect you're not as boring as you seem."

Shaun shook her head. "I really don't know what to say to that."

Saskia shrugged as though she didn't know what to say either. She ate her piece of bacon and licked her fingers. "I heard you're going out to the club tonight. You going to wear that dress that you tried on yesterday? The one you wore home?" She snickered.

"I hadn't really thought about it," Shaun admitted.

Saskia bounced excitedly on the couch. "You totally should. Not only will you look amazing, but you're gonna make all those club bitches green with jealousy. The ones who treat my cousin like shit but would still fuck him if he looked at them twice."

Shaun stared at Saskia silently. Now she really didn't know what to say. She didn't know why any woman would treat

Jozef badly, other than his tendency toward kidnapping, and she really didn't want to hear about him fucking other women. She didn't want to examine why she didn't want to listen to that sort of thing too closely, but she knew that it made something inside her burn with jealousy.

Unable to remain silent, Shaun asked, "What other women?"

"The club whores," Saskia said with an evil grin. "The hotties who hang out there in hopes of catching the eye of one of the Koba boys. They're looking for a good time, drugs, gifts, that sort of thing. They want to get set up in an apartment, be the arm candy."

"Koba boys?"

Saskia nodded. "Yeah, Jozef and his team. You know, Halil, Havel, Terek, Nikolay. Even Karl gets attention, and he's like, old. Basically, anyone who lives or works with us is considered cool by association."

"And these club... women..." Shaun said tentatively, refusing to say the word 'whore' in relation to another woman. "They want Jozef?"

"They want Jozef's money," Saskia clarified. "They want nothing to do with his disability and everything to do with the cash he rakes in for my dad. He's damn good at his job and they know it. They flock to him because he's the baddest bad boy in town and because he can set them up real sweet. But most of them treat him like crap behind his back, tease him because he can't talk."

Shaun appreciated that Saskia was standing up for her cousin. "Ability. Your cousin has a different ability, not a disability. The way he communicates, it's unique and special. It's not a disability, but something to celebrate."

Saskia laughed sharply. "Look at the chick who tried to run away defending my cousin. Cute. You can keep your lecture to yourself. I'll be the first to get in line to cut any bitch who treats my cousin wrong."

Though she was positive the comment wasn't directed at her, Shaun made a mental note never to treat Jozef wrong in front of Saskia. Especially if she was holding a knife.

"Are you coming to the club?" Shaun asked tentatively. Though Saskia wasn't exactly an ally yet, she would be a familiar face in an unfamiliar situation. Not only had Shaun never been to the so-called club, but she rarely went to clubs at all. She despised high heels, loud music, and sweaty, pawing, drunken dancers.

Saskia shook her head. "No, my parents don't like me going. They think I'm too young."

Shaun took an extra hard look at Saskia. The girl had a sophisticated air about her; a hard shell cultivated over years of wealth and being part of a crime family. Her attitude made her seem older than she probably was.

"How old are you?"

"Seventeen," Saskia said breezily.

"You're definitely too young to go to the club," Shaun said with a frown.

Saskia rolled her eyes. "I shot a guy once. I figure that makes me old enough for this sort of thing, but since my family owns the club, the bouncers know better than to let me in without permission."

"Shot a guy?" Shaun asked faintly.

Saskia smirked. "Yeah, he got a little too handsy on a first date and my dad taught me never to put up with bullshit. I only put a bullet through his hand to remind him where he should keep them."

Once again, Shaun decided that this girl should probably be treated with respect.

Saskia winked at her and stood, wiping the crumbs from her toast off her jeans. She made her way toward the door, then stopped and turned back to look Shaun over one last time.

"Wear the silver dress." She cocked her head to the side. "And a pair of very high heels to add to the height you already have. Nothing else. No jewelry and minimal makeup. The mystery of you is going to drive the club whores insane."

Saskia left, closing the door firmly behind her.

CHAPTER TWENTY-TWO

Shaun was escorted to the club by the same guards who'd escorted her to the shops the day before. She smiled warmly at Karl as he held the door open.

Before going inside, she stopped to ask him anxiously, "Did you get in trouble for my escape attempt yesterday?"

He looked surprised at her concern. "No, ma'am. Your attempt was just that, an attempt. It was expected that you would try to leave us, so we were prepared for anything."

She nodded sadly. "I see, so I was always doomed to failure."

He patted her arm and tipped his head toward the vehicle, indicating that she should get inside. Before he closed the door, he said, "Don't let it bother you. The family surrounds themselves with more security than the Queen of England. Not even Houdini would be able to get out."

The door closed on his words and Shaun was left wondering if she felt comforted or even more terrified. She'd only been with the family for a few days, but already she was realizing that, unless something drastic happened, she would need to reconcile herself to the fact that this was her future.

Not a pleasant thought. Shaun had too much to live for, too many things she wanted to do with her life. Becoming the wife of a violent mafia enforcer was not one of her goals. Though Jozef intrigued her, there could be no future for the two of them. She had to find a way out.

The vehicle wound its way down the long driveway and out to the highway where it would take her to the club. She knew nothing about the club other than the family owned it and several women interested in Jozef frequented the place. She was given the impression that the Kobas also did business there, so she wasn't sure what to expect.

Jozef had gone on ahead, saying that he had business in the city before he could meet her at the club. In a way, she was grateful. Jozef messed with her equilibrium, made her head fuzzy. What she knew to be true, that he was a violent killer, became less important when he was near her. There was so much more to him and she was tempted to explore.

Twenty minutes later they arrived at the club. Shaun shifted to the other side of the vehicle and looked up at the building. It was an old four-story brick and marble complex. Similar to the buildings surrounding it, but with a modern and edgy sign announcing that she had arrived at Zmatek.

When Karl opened her door, she asked him what it meant.

"It means chaos." He looked up at the brightly lit sign. "Anarchy."

Another reminder of how different her world was from Jozef's. He embraced a life without restrictions, giving himself god-like decision-making power. Her presence in his life was the perfect example. He'd had to make a decision between keeping her alive and forcing her to marry him or putting a bullet in her head.

Karl reached a hand out and she took it gratefully, allowing him to help her slide out of the vehicle onto the sidewalk. She wobbled for a few seconds on the four-inch strappy silver sandals that Saskia had sent to her room for her. It was a surprising gift; one that Shaun wasn't positive she was grateful for yet.

The heels looked gorgeous but felt like spiky death traps on Shaun's feet. She took several deep breaths while Karl patiently waited for her to figure herself out. Once she was certain she wasn't going to fall over, Shaun reached back into the vehicle for her sparkly silver clutch purse and then headed toward the club with a three-man security detail surrounding her. She felt like a movie star who didn't want the attention. Everyone in the long club line turned to watch her as they made their way up the stone stairs.

Shaun paused next to the door where the bouncer was checking his notes, but Karl took Shaun's arm and tugged her inside without looking at the bouncer. The bouncers respectfully stepped out of the way for Shaun's entourage.

"Wow, I've never felt so important," she said dryly as they walked past the hostess, who bowed her head respectfully, her curious gaze on Shaun as they headed toward the club floor. "I don't even get VIP parking at the hospital in Montréal and I'm head of the neurology department."

Karl chuckled and looked as though he was about to speak, but his eyes caught on something just beyond the doorway where they were standing. His face straightened and he stiffened, stepping away from Shaun and dropping his hand from her arm.

She looked over her shoulder and caught sight of Jozef, making his way through a crowd of people toward her. She turned to watch him approach, absorbing everything about him. His long graceful steps, smooth and confident. He was wearing tailored suit pants but instead of a suit jacket he was wearing his leather jacket. The collar was open at his tattooed throat and he wore no tie. She couldn't help herself, her gaze trailed up and down his body, lingering on his strong hands and the cords of his throat, where the tiny scar became visible as he approached.

Shaun couldn't help it; a smile stretched her lips and she stepped forward to greet him. Instead of greeting her though, he gripped her arm and turned her so quickly she stumbled on her heels. As she caught herself, she straightened and realized that he was signing at her security team.

This dress is not appropriate. You should not have allowed her to come here like this. Everyone is looking at her.

Shaun frowned and glanced over her shoulder, worried that maybe she was underdressed. She quickly dismissed the thought though. The dress she was wearing was revealing, but not more so than any other in the room. In fact, she rather thought her dress was perfectly appropriate in a room filled with glitz and glamour where the patrons oozed sex.

She tugged on Jozef's arm. "I don't see the problem." She waved her hand toward the other people in the club. "I'm just the same as anyone else here."

You are not the same, and this dress is indecent. I will be speaking to my cousins for allowing this purchase.

His frown lingered on her plunging neckline where the shimmering silver stood out in startling contrast next to her rich ebony skin. She realized what his problem was. Jealousy. He didn't want anyone else to see her dressed that way. A glow lit within her and she softened toward him... just a little.

She tugged her arm from his grip and laid her hand on top of his, squeezing lightly. "I feel good in this dress, Jozef. I've worn scrubs for my entire adult life, please let me have this little bit of glamour."

His lake-blue eyes held hers. She saw the softening in them and knew that she had him. He placed his hand over top of hers where it rested on his arm and escorted her deeper into the club. Shaun was not prepared for all the eyes that turned toward them, burning curiosity in most of their depths, outright hostility in others.

She clung tightly to Jozef and followed him as they weaved their way through the throng of people. He didn't pause, though a few called out to him, trying to get him to stop. Shaun glanced around, but Jozef's grip was tight and he moved at a dizzying pace. They continued together up a set of short stairs which led into the VIP area. Long royal blue velvet curtains were tied back, revealing several tables.

Jozef waved Shaun toward a booth and she slid in, grateful to get off her feet. It was a miracle she hadn't fallen on her face in front of everyone.

The waitress sashayed her way up the steps and into the VIP area. "What can I get for you?" she asked coolly, her eyes on Shaun.

Shaun glanced around and saw that Jozef already had a drink at the table. He must've arrived well before she did.

"I'll have a glass of wine." Shaun didn't drink often, and she never went to clubs, so she had no idea what kind of drink was appropriate for a place like this.

Apparently, she'd said the wrong thing. The waitress narrowed her eyes at Shaun and said coldly, "There are many wines available, ma'am. You must choose one."

"I don't know." Shaun glanced around as though a menu would jump out at her. She was so far out of her depth that she had no idea what to do. What varieties of wine did they have in the Czech Republic? The same as the ones in Canada? Not that that would help her much. She tended to buy the cheap red ones, regardless of what variety they were. Sometimes she liked them, sometimes she didn't, but there was no rhyme or reason to her choices in wine.

Before she could answer, or before the waitress could say anything else snarky, Jozef's hand came down on the table so hard both women jumped. Some of the liquid in his drink spilled over the side onto his hand, but he ignored it. He snapped his fingers and pointed at the waitress, tiny droplets of liquor flying, his glare speaking for him. He wasn't pleased with the way she was treating his fiancé.

The waitress's expression shifted rapidly into one of pleasant contrition. She kept her gaze on the floor as she spoke, her tone marginally warmer. "We have a lovely burgundy, direct from the region in France. I think you'll like it."

"Sure, I'll take that." Shaun hoped that nothing terrible found its way into her wine. The whole exchange was making her uncomfortable.

When the waitress left, she took the unpleasant atmosphere with her, leaving Jozef and Shaun in a bubble of their own. Shaun was hyperaware of Jozef at her side, his thigh touching hers, his long, capable fingers tapping the edge of his glass. He lifted a finger to his lips and sucked the alcohol from it. A warm tingle started in her belly as her gaze traced the move.

Shaun jerked her eyes away from him, blushing. The things she was feeling for him were very inconvenient. She needed to remember that she was dealing with a murderer, a man who'd pressed a gun against her head repeatedly. He was muddying the waters of her conscience by doing things for her, like sleeping with her in the prison cell, buying her a new wardrobe, dressing her up and bringing her to an exclusive club. Normally, these things would not turn Shaun's head, but she knew that Jozef wasn't doing them to impress anyone. He was doing them because he wanted to.

She sensed a feral beast lurking just below the surface of the man sitting next to her. For some reason it was the darkness in him that was calling to her just as much as the moments where he was sweet with her. It was the blend of the two that made her sit up and take notice. Jozef could kill in an instant with no remorse, but then curl up next to her while she was being punished because she might get cold.

In an effort to keep her thoughts away from their current path, she turned her gaze on the club itself, taking in and absorbing the opulence. Everything inside was glittering and gold: the tables, the chairs, the ceiling, the columns. It was beautiful, but so far over the top that Shaun couldn't even imagine how much it cost to build the place.

In fact, it was finally beginning to sink in just how much money the Kobas probably had. She'd been so caught up in her own situation, the fear and tension, that she hadn't really given her place of captivity much thought. But the fact was, she was living in a mansion now. She could go on shopping sprees with unlimited funds. She could come to clubs that she didn't have a hope in hell of being accepted to before meeting Jozef Koba. The whole thing was both awesome and unsettling.

Shaun was not one to be distracted by money. Sure, she made a decent salary at the hospital, but that didn't matter. If she cared about wealth, then she wouldn't have taken a volunteer position with Doctors Without Borders. She cared about people, and she needed to remember that. As long as she was under the thumb of a crime family, she would never be free to continue her life's work. She would be languishing in the home of the very types of people who were often responsible for the horrors she saw in the world. They shaped lives and politics, culture and history.

Shaun jumped as Jozef reached out to touch her, tapping her cheek with his finger. She turned her head to look at him and realized he'd been trying to get her attention. He immediately began signing.

Tell me your thoughts.

Shaun dropped her eyes to the table and thought about what to tell him. Jozef was blunt when he communicated, but she supposed that was only natural. Having to get his messages across without using verbal language had probably trained him to become succinct. He spoke only when he had something to impart, rarely for idle chitchat. Which meant he actually cared about her answer.

She hesitated and then told him the truth. "I was thinking about my job, how much I miss it and how much it'll hurt if I never get to practice medicine again."

Jozef's fingers lingered on her cheek, rubbing gently, as though he was testing the texture. Then he signed, *I am sorry*.

She stared at him. "Sorry for what?"

Sorry for taking you away from the life that you loved.

She hated that he used the word 'loved' in past tense. It meant that he had no intention of ever letting her go back to that life. She blinked away tears and concentrated on his face. "You can't be too sorry since it's clear you have no intention of letting me go."

His response was immediate. *I am sorry that you are hurting, but I'm not sorry that I have you with me.*

It felt like the club was closing in on her until it was just the two of them in the booth together. No glittery people, no opulent room, nothing but them.

"But you kidnapped me," she whispered, pain evident in her voice. "You took me from my job, took me from my family and my country. How can you think I will forgive you for these things?"

He thought about it for a few seconds, then signed, *I don't expect forgiveness.*

She shook her head at him. "How can you want to be with a woman who only wants to get away from you?"

He reached out so suddenly that she flinched, thinking that he was going to hurt her. Instead, he took her chin between his thumb and forefinger and tipped her face up to his. His lips were several inches from hers; she couldn't tear her eyes from them. Hard, but so damn sexy they made her heart skip a beat. The scar across his lips only enhanced his appeal.

He stared down at her intently, his blue gaze searching her dark one. Then he dropped his hands and said, *time will reconcile you to this life*.

"I don't believe that," she whispered.

Nonetheless, this is how it must be.

"You're wrong. There are other options that don't include staying with you forever."

His frown was so sudden and so fierce that she stiffened and wiggled in the booth in an attempt to move away from him a few inches.

There are no other options, he signed rapidly, his movements jerky. *You will stay with me. You will not leave and you will learn to adapt.*

"No," she said clearly. "I won't."

He reached out and gripped her by the back of the neck, dragging her against him. Her heart hammered as he held her against his chest, staring down at her with an intensity that sent a chill skittering through her body. He spoke with his eyes instead of his hands and his message was clear. *You will never leave.*

Before they could say anything else though, they were interrupted.

"I see someone let the dog out of his cage."

CHAPTER TWENTY-THREE

A tense silence fell on the table. Shaun's wide gaze moved from Jozef to the man standing next to the table with two bodyguards behind him. She was relieved to see Havel off to the side of the VIP area, his hard gaze on the uninvited guests. She never thought she'd be happy to see Havel, but he was a familiar face who she knew was on Jozef's side should anything happen.

Just as the tension grew so thick that Shaun wondered if somehow an enemy had managed to make his way to their table, Jozef's face split into a wide grin and he slapped the table with the palms of his hands, standing to greet the man. He reached out and they shook hands, then clasped shoulders.

The man's eyes strayed to Shaun, his gaze lingering speculatively before swinging back to Jozef. "I heard that you have new sweetheart." The man had a thick accent, maybe Russian.

Jozef tugged Shaun against his side and nodded at her. She took that as her cue to introduce herself to the stranger.

Shaun took the proffered hand and murmured, "Dr. Shaun Patterson."

His speculative look sharpened and for a moment Shaun was positive he knew exactly who she was. Was there news coverage of her disappearance? She wouldn't be surprised. Though the Ukrainian border with Russia had become largely lawless, and it wasn't unheard of for people to go missing, a woman of her stature, working with Doctors Without Borders, would draw attention. Along with the dramatic hospital exit, Shaun was fairly certain her disappearance was a hot topic. The man didn't mention the kidnapping though.

"I am Klaus, good friend of both the Koba family and this scoundrel here." He looked at Jozef with a wide grin. "I heard you were back in town. Do you mind if I sit?"

Jozef waved him into the booth and pulled Shaun even closer against his side, his hand at the back of her neck sending pleasurable skitters of awareness down her spine. Apparently Jozef had no qualms about public displays of affection. The guards hovered nearby until Jozef waved them away.

"Do you require translation this evening, sir?" Karl asked before leaving.

Jozef hesitated then glanced at Shaun and shook his head. As she watched, Jozef signed, *my fiancé will translate for us.*

Shaun raised her eyebrow. It was clear that Klaus was an important contact, possibly a business associate. It was a dangerous game getting someone like Shaun to translate. She suspected that Jozef didn't want his bodyguards nearby because he wanted to retain some of the intimacy they'd shared before they were interrupted.

"You're looking good, my friend," Klaus said as the waitress came back to drop drinks off. She placed Shaun's glass of red wine in front of her, another drink in front of Jozef and another in front of Klaus.

The club was very good if the waitress already knew that this man would be sharing their table and what his drink preference was.

"Then again, it is hard to be ugly with a woman of such rare beauty at your side." Klaus glanced at Shaun, but his eyes slid away quickly.

Jozef signed, *indeed, she is very beautiful.* Jozef's eyes lingered on Shaun and she could feel her face heating under his scrutiny. He continued, *what brings you to my club? Were you looking for me?*

Shaun translated for Jozef, relieved that it came easily to her. She just had to make sure that she watched his hands carefully and that her attention didn't drift.

"Indeed, I was," Klaus admitted, sipping from his drink. "There are rumours that the head of the Koba clan was captured, but he's now safely home. This incident could make your family appear less in control than they should be. Others might think there is opportunity to bring the Kobas low. You need to be careful, my friend."

Shaun translated, but her curiosity was piqued.

I sent a strong and public message to Vasiliy. Hopefully it will discourage others from taking advantage of our situation.

Klaus shook his head. "It was nasty, what you did to Vasiliy's men."

Jozef's brows drew downward into a frown. *What I did was necessary. The mutilation of Krystoff Koba required a strong response.*

Klaus laughed loudly and downed the rest of his drink before replying. "There was nothing subtle about your message. One dead body and seven fingers definitely sends a message."

Shaun froze as she realized what the two men were talking about. Jozef had killed and tortured someone. Suddenly the club felt less warm, less welcoming. The opulent surroundings now felt garish as they housed the brutality of the people within.

Jozef's hands moved, but Shaun wasn't paying attention.

Klaus continued, chortling as he spoke. "I heard you did the deed on this very table and then sent his men's fingers back to him in a doggy bag. You have a sense of humour, my friend, even if it's a grim one."

Shaun jerked back from the table, her eyes glued to a mark she saw on the opposite edge, one clearly made by a knife. Her heart sped up in her chest and her palms grew damp. How could she possibly forget for one single second who Jozef was?

Shaun jumped in her seat as she felt Jozef's fingers at her neck. She swung her gaze to him. He was looking at her with concern, his fingers gently kneading the back of her neck as if trying to calm her.

"I can't do this," she whispered for his ears alone.

They stared at each other, both knowing exactly what she meant. She couldn't handle that moment; she couldn't handle Prague or Jozef. She couldn't handle being forced to become part of a crime family.

Klaus's voice boomed out again. "You two are so fucking cute together it gives me cavities. Come, let's have some fun and not be so serious."

He reached into his suit jacket and pulled out a small silver box. He opened the box, revealing a small bag of white powder.

Shaun stiffened in her seat, her gaze on the drug. She suspected it was cocaine but couldn't be sure as she didn't have any experience with drugs other than the aftereffects of drug overdose in the hospital. Jozef sensed her discomfort and ran his hand down her back, resting it on her waist. His touch did help to calm her, but she was deeply uncomfortable when he reached out and took the bag from Klaus.

Shaun watched in horrified fascination as Jozef took a pinch of the powder and spread it out on the table, tidying it into three short lines. Everything she'd ever learned about the toxic effects of drugs on the brain rushed through Shaun's mind. Jozef leaned over the table, pressing his finger against the side of his nose and inhaled the powder through his other nostril. He did it so smoothly, like it was nothing.

He bent to take the next line, but Shaun gripped his wrist, stopping him. He looked down at her with a raised brow. "Please don't," she said quietly.

It wasn't Jozef who answered, but Klaus. "Come, loosen up and relax. Jozef has done this many times. It helps him focus, helps him do his job. He is far more fun and social this way."

Shaun swung her glare toward Klaus. "He's fun the way he is." She ignored Jozef's chuckle at her lie and continued, "I'm a medical doctor and there is no chance that I'll condone him or anyone else in here doing this." She waved her hand toward the line on the table, her expression reflecting distaste. "Excuse me, I need to use the restroom."

Shaun pushed her way past Jozef, not giving him a choice but to let her stand or end up with an elbow to the gut. Before she could stalk away from the booth, he caught her wrist, turned her on the spot and tugged her back until she was forced to face him again.

He let her hand go and signed, *keep your bodyguards close and don't be gone long.*

Shaun didn't respond but turned away and hurried from the VIP area, disgusted. She glanced around in frustration, looking for a doorway that might lead to a restroom. She spotted a shadowy hallway off to her left with a sign above it that she couldn't read. Assuming that she'd found the right place, she made her way through the throngs of people toward the hallway.

Before she made it though, a hand came down on her shoulder and stopped her. Shaun whirled around, bringing her hands up protectively. A woman stood behind her, beautiful, angry and ready to tear a strip off Shaun, which Shaun just didn't have enough energy to face. She stepped out of the grip at the same time as Karl showed up, his massive bulk dwarfing the woman who'd touched Shaun. The woman lifted her hands in a gesture of surrender and stepped back.

"I just wanted to say hello to Jozef's new woman." Her angry gaze assessed Shaun in a glance, her frown saying clearly that she found Shaun lacking.

The woman was stunning in what Shaun suspected was an extremely expensive red dress that clung lovingly to every one of her ample curves. Her throat, wrists, and ears were dripping in diamonds. She had long icy blond hair that waved artistically down her back, highlighting the honeyed tone to her flawless skin. As beautiful as she was, Shaun sensed a malicious underbelly to the woman. From her work in the hospital, Shaun was used to assessing people and situations quickly so that she could make snap decisions. This woman was not going to be worth her time.

Instead of responding, Shaun looked up at her bodyguard. "I just need a few minutes to myself. Which way is the rest room?"

He pointed her in the right direction, which indeed was down the hallway she'd been headed. His hand hovered protectively over the small of her back without touching. Shaun broke away from the two and quickly made her way toward the back of the club. Even though there were several stalls in the washroom, Shaun flipped the lock on the main door so she could have a few minutes of privacy. If another woman had to use the washroom she was just going to have to wait.

Shaun stared at her reflection in the mirror over the sinks.

Far from the lovely confident woman she'd been when entering the club, she now looked like a shaken frightened lost girl. She didn't know where she was going, and she didn't know what she was doing. Jozef had narrowed her choices down to none, yet the single choice he was giving her was impossible. How could she possibly marry a murderous mobster who was at that very moment snorting lines of cocaine in a club Shaun would never have stepped foot in on her own?

A sob tore from her throat and she covered her face with her hands. She wanted to hate him, but she couldn't. Every moment she spent with him sucked her in more. Yet every moment she spent with him, she learned something new and terrible about him. This was no way to live.

She had to leave.

Shaun had always been one of those people who scoffed at the ideal of death over oppression. In her opinion, if a person's life were at stake, they should seize it with both hands, no matter what was going on around them. She'd watched too many people fight for their lives after having tumors cut from their brains to take that sacrifice lightly. Yet, here she was, facing an impossible situation where death could be the very real result of another bid for freedom, and she was considering running, despite the risk.

Shaun cleaned her face with a wipe from her purse and then went to unlock the bathroom door. Before she could leave, the woman in the red dress came barreling through, shoving the door so hard Shaun had to jump back. Shaun sighed heavily when she saw who was accosting her.

"Excuse me," Shaun said coolly, attempting to slip past.

The woman grabbed Shaun again, her long, lacquered fingernails digging into Shaun's arm. Before Shaun could demand the woman let her go, she hissed in Shaun's face, "I don't know who you think you are, but I can tell you right now, you are nothing. Whatever this supposed engagement to Jozef Koba is, you can forget about it. I put my name on that years ago and I'm not letting go."

Shaun laughed; the sound weak and incredulous to her ears. She wiped the back of her hand across her eyes. She really didn't want to cry in front of the hostile potentially psychotic woman, but her emotions were getting the better of her.

"You can have him if you want him. I'm sure you two will make a great couple," Shaun said as dismissively as she could manage. "I didn't ask for any of this and now I'm leaving." Shaun tried to sidestep the woman, but she dug her nails in until they cut, causing Shaun to cry out.

The woman spoke as though she hadn't heard Shaun. "He is the only eligible bachelor in that entire family and he's mine. He's only fascinated by you because you know sign language." She eyed Shaun up and down. "And you're exotic."

Shaun rolled her eyes, suspecting 'exotic' meant black, but didn't say anything. There was no point. This woman was determined to be a viperous bitch and Shaun was determined to get the hell out of that bathroom before she was forced to slap the shit out of a complete stranger, breaking her sacred oath to do no harm.

Rather than asking the woman to move again, Shaun jerked her arm out of the other woman's grip, crying out in pain as her nails dragged down Shaun's arm, digging deep grooves in the skin. Shaun cradled her arm against her chest and moved to open the door, but once more was flung back as Jozef and his bodyguards filed in.

Jozef took stock of the situation, his eyes lingering on Shaun's injured arm. He shoved her behind him, causing Shaun to stumble. Havel grabbed her arm to steady her, his malevolent gaze on the other woman.

"Jozef, my love..." the other woman started to say but was cut off when Jozef grabbed her by the throat.

Shaun gasped in shock as Jozef picked up the woman off the ground and slammed her back into the tiled wall. Shaun let out a shriek and grabbed him by the arm, trying to drag him away from the woman.

Jozef ignored Shaun, but Havel didn't. He jerked Shaun back by her good arm just in time to miss the hand that swung back. A loud crack filled the washroom as Jozef slapped the woman, then slapped her again. Shaun cried out, begging him to stop, but he continued to ignore Shaun's pleas. Karl came up behind Shaun and placed his hand on her shoulder, gently pulling her away from the group before she got hit by a flailing arm.

Havel stepped forward, addressing his words to the woman, speaking on Jozef's behalf. "You and your friends will stay away from this woman. If you don't, Jozef will bury you. This is your only chance to comply. Consider yourself warned, Giselle."

Giselle's terrified eyes fell on Jozef and she gave a quick nod. Her perfectly arranged hair was now in disarray and her cheeks were bright red from the slaps Jozef administered. Rather than letting her go, Jozef pulled his gun from beneath his leather jacket, flipped the safety off and held it up to her forehead, emphasizing Havel's point. The woman whimpered in fear, her fingers scrambling against Jozef's wrist where he held her up by the neck.

Unable to do anything to help, Shaun backed quickly away from them, the sight of the gun terrorizing her all over again. The deaths of the two men she'd witnessed at Jozef's hands flashed through her brain as well as the many times he'd held that same gun to her head.

She let out a cry and whirled on her heels, fleeing into the hallway. She looked around her, desperate for an exit. She just needed a couple of seconds of fresh air to calm her panicked heart and spinning head.

She spotted an exit at the far end of the hallway toward the back of the club. She ignored the shouts from behind her and ran for all she was worth, her entire being focused on the exit door. She had to get away from that gun, had to get away from the situation and Jozef. If she didn't, there was no doubt in her mind that Jozef would turn the gun on her next and this time actually pull the trigger and put a bullet in her brain.

CHAPTER TWENTY-FOUR

"Shaun, stop!"

She didn't know who was calling her and she didn't care. The voice gave her the impetus to move faster, pump her arms harder.

Shaun had never felt anything like the driving desire she had to escape her current situation. It gave her the ability to run in heels, to run faster and farther than she'd ever run in her life. She ran straight out the back door of the club and into a throng of happy partygoers. She shoved her way past them and continued running through Prague's busy, touristy downtown. It never once occurred to her to stop and beg for help, she just had to run.

Shaun could hear shouts coming from behind her, but she didn't look back. She ran until the shouts grew fainter. It took her a moment to realize that there were sobs spilling from her mouth; deep gut-wrenching sobs. Tears wet her face, ruining her make up. Nothing mattered except getting away from Jozef, the bodyguards, the Koba influence.

She ran until everything hurt, until her lungs burned, her

legs ached, her feet begged for mercy and a stitch in her side became so bad that she had to stop and bend over, clutching at her stomach. As she doubled over, hands on her knees, she sucked in deep breaths, filling her lungs with air before releasing the toxic panic that had built up inside her. She used the back of her hand to swipe at the tears on her cheeks.

Finally, she straightened and looked around. She was standing in some kind of alleyway, a dead end. Dismally, she crouched, leaning her back against a rough brick wall and sucking in air, trying to calm herself while she waited. She had no doubt Jozef and his men would find her very soon. In the meantime, she needed to figure out what she was going to say to Jozef to get her out of another possible punishment.

Would he look at this is another escape attempt? She hadn't really been trying to escape. She just needed to get out of there, away from the guns and the drugs and the thugs. None of them made sense to her. None of them fit in with her worldview.

"She's here!"

Shaun straightened, pulling herself shakily back to her feet, her hands pressed against the wall to steady herself. She was determined to face her persecutors head on. Her desire to run might have been visceral, coming from a place of panic and anxiety, but now she was calm. Now she could think.

Except, the three men who piled into the alley with her were complete strangers. She squinted into the gloom, attempting to make out a familiar face in the dim lighting coming from the street. It quickly became clear that she knew none of them. They advanced on her, their faces reflecting eager surprise, as though she were some kind of unexpected prize.

One of them spoke, his eyes roving down Shaun's body in appreciation. She couldn't understand what they were saying, the language foreign to her ears. It wasn't Czech, Russian, or Ukrainian, but similar.

"I need help," she tried pleading with them.

They continued to advance; their body language aggressive. Shaun cringed away from them, glancing around for a way out, but there was none. She'd truly managed to find herself in a dead end.

"Who are you?" she asked shakily.

They ignored her. The man who seemed to be their leader spoke rapidly to the other two, pointing at a car parked at the end of the alley. The others nodded and one reached for her.

Shaun slapped at the man and pressed herself against the alley wall. He took her arm in a tight grip, yanking her forward with one hand and slapping her across the face with the other. Shaun went sideways into the brick building, the rough surface scraping against the skin of her back. She gasped and reached for her face.

The men didn't say anything to her but started hauling her out of the alley. Shaun opened her mouth to scream, but the man who grabbed her back-handed her. He growled something at her that she didn't understand, but she suspected he was trying to get her to comply.

Shaun's face was on fire, but she knew that he hadn't done much damage. His slaps were light compared to what they could've been. She was lucky. If he decided to use his entire strength, he could've knocked her teeth out.

Before they could get her out of the alley though, several dark shadows appeared, stalking down the alley toward the trio. A chilling growl made everyone freeze. It was low and guttural but loud enough that it reverberated in the alleyway, raising the hairs on Shaun's arms. It took a second for her to realize that the growl had come from the depths of Jozef's throat.

One of the men surrounding Shaun said something,

laughed unpleasantly, then took hold of her and swung her out in front of the trio. The man pulled a gun from his holster and held it to Shaun's head. Hot bile rose up in her throat. Before the man could speak, or so much as blink, Jozef pulled his own gun and put a bullet through his head. The man went straight backwards, releasing his grip on Shaun's arm.

Shaun tottered on her heels, then whirled around to watch as the man tumbled to the pavement. She dropped to her knees next to him, automatically reaching for his throat, checking for a pulse. It was there for a few seconds, beating strong as his heart continued to pump, then nothing. Shots rang through the alley and Shaun crouched next to the body, covering her head with her arms.

She had no idea how long the shooting went on for, but it felt like an eternity. She flinched with every sound, expecting to feel the agony of a bullet ripping through her flesh at any moment. When the alley finally went silent, she carefully raised her head, peeking through her arms at the carnage surrounding her.

"Oh my god," she gasped.

The three men who'd threatened her in the alley now lay on the ground unmoving. After determining that the first man was dead, she reached for the next, trying to find his neck in the darkness. Before she could locate his pulse, Jozef took her by the arm and dragged her off the pavement, pulling her into his chest. His piercing eyes gleamed down at her as he surveyed her.

"Boss, time to get out of here," Havel said from behind them.

"But..." Shaun twisted around to stare at the dark shapes on the ground in the alley. She was certain all three were dead, but she should make sure, help if she could.

Jozef dragged her out of the alley and looked around.

Spotting their vehicle, he pulled Shaun toward it. He flung the door open and shoved Shaun inside. She scrambled in, her dress riding up her thighs. She didn't care though. She clung to the door on the opposite side of the car, her terrified gaze on Jozef as he slid inside. He didn't look at her, but calmly buckled his seatbelt.

Shaun was shaking so bad she couldn't manage her own seatbelt. She was covered in blood. It was all over her dress, her arms and in her hair. Panic rose up inside her and she began trying to rub the blood away. Trying to erase the violence.

She let out a panicked shriek as Jozef reached across the car and took hold of her. He shoved the seatbelt out of her shaking hands and pulled her across the back seat until she was sitting on his lap. He wrapped an arm around her head and pressed it against his chest while reaching out to tap Karl on the shoulder, indicating he should start driving.

Jozef held her tight, pressing her hard against his chest as the vehicle pulled into traffic. He tipped her chin, forcing her to look up at him. He breathed deeply, taking several breaths through his nose and then releasing with his mouth. He tapped her mouth, indicating she should do the same.

Shaun automatically complied, taking long shuddering breaths into her lungs and then releasing the air. Each deep breath released some of the panic threatening to choke her, until she found herself relaxing against Jozef, listening to his heartbeats and following his lead, breathing in and out in unison.

She was still terrified, yes, and sick to her stomach from what she'd seen, but Jozef had saved her. He hadn't hesitated. He'd simply killed the men accosting her, for no other reason that she could see except that they were attacking her. It'd been automatic, as though he'd been doing it forever.

The tears started to fall, but she ignored them. She dug

her fists into his leather jacket, clinging to the only anchor she had in the choppy seas of the new life she was being forced into. Jozef wrapped his arms around her and held her tightly, telling her without words that he would be her anchor.

CHAPTER TWENTY-FIVE

Once again, Jozef carried Shaun through the house to his suite. This time Shaun didn't care who saw them. She was traumatized by what she'd experienced in the alley and Jozef was her only source of comfort. It didn't matter to her that he was largely responsible for the trauma. She clung to him as though she'd die if he let go.

He strode through the mansion, ignoring his aunt's exclamation as she came hurrying down the stairs toward them.

"What happened?" Dasha asked sharply.

Jozef let out a ferocious growl and continued through the house to his apartment, ignoring Dasha, who rushed after them. Jozef set Shaun down long enough to unlock the door to his suite and then pushed her inside, slamming the door shut behind them and locking it. He ignored his aunt's frustrated exclamation from the other side, took Shaun's hand and pulled her through the sitting room into the bedroom. He slammed the door shut and locked it.

Shaun backed away from him, her previous desire for his comfort quickly evaporating into fear. She'd run away from him again, and as a result he'd killed three men. He was going to be furious. What if he decided to really punish her this time? Maybe he thought she hadn't learned her lesson in the shed.

But when he turned to look at her, his expression was one she hadn't seen before. He looked... contrite.

I'm sorry, this shouldn't have happened. His hand movements were angry and jerky. *I shouldn't have scared you. I allowed my anger with Giselle to eclipse my better judgment.*

She shook her head. "It was my fault," she said dismally, her eyes on his hands because they were easier to look at than his frightening granite expression. "I shouldn't have run like that without thinking about where I was going. I should have realized you might have enemies."

Indeed, I do have enemies, but it's my job to protect you from them. We should have been prepared. You should not have been able to leave the club.

Shaun suspected as much. She'd taken them all by surprise when she bolted out the back door of the club. It was probably sheer luck and adrenalin that carried her as far away from Jozef and his men as she'd managed to get.

She stared at him in despair. This was yet another reminder of how much she didn't fit into Jozef's world. She couldn't go more than a few hours without getting herself into trouble.

"Do you... do you know those men?"

He frowned and shook his head. *I didn't recognize them, but it was dark in the alley. Havel will get back to me with identifications.*

She glanced down at her arms and saw the little flecks of rust red blood drops staining her skin. She automatically began scrubbing at it with her nails. It was a weird sensation being so freaked out by blood. She'd seen plenty of blood, probably far more than the average human, yet she'd never seen it spilled in violence until she met Jozef.

"I need to take a shower." She tried to keep the edge of panic from her tone.

Jozef nodded. *I will have some tea sent up. It will warm you.*

She realized that she was shivering. The shock of the past hour was rushing through her veins and giving her the shakes.

"Can you have them send up something a little stronger?" she asked.

A small smile stretched Jozef's lips and he nodded. *Of course.*

Shaun turned away and headed toward the bathroom, reaching behind her to unzip the dress as she walked. She jumped when Jozef's fingers brushed hers aside. He placed one hand on her hip while drawing the zipper down to the small of her back with the other. His fingers lingered against her skin, warming her and sending tiny sparks through her body. He gently pushed her away, encouraging her to step into the bathroom.

Shaun closed the door and allowed the dress to fall down her arms, pooling on her hips before it dropped to the floor in a beautiful, bloody silver waterfall. She bent in half, reaching down to unbuckle each sandal before stepping out of the mess of dress and shoes. She groaned out loud in relief as she stepped onto the cool bathroom tiles. She slipped her thong off and tossed it on the pile. She was going to burn every item once she figured out how to work Jozef's fireplace.

She turned the taps on in the shower and waited for the water to heat before stepping under the spray. The shower was one of the things she appreciated most in her bizarre situation with Jozef. It was a huge earth tiled monstrosity with four heads; one that sprayed directly over her head in a rainfall, another that hit her body at an angle and two more on the other side of the shower for someone else to wash at the same time.

The glass door quickly steamed up, which meant Shaun

didn't initially see Jozef through the clouds of steam as he opened the door and stepped into the bathroom with her. She lifted her face into the spray and allowed the soothing feeling of hot water to drain some of the gut-wrenching fear from her. During a normal week she would be careful not to get her hair wet unless she had time to deal with the chaos that would ensue. Today, she didn't care. She just wanted to feel clean.

She felt a rush of cool air skitter over her body, raising goosebumps all up and down her legs. She pulled her face out of the stream and blinked the water from her eyes. When she turned her head, she saw Jozef standing on the other side of the glass door, his frowning gaze on her naked body.

"Jozef!" Shaun gasped and took a step back, out of the spray. She wrapped her arms around herself. "What do you want?"

He opened the door and stepped into the shower with her. He'd taken his leather jacket, shoes and socks off, but otherwise he was still fully clothed. He didn't seem to notice as he stood on the other side of the water from her, watching her through the clouds of steam.

Shaun stood frozen, unsure what to do. Her heart was pounding in both anticipation and fear. Was he here because he wanted her, or was something else going on? She couldn't think of a reason for him being in the shower with her.

He reached up to touch her face and she flinched away. He stood patiently with his hand out, the sleeve of his shirt getting soaked as he reached through the water. Shaun stood completely still as he closed the last few inches between them, brushing his fingers over her cheek. A sharp pain radiated through her face and she realized he was touching the bruise the guys in the alley had given her.

"It doesn't hurt," she whispered.

He nodded slightly, then dropped his hand to her arm.

His fingertips very briefly caressing the side of her breast. She sucked in a breath as her nipple peaked in reaction.

He lifted her arm, turning it over in the water. Shaun let out a gasp of pain as she realized there were long deep scratches all up her forearm. She'd been so distracted that she hadn't remembered the wound where Giselle had grabbed her and dug her talons in. Jozef gently rubbed the specks of blood from her arm, turning the water pink as it went down the drain.

The move was so sweet, so uncharacteristic of his bad guy persona that it melted Shaun. She couldn't help but stare at him as his light blue shirt grew wetter and wetter and became plastered to his chest. She could see every muscular ridge through the fabric of his shirt. When she dropped her gaze lower, she could make out the outline of a sizeable cock behind the zip of his pants.

Her mouth grew dry and when she lifted her gaze to his, his expression had changed from concern over her injuries to pure lust. Warmth spread through her belly as his gaze dropped down her body, leisurely taking in every part of her. She wondered what he saw. Were her smallish breasts with their wide black areoles a turn on for him? She burned with embarrassment as his perusal continued down.

Shaun didn't have a lot of time for grooming, so she only shaved her bikini area when she anticipated a sexual partner. She hadn't thought once about sex with Jozef. There was a definite attraction between them, but she'd been in survival mode from the moment Jozef kidnapped her from the hospital. Now, he was caring for her, showing her another side.

"Jozef..." she whispered uncertainly.

She wasn't sure what she was about to say, and she didn't get a chance. Jozef rushed at her through the water, pushing her back against the shower wall and covering her lips with his. Shaun reached up and gripped his shirt, which was about all she could grab hold of during the tempest of Jozef's kiss. To say he devoured her was putting it lightly.

He took her mouth with more passion than she knew was possible. She clung to him, digging her nails into his skin through his shirt as his tongue battled with hers and his teeth forced her mouth wider. When she wasn't fast enough to give him what he wanted he gripped her by the hair, burying his hand in the soaked mass and dragging her head back.

His lips trailed down her throat licking and biting. It felt like he was everywhere at once. His hands on her skin and her hair, his tongue on every inch of skin he could reach. It was like being fucked by a storm. Her heart soared as explosions went off beneath her skin.

She wiggled her hands between them and tried to undo a button but her shaking slippery fingers refused to comply. Jozef pushed her hands aside, gripped his shirt and tore. Buttons flew everywhere and Shaun let out a breathless laugh. He slammed his mouth over hers, swallowing her laughter and reminding her of exactly what he wanted.

Shaun knew she would regret this. She knew this was a bad idea. There were consequences to this sort of thing, aside from Jozef being the mobster who'd kidnapped her.

She didn't care. She was doing it anyway. She desperately needed the release of fucking her captor. She needed the physical and emotional connection. She needed to feel something other than terror for however long she could.

Reaching between them, she tried to unbuckle his belt. Just as the thick leather gave way under her determined hands, Jozef stepped back, dragging Shaun with him. He brushed her hands away from his crotch and pulled her from the shower. Before Shaun could even think about reaching for a towel, Jozef dragged her dripping from the bathroom. He swung Shaun around and shoved her.

Shaun let out a shriek as she fell backwards on the bed,

her limbs flailing. She yelled again as Jozef fell on top of her, his hands capturing hers and holding them while he fucked her mouth again with his all-consuming kisses. He broke contact with her lips and worked his way down her body, touching her here and there, digging his fingers into the skin of her breasts and hips as though revelling in the silken resiliency.

Shaun shot up in the bed when he settled between her thighs, but he shoved her back onto the mattress so hard she bounced. And then she didn't have time to overthink the hair she would normally have removed, what she tasted like or how she smelled. It all disappeared into a haze of intense sensation as he attacked her vagina with his tongue in the same way he'd attacked her mouth.

"Oh... fuck!" she gasped, her hips bucking off the bed and into his face.

Jozef wrapped his hands around her thighs, digging his fingers into the muscle and holding her still while he lavished her pussy with all the attention she could ever want.

Shaun hadn't had many sexual partners; her career made finding potential partners difficult. Not a single person she'd ever been with had gone down on her the way Jozef was. He was touching nerve endings she didn't know existed as he slid his tongue through her folds, then flicked her clitoris, then back down to shove his tongue as far inside her as he could get.

Then he took it to the next level, replacing his tongue with his fingers, shoving them deep into her body. There was no hesitation, no single digit probing to see if she was ready for him. He shoved two fingers up inside her, slamming them home, then pulled out and did it again. Every time he bottomed out, he pressed his fingertips hard against her g-spot, scraping his knuckles against her inner walls.

Shaun let out a shout of sheer pleasure and gripped his

hair with her fists. It was too short to get an actual handful, so her fingers just scrambled over his scalp. He either didn't notice or didn't care as he continued to drive Shaun closer and closer to the edge of a colossal orgasm.

Finally, she was there. She lifted her hips right off the bed and slammed them back down as she let out a keening scream. Jozef tightened his hold, pinning her down while she wiggled and shouted her orgasm. She felt a gush of fluid leave her body as the waves continued.

CHAPTER TWENTY-SIX

When Jozef looked up at her, his eyes were so dark blue they looked black. He looked like the big bad wolf about to eat a sheep. And she was his meal, staked out on the bed. He stood, his hands dropping to his pants. He unbuttoned and unzipped then dropped them to his feet. He wasn't wearing underwear.

His penis was an awesome sight. Not because it was the biggest or longest Shaun had ever seen. She was a doctor; she'd seen a lot of cock in her career. It was beautiful though, long, thick and fully erect.

No, what drew her was the man himself. His confident nudity. The power emanating from him. He was a conqueror and she was his prize. It suddenly made sense to her, even though it wasn't logical. He'd seen her, he'd wanted her, he'd taken her. Shaun had never experienced that kind of desire. The consuming drive behind a courtship.

Maybe their circumstances drove them together. His need for a doctor and her being in the right place at the right time to fulfill his need. But it wasn't the doctor he wanted now; it was the woman. And that knowledge was extremely heady.

Shaun reached for him as he dropped onto the bed, wrapping her arms around his shoulders and clinging to him as he pressed his lips into the sensitive spot between her neck and shoulder. She wiggled underneath him until he wrapped his arms so tight around her, she could hardly move. Instead of feeling trapped though, she felt safe.

He reached down between them, guiding his rock-hard cock to her entrance. Shaun gasped as he pressed himself inside her, taking his sweet time as he filled her completely, pushing inch after inch inside as she lay gasping and soaring from the rush of endorphins washing over her. Even though he had a big cock and it'd been a while since Shaun last had sex, she took him without too much discomfort. He'd prepared her to the point that she was dripping for him.

Shaun could feel the tension thrumming through his body as he held himself rigid above her. He lifted his head to look down at her, wrapping his big hands around her head and holding her. The look in his eyes was so intense it melted her. She read him without words. He was concerned for her comfort, but he desperately wanted to fuck her.

She smiled tremulously and whispered, "I'm okay."

His eyes darkened to cobalt and he gave a slight nod. Then he began moving his hips, pulling out of her almost completely and then filling her again. Even though his thrusts were slow, she was left gasping, her heart hammering, her body vibrating with tension. She felt incredible.

She stretched beneath him, luxuriating in his long, slow strokes before reaching up to grip his strong arms. She lifted her legs to wrap them tightly around his waist, then tilted her hips and thrust forward in one smooth move as he pushed into her.

His eyes flared in pleasure and he let out a guttural groan.

Shaun grinned and wiggled her hips again, tightening her kegel muscles.

Jozef let out another growl, this one more ferocious than the last. He gripped her so hard she let out a squeak, then he slammed into her hard enough to thrust her up the bed. Shaun let out a shriek and gripped the sheets while he took hold of her waist and dragged her back down the bed, continuing to fuck her in a flurry of aggressive thrusts. It was like fucking a hurricane. She had no choice but to hold on and take it.

Shaun twisted her head to the side and hid a grin in the pillow next to her. It felt fucking amazing! She hadn't let free and allowed herself to enjoy the sheer bliss of a good fuck in so long she was starting to wonder if she'd ever really had a good fuck. She'd only ever hooked up with doctors or one-night stands from the bar. She could definitely say nothing had compared to this.

All she could do is hang on as he pounded into her, his hands wrapped around her hips, holding her in place as he took his pleasure from her body while giving her just as much in return. Shaun flew higher and higher toward the shining peak. This sensation was different though; she'd never come through vaginal penetration. Hell, she'd been pretty sure it was a myth.

As it turned out, not a myth. With each thrust he sent her soaring, tilting her hips at just the right angle so that he was hitting her g-spot again. Shaun let out a high-pitched cry as he shoved her right over the edge of another incredible orgasm. Her brain went fuzzy and blank while her hips pumped of their own volition, milking him of every ounce of pleasure he had to give.

Jozef gripped her so hard Shaun had a brief second to wonder if he might actually be able to crush her hips before he let out another guttural growl and followed her over the edge. She felt hot jets touch everything inside her, bathing her with his semen. She gloried in the feeling, stretching her arms wide and grinning.

Jozef gripped her face, forcing her to look at him. His expression was serious, but his eyes were soft. He dropped his forehead to hers and stared at her, allowing her to see the shifting emotions. Her heart pounded and she suddenly felt vulnerable, like they'd just had a life changing moment together. But it was only sex. It wasn't that important. Something they'd both done before with other people.

A sensation ran through Shaun as she thought about Jozef with other women. With Giselle, who clearly thought she had some kind of claim on him. The feeling of vulnerability intensified until Shaun thought she would suffocate if she was forced to lay underneath Jozef for another second.

She shoved his shoulders and said in a high thin voice, "I need to get up."

When he didn't react quickly enough, she slapped her palm against his bare shoulder and said in a louder voice, "Jozef, let me up!"

He frowned at her and a shutter dropped over his expression. He rolled to the side, releasing his grip. Shaun scrambled off the bed and stood shaking next to it, her arms wrapped around herself. She must have looked truly stricken because he frowned in concern and sat up, reaching for her. Shaun jumped away and shook her head. "I just need a minute, okay?"

He studied her for a second, then nodded. Shaun ran for the bathroom, slamming it shut and leaning against it. She didn't bother locking it. She'd locked it before and Jozef had let himself in without even alerting her. She covered her face with her hands and tried to get a grip on herself. She felt like she was in shock. Her heart was racing, she was shaking, tears were pricking her eyes.

Did she regret what they'd just done? She thought long

and hard about it and decided she did not regret having sex with Jozef. It was easily the most pleasurable moment of her life and she was going to treasure it as a perfect memory.

Then why was she so fucked up over it? She pushed away from the door and paced the bathroom.

"Oh god," she moaned as semen and vaginal fluids dripped down her thighs.

She grabbed a towel and pressed it against herself, trying to wipe away the evidence. Then it hit her. They'd fucked without a condom. Shaun never had sex without protection. EVER. This moment was unprecedented in so many ways. What if Jozef had an STI? Shaun certainly didn't, but he didn't know that. They'd been reckless.

Then there was that possibility of a baby. Shaun wasn't on birth control because she'd been too busy with her job in Ukraine to re-administer her Depo-Provera shot. She hadn't worried though, because she hadn't intended on hooking up with anyone. She was too busy for even a casual fling.

Apparently, she wasn't too busy to fuck her captor.

"Oh god," she said again.

There was a knock at the door and Shaun jumped in surprise. Since when did Jozef knock before entering a room? She hesitated and then reached for the doorknob. She suspected he was being polite, giving her the few minutes of space she'd requested. But his concern would only extend so far. If she didn't open the door then he would come in anyway.

He stood on the other side, still naked, a bathrobe in his hands. He held it up and jerked his head, indicating she should step into it. Shaun obeyed, feeling instantly better when she was enveloped in fuzzy warmth.

"Thank you."

He leaned toward her, capturing her chin when she tried to move back. He did the same thing he'd done while they were fucking, he dropped his head to hers, pressing his forehead against hers. It was a strange moment of solidarity that gave her strength.

"We didn't use a condom," she told him.

He nodded his head in acknowledgment then gently tugged on her arm, leading her back to the bed. Shaun crawled on top, blushing when she climbed over a wet spot made of their combined fluids.

Jozef sat on the bed and leaned back against the headboard. He reached for her and she thought he was going to pull her against his chest, but he didn't. He maneuvered her so she was facing him, their knees touching. He tugged on the lapels of the bathrobe, closing them against her throat so she wouldn't get cold.

Shaun realized what her problem was; he was getting to her. Not just physically, but emotionally. Their sexual encounter had made such an emotional impact on her that she couldn't deal with the aftermath. Couldn't deal with wanting him, liking him, enjoying his body, but knowing they had no future. The idea of not being with him forever felt horrible. Yet she shouldn't be this attached. They barely knew each other. He'd abducted her. He was a murderer. There was no scenario that ended with a happily ever after.

Jozef began signing. *I'm clean, you don't need to worry about S-T-I's.*

"How do I know?" Shaun asked, her voice shaky with emotion.

Jozef gave her a stern look. *I will never lie to you. I have always used protection with other women.*

Shaun nodded. She believed him. "I'm clean too," she told him.

He laughed, the sound strange and shocking. It was a bark, not loud, but sharp and unexpected. She realized how rare it was to hear him laugh and the sound was always off, like whatever happened to his voice had affected his laugh too.

I think it goes without saying that you are clean.

Shaun frowned at him. "That's quite an assumption. I'll have you know, I was quite the busy girl in my early years of med school."

Jozef grinned at her, showing his even white teeth. Again, Shaun was surprised. She hadn't seen this much joy from him. He was truly loving the after-sex moments, the banter, being with her. It gave Shaun a warm glow.

Busy doing what? Burying your nose in a book.

Shaun laughed and shook her head. "Nope, I had a pretty normal college experience. I was the queen of multitasking, juggling my books in one hand and the football team in the other."

I admit this surprises me. His smiling face slowly became stern. *Time to stop talking about your conquests though. You seem to bring out my jealous side.*

"Really?" Shaun asked, the warm glow spreading.

She wanted to roll her eyes at herself. Here she was, blushing like a schoolgirl and eating up his compliments. She was a grown woman; she should be kicking his ass for not using protection.

Really, he signed. *You make me feel things that I shouldn't feel.*

He looked serious and Shaun felt the moment shift from light to heavy.

"Me too," she admitted. "It scares me."

Jozef reached for her face and placed his hand over her mouth. She frowned from behind his hand, wondering what he was doing. He lifted her hands and held them aloft, wiggling them when she looked at him with confusion.

"You want me to use...?" he cut her off again with a hand over her mouth.

Shaun nodded. "Okay, but I'm rusty - "

He frowned and tightened his hand, indicating she wasn't to speak again.

Shaun signed, *this feels awkward.*

He let out a growling laugh and she stared at his lips in wonder. The sounds he made meant different things. It wasn't just one sound for everything. He had a barking laugh and a soft laugh. He had an angry growl and a sexy growl. Actually... all of his growls were sexy, but they had different meanings.

I like communicating with you this way, he admitted.

As the silence surrounded them, the warm glow of the fireplace bathing them, Shaun agreed, there was more intimacy in soundless communication. They were wrapped in a private bubble that belonged to only them.

I like it too, she told him.

Jozef relaxed against the headboard, pushing himself into the pillows and getting comfortable. He was completely confident in his nudity, unfazed that his now flaccid cock rested on his thighs. Shaun sneaked as many glances as she could without being completely obvious.

Talk to me, he signed.

Shaun grabbed a pillow and pressed it against her stomach. *What do you want to know?*

Anything. Everything. Tell me about your life in Canada.

Shaun thought about saying no; telling him that talking about her home country was too raw. Especially with her kidnapper. But she reconsidered. She felt the desire to share parts of her life with him. It couldn't hurt. Maybe he would hear the love and longing in her words. Understand that it was wrong to take her away from the places and people she loved. Maybe he would let her go.

I have a cat, she signed.

He grinned, his face creasing in humour, dimples flashing in his cheeks. *I remember the cat. His name is F-I-T-Z-Y and he's a big orange tabby who eats the neighborhood birds.*

Shaun stared at him, surprised he remembered the things she'd told him during their desperate van ride into the forest. She hadn't thought he was listening.

What I didn't tell you was how I came to own him. She grinned fondly at the memory. *He somehow got into the hospital during a night shift. He was very mischievous, leading the security guards on a merry chase. I could hear updates on the PA system. Cat spotted in radiology. Cat is now in kinesiology.*

Jozef laughed with her, mesmerizing her with his easy joy. She wondered if he was always like this when he was at home or if relaxation was rare for him.

Shaun continued her story. *Of course, I had to adopt the cat after listening to his hospital escapades all night...*

CHAPTER TWENTY-SEVEN

J ozef was in trouble.

He was falling for his fiancé, which was a problem. He could have no weaknesses in his line of work. Mafia wasn't what it used to be, back when there were rules to govern behaviour. When it was a brotherhood. Now there were insidious commonalities among the vicious young mobsters who worked according to their own rules while attempting to set themselves apart. Family was now fair game, human trafficking was wildly popular and substance abuse was rampant. The brotherhood still existed. Krystoff insisted that his own organization observe the old rules. They did not target family; they did not peddle in flesh and they were controlled at all times while on the job.

Jozef lived somewhere between worlds. He had to be as harsh, brutal and unfeeling as the rest of his contemporaries if he wanted to stay on top of the game. Any weakness would make him a target. Drugs and alcohol were rampant but he limited himself to the occasional drink, joint, or line of coke.

He gazed down at Shaun who was curled on her side, pressed against his leg, her head tucked into his hip. He shifted until he was leaning over her and able to see more of her lovely face. He brushed his fingers down her ebony cheek and over her plush lips. She was so beautiful it made him ache. It wasn't her outward beauty that captivated him, though she was certainly attractive, but her inner glow. It radiated out of her as an energy filled with kindness and purpose.

She epitomized everything he couldn't be, but he was discovering he wanted in his life. He wanted to put her personality in a jar and keep it with him, so he always had her, even when they were apart. He knew keeping her was selfish. He could have found a way to keep her alive and let her go. He could put her on an airplane back to Canada right now and she would be safe on the other side of the world. Safe from him. Safe from his family.

He wouldn't do it. Selfishly, he wanted to keep her forever. He wanted to hold onto everything that made Shaun special. He couldn't bring himself to let her go. They'd only known each other a week, but he was captivated. He could feel his world shifting irrevocably and he couldn't bring himself to regret it.

"Hey."

Jozef looked down. She was blinking sleepily up at him with a quizzical look. He must've woken her when he touched her cheek. He looked at her, wanting to tell her to go back to sleep but not wanting to stop touching her to make the signs.

She wiggled against him and closed her eyes, sighing deeply. He thought she went back to sleep, but then she spoke, her voice quiet and serious, "What does it feel like to kill someone?"

Jozef froze at the unexpected question. Her eyes were open now, and she tilted her head so she could look at him. Her gaze was curious rather than accusing. Jozef thought about what to say. Did he tell her the truth, or did he tell her something that might make her feel better? Did he know her well enough to know what she might find comforting?

Maybe it was good that she knew about him, knew how rotten his soul was. She should know exactly who she would be marrying. And if she didn't like it, she would have to learn to live with it, because she wasn't going anywhere.

Jozef twisted until he was half facing her and she could clearly see his hands. She lifted her head off the pillow to watch as he signed. *I was sixteen when I became Krystoff's enforcer. I was young, cocky, full of myself. I had this friend, another young guy, M-A-X, who worked the streets with me. He was one of our recruiters. We grew close. Played video games together, worked together, partied together. I ate meals at his house, prepared by his grandmother. I took their food and their friendship.*

"Oh god," she whispered, as though she knew what was coming. He didn't stop.

My friend started skimming profit. Krystoff's accountant blew the whistle and I was charged with taking care of the matter. It was my job to put my best friend in the ground.

"Wh-what did you do?"

He shrugged. *I pulled the trigger.*

"Why?" she demanded angrily. "Couldn't you have warned him, sent him away or something?"

He stared at her steadily and then shook his head. *As the family dog, it is both my duty and my pleasure to enact the orders of my uncle. I am effective because I'm loyal to those who are loyal to me.*

"Who are you to decide who deserves death and who doesn't?" she sputtered, pushing away from him, her voice rising in anger. "You destroy families! What about his grandmother? You took away her grandson, someone she loved."

Jozef took a deep breath to calm the pain her words were causing. They hit too close to home. *You wanted to know how it feels to kill someone?*

She nodded, her eyes golden pools of accusation.

I remember every face, every name, everything about them. I accept the pain I have caused their families and I take it into myself. With every kill, another piece of my soul is torn away. I kept track of M-A-X's grandmother until the day she died. I made sure she was taken care of, sending food and money anonymously. I will never forget her face, nor the way she looked at me on the day of his funeral, knowing that her grandson's killer was standing next to his casket.

"Then why do you do it?" she cried out.

It is my duty.

The stricken look on her face told him she either didn't understand or she couldn't accept his words. He didn't want her to hate him, especially not after the moments they'd shared over the past several hours. He wanted to grab her and force her back to his side, force her to touch him willingly again. But of course, he couldn't. He couldn't reassure her, either. There needed to be truth between them.

This is the world I live in. There are no good guys or bad guys. Some people need to die, and in this family, it's my job to make those decisions regardless of my feelings.

"I didn't deserve to die," Shaun cried out, her voice filled with the anger and trauma of their first day together.

Jozef's heart ached for her. She was confused, hurt, scared, and he couldn't be the one to reassure her. She was part of this life now and she needed to adapt. He reached out and took her chin in his hand, forcing her to look at him.

No, you didn't deserve to die.

"But you would've killed me!" Her voice broke on a sob.

He nodded solemnly. *I would have done my job.*

"Why didn't you?" She swiped angrily at the tears that started to fall.

He sighed and rubbed a hand over his short hair. He thought about her question, thought hard, but he couldn't come up with an answer. When he imagined the scene, he could see it clearly, as though it'd just happened.

He was in the forest clearing with her again, looking down his gun at her, his finger tightening on the trigger. Their eyes locked and she told him silently she would die with dignity. She would go into the afterworld with her head held high and no regrets. In the seconds between pulling the trigger and not, Jozef decided he needed that fierce spirit in his life. That he would not live with the regret of putting this spectacular woman in the ground. He would keep her.

I couldn't pull the trigger, he finally told her.

"But why?" she demanded again, anger and passion colliding in one irresistible woman.

He gripped her head hard and gave her a little shake to show his frustration, then dropped his hands to sign, *it doesn't matter, let it go*.

"It does matter!" she shouted, wiggling backwards, trying to put more distance between them. "I need to know what stopped you; I need to know it can never happen again. I have to know that you'll never decide to change your mind."

Her voice was edging toward hysteria and Jozef was caught between his own anger that she wouldn't listen, that she was ruining their perfect moment, and his desire to calm her, to hold her and promise she never had anything to worry about.

He grabbed her by the waist and dragged her toward him.

This time she fought him, striking out and slapping his arm while flailing her legs. Jozef growled and rolled her underneath him.

He pinned her to the bed until all she could do was thrash inside the cage of his arms. He let her tire herself out until she went limp, glaring up at him.

Jozef tried to take her mouth in a kiss but she turned her head away. This annoyed him more than anything else she'd done so far. He didn't care if she tried to deny him her body, her feelings, her words, but she would not be allowed to deny his kisses. This is where their intense spiritual connection merged with their physical bodies. Everything he needed to tell her but couldn't was conveyed in a kiss.

He gripped her by the neck, yanking her head off the bed and slashing his mouth over hers in a rough kiss. She gasped as he attacked her lips with his teeth, forcing his way into her mouth. She was too shocked to resist, and he took advantage by sweeping the dark recesses within over and over until she had to fight for breath.

He dragged the bathrobe open and squeezed her breast, rubbing his thumbnail over the nipple. Earlier he'd shown his caring side, bringing her to orgasm well before entering her and then carefully guiding her desire back up. This time he was going to show her his dark side. The mob enforcer who took what he wanted with no consequences. She would feel his power. She would know all of him and she would love it.

He reached further down her lithe body until he found her still slippery pussy, shoving two fingers deep inside without preparation. Her tight pussy fought him for a second then gave way as he thrust deep inside, found her g-spot and rubbed it hard. She screamed into his mouth as pain and pleasure collided and sparks went off all around them.

Jozef began to sweat as his cock leapt to life again, weeping at another opportunity to fuck this beautiful woman. She bowed on the bed, her body pressing up against his. The fit was tight, but he continued to slam his fingers in and out of her, swallowing her cries as they came closer and closer together. Before she could reach her orgasm though, he pulled his hand from her pussy, grabbed hold of her and flipped her over.

Confused and disoriented Shaun flailed on the bed and tried to push herself up on her hands and knees. Jozef gripped the bathrobe at the back of her neck and wrenched it off her. She gasped as she was dragged up onto her knees, then fell onto her hands again once he tossed the robe away. She looked at him over her shoulder, fear and excitement lighting her expression.

"Jozef..." she pleaded.

He slammed into her from behind, dragging her hips back as he thrust. She let out another scream and clawed at the blankets in front of her. Jozef took her with ferocious pumps, staking his claim in a way that she would never be able to question. He didn't want her talking about how he'd almost killed her. He didn't want her talking about STI's and condoms. She was his. Period. No questions, no negotiation, no escape.

Shaun stopped fighting him and began rocking her hips back, primitive sounds of unbridled pleasure spilling from her lips. She was completely lost to him, exactly where he wanted her. He grabbed her hair, tangling his fingers in the curly mass and dragging her back for a kiss that was so passionate, so primal, his teeth cut her soft inner tissues, making her bleed.

He shoved her back down, pressing his hand against the small of her back as he approached his orgasm. His balls felt like they were made of steel, they were so tight, so ready to blow. He slammed into her, fucking himself dry as he shot his load deep into her body.

He didn't remember hearing her come, so when he finished, he pulled out and replaced his cock with his fingers. She shouted as she instantly flew up into the embrace of an electric pleasure that could only come from having someone attack her g-spot. As he continued to slam his fingers in and out of her, he used the juices flowing from her body to ease the entry of his finger into her tiny asshole.

She tried to jerk away, but he caught her hips and dragged her back, slapping her ass hard enough to make it bounce and draw a shriek from her. She moaned as he slid his finger into an ass so tight, he'd bet his fortune it was virgin. Pleasure sizzled through him, making his tired cock sit up and take notice. This ass was his and one day soon he was going to take it.

"I'm coming!" she keened desperately.

Fluid washed over his hand as he continued to pump in and out of her. Her hips thrust back in unison with his hand while her ass spasmed around his finger, her orgasm setting off every nerve ending he was touching. She felt like silken fire in his hands and he couldn't wait for her to recover enough to do it all over again.

As she collapsed to the bed, he climbed over top of her, took her jaw in his hand and shoved it to the side. He sank his teeth into her throat, biting her hard enough to break skin. She jerked, cried out tiredly and gripped his head as he sucked hard on her flesh, leaving his mark. When he finished stamping himself into her soft flesh, he moved his lips to her ear and let out a low possessive growl. She shivered against him and allowed him to gather her against his chest, tucking her into his side for the rest of the night.

CHAPTER TWENTY-EIGHT

"Are you listening?"

Shaun looked up sharply, a guilty expression on her face. She had not been listening to Dasha; she'd been daydreaming about her night with Jozef. She shivered as she thought about it. He was so intense, so demanding, so different from any man she'd ever known. The sex was glorious and definitely something she wanted to try again.

Then guilt hit her like a fist to the chest. She was forgetting her situation, something that seemed to be happening more and more frequently as the days passed. Her mother must be frantic, devastated, sick with worry over her daughter's disappearance. Shaun needed to concentrate on getting a message to Fatima, not daydreaming about her mobster fiancé.

"I'm sorry," she murmured to Dasha. "My mind was drifting, what were you saying?"

Dasha gave her a sharp look. "I was saying that I think the colour scheme should be gold and black. Classic with a twist. We don't want white or silver because obviously we want to save those colours for the wedding. What do you think?"

Dasha's long, beautifully lacquered magenta nails flashed as she fanned out an impressive spread of colour samples across the coffee table in front of them. Shaun had managed to live 34 years without knowing that there were so many different shades of gold.

"Uhhh, that one." She pointed at one of them.

Dasha frowned at the sample, picked it up off the table and held it a few inches from her face. "Are you sure? I think this one's a little dark. It won't complement the black. What about this one?" She picked up a lighter sample with a tiny amount of sparkle to it.

"It's beautiful," Shaun murmured, then smothered a yawn.

Dasha's frown amped up a notch as she surveyed Shaun critically. "Are you okay, my dear? We can go over the samples this afternoon if you need a rest."

Shaun wanted to point out that, no she was not okay, she was still the victim of a kidnapping. Also, she'd spent the entire night previous getting her brains fucked out by the woman's nephew and was still a little fuzzy from the happy hormones.

Since neither response seemed appropriate for the Koba matriarch, she said, "I'm fine, thank you. It's just that I have no experience with party planning and your decorating skills are stunning." Shaun waved her hand around the sitting room where they were having their meeting. It was a combination of heavy woods, gold and beige trimming and the occasional pop of modern. Really, every room Shaun had visited so far had been a feast for the eyes. "I think this engagement party is better left in your capable hands. I will happily bow to your expertise."

"Lovely, dear." Dasha beamed at her and squeezed her hand. "You won't regret this. A few years ago, I threw a 50-

year anniversary party for the Baroness Von Grieger. European society is still talking about it. Never mind Leeza's wedding. Now *that* was the event of the decade..."

Shaun checked out while Dasha described her daughter's lavish wedding in meticulous detail over the next hour. Since it was impossible to get in a word edgewise, Shaun didn't think Dasha would notice that she wasn't paying attention.

Shaun sipped her tea which seemed to magically refill with hot tawny liquid before she could reach the bottom of her cup. The weird part was she couldn't once remember seeing a servant. She suspected they were quick and stealthy, neither seen nor heard by the family unless called upon. In Montréal, Shaun had a housekeeper that came in twice a month to make sure she didn't get too far behind on cleaning when she was working long hours.

"I think we'll go with the choices of prime rib or salmon for the reception dinner with a vegetarian alternative. We'll add roasted garlic rosemary potatoes, fresh greens and fresh-baked sweet buns. That should do for the Westerners, and we'll serve *vepřo-knedlo-zelo*, roast pork with dumplings and sauerkraut for the locals. Oh, I forgot to ask, do you have any dietary restrictions?"

Shaun blinked at Dasha as her brain kicked in to repeat the question. "No, nothing. I don't eat a lot of red meat and I try to limit sugar and alcohol, of course."

"Of course." Dasha squeezed her knee. "You're a doctor; you would know best how to protect your body."

Shaun started to snort and cut it off so as not to offend Dasha. She clearly did not know how to take care of her body, as it had been through the wringer the past several days. She'd been kidnapped, pushed around, attacked with guns, accosted in a women's washroom, and forced to sleep in a cold dank prison cell. She wasn't doing awesome at taking care of herself, but most of that wasn't her fault.

"I vote for the prime rib." Saskia wandered into the room, though she'd clearly been standing near the doorway for longer. "With mashed potatoes, gravy, biscuits and green beans smothered in fresh butter. Our English and American attendees will love it."

Shaun decided to cast her vote for Saskia's menu. It sounded amazing. "People will come that far for a last-minute engagement party?"

"Of course they will, we're extremely rich, dear."

Shaun had to smother a laugh. This was the second time Dasha had reminded her of the Koba wealth as though it should be perfectly obvious the family would get whatever they wanted.

Dasha turned the full force of her frown on her youngest daughter. "You shouldn't eavesdrop; it's not ladylike."

Saskia dropped into the ornate chair sitting opposite the couch and reached for a cucumber sandwich, stuffing it into her mouth before pulling her legs up underneath her and getting comfy. "The menu for Jozef and Shaun's engagement party is hardly top-secret business."

Dasha glared at her daughter as she cleared the samples off the table. "I can hear your sarcasm, daughter, and I don't like it. You need to do something with your life rather than wander the house looking for mischief."

Saskia straightened in her chair and glared fiercely at her mother. "University isn't a waste of time!"

"This family is where you should focus." Dasha stood regally. It looked like magic to Shaun, the way she simply stood up from the rather low couch in her four-inch stilettos, the epitome of grace. "You spend far too much time with your head in the clouds and not enough on building the family business."

"You want me to help run drugs and weapons?" Saskia snapped, fire in her eyes. "Sure, mother, just tell me when and where. I'll be sure to bring my most bedazzled Uzi for protection."

As mother and daughter bickered, Shaun was given the impression that this was not a new argument. Saskia clearly wanted something she wasn't getting in the mansion and Shaun suspected it was an education.

"This free ride won't last forever. You must watch your tongue and act like part of the family if you wish to continue the benefits of such luxury living," Dasha lectured.

Saskia jumped up from her chair, her short compact body rising with a burst of energy. "I don't want it to last forever! You're the ones who keep me here like some kind of prisoner."

As soon as the word 'prisoner' flew out of her mouth, Saskia gasped and smacked her palm over her lips, her gaze going to Shaun.

Dasha took advantage of the momentary silence by saying coolly, "I'll see you both at dinner. Saskia, I expect you to keep a civil tongue in your head."

Dasha walked away, her steel tipped heels tapping against the hardwood flooring as she walked, her long flowing scarf exiting the room after her as though the accessory was choreographed perfectly to her every movement.

"Are you okay?" Shaun asked quietly.

Saskia was standing with her fists and teeth clenched, staring at the doorway where her mother had just disappeared. She looked at Shaun in confusion then seemed to snap to the present. Her expression smoothed out and she reached for another sandwich before dropping back into her chair.

"I'm fine," she mumbled, then said more clearly, "I'm sorry I made that comment about being a prisoner. I've been told sometimes I can be insensitive."

Shaun smiled kindly at her. "I think you're genuine, not

insensitive. You say what you think. I knew you didn't trust me the moment I walked in the dining room, yet here we are, chatting like friends."

Saskia narrowed her eyes. "I still don't trust you."

Shaun laughed and reached for a sandwich, feeling more comfortable with the youngest Koba than she had in Dasha's presence. She kicked off her shoes and curled her legs up on the couch.

"So what do you want to study in University?"

Saskia shrugged, her shoulders slumping.

"If you don't want to talk about it, I understand," Shaun assured her, eating the surprisingly delicious sandwich. Who knew cucumber and mayo on bread would taste decent? "I'm not a bad person to run some ideas by since I have eight years of University experience. I can probably answer any questions you might have."

Saskia glanced up, her face a heartbreaking mixture of hope and despair. This really was a dream she wanted but couldn't bring herself to hope for because her family didn't approve. Once again, the strangeness of the alternate world she was inhabiting hit Shaun. The Kobas were fine with Jozef committing murder and kidnapping, but they didn't approve of their youngest daughter furthering her education.

"I was thinking about linguistics. I'm really good at learning new languages and understanding the origins of words. I love reading books in other languages, so my brain stays sharp." She glanced at Shaun under her lashes. "I guess it's not as important as being a doctor..."

"Are you kidding?" Shaun jumped in enthusiastically. "Language is so important. Honestly, learning multiple languages is a huge achievement that you should be proud of. Language is just as important as medicine. My job would be much more difficult if I couldn't communicate with my patients. I once had a patient who was brand new to Canada come into Emergency while I was on shift, presenting with acute appendicitis. He was from Syria and he couldn't speak a word of English. His eleven-year-old daughter translated for us. Without her we wouldn't have known he had a deadly allergy to propofol, a common general anesthetic. We could've killed him during the surgery if she hadn't been there to help us."

Saskia's eyes were round as she absorbed the story. "Was... was he okay?"

Shaun smiled. "Yes, very much so, and the hospital staff got to know his entire family while he was recovering." She stopped speaking verbally and started using sign language. *Translators are extremely important people. They work with the U-N, Doctors Without Borders, the W-H-O. They are invaluable. There are so many wonderful things you can do with a degree in linguistics.*

Saskia grinned from ear-to-ear and signed, *I want to do it. I'd love to travel around the world doing translation work for important organizations.* She glanced shyly away. *Sort of like what you do with Doctors Without Borders.*

Shaun's heart swelled and she felt as though she was forging a genuine friendship with the younger woman. "There are plenty of translators working with Doctors Without Borders. It would be an excellent choice."

Saskia's look of hope melted away as quick as it came. Only instead of the carefully cultivated scowl she usually wore, she now looked crestfallen. "My parents will never go for it. They want me to marry into the life and have babies. Like Leeza. They look to us to spread the Koba genes."

"And you don't want that sort of life?" Shaun asked gently.

Saskia blanched, her face going pale. She looked visibly shaken which Shaun thought was an extreme reaction for a pretty basic question.

Concerned, Shaun asked, "Are you okay?"

"Yes, of course I am." She stiffened her shoulders and

hardened her gaze. "I will do as my parents ask. My duty is to the family."

Saskia's statement sent a chill through Shaun. The Koba family went beyond just tight knit. Their obsession with family bordered on cult-like. As far as she knew, anyone with even a drop of Koba blood lived either in the house or on the grounds. She'd found out the day before that two of the men on Jozef's team were cousins to the family and several members of security were distantly related. She wasn't surprised that someone holding the position of daughter to the boss would be closely monitored, her life mapped out for her. Like royalty, only Saskia was mafia royalty.

It was a grim insight into Shaun's own future and any possible children she might have with Jozef. This thought sent her mind spinning into an abyss of emotion. The idea of having Jozef's child made her feel inexplicably happy, yet she barely knew him. She couldn't trust him to do the right thing when it came to children. She didn't want to raise a family in the Koba household, under the thumb of mobsters. A group of people who would have thought nothing of her execution. Yet, she might already be pregnant.

"Everything okay over there?" There was an edge of sarcasm to Saskia's tone.

"I'm fine, thank you." She tried to shake off the feeling of someone walking across her grave and focused back on the conversation at hand. "If you really want to go to university you should push for it."

"How?" Saskia asked skeptically. "Have you tried asking my parents for something you know they won't approve of? It's worse than just a no. They'll have you watched every minute of every day to make sure you don't take a single step out of line. They're worse than cookies, or whatever the internet uses to ferret out every detail of our lives so they can come at us with personalized advertising, like I ever asked for a unicorn shaped dildo."

Shaun giggled at the descriptive complaint before sobering. "I'll help you," she assured the other woman. "We just need to tell them something they want to hear. I bet your family could use a translator with some of their business associates."

Saskia's eyes grew round and she straightened in her seat. "They do use translators sometimes!" she said excitedly, but then her face fell again. "But I don't want to do that kind of work. It's not as... important... as the things you do."

The glow within Shaun began to spread. She really had managed to pick up an ally in this fierce young woman. "You don't have to work for your family; you just need to convince them to let you go to university. Once they agree, you'll have four years to pick out your dream job and work on them from the inside. When you graduate, they'll be so proud of your accomplishments that they'll have no choice but to let you work wherever you want."

Saskia looked completely blown away by Shaun's logic. "That's brilliant!"

Shaun laughed. "I've been known to have a good idea from time to time."

"No wonder you're a doctor," Saskia said emphatically. "You're a fucking genius."

CHAPTER TWENTY-NINE

Over the next several days the mansion was turned upside down as they prepared for the engagement party. Servants clogged the hallways as they moved furniture, carried bolts of cloth, brought in brand new kitchen equipment and hauled armloads of groceries. More staff was hired to cook and serve while still more were hired to help the head gardener and his team make sure the grounds were immaculate.

The entire weeklong process left Shaun speechless. She couldn't fathom that a party of this opulence and magnitude was being pulled together so quickly. The amount of resources going into an event meant to celebrate the engagement of two people who only met a few weeks ago was simply stunning. Yet no one seemed concerned about the bride and groom's lack of history together.

"More flowers arrived."

Shaun turned from where she was standing next to a long serving table in the massive ball room. Dasha had tasked her with making sure it was in the correct place. Shaun had no idea what the correct placement might be, but if there was anything she'd learned about Dasha since arriving in Prague, it was that a person simply nodded and quietly excused themselves to immediately go do whatever it was Dasha asked for. Life was pleasanter, it seemed, when Dasha was happy. Shaun liked to think of her as a loving, pleasantly kind matriarch who could turn into a fire-breathing dragon in the blink of an eye if she wasn't happy about something.

Leeza stood hesitantly in the entrance of the ballroom holding a massive bouquet of flowers. Unlike the other flowers arriving, these were big and bright, much prettier than the carefully chosen bouquets from Dasha's personal florist. Displays had been pouring in all week; black roses dipped in some kind of liquid gold, which made them look like they were dripping. The arrangements were set high on pedestals all around the perimeter of the ballroom. Shaun hadn't known roses could come in black, but was quickly learning that if Dasha wanted something, she always got it. Shaun was told the roses were native to Turkey and extremely expensive.

According to Saskia, Dasha set up a flower donation fund for anyone who couldn't attend the engagement party. They sent money into the florist, which paid for an arrangement of Dasha's choice. Shaun didn't understand the system, since the Kobas could easily afford the flowers themselves. The super-rich baffled her. Whoever had sent this display hadn't gotten the colour coordination memo.

"Thank you." Shaun approached Leeza carefully. They hadn't spoken more than a few words since Leeza had pointed a gun at her. Shaun supposed it was only natural that their budding relationship would become stilted after such a thing. She reached out to take the card from the flowers.

She glanced at the card and started laughing. "This has to be a joke."

"Who's it from?" Leeza asked, setting the heavy arrangement down on the nearest table.

A servant gave the flowers a scandalized look and whisked them out of the carefully decorated black and gold room before Dasha could see them. Shaun didn't blame the staff member for his concern. She'd seen things that week that would make a drill sergeant flinch, and now had a new respect for anyone who worked on the Koba grounds.

"The card says it's from Buckingham palace," Shaun said with another laugh. "It says, best wishes on your upcoming nuptials. Yours Sincerely, the Duke and Duchess of Wales."

"Yes," Leeza said with a knowing nod. "Mom went to boarding school with a few royals. The families occasionally hunted together when my grandparents were in England."

Shaun felt dizzy and reached for the nearest chair. "Who exactly is coming to this party?"

Leeza's face creased in understanding and she took the chair next to Shaun, reaching for her hand. Shaun stiffened at the contact, the image of a gun in that delicate hand haunting her. Then she shook the thought away and forced herself to relax. Leeza was just trying to put her at ease, like she'd done the first day Shaun spent in the mansion.

"You really don't want to know," Leeza assured Shaun, humour in her accented tones. "It doesn't matter though. They're still people, with or without their money. Their shit still stinks, just like the rest of us."

Shaun laughed out loud, covering her mouth with her hand. "I don't think you can put yourself in the 'un-monied' category with the rest of us."

Leeza grinned. "Yeah, well, my shit smells like roses, so I guess we know which side of the aisle I'm on."

"The groom's, definitely the groom's," Shaun quipped and they both dissolved into laughter.

Shaun was wiping tears from her eyes when a child came

running into the ballroom as though his pants were on fire, fat tears rolling down his cheeks. Shaun was startled for a moment until he flung himself at Leeza, climbing onto her lap and wrapping his chubby arms around her neck. Still smiling, Leeza hugged him back, holding him against her chest.

She tipped him back in her arms, smoothed the hair on his forehead and kissed him. He squirmed but didn't try to leave. Leeza's eyes met Shaun's and she said proudly, "This is my son, Kristoph."

Shaun reached out a hand to the little boy. "Pleased to meet you."

He straightened on his mother's lap and reached out to take Shaun's hand, squeezing it in a surprisingly grownup handshake. His eyes slid past her, focusing on something behind her. Shaun remembered that he was autistic. He had a head full of shaggy hair, the same shade as his mother's. His face was heartbreakingly beautiful, with large golden eyes and round cheeks flushed with colour.

Leeza hugged the child protectively against her chest. "He's mostly non-verbal, like Jozef. He speaks sometimes, but never to strangers."

"It's fine," Shaun assured her. "Is he alright?"

Leeza held him away from her chest and spoke to the child in Czech. It almost seemed jarring to hear the language, despite that they lived in the Czech Republic. Since coming to the mansion, Shaun had only heard English spoken.

Shaun enjoyed watching mother and son together. Though they both lived in what could be described as a completely dysfunctional household, considering it existed solely based on mafia affiliations, Leeza and her son clearly had a bond that transcended their surroundings.

Kristoph frowned and clutched his arm against his chest. He started signing with one hand as though born to the language. His movements were so fast and over so quick Shaun didn't catch what he was saying.

Leeza looked concerned as she gently took his arm, pulling it away from his chest. "I don't see anything."

"What did he say?" Shaun asked.

"He says he hurt his arm."

Shaun noticed a slight mottling of the skin. "Can I have a look?"

Leeza looked surprised for a moment, then relieved as she remembered Shaun was a doctor. "Please." Leeza set Kristoph on the ground and gave him a small push toward Shaun.

Shaun gently took both of Kristoph's arms and pulled them out straight in front of his body. When he didn't seem distressed, she leaned over for a closer look, running her hand over the skin. He winced and jerked in her hold. One arm was definitely more swollen than the other. "Can you tell me what happened, sweetheart?" she asked him in her professionally calm voice.

He glanced guiltily up at his mother before answering in sign language. This time Shaun was expecting it and was able to understand him. *I fell out of a tree I'm not supposed to climb.*

Leeza kissed the back of his head. "I'll let it go this time, especially since it looks like karma got your arm anyway."

What's karma? He looked curiously at his mother while Shaun continued to examine him.

"Fate," Leeza said laughing. "Something that is meant to be."

Kristoph twisted around to glare up at her. *My arm isn't fate, mama. You should never say bad things like that.*

Shaun and Leeza shared a private glance while Leeza tried to soothe his ruffled feathers.

"I don't want to alarm you," Shaun said to Leeza. "But he does need to go to a clinic. They need to ex-ray this arm and possibly put it in a cast. I suspect he's suffering from a greenstick fracture." Leeza blanched and Shaun rushed to reassure her. "It's very common among children. Their bones are still growing so there is some elasticity to them. Which means when they fall, instead of splintering, the bones will get tiny cracks called hairline fractures. They aren't nearly as bad as other types of fractures."

Leeza looked marginally better, but was quick to stand up clutching Kristoph's good hand. "Thank you, Shaun. You must excuse us though; I must get him to our doctor right away."

Without waiting for a response, Leeza rushed from the room, her voice ringing in the hallway as she shouted. The sound of her voice echoing back into the ballroom was reminiscent of Dasha. Perhaps that apple didn't fall far from the tree.

Shaun glanced at the serving table, shrugged and decided to leave the decision of its placement to Dasha. Instead, she went back to Jozef's apartment where she could have a few minutes alone, making a detour into the kitchen to grab a snack. Munching on a handful of nuts and raisins, she nodded at the man guarding Jozef's door. He unlocked and opened it for her.

She wasn't thrilled with the presence of security on the door, but she'd kept her discontent to herself. She wasn't sure if security had been stationed there before her arrival or if it was special for her. She didn't particularly care. She'd decided that escaping from the mansion directly would be impossible anyway. She'd have to wait until she was in the city and an opportunity presented itself.

She was surprised to find Jozef standing in their bedroom with his back to her as she entered. She stopped, feeling awkward. Though they slept in the same bed and made wild passionate love to each other, she couldn't seem to look him in the eye in the light of day without blushing. When he turned to look at her, the awkwardness melted away. It was impossible not to feel wanted when his eyes glowed with sexual tension and possessiveness. His expression took her breath away.

Jozef lifted his hand and crooked a finger at her, telling her to come to him. Shaun hesitated, knowing she should resist the insane lure of their combined chemistry. She was helpless though. Jozef was everything she should despise. He was a criminal, a killer, a kidnapper, and the list could easily go on, but he was also everything she wanted. He was tough, sexy, and intelligent. His desire for her was an aphrodisiac she couldn't ignore.

Before she could make up her mind, Jozef crossed the room to her, his gaze intent. She watched him, her eyes widening as he reached for her. He dragged her against his chest and kissed her. Not a kiss of greeting, but one of passion, one of possession. He was staking his claim.

It took only seconds before Shaun was lost to the pressure of his lips on hers, the aggressive thrust of his tongue and the sweep of his hands over her back, holding her and feeling her at the same time. She held him, pressing her body against his, inhaling his incredible masculine scent. It sent every thought fleeing from her brain until all she wanted to do was keep her lips pressed to his and spend the day smelling him.

Finally, Jozef broke the kiss, but continued to hold Shaun, pushing her back only far enough to lift his hands between them.

I want to take you out into the city, he signed. *Will you come with me?*

Was he asking? So far, asking her permission for anything hadn't been a strong point in their budding relationship.

"Okay," she said carefully.

He shook his head and grabbed hold of her wrists, holding

them aloft and wiggling them. Shaun laughed and nodded her understanding. She signed, *what are we going to do in the city?*

His deep blue eyes held hers in thrall and she had to force herself to drop her gaze so she could concentrate on his hands. *I want us to start over. I want you to get to know me....* He paused, as if thinking about what he wanted to say. Finally, he decided to go with blunt. *I want you to forget the Luhansk hospital, forget what I did to you, forget the guns. Get to know me, I think you'll learn to like me.*

That's what Shaun was afraid of, because it was happening already. The more she got to know Jozef, the more she liked him, and the more she was willing to compromise her values for just a few more hours and days with him. She knew deep down that eventually she would have to extricate herself, go home and pick up the pieces of her shattered life. Sadly, it wasn't the trauma of her kidnapping and subsequent events that would occupy her thoughts for years to come, it was the loss of Jozef. An enigmatic man, determined to marry his witness, thus saving her life.

Yes, let's go into the city, she signed. *I could use a night away from party planning.*

Jozef flashed her a look of simple pleasure. He was pleased that she agreed to his plan without a fight.

Do I need to change? she asked.

He looked her over and shook his head. *You're perfect the way you are.*

CHAPTER THIRTY

Security hovered around the couple as they made their way through Prague. Jozef took Shaun to wander down by the beautiful Vltava river and visit nearby tourist sites. He touched her as often as he could, his caresses gentle and solicitous, never crossing the line into darker territory. When he wasn't touching her, he was signing rapidly, giving her information about the sites they were visiting, telling her anecdotes of his youth and guiding her through a city steeped in history.

It was an exciting opportunity for a person from Canada, a relatively young country where history could only go back so far. Jozef showed her St. George's Basilica at Prague castle. Built in 920 it was one of the oldest churches in the Czech Republic. As they walked the castle grounds, Jozef pointed at a huge golden chapel, St. Vitus Cathedral, its grand architecture breathtaking as the sun lit up its gold turrets. Shaun watched his hands as he explained, *my aunt and uncle were married in this church. It was one of the last weddings performed here. Now it is a tourist attraction, though there is still the occasional service.*

Shaun asked, *were you born yet when they married?*

He nodded. *I was a child, too young for the event, but my parents attended.*

She wanted to ask about his parents but didn't know how to broach the subject. Based on some of the gossip she'd heard around the mansion and knowing that Jozef was raised by his aunt and uncle, she guessed that there was a story behind their deaths.

Next, Jozef took her to a restaurant. At first, Shaun was hesitant, as it was clearly a high-end restaurant, probably more extravagant than any restaurant Shaun had ever been in, and she was wearing a pair of jeans, a light pink blouse and a patterned scarf. Jozef didn't seem to care about a dress code though. He walked confidently up to the host with his hand firmly wrapped around Shaun's.

"Ah, Mr. Koba, we have your table ready. Please follow me."

The host turned and weaved his way between tables to the back corner where a table was set aside. He pulled out the chair for Shaun as she sat down and reached to place a cloth napkin over her lap. Jozef caught the napkin, tugging it away from the man and waving him away. Jozef smoothed the napkin over Shaun's lap while she blushed at the small intimacy.

"Do you come here often?" Shaun asked, taking a gulp of her water to chill her burning cheeks. What she really wanted to know was if he brought dates here often, but she wasn't willing to ask that question.

Jozef frowned and tapped her arm impatiently. *Speak to me in our language*, he signed, then he answered her question. *I've been here only a few times. My uncle owns the place and this table belongs to the family. He likes to bring Aunt Dasha here.*

Shaun was happy that she had nothing to be jealous about, but then gave her head a small shake. She didn't have any business being jealous about anything related to Jozef, let alone his past conquests. What was wrong with her? She never cared about this sort of thing. Never became possessive of a man, especially one she knew wasn't good for her.

To distract from the moment, she asked, *so your uncle owns both the restaurant and the club?*

Jozef shook his head while signing, *no, my uncle owns this restaurant and several other local businesses. I own the club.*

Shaun was surprised. The Koba clan tended to think in terms of family, not individuals, so she assumed the club was family owned. *Why do you own the club?*

He shrugged. *It was a good investment opportunity. There's no point in having a fortune if you don't spend it.*

Shaun knew enough about the mob to understand that they often owned businesses to funnel dirty money through, making it legitimate. She didn't suppose Jozef would explain the process to her.

Their waiter approached the table, beaming obsequiously at Jozef. "Sir, we have informed the chef of your presence and he respectfully requests that you allow him to prepare a menu for you and your..." His gaze slid to Shaun. She didn't know what to say but was saved having to clarify her status in Jozef's life when his second-in-command, Havel, appeared from out of the shadows.

"Dr. Patterson is Mr. Koba's fiancé," he said coolly, his gaze fixed somewhere past the waiter's shoulder. "She must be treated with the same respect as any member of the Koba family."

"Of course, sir," the waiter agreed, his gaze falling to Shaun. "My apologies, Ms. Patterson."

"Dr. Patterson," she corrected. She'd learned long ago to take pride in the title she'd achieved. It was her opinion that women were told to be humble, and that it was bragging to lay claim to their achievements. Shaun thought it was bullshit. Women needed to embrace their achievements and tell the world about them.

"Dr. Patterson," the waiter repeated. "Would you like something to drink?"

Shaun decided a chilled white wine would be perfect after a few hours of doing the tourist thing at Jozef's side. The waiter suggested a New Zealand Chardonnay and Shaun agreed. He didn't ask Jozef for his drink order and Shaun assumed he already knew it.

When the waiter left, Havel melted back into the shadows. It occurred to Shaun that she hadn't noticed Jozef's security team follow them into the restaurant. They fit seamlessly into the background, moving with the crowds and making themselves scarce unless needed. She glanced around, attempting to spot more of them, but saw no one she recognized.

Shaun signed to Jozef, using his preferred method of communication, *your men are very good at their job, aren't they? I know they were with us, but they're almost impossible to spot.*

Jozef nodded, his eyes glowing in warmth over her use of sign language.

Yes, they are always near. I will not take chances with your protection; you will be escorted at all times.

She shook her head. *I'm not used to this kind of protection. I never needed it before.*

His eyes bored into hers, his expression becoming deadly serious. *Yes, you did. I was able to take you right out of a hospital that should have been safe for you.*

A chill ran through Shaun as she was reminded once more that she was in the presence of a criminal. He refused to let her forget it yet seemed determined to show her another side to him. A more human side. The dichotomy confused her, made her want to put more distance between them.

"Excuse me," she whispered, pushing herself back from

the table. "I... I need to use the washroom." It was the same tactic she'd used in the club, but if it worked, why mess with a good thing? She needed space and she needed it now.

Jozef captured her wrist before she could leave the table and gave her a penetrating look. She read what he wanted to know in his gaze. It amazed her how expressive he could be. Before she'd marvelled at how much he was able to hide for a man whose primary method of communication was signing. Now he was giving her the opposite, he was forcing his expressions to do the talking when sign language wasn't enough.

"I'll be okay," she told him, unable to hide her vulnerability. "I just need a minute."

He nodded, but held her hand for a moment longer, finally pressing a lingering kiss to the back before releasing her. Shaun pressed her hand against her thigh, savouring the burn of his kiss on her flesh.

She realized about halfway to the washroom that a man was trailing her. When she glanced over her shoulder, she recognized Halil. She nodded in acknowledgement and continued on her path. Jozef hadn't been lying, his men were to follow her everywhere she went. On the surface she'd known this would happen, had seen other members of the family arrange their security when they left the house. But this wasn't her world and she couldn't imagine herself living it forever. She was still the ambitious doctor fighting for a residency in a busy Montréal hospital.

She shoved open the washroom door and reached for the counter, breathing as though she'd run a marathon when all she'd really done was cross a room. She stared at her face in the mirror, devoid of makeup but flushed with emotion.

"What are you doing?" she whispered to herself.

She knew what she was doing, and she knew why it was so terrifying. She was crossing over into their world, beginning to accept the things her kidnappers were telling her as her new reality. She did belong to their family now; she was engaged to Jozef Koba and the life she once knew and loved was over.

"No," she said firmly to her reflection. "This isn't me; I'm not one of them and I don't have Stockholm."

But she knew she was exhibiting textbook symptoms. She was genuinely sympathetic to her captors and didn't want to see them harmed, despite the ongoing danger to herself. She was forming an emotional bond with Jozef that was growing tighter with each physical encounter. Every time he touched her, he sent her hormones into a tizzy until she couldn't think straight.

"It's just oxytocin telling you that you have feelings for him," she told herself. "Get a grip, oxytocin is a lying bastard and you know it."

A woman chose that moment to walk into the washroom. She gave Shaun a half-smile before choosing one of the stalls. The washroom was large, with spacious stalls which were completely enclosed in frosted glass paneling that allowed the occupants privacy. Shaun took advantage of her own few minutes of privacy by splashing water on her face, washing her hands and drying them with a paper towel.

Feeling slightly better, she made her way back to her table, ignoring Halil who shadowed her every step. As she sat down, she was able to smile at Jozef. She felt more normal, more herself, some of her confusion ebbing. Life wasn't black and white but filled with grey shadows. It wasn't such a surprise that she liked her captors. They presented themselves as a normal, albeit very wealthy, family, with all the accompanying family issues. Shaun could relate to them on some level and it made her feel sympathetic toward them. That didn't mean she had Stockholm. She could and would leave when the timing was right.

Shaun and Jozef had a pleasant meal, conversing entirely in sign language until their food arrived. Jozef regaled Shaun with more anecdotes about Prague, his childhood and his travels. Under his uncle's patronage, Jozef travelled the world with his team, doing odd jobs and ensuring lucrative business for the Kobas. While he didn't go into great detail, he gave Shaun enough of a picture that she understood their reach was far and wide, spanning the world over, including Canada, where the Kobas had shares in lumber.

They stopped talking when their food came, falling into a companionable silence.

The chef had prepared a tomato bisque soup to start, followed by thin slices of prime rib served over horseradish mashed potatoes with grilled asparagus spears on the side. It was a simple dish, but one of the best things Shaun had ever eaten. Each bite was an orgasmic experience in her mouth, and she couldn't help moaning out loud.

When she looked up, both Halil and the waiter were watching her with fixed expressions, Jozef with a scowl. Halil was the first to look away when Havel smacked him in the head, while Jozef turned the heat of his annoyed stare on the waiter who rushed to apologize.

When Jozef's gaze swung round to meet hers, the ice in his eyes melted away, leaving his expression warm and glowing once more. He hadn't minded the way she was acting, but he didn't like the men surrounding them to watch.

He was jealous, Shaun realized.

It wasn't the first indication she had that he was jealous, but before she'd chalked up his behaviour to protectiveness. He'd wanted to protect his family name and his reputation from gossip and wanted to make sure Shaun was treated with respect. Now she wasn't so sure. His glares and growls felt more personal. As though he wanted to shield her personally from all other men and the world surrounding them.

It was a fanciful thought, one she reminded herself she shouldn't be having. Jozef had about as much business being jealous over her as she had of being jealous of his other women. They'd barely known each other a few weeks. He didn't even know who she was before kidnapping her, which meant he had nothing to be jealous about.

They finished their meal and waited silently as the dishes were taken away. Jozef asked Shaun if she was satisfied and she smiled at him, rubbing her belly. "That was wonderful, I'd love to come back here sometime."

We will, I'll make sure of it, he answered.

Shaun was beginning to feel sleepy. *Are we going home soon?*

Soon. He looked at her enigmatically. *I have something to show you first.*

He led Shaun from the restaurant without paying and she assumed either one of his men would pay or he didn't have to because his family owned the restaurant. It was a weird feeling, leaving without paying. She felt like a dine-n-dasher.

Jozef threaded his fingers through hers and together they walked through the brightly lit downtown Prague. When Shaun shivered, Jozef dragged her into the nearest store, a leather boutique, and purchased a jacket for her. She was stunned when in the space of five minutes he bought her a $500 jacket so she would be warm as they continued meandering through Prague.

They walked through Old Town, toward the famous Charles Bridge. Shaun was awed by the beautiful architecture as they took the path onto the bridge. About halfway across, Jozef stopped. Shaun looked at him curiously. He nodded toward the direction they'd come from and she dutifully looked. The buildings lining the street next to the river glowed a warm yellow from the streetlights. The river itself shone in the inky darkness, shifting and sparkling, giving the impression of life as it flowed lazily through the downtown core.

Shaun sighed happily, acknowledging to herself that she would never have enjoyed this sight if Jozef hadn't brought her to Prague. She told herself it was okay to enjoy the simple pleasure of a stunning view as long as she never lost sight of her reality. She glanced to the side to find Jozef's gaze on her face, his expression wistful, as though he felt the magic of the evening too. She couldn't see what was going on in his brain, but she read admiration in his eyes. She couldn't help but lift her lips in a smile.

You are a goddess, he signed, his hands flashing beneath the streetlight. Then he sank to his knee on the pavement. Shaun gasped as he reached into his pocket pulling out a jewelry box. Heart hammering, she shook her head in denial, wanting to beg him to put it away, to stop ruining the perfect moment they'd been sharing.

He didn't put it away. He opened the lid to the box. A huge solitaire diamond in a white gold setting sparkled as it captured what little light filtered down from the overhead lamps. It was a silent, sinister reminder of Shaun's place within a crime syndicate.

Jozef didn't attempt to sign the question. He didn't need to. There could only be one outcome in his mind; Shaun would become his wife.

Even as he took the ring from the box, dropping the velvet package to the street, Shaun shook her head in denial. "No."

Jozef's head came up swiftly and any warmth he'd been harbouring in his blue eyes froze to hard uncompromising chips. He stood, glaring down at her. Shaun tried to step away, tried to tug her hand from his grip, but his hold became painfully tight. If she continued to struggle, he could break her fingers. His gaze continued to capture hers as he shoved the ring onto her finger.

He looked past her and snapped his fingers. Shaun glanced over her shoulder as Havel strode from the shadows, announcing, "The car is on its way."

CHAPTER THIRTY-ONE

The drive back to the mansion was done in tense silence. Jozef stared broodingly out the window, his scarred visage flashing in the dim streetlights that they passed. Shaun didn't know what to do with herself, so she sat as quietly as humanly possible, not wanting to draw attention. She didn't know how to feel. Part of her was upset that she'd ruined their perfect night, even though she couldn't possibly accept Jozef's proposal.

The other part of her was angry at Jozef for pulling such a stunt. He had to have known what her answer would be. Didn't he?

Maybe he didn't. She glanced at him out of the corner of her eye, watching his frozen expression. He sat completely motionless as though lost in thought. Maybe he really did think Shaun would want to marry him. What in his experience had taught him otherwise? He was born and raised in a violent lifestyle with a cutthroat family. The violence and trauma of her abduction, when seen through his eyes, probably wasn't as big a deal as it was to her. It was business as usual for the Koba enforcer.

What Jozef saw when he looked at Shaun was a woman he got along with, someone with an intelligent brain and a solid moral compass. A woman he was sexually attracted to, who was attracted to him as well. What seemed like an extraordinary set of circumstances to Shaun was Jozef's every day. Well, she doubted he picked up a new fiancé every day, but the extremeness of the situation wouldn't be too far out of his experience.

So, it was entirely possible Jozef would have expected a yes when he proposed.

He had no real understanding of Shaun, of her actions or reactions. She was too far out of his realm of experience. They were from two different worlds.

She was so deep in thought that she didn't notice them turn into the long winding driveaway of the Koba estate until the vehicle came to a halt. She looked up, blinking in the gloom and glanced at Jozef who was already halfway out his door.

Shaun unbuckled her seatbelt and reached to open her door, but it was jerked from her hands. Jozef grabbed her arm and pulled her from the SUV, not waiting to see if she was clear before dragging her toward the house. His tight grip and the set of his shoulders told her he was angry.

"Jozef, stop it!" she gasped as she tripped on the pavement and nearly fell.

He paused only long enough to allow her to regain her footing before he pulled her into the house. Shaun blinked at the bright chandelier-lit interior of the foyer.

"Hey," Saskia greeted them as they passed her in the hallway on their way to Jozef's suite. She held a melting ice cream cone in her hand and her lips were smeared with chocolate. "How was your date night?"

Jozef ignored his cousin.

"Is everything okay?" Saskia asked, turning on the spot and watching with concern.

Shaun glanced over her shoulder but didn't have time to answer.

Saskia's concerned gaze followed the pair as they disappeared around a corner and entered Jozef's wing of the house.

He pulled keys from his pocket and unlocked the door, shoving Shaun inside before following her. He closed the door with a bang and reached out to grab her, wrapping his fingers around her upper arm and swinging her around until she was shoved up against the hard wood.

They stared at each other for long seconds, then Jozef dipped his head, slanting his mouth over Shaun's.

She pushed at his chest, but he was impossible to move.

He gripped her jaw, forcing her mouth open. The second his tongue was inside her mouth she slammed her teeth together. Jozef pulled back just in time.

"No, you do not get to kiss me without permission!" Shaun angrily wiped her mouth with her sleeve and glared at him.

He looked startled for a moment, as though only now realizing she hadn't actually been participating in the kiss. Then his eyes narrowed, his expression hardening. He reached for her again, but Shaun slid sideways away from the door and backed away from him. He stalked her through the outer room until her back was up against the bedroom door. He stopped a few feet away and she breathed a sigh of relief. Then she realized he was only giving her space so he could communicate.

You don't get to say no to me. I am law and order here. I take what I want.

"It this what you want?" she answered back, glaring at him. "You want an unwilling bride?"

Instead of answering the question he gripped her by the head and shoved her back against the door. Though he was taller than her at 6'3" she was tall enough that they were able to look each other in the eyes. He continued to hold her head, his fingers spanning her skull, but didn't make any further moves. Shaun took the opportunity to attempt to reason with him.

"Is this the life you want? To get told who you have to marry based on one violent incident? This life of yours is dangerous. It's brutal and it'll eat away at you. What's the life expectancy of a mobster? If I had to guess, you guys probably don't die of natural causes."

When he continued to silently stare at her, she pressed on, "You can't possibly want to be forced to marry a woman you barely know. There's still time to call this whole thing off."

The words had barely left her mouth and he was kissing her again, his lips moving over hers, trying to coax a response. She shoved at him again, turning her face to the side.

"I said no."

Jozef slammed his hand into the door over her head, shaking the thick wood with the force of his strike, then he dropped it to turn the knob, pushing her into the bedroom.

"Jozef, stop it!" she shouted as he reached for her new leather jacket, yanking it down her arms, trapping them at her side.

He shoved her backwards and she fell across the bed, unable to catch herself with her hands. He stood over her, his spread legs on either side of hers. He pointed down at her, using his commanding presence to intimidate her when he couldn't use words. It worked. He looked utterly terrifying. His big body was tense, coiled and ready to spring. His expression was fiercely determined. The tattoos on his fingers and neck seemed suddenly much more sinister.

She was sharply reminded that she barely knew this man and could not reliably predict his moods. She wiggled her arms out of the jacket and pushed herself up until she was sitting.

Jozef's expression said it all; her place in the Koba household was either going to be next to Jozef or under him. It was her choice. She stared back at him defiantly, refusing to drop her gaze. She wanted him to know that pushing her around and bullying her was unacceptable.

"No more, Jozef. I mean it."

He growled angrily. *You don't get to decide when you've had enough, I do. I will soon be your husband; my word is law. My actions are law.*

Shaun hated everything about Jozef's lifestyle. Hated his tendency toward autocracy and his ability to shrug off the brutality of his chosen profession. Despair washed over her as she acknowledged to herself that no matter how much she was growing to care about the man, she could never be with him.

"I can't live like this." She felt crushed as she looked up at him. "I need to be free."

Her words seemed to anger him even more. He pointed at her, punching the air with his finger before signing, *you don't need to be free; you want to be free. There's a difference.* His lips twisted with scorn. *You westerners have been spoiled. You hold freedom as an ideal, even above your own welfare. You can live a full life as my wife.*

"As your captive wife," she said sadly, realizing he wasn't going to relent.

If need be, as my captive wife, he agreed.

"I refuse to participate in this farce."

You have no choice.

They were at an impasse.

Shaun tried to roll away from him, determined to climb

off the other side of the bed and put distance between them, but he grabbed her and flipped her onto her back, dragging her. She fought him as he started pulling her clothes from her body. She quickly realized his intention when he leaned far enough into her that she could feel his steel-hard cock through his jeans, pressing against her thigh.

Once again, they were speaking a different language. Nothing in Jozef's experience had taught him that it was wrong to force a woman's compliance, whereas Shaun had been raised with the truth that consent was everything and betrayal of that consent was life-altering. She had to somehow make Jozef see that it would be wrong to force her before he made her life with him completely impossible.

She grabbed hold of his face as he reached between them, his hand landing on her midriff and dropping to the button on her jeans.

"Please, listen to me." His gaze met hers with angry challenge in their depths. She prayed that he felt something for her, anything. "If you do this, it will destroy anything we've managed to build since you took me. I won't be able to look at you the same. You'll always be the guy who... who... raped me. Is that what you want?"

He glared down at her, his body tense against hers. She felt the indecision and wondered if there was anything else she could say or do. She knew fighting him would prove useless, but if he pushed, she would fight with everything she had. She wasn't going to have sex with him, not like this.

He continued to pin her to the bed, but moved back until he could sign, *you already see the men I have killed when you look at me. Why should this be any different?*

She thought about his question and tried her best to come up with an answer. "I don't know, it just is. My body is mine, but if you take it in violence, I will change. I've treated enough traumatized victims that I know for sure I will be altered if you hurt me that way." She paused and then added, "And I don't see dead men when I look at you. I should, but I don't."

Jozef nodded, some of the tension draining from his body. He leaned over her, caging her in his arms. Shaun tensed in fear, but all he did was drop a kiss onto her lips before rolling to the side and stretching out next to Shaun. He glanced at her to make sure she was watching before he lifted his hands to sign.

You're wrong about one thing. No one has the power to force me to marry. Not my uncle, not anyone. I'm marrying you because I want to.

Shaun smiled; she couldn't help herself. The entire situation was beyond fucked up, but hearing him say that he wanted her, that he was choosing to marry her, somehow made everything a little better.

"Thank you for saying that," she whispered.

Jozef grabbed her hand and waved it around, Shaun's wrist flopping in the air. She laughed as he dropped it back onto the bed without ceremony.

I want you to use sign language only, he demanded.

Shaun raised an eyebrow at his highhandedness, then complied. *Isn't it easier for me to speak verbally? We can converse faster and more efficiently.*

I don't care about fast or efficient, he was quick to respond. *I prefer to communicate this way. It feels... intimate.*

Shaun knew what he meant because she felt it too. *Like our own little bubble.*

He nodded his agreement, then signed, *talk to me, tell me about yourself.*

What do you want to know?

Anything, everything. Just talk to me.

He loved to hear about her life and often made this request when they were in bed together.

"Okay," she whispered.

Jozef rolled against her and covered her mouth with his hand giving her a stern look. She rolled her eyes and shoved his hand away.

Okay, okay, it'll take me some time to adjust to non-verbal.

It really was going to take Shaun time to adjust. She'd been extremely rusty with her sign language before Jozef grabbed her. Though she was quickly relearning, she wasn't entirely there yet. She did silly things like stopped breathing while she was signing. If Jozef wanted her to sign as much at it seemed he did, then she was going to have to learn to sign and breathe at the same time or risk passing out. Her mom used to gently make fun of Shaun's inability to multi-task. She would shake her head and laugh that it seemed appalling that such a promising young doctor couldn't even walk and chew gum at the same time.

Shaun realized she knew what she wanted to talk about. She would give Jozef what he wanted, insight into her life, while working on a way to reconnect with that life. She would talk about the life she left behind as a way to deal with her grief over losing it. She would talk about her mother.

Shaun pushed herself up into a sitting position and wiggled around on the bed until she was facing a reclining Jozef. She took a deep breath and started signing.

My mom's name is F-A-T-I- M-A.

He nodded and signed back, *I remember, you told me about her in the van.*

While he was driving her into the woods to shoot her. Though the memory still made her heart beat faster, she was able to think of it without the icy fingers of terror stealing down her spine. She was impressed that Jozef remembered what she'd told him. At the time, he'd acted as though he hadn't heard a word.

I'm half Iranian, which most people don't know about me because

I look more like my dad. My mom was born in Iran but moved to Detroit with her family when she was a child. She met my father while he was taking his residency in Detroit. After a few years they moved to Canada and got married. She's really smart; she's fierce and compassionate. She's involved in all kinds of charities...

CHAPTER THIRTY-TWO

Their truce lasted less than a day. Shaun had spent a good part of their evening together telling Jozef all about her upbringing and her love for her family. He'd nodded in all the right places, his face softening as he listened to her. He even pulled her in for a hug when she told him of the devastating loss of her father. During their conversation, Jozef looked much less like a gangster and more like a man she would actually date.

So it came as a shock to her when he refused to listen to reason when she requested a phone call to her mother. He stood firm, his face a granite carving as she'd pleaded with him. He was unmoving though.

"But if she knows I'm alive, she's much more likely to stop looking for me. I can't know for sure, but if I know my mom, she's pulling in every connection she and my dad had to try and find me. If even a single person in that hospital recognized you, she'll be able to find me. Plus, you aren't exactly low profile, going to clubs and flaunting a black woman among your predominantly Caucasian friends."

Still, he refused to listen to reason. He did try to give her an explanation, but it only made her angry.

If your mother is anything like you, she won't stop digging. Hearing your voice will only make her try harder to find your location. It would be cruel to give her hope when she can't see you.

"What's the big deal?" she asked. "If I – "

He cut her off by lightly slapping her mouth and grabbing her hands, waving them in the air. Far from thinking it was a cute gesture, as she'd done the night before, it enraged her. She shoved him, but he didn't move, which forced her to take a step back.

She growled her frustration, then took a deep breath, seeking the deep dark depths of her patience for just a little more.

She signed, her hands moving in angry jerky movements, *don't hit me and don't cut me off when I'm speaking.*

He narrowed his eyes at her, then nodded. She wasn't sure if he was agreeing to her demands or if he was acknowledging that she was using sign language. She felt if she didn't conclude this conversation quickly, she was probably going to stab him, and she knew how to make sure he bled out in under a minute. Why did she ever think she was attracted to this man? Oh yeah, fucking pheromones.

If I tell my mom it was a misunderstanding that's been taken care of, I can probably convince her not to come searching for me. But I have to talk to her, to reassure her and get her to call off any searches she might have started.

Jozef shook his head. *No phone calls.*

So you're content allowing me to think you're some heartless asshole who would stop his bride from talking to her mother?

He glared at her, making his displeasure known through his facial expressions. He didn't need to sign his thoughts.

Shaun took a step away from him so she wouldn't get

smacked again. "If you won't give me what I'm asking for, then I won't give you what you want."

He took a threatening step toward her, a shutter slamming down over his expression, leaving blankness in its place. *You won't have a choice.*

"Watch me."

He grabbed her, crushing her lips beneath his. Shaun fought him, but Jozef was extremely adept at subduing a person. She found herself locked into place and shoved up against a wall while he ravished her mouth. Butterflies swirled in her stomach, while her brain went wild with anger that he would do such a thing after their night together.

Finally, he stopped, lifted his head and gave her a cold look. A look meant to tell her everything he couldn't and wouldn't say.

"Coward," she accused him scathingly. "You don't want to say it because then you have to own it. You're hiding behind your lack of voice. If you want to turn me into a mindless fixture, then tell me the rules. Stop making it seem like you care about what happens to me and then crush my hopes in the next breath. I'm done with it, and I'm done with you."

She shoved him hard enough that he moved this time. When she tried to storm past him, he grabbed her arm in a grip so tight it told her she'd scored a point with her cruel words. She'd meant them, though. He was hiding behind his lack of voice, refusing to give her the unvarnished truth while allowing his actions to speak for him. Which was dangerous for a man in his position. He was a killer, and if he wanted his actions to do the talking, they weren't going to say anything good.

"Give me a phone call and we can talk about my position in your life."

He released her arm and turned away from her in disgust.

"I'll be in the garden," she told him dejectedly.

He allowed her to leave the oppressiveness of their shared rooms. She made her way quickly out to the gardens, which she'd been visiting more and more often during her time at the mansion. It gave her reprieves from her host and his family. Jozef was so intense and they rarely agreed on anything. If they actually somehow made it to the marriage stage of their false relationship, they were likely going to kill each other before they made it to the honeymoon.

Shaun was so distracted as she wandered through the garden, she almost stumbled over Krystoff who was on his hands and knees, half buried in a rose bush. "Mr. Koba!" she exclaimed as she accidentally kicked his rubber boot. "I'm so sorry, I didn't see you."

He slowly unfolded himself from the bush and looked up at Shaun. She couldn't see his expression, as the sun was shining in her eyes. He climbed to his feet. "Nonsense, I was half-hidden. You couldn't have known I'd be down here."

The moment felt awkward for Shaun. This was the man who held her life in his hands, the man who was directing her to marry his nephew. Sometimes he seemed like the powerhouse he was; the head of a powerful crime family. He could freeze a person with a single glance. His commands were followed to the letter by a household used to following where this man led. Yet, in moments like this, he seemed human. If they'd been in Canada, he might be a retiree, puttering around his garden, building a hobby to keep himself occupied in his retirement.

Shaun didn't fool herself for one moment that Krystoff Koba might be considered a harmless retiree. "Do you work out here often? I thought you had gardeners," she ventured, trying to dispel some of the awkwardness.

He smiled and pulled his gloves off, slapping them against his work pants and sending up small puffs of dust. "Indeed, we do. But I enjoy the quiet solitude," he said agreeably. "I try to come out here as often as I can. Please, will you sit with me?"

He nodded toward a stone bench nestled amidst the bushes. Shaun allowed him to take her arm and lead her to the bench. He helped her sit, like an old-fashioned suitor, before taking his place at her side. Together they sat in companionable silence, gazing out across one of the most beautiful gardens Shaun had ever experienced. It was lush and green with splashes of colour from the strategically placed rose bushes. Most were red, but some were white and pink.

"How's your finger?" she asked, glancing at him.

He held his hand up to show her and she took it, setting it in her lap to examine the bandage. He'd transitioned from her care to his regular physician. The bandage was clean and Krystoff couldn't be in too much pain or he wouldn't be in the garden. She let his hand go, satisfied he was healing.

It seemed incongruous but oddly comforting to sit with Krystoff. He was such a formidable character. She could easily imagine his hands soaked in the blood of his enemies, then going out to his garden to meditate on the miracle of life. The dichotomy of violence and peace was strangely appealing to Shaun.

"The operating room is my garden," she murmured. When Krystoff glanced at her, she added, "I find peace when my hands are buried in someone else's body. The blood flowing beneath my fingertips, the power of their life force at my mercy. The knowledge that I am the only person in the world who can fix them in that moment. I choose whether they live or die. It's intoxicating."

Shaun had never spoken that way before, had barely allowed herself to have the thought, yet sitting next to Krystoff, she felt that the mafia world finally made a strange sort of sense to her. There were studies done that suggested surgeons were among the top ten most psychopathic professions. It took a certain amount of ego and lack of fear to dig around in someone else's body. Doctors played god with their patients, and while Shaun didn't think she was a psychopath, she was no different than the average surgeon. She got a rush from the power of preserving life.

"There is happiness to be found in the release of that power, too," Krystoff said quietly. "Of deciding when to stop and find a new path."

Shaun looked at him sharply. Was he talking about his situation or Shaun's? Perhaps he was telling her that she could find equal happiness in giving up her chosen profession to live under the umbrella of the Koba family, married to his vicious nephew.

"I don't agree," she replied flatly. "When you spend a lifetime working toward one shining goal, a new path feels like misery."

"Misery is better than death."

Shaun sighed her annoyance. Krystoff sounded just like his nephew. They were all telling her to settle down, to forget her old life, but how did she forget the career she'd spent their entire life driving toward and the loving family that had supported her every step of the way?

"I don't think so," Shaun disagreed. When Krystoff looked up sharply, she was quick to add. "Don't worry, I don't have a death wish. I'm just getting sick of being told by this family that my life is being decided for me and it would be best to just settle down and forget my past life. You wouldn't be saying any of this if I was a man."

Her words were bold, and she briefly wanted to recall them. What was she doing mouthing off to a guy who called entire countries allies? The man who made massive life-altering decisions as though he was choosing a tie. He could easily decide she was too much of a pain in the ass to keep around and order her killed and buried under one of his rose bushes.

Instead, he chuckled and said just as bluntly, "If you were a man, you would be dead."

His words sent a chill through Shaun. He was right. The ease in which Jozef put a bullet in Danilo's head told her that the Kobas had no problem killing innocent men. She was very lucky that she was not only a woman, but a woman Jozef found attractive. It was likely the only thing that had saved her life.

Krystoff reached for her hand and squeezed. "You are part of the family now; you have nothing to worry about from us." He turned on the bench to study her, his sharp blue eyes seeing far more than Shaun was comfortable with. "You helped my grandson when he broke his arm. This is not something I will forget."

Shaun felt the significance of the moment. The Godfather of Prague was basically telling her he owed her one. Since she didn't think she could ask him to forget the whole marriage plan and send her home, she wasn't sure what his protection would mean for her.

"I didn't do anything but diagnose an easy break. How is he doing? I haven't spoken to Leeza since yesterday."

"He was just out here skipping around the stone path. He's fine," Krystoff assured her. "He took a rougher tumble than usual, and it scared him. He'll be back to normal once the cast is off."

Shaun was relieved that the injury was as minor as she'd thought. She imagined there would be hell to pay if any member of the Koba family came to harm. She wondered if their fierce loyalty would one day extend to her. Maybe it already did.

Krystoff squeezed her hand again and stood. He looked down at her, his eyes squinting against the sunlight. "One day you will find your normal again. It might seem difficult now, but you are resilient."

He reached behind the bench and, using the gardening shears he pulled from his baggy pocket, cut a red rose. He held it to his nose for a few seconds, enjoying the simple pleasure of a fragrant flower. Then he handed it to Shaun and walked away.

CHAPTER THIRTY-THREE

The moment Shaun walked out of their suite, Jozef sent his fist flying into the nearest wall. Luckily it wasn't one of the stone walls. A thought that didn't occur to him as his hand sank through the plaster, sending dust flying in the air. He growled and yanked his fist out.

He'd never been so emotional that he couldn't hang on to his temper. His uncle had raised him to make calm, cool and logical decisions so he could always do what was best for the family. Emotion was a liability and therefore stamped out of him at a young age.

So why couldn't he control himself around one particular woman? Women were for fucking, not fucking with his head. Shaun made him feel out of control. Yet he couldn't consider a life where she was dead, especially by his own hand. He had no choice but to keep trying with her.

He was starting to realize his lack of control with her wasn't his only dilemma. Her inability to settle down and accept her new position was problematic. Jozef had been naive in his belief that bringing her home and forcing her to accept her place at his side was going to work. He'd yet to meet a woman who wasn't compliant with him, but then again, he'd never really thought about women at all, except in fantasy when he was jerking off.

Maybe he did have prejudices toward the weaker sex. Maybe he shouldn't think of them as the weaker sex. Shaun sure as shit wasn't weak. She was the strongest woman he knew. Not physically, but mentally, she won every skirmish they had, persuading Jozef to do things that were out of character for him.

Maybe Shaun was right. Maybe they shouldn't be together. Jozef knew nothing about how to treat a woman of Shaun's caliber. She was no whore, but her responses in bed were utterly intoxicating. Addictive. For that reason alone, he didn't want to let her go. But aside from sex, there was so much more to her. She had dignity, a sense of responsibility, she had solid morals. She made Jozef feel deficient in every way. Yet he liked it. He liked the challenge she presented.

He frowned. Was he a closet masochist?

No, definitely not. He didn't enjoy pain himself, just enjoyed inflicting it. He leaned more toward sadist, but he had no desire to hurt those who didn't deserve it. Was selective sadism a thing? Yeah, he was a selective sadist. For the right kind of guy, he was willing to pull out his tools and set to work.

Jozef decided that brooding, pacing and scowling at the hole he'd put in the wall wasn't getting him anywhere. He needed to find Shaun and try to talk through some of their issues. It seemed like the sort of mature thing Shaun would do. Jozef would try his best to play by her rules without losing his temper. He would also find a servant to patch the hole in the wall, so Shaun didn't find out he'd already lost his temper before going to find her.

He jerked the door to his suite open and was surprised to find Havel on the other side, his fist raised to knock on the door. The expression of surprise on Havel's face was enough to draw a slight smirk from Jozef.

Jozef raised a brow in greeting and waved his hand inside, indicating Havel should come in. Havel dropped his hand and walked past Jozef, heading straight to the mini bar. "Got some news." He picked up a bottle of Jozef's Scotch and raised an eyebrow.

Jozef thought about it and shook his head. It was common for the two men to meet in the afternoons to discuss business and security. They usually had a few drinks while they talked, but today Jozef couldn't get the image of Shaun out of his head. If he was going to find her after his meeting with Havel, then he should do it with a clear head. She hadn't liked it when he took those lines of coke; her expression clearly shocked and disapproving before she'd run off to the restroom. Jozef didn't usually care what people thought of him and his habits, but for some reason the look on her face, the disappointment, was enough to make him rethink a few life choices that had seemed so automatic before.

Havel poured himself a generous glass of Scotch, replaced the lid on the bottle and settled his large frame on the couch. Jozef joined him, sitting in the chair next to Havel.

Jozef opened the conversation. *What news?*

Havel took a long swallow of his drink and licked his lips appreciatively before setting it down on the table in front of him. He leaned back in his seat and crossed an ankle over his knee. He looked relaxed, as though the jobs of security specialist for the Koba family and Jozef's second-in-command were a breeze. Jozef knew better. He knew how seriously Havel took his position.

Havel had been a rescue from another organization that

had erroneously fingered him as a traitor. They'd beaten him to within an inch of his life and left him to die. Havel was stronger than death, though, and had made it out of the situation. Once he'd healed, he'd gone to the Koba family in retaliation and handed them their competitors on a silver platter. Jozef had been fourteen at the time and Krystoff had appointed Havel as his protector and mentor.

"Vasiliy wants a meeting with Krystoff. He says he has information that will explain his motives for kidnapping your uncle."

What do you think of this development? Jozef asked his second-in-command. Part of their job was keeping Krystoff safe at all times. While Krystoff was head of the family, he made no real decisions without Jozef's backing, since Jozef would provide the skill and muscle.

"I think it's bullshit," Havel announced, taking another sip of his Scotch and leaving a wet ring on the glass table. He never used the coasters, despite Jozef having plenty to go around. "Vasiliy hasn't shown his face. It's as though he wants to stay hidden while his men do the work. I would almost say it was his son acting in his name, rather than the old man pulling the strings, but the lad is a complete incompetent. He couldn't plan his way out of the bottom of a pint glass. And now Vasiliy wants a meeting? I'm tempted to agree to one just so we can finally get him in a room. I want to ask him what the fuck he was thinking. Clearly whatever he was attempting to do when he took Krystoff didn't pan out, as there were no demands."

We still don't know what he wanted with my uncle? Jozef asked, knowing the answer.

"No, we never figured out a motive. It's like he came out of thin air to poke your family. There's a lot of history though... with your mother." Havel paused to see if Jozef would add anything, but he remained silent. Havel continued,

"Over the past several years, Vasiliy has lain low and avoided your uncle. It seems strange that he would come out of nowhere to kidnap Krystoff, cut off his finger then allow him to be taken back without resistance."

Jozef nodded. Everything Havel was saying jived with his impressions of the situation, right down to the ease in which they'd rescued Krystoff. There had been very little security on the property and Jozef would have been surprised if Vasiliy himself was at the house. He'd likely been tucked safely away at one of his vacation estates.

You think they knew we were coming?

Havel nodded. "They had to. Either that, or they're by far the most incompetent kidnappers I've heard of. They let us walk right in unmolested and leave with the only leverage they had. It works with our theory that someone inside our circle was involved. We had Krystoff locked down tight; he should never have been taken while he was visiting Kiev."

They fell silent for a few minutes as they contemplated the strange and bungled kidnapping. Finally, Jozef signed, *I think I take the trophy for worst kidnapper. My victim hates me, is refusing to marry me and is now likely plotting her escape from the rose garden.*

Havel looked somewhat taken aback at Jozef's admission. They didn't usually talk about their personal lives. Then, they didn't exactly have personal lives, beyond the most recent piece of tail one of them was sampling. Shaun was different, she hovered between personal and business.

"Hate to say it, buddy," Havel started, "But you should've —"

Jozef held up a hand, stopping the other man from continuing. *Don't say it. I don't want to make an enemy of my best friend.*

Havel nodded slowly, digesting the implications of what Jozef was saying. He was telling his second-in-command that

Shaun was more to him than just his kidnapping victim, or another piece of tail. She was his future wife. She was someone he was rapidly coming to care for.

"Then I won't say what I think. Instead, I will say this." He looked at Jozef seriously. "Classy bitches, like the one you have, are high fucking maintenance. And yours is worse than the usual. She has ethics. Prepare to spend your life grovelling, my friend, because every time you fuck up, she'll expect you on your knees. And I have no doubt you're going to fuck up a lot."

Jozef reached over to slap Havel in the side of the head, but Havel dodged him, picking up his glass and downing the rest of his scotch.

When Havel was looking at him again, Jozef signed, *one day you'll find a woman who fucks with your head and I will take pleasure in your misery.*

Instead of laughing and giving a snappy comeback, Havel's face fell into serious lines and his thoughts wandered to somewhere else. He pushed himself off the couch and made his way to the door, only speaking as he was about to leave.

"If you love her, make sure you do everything in your power to keep her. Don't fuck it up." He left, closing the door behind him and locking it. He never left the family's security up to chance.

Jozef was stunned by Havel's parting words and not just because they were downright romantic, but because they were spoken by one of the toughest, most staunch bachelors Jozef knew. It was Havel's position that Shaun should've been killed in the basement before ever getting to know any of them. It seemed strange that now Havel was advising Jozef to keep her. Had Havel loved and lost? And when had it happened? Havel had been with the family for decades, since Jozef was a teenager. Jozef didn't remember any point at which a woman featured in the older man's life.

Then Havel's words struck Jozef like a punch to the chest, leaving him stunned, his mouth open and his hands clenched on the arms of his chair. He wanted Shaun more than he'd ever wanted anything.

He loved Shaun.

CHAPTER THIRTY-FOUR

Shaun spent most of the afternoon avoiding Jozef, which wasn't a difficult feat considering the size of the Koba mansion and the level of activity going on inside. The engagement party was in two days. Flowers were being brought in and placed in a special refrigerator to keep them fresh. The extra staff Dasha hired for the event were arriving in droves to join the fray. Shaun was amazed at their ability to immediately pick up their tasks and carry on like they'd been there for years. They looked as though they belonged far more than Shaun did.

Shaun trailed after Dasha for a while, who generously tossed a few party planning tidbits Shaun's way. Dasha already had her mind made up about everything so Shaun's opinion was often overridden or ignored entirely. It wasn't out of maliciousness. Dasha knew what she was doing, and she was in her glory doing it. She was like a military general with armies of servants and boatloads of money at her disposal.

"Silver or gold for napkin rings?" Dasha held up two rings, which sparkled their shiny best in the lights of the formal dining room.

"Uh…" Shaun had heard of napkin rings, but she'd never seen one. "Silver?"

Dasha shook her head, her dark, perfectly arranged waves bouncing around her shoulders. "No, I think the gold will be more effective. We have a gold underplate with white china place settings, silver cutlery and silver lined teacups. A little more balance is needed." She nodded sharply to herself. "Yes, the gold."

She handed the gold ring to a hovering servant, who hurried away with it to presumably find more. Dasha turned on her heel and walked briskly to a wall lined with rows of windows and French balcony doors. The formal dining room and ballroom faced the gardens, with doors opening out onto the terrace, leading into the plush green paradise.

"I'm not convinced this drapery will do. It is perhaps too heavy for the season." She fingered the heavy rich brown fabric with silver strands throughout. "I think something lighter, maybe saffron velvet with a sheer gold overlay. We'll save white for the wedding day. What do you think?"

She turned to look expectantly at Shaun.

Shaun marvelled over how impossibly perfect the older woman looked while orchestrating an engagement party likely to become the event of the season. She wore a pencil skirt suit, with pink frills at the throat and sleeves. Instead of looking overly feminine, the delicate fabric somehow comple-mented the severity of the suit. Dasha's dark hair was shot through with honey-coloured highlights and styled to perfec-tion. Shaun wondered if the woman had a professional stylist on her payroll.

The amount of money flowing through the Koba empire was staggering. Being surrounded by that kind of unimagin-able wealth was definitely a learning curve for Shaun, who still lived out of boxes three years after moving into a cute and modern condo townhouse situated between the hospital and her family home.

"Shaun, are you with me, dear?" Dasha said impatiently, snapping her manicured fingers.

Shaun blinked and looked up, trying to force her lips into a smile. "Sorry, I was daydreaming about Montréal."

Dasha's face reflected sympathy and she rejoined Shaun, leaving the problem of the drapery for a few minutes. She put her arm around Shaun and gave her a squeeze. It was an awkward perfume-filled half-hug, but Shaun was grateful for the sentiment.

"It's only natural that you should be thinking about your homeland at such a time. You're far from home during this very significant event in your life. Your friends and family aren't here to support you and you probably feel at sea with all this." Dasha smiled warmly at Shaun. "I hope you know you can come to me about anything. I've been a source of great comfort for my daughters and Jozef in their times of need. I can be the same to you."

Shaun stared at Dasha in bewilderment. Was she delusional or was this her attempt at comfort? It was like Shaun had never been kidnapped and forced into their lives against her will. A significant part of her wanted to start shrieking like a banshee at the strange unfair turn her life had taken. She wanted to scream at the top of her lungs that she was their captive and no amount of golden plates and opulent parties was going to change that.

Then she caught the hard glitter to Dasha's eyes. She was standing next to Shaun, her body carefully arranged in a picture of beauty and poise, but Shaun sensed the shark under the manicured exterior. Dasha would always say and do the correct thing, but her thoughts were carefully guarded.

Instead of shouting that she'd been kidnapped and of course she missed her friends, family and home, and no it had nothing to do with the upcoming sham of an engagement party, Shaun forced a smile and said, "Thank you, I really appreciate all that you're doing."

There was no point in alienating the people living under the Koba umbrella. She needed them if she was ever going to get back to her real life. They'd made sure escape was impossible and most likely dangerous. Shaun's best play was to appeal to their human side. The family's interactions with each other proved that they had finer emotions, even if they were cold and calculating toward the outside world. If they were prepared to embrace Shaun as part of their family, maybe she could eventually appeal to them to send her home.

It was long shot, but it was all she had at this point.

Dasha seemed to accept Shaun's response, her face creasing into genuine happiness. "I just know you're going to make an excellent part of the family." She gave Shaun a quick hug. "Now, back to the drapery."

Shaun would rather give stitches to an injured grizzly bear than try to choose drapery with Dasha. "If you'll excuse me, I've had a long day. I'd like to go back to Jozef's... to our suite."

"Of course." Dasha's face took on a look of concern that Shaun was becoming quickly acquainted with. The woman was a master of her emotions, arranging them for whatever was most appropriate in the moment. "I'll have a tea setting sent up for you. You just need a little snack and some caffeine, and you'll feel fine."

Shaun smiled wanly, backing toward the dining room entrance. "Thank you, you're probably right."

Shaun turned and left, relieved to be out of Dasha's energetic presence. Shaun couldn't pin down the other woman's motives. Sometimes she seemed sweet and understanding and other times she was the hardened matriarch of a mafia dynasty. Was she both? Neither? The entire family made

Shaun feel like she was standing on quicksand, shifting around and trying to find where she belonged.

She stopped walking when she realized she had no idea where she was going. She didn't want to see Jozef, which meant their suite was out of the question. She smiled in amusement when she realized Jozef was about to get an unexpected tea setting. She thought about the garden, but there was little to do out there other than contemplate her strange new Alice in Wonderland life. Besides, she didn't want to run into Krystoff.

She was standing in the hallway undecided, when the decision was taken from her hands. Saskia came rushing down the hall toward her, her pace so fast that Shaun took a step back, thinking the younger woman was about to walk right into her. Instead, Saskia took her arm and tugged.

"Come with me, I have something for you." Her words were rushed, her face was flushed, and she was glancing around as though someone was after her.

Shaun was intrigued. "What do you have for me?"

"Come on, we can't talk here."

She dropped Shaun's arm, spun around and walked rapidly in the direction she came from.

"Uh, sure..." Shaun followed after her, both confused and amused.

Saskia climbed the wide staircase, her high-top running shoes noiseless against the hardwood flooring. Shaun was wearing heels again, since it was expected that she dress appropriately for a meeting with Dasha. She struggled to keep up and almost lost sight of Saskia when they reached the top of the staircase. She looked both ways down wide opulent hallways, completely lost. She rarely came up to the second floor, as Jozef's suite was on the main floor at the back of the house. She knew Dasha and Krystoff's rooms were on the second floor, and Leeza's family occupied a cottage on the estate grounds.

Shaun guessed that Saskia was leading her to her own suite.

She stopped abruptly at the top of the stairs, looking around and trying to figure out which way to go. Saskia's head popped out from one of the doorways. "Come on!"

Shaun entered the suite and stared in bemusement. Considering Saskia tried to pass herself off as some kind of badass, Shaun was not expecting a suite that looked like the girly girl's pink monster vomited all over it. Wherever she turned there were frills, pillows, stuffed animals, dolls and gold, white and pink striped wallpaper. The whole effect was chaotic, disorienting and over the top.

It felt human.

"This is your room?" Shaun asked as she stared around.

"Uh huh," Saskia said, grabbing a stuffed unicorn and dropping onto a pink couch covered in so many frilly, flowery pillows that Shaun wasn't sure where she should sit. "I know it looks like a little girl's candy shop, but I like it. I feel comfortable in here."

Shaun couldn't image why. The creepy porcelain dolls were arranged in lifelike poses behind the glass walls of their cage, their soulless eyes following her every move. But what she thought didn't matter; this was Saskia's sanctuary, and after experiencing the chaos of the Koba family, Shaun didn't blame her for creating her own version of paradise.

Shaun tried not to look at the dolls as she lifted a few pillows off the couch and carefully set them down next to the coffee table. She sat gingerly, lifting one of the oversize teddy bears and setting it on her lap. She tugged its ear, enjoying the super soft faux fur against her skin.

"What did you want to show me?" Shaun asked.

"You have to promise not to tell anyone." Saskia's words

came out in a rush and she glanced guiltily at the door. "This house has ears and it's impossible to keep anything a secret. My parents can't know. Jozef definitely can't know."

Shaun frowned, her concern growing. "Maybe you shouldn't show me then. I don't want you to get in trouble."

She looked at Shaun, her eyes wide with excitement. "It's not me I'm worried about. Well, not as much."

"You're worried about me?"

"Yes, no, sort of. This surprise is definitely not allowed, but you deserve it and I don't want to see you suffer anymore."

Shaun blinked, trying desperately to decipher Saskia's words. Oddly, she was comforted by Saskia's declaration that she didn't want Shaun to suffer. In a family whose staunch loyalty to each other made Shaun feel like an outsider, Saskia was the one she felt most comfortable with. Perhaps it was the other woman's blunt honesty, her youth, or her ridiculously over-the-top suite, but Shaun didn't think she would lie. She was not nearly as carefully calculated as the other members of the family.

Saskia projected herself as a world-weary adult. It was easy to forget her youth until she let her guard down. The nervous excitement surrounding her now made Shaun realize Saskia needed an adult to guide her. She was looking for permission, though she was attempting to control whatever surprise she had for Shaun.

"I think you'd better show me what you have," Shaun said gently. She was careful not to promise not to tell Saskia's parents. She didn't know what the surprise was, and some things simply couldn't be kept secret. If Saskia showed Shaun something potentially harmful to herself or others, Shaun would have to take the knowledge to Saskia's family.

Saskia either didn't notice or didn't care about Shaun's lack of promise. She bit her lip, glanced at the door one more time and then reached into her pocket, digging out an object. She extended her hand toward Shaun.

"A cell phone?" Shaun asked bewildered.

"A burner phone," Saskia said gleefully. "Untraceable. I got it from a friend, but he doesn't know why I wanted it."

"And why do you want it?" Shaun asked carefully.

"It's for you." Saskia couldn't help the grin that spread across her face as she gave Shaun the news. "So you can call your family and tell them you're okay."

Hope hit Shaun so hard she felt dizzy. Tears immediately rushed to her eyes and she had to dash them away as she reached to take the phone from Saskia, squeezing her hand as she took it. Emotion choked her voice as she tried to thank the younger woman. "I don't know what to say. Thank you so much. This is... this is..."

Saskia's bright eyes dimmed a little as she took in Shaun's flustered stammering. "You don't have to thank me. It's the least I can do after what my family did to you."

Shaun dipped her head and nodded, overcome. Clutched tight in her hands was the lifeline she'd been waiting for.

Saskia stood up. "Do you mind making the call in my bedroom closet? It's big so you should have lots of room. I don't want to risk anyone finding out."

"Of course." Shaun stood and dashed her tears away as she followed Saskia into the bedroom.

She let out a quickly stifled laugh as she saw that the insane pink frilled theme had spilled into the bedroom as well. There was a huge four-poster bed with pink and white striped hangings, covered in a shiny pink and purple bedspread and piled high with frilly pillows and stuffed animals.

Saskia opened her closet and stood back. It really was like stepping into Wonderland. Saskia's clothes trended toward black with chains, skulls, rips and T-shirts with anarchist slogans. The difference in Saskia's style preferences was so wild that Shaun determined to one day find out how Saskia had evolved into such a fascinating young woman.

"I'll give you some privacy." Saskia closed the door to the closet, leaving Shaun alone inside.

Shaun looked down at the phone.

Every instinct in her body told her to call her mom, but she had to be smart, think first, then make the call. She didn't know how much time she had, didn't know if she'd be able to make more than one call, and she had no idea what she was going to say. She could call the authorities, but how? She didn't know the emergency number for the Czech Republic. It was usually different from country to country.

Then she'd have to hope the person who answered the call spoke enough English that she could communicate her predicament. After that she didn't know. Would the authorities contact her consulate? Would they come into the mansion with guns blazing? The thought of anyone in the Koba family being killed sent a shaft of remorse through her.

She stared down at the phone with indecision, hyperaware of every second as it ticked by.

She had every right in the world to call the authorities. To bring hell down on a crime syndicate that thought nothing of murdering innocents. Jozef had shot Danilo without a second thought. He not only took away a life, but a future too. Anything Danilo would have accomplished. Wife, family, career, gone. Jozef deserved jail time. Yet she couldn't imagine him living the rest of his life behind bars. He was like a wild animal, watching, prowling, hunting. He would die if he was caged.

Shaun never imagined this kind of heartbreaking indecision when she finally got her hands on a phone. It was gutwrenching and she knew, no matter what choice she made, it would be life-altering. Finally, she decided to call the only person she really wanted to talk to.

Luckily, she had Fatima's cell phone number memorized. It was the middle of the night in Montréal; Shaun hoped her mom would answer.

The phone rang once.

"Hello?"

CHAPTER THIRTY-FIVE

"Mom?"

There was a long tension-filled pause. "Shaun! Oh my god, is that you?"

"It's me, Mom." Tears rushed to Shaun's eyes as the sound of her mother's voice reached out to her. It was like she'd been swimming in a dark void these past weeks, never knowing which way to turn, terrified for her survival, and hearing her mother was like a lifeline.

"Oh, my baby, oh my god!" Fatima's words came out in a panicked rush. "Where are you? Are you hurt? What happened?"

"Mom, calm down, I'm okay."

Shaun could hear fumbling in the background and something dropping. "Hang on, I'm calling the consulate."

"No!" Shaun exclaimed, pacing inside the closet. "You can't do that."

"What the hell do you mean I can't call? You were kidnapped from a hospital, for god sakes. Someone was killed! Of course, I'm going to call the authorities. Tell me where you are."

Shaun smiled grimly. This was Fatima Patterson, a force to be reckoned with. When her daughter was threatened, she would go to war like an Amazon queen. "I know, Mom, I was there. But things are complicated. If you call in the authorities, things could get even messier."

"Shaun, tell me where you are right now." Fatima tried to use her authoritarian mom tone, but the strain and worry in her voice were impossible to hide.

"I can't do that." Shaun sank to the floor of the closet and slumped against a chest of drawers.

"Why?" Fatima demanded.

Shaun could hear the creak of bedsprings as Fatima sat down.

"The people who took me... they're into some dangerous stuff."

"No shit," Fatima growled. "They killed that young man at the hospital and kidnapped you. God... I thought we were going to find your body somewhere."

Shaun had a flashback to the shadowed woods where Jozef took her to end her life. Fatima had no idea how close Shaun had come to fulfilling Fatima's nightmare.

Fatima burst into tears which caused Shaun's own tears to spill over. She cried freely as she listened to her mother's sobs and tried to reassure her over and over. "They didn't hurt me. They kidnapped me so I could treat a man who was injured. I saw too much though and they couldn't let me go."

"You have to get out of there," Fatima insisted. "I'm calling the consulate."

"Don't!" Shaun said impatiently. "I'll hang up and I really don't want to. I want to stay on the phone with you for as long as I can."

"But why?" her mom said just as impatiently. "What's going on? Are they holding you hostage? Do they want anything? We'll pay it. Anything, I'll find a way to get it. Your father had a lot of friends in high places. I'm sure we could scrape together as much as we need."

Shaun sighed and pulled her legs up, placing her head wearily on her knees.

"No, they don't want ransom."

"Then what? They have to want something, or why are they keeping you there?"

Shaun thought about telling her mom about the engagement but decided to keep it to herself. As much as she wanted to talk to her mother about everything, she didn't want Fatima worrying more than she already was. Finding out her daughter was about to be forcibly wedded to one of the most terrifying men in Europe might put Fatima over the edge.

"I don't know, mom. I guess they have to keep me since I saw their faces and know who they are."

"And you can't tell me?" Fatima asked again, desperation in her voice.

"I'm sorry," Shaun whispered.

There were a few seconds of silence and then Fatima said, her voice calmer, "No, I'm sorry, baby. I shouldn't be trying to force information from you that you clearly can't give. I'm just so grateful to hear your voice. It's been hell. I haven't slept in weeks."

Shaun nodded, though her mother couldn't see it. "Me neither."

"Are they treating you okay?" Fatima asked helplessly.

"Yes, please don't worry about that. I've been assured that I won't be harmed as long as I stay with them. In fact, I'm being treated more than fairly. They took me shopping to replace my clothes. I'm getting all my meals and then some. More than anything, I'm suffering from boredom. I'd kill for a surgery."

Again, Fatima paused as she digested what her daughter

was telling her. "You're not... are you... getting attached to these people?"

"I don't have Stockholm, if that's what you're thinking." Shaun crossed her fingers in case she did actually have Stockholm Syndrome and was lying to her mother. "I'm just trying to make the best of a bad situation."

"Okay, but I don't want you to ever forget that they killed somebody. No matter how kind they are to you now, they're killers, Shaun. I feel like..." Fatima choked on her words and paused to take a few deep breaths and gather herself. "I feel like I just got you back after thinking you might be dead. I can't handle knowing you're alive and well somewhere, only to find out they killed you anyway. I know you can't tell me much, but I promise you, Shaun, I will do everything I can to find out where you are. I swear to god, if they've harmed a single hair on your head, I will kill every last one of them with my bare hands."

Shaun choked back her tears as best she could as mama bear Fatima showed her claws. "Thank you," she whispered.

They remained silent for another minute as they tried to calm down enough to talk. It hit Shaun for the first time since getting on the phone with her mom that Fatima didn't sound like she'd been asleep. It should be very early morning in Montréal.

"Mom... where are you?"

"I'm in Kiev. I got here a few days after you went missing."

She didn't know why it hadn't occurred to her before that Fatima would travel to where Shaun had gone missing. Shaun would have done the same if her mother had been kidnapped. It made her heart ache to know her mom was relatively close, less than a day's drive away, yet they couldn't see each other; might not ever be able to see each other again.

"I'm sorry you've been put to so much trouble."

"Oh baby!" Fatima exclaimed. "There is no trouble. You are my one and only, I will do whatever it takes to get you back."

Shaun smiled and nodded. "Thank you, it feels good to hear that. Will you go back to Canada now that you know I'm okay?"

"No," Fatima said, her voice stern. "I'm not leaving without you. I promise, Shaun, I won't stop looking. It's only a matter of time."

"I'm scared for you," Shaun admitted. "These people are unpredictable. As you know, they aren't afraid to kill people they think are obstacles. I won't be able to survive if anything happens to you."

"I feel the same about you." Fatima sounded exhausted and Shaun regretted putting her 61-year-old mother through the strain. Fatima was healthy and strong, but she shouldn't be spending her retirement searching all over the world for her grown daughter.

"I'm so sorry about all this. I didn't mean for any of it to happen."

"I know, baby," Fatima assured her. "You're doing everything right. You continue to give the people who took you what they want. I'll find you, and when I do, we'll go home together."

Shaun felt a wave of homesickness so strong she began silently crying again. She had to choke back tears as she said, "I want that so bad."

They continued to talk for several more minutes until a soft knock sounded on the closet door. Saskia opened the door a crack and peeked around, her concerned gaze on Shaun tear-soaked face. She whispered, "Jozef is asking the staff where you are."

Shaun nodded and said to her mom, "I have to go."

"Can you call me again?" Fatima asked sharply. "Is there a way for me to contact you?"

Shaun looked at Saskia, who guessed at the question. She shook her head, her expression apologetic.

"I can't, mom," Shaun said, despair leaking into her voice. "I'm always watched and even this one phone call puts the person who gave it to me at risk. I can't do it again."

"I understand. You don't stress about it, I'll content myself with this conversation, with knowing you're alive and healthy. It's enough, for now."

Shaun realized how much it took for her mom to agree to no contact. Not that she had a choice, but Fatima could get quite vocal if she wanted something. She was trusting her daughter's judgment in this. "I love you, mom."

"I love you too," Fatima said, her voice strong despite the tears choking her. "I will keep looking for you. Never doubt it, baby."

They hung up.

Overcome by emotion, Shaun curled onto her side on the floor of the closet and sobbed, her longing for her mother, for her home, so strong that she didn't know how she would manage to get up again. To keep living. To walk out of the closet and go back to pretending everything was perfect in Wonderland.

She felt movement beside her as Saskia sat down. After some hesitation Saskia's hand came down on her shoulder and she patted Shaun awkwardly. As Shaun's tears began to dissipate a tissue box landed on the floor in front of her nose.

"Are you trying to comfort me?" Shaun reached for a tissue and blew her nose.

Saskia looked sheepish. "Yeah, sort of. We're not a really huggy family."

Shaun let out a watery laugh. "I found that out when your mom hugged me earlier."

"Oh, she's the worst," Saskia said with a quick grin and a fake shudder. "Like being hugged by the grim reaper. Creepy and boney, but weirdly comforting at the same time."

Though Shaun laughed at the assessment, she couldn't help but agree. She pushed herself up on the carpet and sat next to Saskia, both of them with their backs pressed to the chest of drawers.

"Your mom was upset?" Saskia asked tentatively.

"Yeah," Shaun sighed.

"Mine would be too."

They sat in companionable silence until Shaun's tears stopped and she felt well enough to stand again. She handed the burner phone to the younger woman. "I don't know how to thank you for this. If there's anything I can ever do for you, I don't want you to hesitate. I'll do whatever I can."

Saskia nodded; her head tilted to the side thoughtfully. Then she handed the phone back to Shaun. "It can't be traced back to me. You keep it... in case your mom tries to call back."

Shaun took the phone and held it to her chest. It meant a lot to her that Saskia was willing to make such a sacrifice. Saskia had to know that by giving the phone to Shaun, she was risking her entire family. Shaun could walk out of her suite and immediately call the police, bringing hell down on the Kobas.

"Thank you," Shaun said with heartfelt gratitude.

CHAPTER THIRTY-SIX

Jozef was in their suite when Shaun quietly opened the door and let herself inside. At first, he didn't see her. He was sitting on the sofa, the TV blaring a music video. The lyrics for Journey's "Don't Stop Believin'" filling the apartment as Jozef tapped on his phone, texting someone. Shaun was surprised he enjoyed retro music. Based on the club, she would've pegged him as more of a DJ kind of guy.

Shaun wasn't ready for a confrontation with her intense captor, so she quietly closed the door and moved noiselessly toward the bedroom. It was a mistake. Something must've alerted Jozef to her presence because he was on his feet instantly with his gun in hand pointing it at her. Shaun made a terrified squeak and jumped away, bringing her arms up to protect herself, as if they could stop bullets.

Once Jozef recognized her he put his gun back in the holster strapped to his chest.

I'm sorry, I didn't realize you were here, he signed, remorse bright in his eyes. *I promised I wouldn't point my gun at you and already I've broken this promise.*

Shaun believed he was truly regretful.

It's fine, you only startled me. She approached him slowly. The man looked incredibly good in casual clothes; a pair of jeans and a T-shirt with his leather jacket. *I suppose you don't like people creeping around behind you.*

He dipped his head in a nod, his lip quirking. *Anyone trying to sneak up on me is usually trying to kill me.*

Shaun took another step closer to Jozef. *Has that happened before?*

Yes.

Jozef took the final steps between them, standing closer than a casual acquaintance would, but still not touching her. His gaze caressed her face, then dropped down her body. It wasn't a particularly lascivious look, but the air around them began to feel heated and Shaun's heart picked up in anticipation.

Jozef lifted his hand slowly, as if trying not to startle her again. He brushed the backs of his fingers down her cheek. *You've been crying.*

Shaun's eyes widened. In her haste to get a little alone time after her call with her mother, she'd forgotten what a mess she must look like. She scrubbed her hands over her cheeks to erase the tear tracks. Jozef took her hands in his and gently lowered them.

Why? he asked.

Shaun glanced away, her gaze landing on the TV, which was now playing the music video for Blondie's "Heart of Glass". Despite the upbeat track, the atmosphere surrounding them had a distinctly intimate feel. When they communicated without speaking, it wrapped them in a silent bubble, one where they were the only two people in the world. Shaun felt as though she couldn't lie to Jozef. She wasn't sure why. After everything he'd put her through, she didn't owe him her loyalty.

Still, she wanted him to know. *I miss my mom.*

Pain darkened his eyes and she realized he actually cared. He didn't want her to feel the anguish of missing her mother. He shook his head as though he didn't know what to say. Then he looked at her, his eyes blazing as though he'd made a decision.

I will find a way for you to speak with her, at least send a message.

Shaun was speechless. He was going back on his decision not to allow her a phone call. The moment was deeply significant. It felt like he was taking a major step toward trust. She knew it was stupid, but she wanted to trust him back. She felt like she had to tell him the truth.

I already called her. She watched his face carefully as she told him.

There was an instant blankness to his expression that told her he was shutting down their moment and she couldn't stand it. She took the final step between them, leaving only a tiny space so she could sign to him. *Please don't be angry. I had to. It was killing her thinking I was dead.* When he didn't move, she added, *think how your aunt would feel if she thought you were dead.*

When he didn't respond, but still stared at her with his icy gaze, despair started to sink in. She'd been stupid tell him about the phone call. Of course he was going to be angry; she'd done something he'd expressively forbidden. Still, she hadn't had a choice and if he couldn't see that, then that was his problem.

Shaun tried to step away from him, but he grabbed her arms and held her still. She stared up at him. Slowly he released her as though waiting to see if she would bolt. When she didn't, he began signing. *Your conversation has upset you. Tell me.*

He brushed his fingers down her cheek again.

Shaun gave herself a brief moment to savour his gentle

touch, closing her eyes and leaning into him, allowing his wildly masculine scent combined with a subtle and expensive aftershave to wash over her. She nodded her head and he cupped her cheek. Then he dropped his hand and took hers in a strong grip. He pulled her toward the couch, indicating she should sit with him.

They sat facing each other, Shaun's legs tucked cross-legged beneath her. He watched her steadily, giving her the chance to tell him about the conversation.

Shaun began signing. *It was bittersweet to hear her voice. I always miss her when I'm travelling but I've never felt this way before. As though I might not see her again. Our conversation had a desperation to it, like we were both saying goodbye in case it was the last time we talked.* Tears began spilling from her lashes, but she kept signing, knowing her emotions were causing her to mix up the words, but not caring. Jozef would understand what she was trying to say. *I can't stand the thought that I might never see her again. She's the most amazing woman and mom, and after my father passed, we leaned on each other. Now I need her more than ever and I can't have her. It hurts so much.*

When she stopped signing, Jozef gave her a moment to compose herself. She used the edge of her sleeve to wipe the wetness from her cheeks. A hiccoughing sob jumped from her throat and out of her mouth. She covered it with her hand, while Jozef watched her with a warm glow in his eyes.

When he'd made sure she was calm enough to watch, he spoke. *I remember the sound of my mother's voice. It's the only thing I remember about her.* His gaze was steady on hers and she understood that he was telling her something he'd probably never told anyone before. *I can't remember her face, or what her touch felt like, but I remember the sound of her voice. Not the words, just the sound. I think she used to like singing to me.*

Tears leapt to Shaun's eyes, but this time for a different reason. Jozef could understand her pain because he'd been separated from his mother too. It was strange, having a moment of shared pain like this with her captor. He was the cause of her pain, yet he was also the one making her feel better. He wasn't making false promises either, telling her she would see her mother one day. She respected him more for not lying to her.

Fatima's words about Stockholm floated through her brain but she shoved the thought aside. Even if she had Stockholm, she was helpless. She was navigating a new world with a new set of rules. Her old ones didn't apply. If Stockholm helped get her through this nightmare, then so be it.

Yet, as she looked at Jozef, she began to realize that she wasn't living in a nightmare. Not really. Sure, it was terrifying to be constantly surrounded by armed men, with the knowledge that one false move could get her killed, but she couldn't exactly call her situation a nightmare. She was being waited on hand and foot, given anything her heart desired as long as it didn't relate to her being set free. Although, none of those things really mattered to her, and she suspected she was going to become quickly bored with having such easy access to everything. It was Jozef who made her look forward to waking up each day, despite waking up in a mansion filled with intrigue and criminals. She could no longer deny it, she was falling for her darkly handsome kidnapper.

CHAPTER THIRTY-SEVEN

Shaun reached out tentatively and touched the scar on his throat. "When did it happen?"

He hesitated, as if deciding how to answer. She suspected this was a topic he didn't enjoy talking about, which was why she hadn't brought it up before. Now that he seemed more willing to share with her, she wanted to know about him. About the kinds of things that had shaped the man he was now.

Finally, he told her, *I was stabbed in the throat when I was seven. I don't remember anything except waking up in the hospital with my aunt and uncle by my side. They told me my parents were both dead.*

Shaun frowned and scooted closer to him on the couch, leaning in to examine the scar. This close she wasn't able to sign, so she whispered, "Whoever stabbed you would have damaged your trachea, causing vocal cord paralysis. This is why you can't speak, isn't it?"

Shaun had suspected, but she hadn't put a lot of thought into why Jozef communicated nonverbally. His lack of speech could have been something he was born with, completely unrelated to the knife to his throat, or it might have been psychological.

Jozef nodded, his head brushing hers as she leaned in to look at him.

"Whoever did this was either really bad at aiming, or they weren't trying to kill you," she murmured, almost to herself. "If I had to guess, I would say you were stabbed, straight in, straight out with a short blade. Your attacker was trying to damage your vocal cords."

She glanced up at him and realized how close she'd gotten when his velvet blue gaze met hers, their face only inches apart. "Someone was trying to keep you from speaking."

A slight frown pulled at his brow, as though she was giving him information he hadn't known before. She wanted to ask him if he remembered anything, but he already told her he didn't and she didn't want to push.

She touched the rigid scar on his neck, running her fingertips over it and then lifting her fingers to touch his scruffy chin. He needed a shave. His facial hair grew quickly and even when he shaved in the morning, he usually needed another by the time evening came around. The dark hair against his pale jaw was sexy as hell.

The air surrounding them became charged with sexual tension as Shaun continued to stroke her fingers down the side of his face. She shouldn't be doing it. She was reaching out and touching the forbidden, and if she wasn't careful the forbidden was going to get her killed. Yet she felt helpless against the swirling chemistry that came to life whenever they were near each other. Like oppositely charged magnets, they were drawn together, even if they were better apart.

Slowly Jozef dropped his head to hers, resting his lips on hers. He waited, giving her the power to decide. Blood was rushing through her veins and each breath she took stuttered in, then whooshed out. She'd never felt this way with anyone before. As though she was sitting next to the one person on the planet who could possibly complete her. The idea was so wildly disconnected from all her usual cool logic that she was left floundering in a strange new world with only Jozef as her anchor.

She reached for him, sliding her arms around his neck and wiggling closer to him on the couch. She tilted her head up, pressing her lips against his. He didn't hesitate. He took her invitation, gripping her around the waist and dragging her onto his lap until her knees fell open on either side of his body. He gripped her hard around the back and slashed his mouth across hers, kissing her with brutal desperation. It was painful, but also fierce and exhilarating, as though they couldn't contain themselves anymore.

The kiss progressed quickly until Shaun was dragging Jozef's coat from his shoulders, her hands clutching at the muscles of his back, while Jozef gripped her thighs so hard she was positive she would bruise.

He pushed her back on the couch, never breaking their kiss, and leaned across her, his chest pressed to hers. Shaun finished yanking his coat off, then lifted her shoulders off the couch so Jozef could pull her shirt over her head. Then they were kissing again, their heated passion flaring higher and higher with each touch. Josef was gripping her with painful fingers one moment then shoving her back the next so he could strip her pants from her legs.

Shaun tried to help, but it was hard since all she wanted was his lips on hers. Every time he broke their kiss, she trailed kisses down his neck and chest before gripping his shoulders and dragging him in for another lip-lock. Her passionate enthusiasm was driving him crazy. She could tell by the way his hands shook as he tried to stop himself from grabbing her too hard and bruising her.

His care for her well-being melted her until she couldn't

remember a single argument against sex with the mob enforcer. Everywhere he touched burned so good she felt consumed by him. She couldn't stop even if she wanted to.

Soon her clothes lay in an untidy pile next to the couch and Jozef's hands were everywhere, worshipping every inch of her he could reach. Though his touches weren't gentle, she'd never felt safer in his hands. He was in complete control and she trusted him to hold on to her. She wanted to give herself to him, feel him all over and inside her.

She reached between them and unzipped his jeans while he moved his hips so she could reach him. Her fingers were shaking, and her breath was puffing out in short gasps as though she were running a race. Dragging his belt through the loops, she opened his jeans and reached inside, touching him, circling him with her fingers, feeling the raw strength running through him as blood engorged his cock. She pulled him free, tightening her knees against his hips.

He took her wrist in one hand, pulling her away from his cock and dragging her arm over her head. He used his other hand to reach down between them, dragging his knuckles through the wet folds of her vagina, pulling a gasp from her. Her hips surged up in wild supplication. He rubbed his thumb against her clit, dragging cries from her as she writhed underneath him, waves of pleasure already rocking her body and she hadn't even peaked yet.

Jozef pressed his fingers into her tight passage, filling her with excruciating slowness as she wiggled against him, trying to find a rhythm so she could get off. Jozef had other, more tortuous ideas. He gave her a heated look, his gaze capturing and holding hers while his fingers sought and found her g-spot. It was so intimate, having his eyes touch hers with such knowing, while his fingers played inside her vagina, pushing her higher and higher until she thought she would die if she didn't come.

Sparks of light burst through her skull as she clawed for the release that was just out of reach. Before she could take hold of it, Jozef abruptly pulled his fingers out of her. She yelled her frustration and hit him in the shoulder with her fist. He made a grunting sound and her eyes flew open as he took her free wrist and captured it with the other above her head. Then he took her chin in hand and forced her to look at him as he surged inside her.

He filled her completely as he slammed to the hilt, the scent of her own arousal reaching her from where his fingers touched her face. It was the most erotic experience of her life. It was beautiful, raw and honest.

Jozef fucked her with long deep strokes, his rhythm even until the very end, each stroke igniting the fire in his eyes to a fever pitch. She was burning up with him, reaching for her orgasm while laying helpless beneath his masterful body. She felt his cock growing bigger inside her, tighter, and knew he was close. She yanked her wrists from his grasp, reached up and dragged his face down to hers, wanting to see every expression as passion took over and controlled his body. She saw the glassy hardness of his eyes, felt the breath whoosh from him and rush over her face, heard the guttural grunts as he was pushed over the edge.

His hands tightened almost unbearably, pushing Shaun into her own orgasm. She let go of him, reached over her head and took hold of the couch cushions, pushing her hips up into his and taking every drop of semen rushing into her body.

They came down together, the shock of unplanned intense sex visible on their faces. Jozef rolled to the side, pulling Shaun with him until he lay with his chest pressed against her back. He held her in a bear hug, his fingers lacing with hers and resting on her belly. He was cuddling with her, floating with her through the aftermath of the best orgasm she'd ever experienced. She wanted to know if he felt the same but didn't want to ask.

She tipped her head up to look at him and found his gaze steady on her face. His lips softened, not quite into a smile, but something close. His arms tightened around her and he watched her as her muscles began to relax and her breathing evened out. Before she fell asleep, the last thing she noticed was a blanket being pulled across her naked body and tucked around her.

CHAPTER THIRTY-EIGHT

Jozef wanted nothing more than to spend the rest of the evening holding Shaun in his arms while she slept, but he had a meeting to attend. Krystoff wanted to talk to him about some information Jozef's team had dug up. They'd finally managed to discover the whereabouts of Vasiliy Stanovich, the mastermind behind Krystoff's kidnapping. Unfortunately for them, Vasiliy was holed up in the neighboring country of Poland.

Jozef suspected his uncle was going to send him on an out-of-country job, not something Jozef wanted to do while he was still unsure of where he stood with his fiancé. Would she try to leave him the moment he was out of the country? Would her heart grow cooler with distance? He didn't want to risk their budding relationship on a job, but his uncle's word was law, and if Krystoff ordered Jozef and his team to go on a job, they didn't have a choice but to go.

It was the way they had always done things. Krystoff was head of the organization, Jozef was his loyal dog. The power imbalance they held was beginning to make less and less sense to Jozef. He'd never questioned his uncle's autocracy, since Krystoff always treated his family well, and Jozef got to make most of the security related decisions. But it was Jozef who'd put his team together, trained with them, ensured they were the best in the business. He should be the one making the decisions. It was something he'd have to bring up with Krystoff.

Knowing his uncle would send someone to find him if he didn't get moving, Jozef gently pulled his arm from beneath his slumbering woman and slowly crawled over top of her.

She rolled onto her back and let out a soft snore before flinging an arm over her face and falling into a deeper sleep.

Jozef had noticed that about Shaun. She slept soundly no matter where she was or how cramped the sleeping conditions were. He supposed it was her experience as a doctor, working long hours on her feet, that allowed her to sleep so soundly. Jozef was a light sleeper, always had been and likely always would be. That particular character trait could one day save his life.

He pulled on his clothes and then searched through her pockets until he found the burner phone. Stuffing it in his pocket, he made his way quietly out of the suite, locking it behind him. He should be wearing a suit for meeting his uncle, but he didn't want to take the time to change. Krystoff wouldn't care, but Jozef had trained their men to respect the family patriarch at all times, which meant dressing appropriately and using the correct language and grammar.

Krystoff's office was on the first floor, opposite the formal dining room. Jozef knocked briefly, waited for the summons and opened the door. Krystoff was standing next to the floor to ceiling windows, which opened to a spectacular view of Prague in the distance. The older man was drinking cognac from a crystal highball glass. He turned when Jozef entered the room and lifted his glass with a raised brow.

Jozef shook his head, his mind flashing to the woman snoring on his couch. He wanted round two when he was finished his meeting and he suspected she wouldn't want him coming to her bed smelling of alcohol. He didn't think she was a prude, but the look on her face when he'd taken that line of cocaine in the club haunted him, reminding him they were from two different worlds. He was used to a life filled with vices. He knew how to moderate himself, but that didn't mean he had to flaunt his lifestyle while wooing a woman who meant something to him.

"Sit, Jozef." Krystoff waved his hand toward a pair of immaculate leather chairs in front of the fireplace. There was no fire yet as it was warm outside, but Krystoff tended to prefer the leather chairs when he was meeting with Jozef or another member of the family. If the meeting was of a more professional nature, or if there was a darker purpose, he would seat his guest opposite him, the oak desk between them.

Jozef dipped his head in acknowledgment and took a seat, accepting a glass of water from his uncle. Though he'd refused an alcoholic beverage, Krystoff would never allow a guest to go without a drink.

"How are things, my boy?" Krystoff asked jovially, dropping into the chair opposite Jozef and crossing his ankle over his knee.

I'm doing well, Jozef signed. *Are you fully recovered from your ordeal?*

"Indeed. That week off was almost a vacation," Krystoff said with a half-smile, holding up his hand with its missing finger. "Your girl did an excellent job of patching me up."

Rather than prolong the meeting, Jozef asked bluntly, *what's the job?*

Krystoff looked taken aback. Krystoff led the meetings, not Jozef. He talked business when he was ready to talk business. However, Jozef was impatient to get back to Shaun and unwilling to engage in light banter.

"I want you to go to Poland," Krystoff said, switching gears. "Get what you can out of Vasiliy, take care of him and come home. Make sure there is no evidence of your existence. Our Polish allies have made it clear: we do not conduct business in their territory without their permission and we don't have permission for this particular operation."

Jozef dipped his head in a nod. He'd been right about why Krystoff summoned him. Terek, Jozef's 'hunter,' had traced every move Vasiliy had made over the past few years and discovered the man owned a small rustic cabin in Poland. They'd sent someone to check and sure enough, Vasiliy had holed up, disappearing from the mafia radar. He'd probably chosen Poland specifically because the Kobas couldn't move as easily through the territory. Vasiliy was about to find out otherwise.

When do we move? Jozef asked.

"Tonight." Krystoff's voice held a hard edge to it, as though daring Jozef to argue. "You'll have to be back in time for the engagement party."

Fuck. Krystoff was cutting it close. It would take a minimum of twelve hours to travel to Poland, dispose of Vasiliy and travel home. The party was scheduled for the next evening. Jozef was going to be coming in right under the wire, and he was more afraid of what his aunt would do to him if he missed the party than what Krystoff would do to him. Why weren't they waiting until after the party? A few extra days would allow Jozef to come up with an adequate plan that would ensure the safety of him and his team, as well as give him the opportunity to prepare Shaun for his absence.

Jozef didn't want to leave Shaun in Prague while he travelled to Poland. It would only take a day, but that was still a day too long to be away from her. Of course, bringing a woman on such a dangerous mission wasn't an option. Krystoff would never allow it. Though often progressive in his thinking, when it came to the women of his family, Krystoff still held old-fashioned values. The women stayed home and, for the most part, stayed out of the family business. They helped run the home, went shopping, supported charities and met up with socially acceptable friends.

As if reading Jozef's mind, Krystoff said, "I ran into Shaun in the rose garden this morning. She seemed upset."

Jozef frowned. Shaun hadn't said anything about meeting up with Krystoff.

Krystoff studied his nephew with a keen eye. "I've said it before, and I'll say it again. She won't settle easily into this life, son."

Jozef nodded his head in agreement. There was no point in arguing the obvious. *She won't have a choice.*

"How do you intend to control her?" Krystoff leaned back in his seat, his sharp eyes on his nephew.

Jozef didn't like what his uncle was implying. As if Shaun was some kind of dog that needed to be leashed and controlled. She was a kind and intelligent woman with a quick brain and a compassionate nature.

This is not your concern, Jozef signed, trying to shut down the topic.

A frown deepened the grooves between Krystoff's thick grey eyebrows. "I disagree. Her actions will have an effect on this family. I had hoped the lures of our lifestyle would have helped her settle down, but the conversation she and I had this morning has left me concerned. She won't be happy here."

Jozef wanted to growl at his uncle to stay the fuck out of his business. Jozef was an independent man. He stayed in the family home at the request of his aunt, but he owned a building in downtown Prague, the same building the club was in. Many of his men stayed on the middle floors above the club when they were in between jobs. It was times like this, when his family became overly involved in his life, that Jozef wanted to move away from the family estate.

"She called her mother earlier today," Krystoff said quietly, his sharp gaze on Jozef's face, as though trying to decide if Jozef knew.

How do you know? Jozef demanded.

Krystoff's gaze softened. "My apologies, son, but I fear I did something you won't approve of." It was unusual for Krystoff to apologize for anything, but then, he didn't often involve himself in Jozef's personal life. "I made sure she would have access to a phone."

Jozef frowned, anger and disappointment rising within him. His uncle was supposed to be his greatest ally, the man who always had his back. And he was trying to set up Jozef's woman? Unacceptable.

You were testing her?

"Testing you," Krystoff admitted. "You told me you would control the woman, but the first thing she did when given the opportunity was make a call out."

You have the recording? Jozef demanded. *Give it to me.*

Krystoff pulled his phone from his pocket, tapped for a few seconds then held it up as Shaun's voice filled the space around them. Jozef and Krystoff listened to the entire conversation in silence. Some of Jozef's tension eased as he heard Shaun repeatedly deny her mother's inquiries. Whether to keep her mother safe, or because she didn't want to cause problems for the Kobas, Shaun had refused to give up her location. The parts where she and her mother cried together tore at Jozef's heart. He was the cause of such misery.

When the recording finished, Krystoff put his phone away.

"I must admit," Krystoff said thoughtfully, "I thought she would have given us up as her kidnappers. Her refusal is a point in her favour."

Jozef was seething. *What would you have done if she'd given her mother the information?*

Krystoff looked at him steadily, his expression telling Jozef everything he needed to know. Krystoff would've had Shaun removed, any evidence of her contact with the Koba family erased and he likely would've done it without Jozef's permission or knowledge. It would have been as though she never existed to them.

She needs more time, Jozef insisted.

Shaun's compassionate personality was already softening her toward him, and he could tell she was bonding with Saskia. Given more time, Jozef was positive Shaun wouldn't want to do anything that could harm Jozef or his family. She may never fully reconcile herself to Jozef's lifestyle, but she wouldn't wish to hurt him either.

"We don't have the luxury of time," Krystoff said, his voice hardening. "Do what you must, but if you wish to keep this woman, you need to crush her spirit and ensure her loyalty."

Jozef's gaze hardened and he leaned forward in his seat, pinning his uncle with the heat of his anger. *Do not make the mistake of thinking you can have Shaun hurt or killed and expect no retaliation from me.*

Krystoff looked taken aback by Jozef's aggression. He wasn't used to anything less than complete loyalty from his guard dog. Yet both men knew who held the real power in the Koba family. Jozef could walk away from his family and take most of their business. He was the man on the ground, the person their contacts trusted.

Are you threatening me? Krystoff asked, using Jozef's preferred method of communication.

Jozef recognized what his uncle was doing by speaking in sign language. The older man was trying to draw Jozef's sympathy, remind him of their shared history. Krystoff had learned sign language so he could communicate with his nephew at any time, though he tended to use verbal communication. Jozef hadn't thought about it before, but he wondered if Krystoff did it as a power move. He had something Jozef didn't: a voice.

If that was Krystoff's tactic, then it was pointless. Jozef had never felt powerless from his lack of voice, because he didn't lack for anything. He could make himself heard. Sometimes his bullets, knives or fists did the talking, but in the end, people knew what he was trying to say.

I am no threat unless something happens to my fiancé.

And if something happens to her? Krystoff pushed.

Jozef pinned his uncle with a cold look. *Then I will not rest until I've found and removed the persons who caused her harm.*

Krystoff nodded thoughtfully. "You have my word that no harm will come to Shaun while she is under my roof."

Though it sounded like Krystoff was capitulating to Jozef, he'd worded his concession carefully. As long as Jozef resided under Krystoff's roof, remaining under his control, then Shaun would not be harmed. If Jozef moved with Shaun, then she would become fair game. Jozef needed time to think and decide his next move. Things were changing in the Koba household.

Jozef stood. *I will hold you to your word. Shaun is to be treated like family while I'm in Poland.*

"You have my word," Krystoff assured him.

Jozef dug the burner phone from his pocket, crushed it in his hand and handed it to his uncle. *No more tests.*

Krystoff's face stiffened but he nodded his acquiescence.

As Jozef turned to leave the office, Krystoff's voice reached out to him. "Don't forget where you belong, son. You are a Koba. Loyalty, pride, family."

Jozef looked down at his hand resting on the doorhandle. The words *vernost*, *hrdost* and *rodina* were tattooed on his first three fingers. Loyalty, pride, family.

He jerked his head in a nod, opened the door and left.

CHAPTER THIRTY-NINE

There's no security that I can detect. No men, no cameras, no alarms.

Jozef nodded as his man filled him in. Terek had gone ahead to meet up with their Polish contact and to stake out Vasiliy's hideout. Despite Terek's assurance that the house wasn't wired, Jozef wasn't taking chances with the safety of his team. With the tight timeline they were on, they'd only had a few hours of surveillance, rather than the minimum of two days Jozef would normally insist on.

Is he inside the house? Jozef asked.

Terek lifted his shoulders in a shrug, his look of frustration mirroring Jozef's, who was silently cursing his uncle for setting up such a disorganized hit. Twelve years earlier, when Krystoff had wanted to up the Koba game in the global market, Jozef had suggested putting together an elite team of mercenaries for hire. His team consisted of the best people he could find in the areas of security, explosives, surveillance, investigation and tech. He'd worked with them until they became a well-oiled machine. He always had a five-man team who travelled with him, a two-person tech team at home, and a secondary B-team in training. After years of taking jobs, Jozef had come to understand exactly what he and his crew needed for each job: time to plan, time to train, time to surveil, and the correct equipment. They'd had the opportunity to do none of that for this job, meaning they were forced to go in blind.

Jozef hated the idea of doubting his uncle, the man who had adopted and raised him, but it seemed strange that he was being sent on such a rushed mission when he could have easily done the job after the engagement party. That would have given his team a few extra days, enough time to plan, and enough time for Jozef to make sure Shaun was well settled.

He'd hated leaving her behind. She'd simply nodded when he told her and remained silent, a frown creasing her forehead. He could see the questions lining themselves up in her mind: where is he going, what is he doing, is he planning on killing someone? But none had passed her beautiful lips. Before he left, she'd told him to stay safe. He'd held those two words next to his heart, determined that he would do as she asked. He would stay safe for her.

Halil and Havel will go through the front gate while Nikolay provides backup, Jozef signed to Terek, adjusting night vision goggles over his eyes. It was 2:00 AM, and the entire team would be equipped with goggles to help ease their entry into the house. They would also have the element of surprise if Vasiliy was sleeping. There was no light shining through any of the windows, though they could be covered with blackout curtains. *I will go through the back gate while you follow.*

Jozef, Halil, Nikolay and Havel had discussed the plan in detail on the ride into Poland, but Terek had gone ahead of them and wasn't privy to their discussion, which was why he was being given the safest position of rear backup.

Jozef tapped out his commands into his earpiece, reiterating the plan to the others. He and his team had learned morse code so they could easily communicate with Jozef. The uses went far beyond Jozef being able to give orders to his men via radio coms, though; the entire team used a combination of morse code and sign language, which allowed them seamless and silent entries and exits from their jobs, stealthy communication, and a way to let the tech team know what was happening while they were on radio silence. The method was much less cumbersome and less visible than messaging.

Once the entire team acknowledged Jozef's commands, Jozef gave the order to move. Like a team of wraiths moving swiftly through the pitch-black night, they moved so fluidly through the trees they would have been invisible to the naked eye.

Havel and Halil went through the front gate, breaching the perimeter first. Nikolay stayed at the gate to provide cover for the team while they were inside. Two taps through the radio told Jozef they'd made it safely to the front door. Jozef acknowledged and then pushed the back gate open, crouching as he went through, sweeping the area with his goggles. Nothing moved, no heat signatures. Terek came in behind him and they made their way through the shrubbery to the back door. Per protocol, they waited and listened for twenty seconds before letting Havel know they were in position.

Three seconds later, they breached the cabin, throwing smoke grenades and moving through each room in rapid succession. Jozef met Havel in the hallway and together they moved through to the bedrooms, while the other two covered the front and back entrances so no one could come in behind them. Havel stood next to the first bedroom door, his gun up and ready while Jozef flung the door open, threw a smoke grenade and swept the interior. It was empty. They hit the next room, which was also empty.

They paused, regrouping. The cabin appeared to be empty, and now they'd lost the element of surprise. If anyone was home, they would know that they'd been discovered.

Havel tapped Jozef's shoulder, catching his attention.

Underground? Havel signed, his face reflecting his annoyance. Jozef felt the same way. If they'd had enough time for proper surveillance, this wouldn't be happening. They would know Vasiliy's routine, would know if he was home or not. They would have had time for a phone tap and surveillance, which might have given them an edge.

Jozef had to think quickly. He couldn't spend precious seconds trying to make a decision. He nodded at Havel, indicating that he should search the front of the cabin while Jozef searched the rear. The team reconvened and started swiftly searching for a trap door or loose floorboards.

It was Jozef who found the tunnel. Like a scene straight out of a movie, he leaned against a bookshelf as he was bending to flip over an oriental rug in the office. The bookshelf moved a few inches.

Jozef turned swiftly, took hold of the top of the shelf and pulled. It swung easily out, opening into a stone stairway leading into an underground tunnel. Jozef tapped furiously on his earpiece, bringing the team running to the office. He gave Halil and Terek instructions to watch the entrance, while he and Havel descended the stairs.

Now that they had an idea of where Vasiliy had gone, they moved swift and sure, back on target. The tunnel ran about a hundred yards from the house; a crude dugout reinforced with wooden beams every few yards. They swept through at top speed, running until they reached a door, which was slightly ajar, light pouring through. Jozef reached for a smoke grenade on his belt but was halted when he heard the sound of music drifting into the tunnel.

He frowned as he was able to pick up the haunting sounds

of an Italian opera. The whole scene felt like a setup, but he had to press on. This was his mission and he'd never failed to complete a mission.

Rather than throw the grenade, he replaced it on his belt and carefully pushed the door open, his gun up and ready. What met his eyes was such an incongruently strange scene compared to what he'd expected, that he stood and stared for several long seconds, finally reaching up to pull his goggles from his face so he could get a better look. Havel covered his back as Jozef stepped into the room.

"I've been waiting for you."

An older gentleman, probably in his 70's, spoke without looking up. Vasiliy. Though Jozef had seen pictures of the man, he hadn't met Vasiliy in person. He was a robust man, with wide shoulders and a round belly. He sported a snowy white head of hair and a beard that reached halfway down his neck. In his hand was a fine-tipped paintbrush. He was carefully applying red paint to what looked like a doll's face.

It took Jozef a moment to realize that he was looking at an underground workshop, not a safe room. The room was filled with tables piled high with all sizes of *matryoshka*, or Russian nesting dolls, in various stages of completion. One of the tables was filled with paints, jars, brushes and carving tools. A quick sweep of the room revealed a set of stairs beneath a trap door. Jozef guessed it would lead outside, set purposely away from the cabin in case the occupants needed a quick escape. It would have worked if Vasiliy had chosen to run. There was no one else in the room besides Vasiliy and there were no visible weapons besides the carving tools, and those were safely out of Vasiliy's reach.

Finally, Vasiliy dropped his paintbrush into a nearby jar, set aside the doll and stood, stretching until his back cracked audibly. Jozef could feel Havel move behind him, bringing his gun up so he was aiming at Vasiliy's heart.

"I'm sorry, I don't know how to communicate in your language," he said to Jozef, sounding genuinely regretful. "If you wish to speak to me before you kill me, we'll need a translator."

Jozef was completely taken aback by Vasiliy's attitude. Instead of acting like a rat on the run, he was holed up in a wood smith's paradise, calmly facing death as though it was another to-do on his checklist.

"What do you want to do, man?" Havel asked Jozef, breaking protocol and speaking so he wouldn't have to put his weapon down.

It was Vasiliy who answered. "I can move away from the table, if you like, and keep my hands raised where you can see them. I promise, I have no motive other than to speak to you before you kill me."

Though he was tempted to put a bullet in Vasiliy and be done with this strange job, he wanted to hear what the older man had to say. He nodded toward Havel, indicating it was alright to put the gun down. Havel did as Jozef asked, then said to Vasiliy, "Move there." He pointed. "Hands up and out to the side, fingers spread. If you twitch wrong, I will put a bullet between your eyes. I guarantee I'll be faster than you if you reach for anything."

Havel was the fastest man on their team. He was bigger than the rest of them, but able to move like a speed demon when he needed to.

Vasiliy complied.

Once he was standing in the middle up the room, his arms up and out to the side, Jozef relaxed enough to sign while Havel translated. *What do you want to tell me?*

"Thank you for trusting me." Vasiliy caught the look on Jozef's face and added, "Yes, of course you don't trust me. What I mean is, thank you for trusting me enough not to shoot before I get the chance to speak."

Jozef gave him the universal 'hurry up' signal, which Havel didn't need to translate.

"Right, right, of course," Vasiliy said hurriedly. "You'll be in a rush to leave." He didn't sound at all like a man who was facing death. Where was the begging? The bribery? Jozef wondered if he was less frightening than he thought. He glanced at Havel. Nope, the fatigue-clad crew, loaded with weaponry, would look scary as fuck coming through a door, weapons drawn.

"I didn't order my people to pick up your uncle." Vasiliy spoke earnestly, the words sounding planned, as though he knew what he wanted to say once Jozef arrived and had been practicing. "I've been retired for three years, living in this peaceful section of Poland. I had no idea Krystoff had been abducted until my son called to tell me."

Jozef frowned his disbelief. Yet... some of what Vasiliy was saying rang true. The older man hadn't been seen in public in years. Rumours had abounded through the Underworld circles that he was in hiding, embarrassed after being pushed out of the game by the other Vory. The fact was, Vasiliy had never been an effective mobster. He was weak.

Or that was the rumour. Jozef was beginning to wonder if it was something else. Maybe Vasiliy had too much heart for the mob. His cabin was filled with warmth: quilts, books, music. His workshop showed a love of manual labour and fine carpentry.

Jozef had been told his entire life that this man was dangerous but stupid. He'd never questioned it before, just like he didn't question orders coming from his uncle.

Did you send those men to my club to negotiate with us? Jozef demanded, while Havel translated. *Did you get my message?*

Vasiliy looked confused. "I did not. What message did you send?"

Several fingers, one head. Jozef didn't need to expound,

anyone in the mob would understand he was being quite literal.

Vasiliy nodded thoughtfully, his face reflecting some surprise, but not shock. As though he was hearing about the club incident for the first time, but he wasn't completely blindsided by the news.

"I hope you didn't kill anyone I like," Vasiliy mused.

Jozef was done messing around. *You know why I'm here; I won't leave without completing my mission. Tell me what you wanted to talk about, or we're finished here.*

Havel translated.

"You can protect her," Vasiliy said, his voice going from calm to anxious. "She's young and impetuous, but very, very smart; an incredibly talented genius. With every job she learns more, perfects her routine. She's striking out on her own, but she is still too inexperienced to be allowed to run around unsupervised. She's filled with anger and I worry that she will become reckless."

Who? Jozef was getting angry. He hated when people talked in circles; it made communicating so much more difficult. He wanted to tell the man to hurry up and fucking spill so Jozef could kill him already.

"My daughter," Vasiliy admitted.

Jozef and Havel looked at each other. A daughter? Vasiliy only had a son. The families had been close enough at one time that Jozef would know if there was a daughter. Yet, he didn't think Vasiliy was lying.

Who is your daughter? Jozef demanded.

"She calls herself the Phantom."

In the car, when they'd been bringing Krystoff home from Ukraine, his uncle had said something about a person calling themselves the Phantom. And again, in the club, Krystoff had tried to get more information from Vasiliy's men. Jozef had looked into it but had unearthed no leads on a so-called

Phantom. So, the Phantom was a woman. Not a common thing in the mafia, where women typically didn't hold positions of power.

Who is the Phantom? Jozef asked, taking a few steps closer to Vasiliy. *What is her name?*

Vasiliy shook his head. "That I will not give you." When Jozef lifted his gun threateningly, Vasiliy didn't flinch. He smiled sadly. "Until I can be assured that she will be safe from harm, I will not give you her name."

Jozef frowned. *You stayed here, knowing we would hunt you down and kill you, just so you could tell me about your daughter, but then you refuse to give me her name. Will you tell me where to find her?*

"No," Vasiliy said grimly. "Not until I know for certain she will come to no harm." When Jozef gave him an annoyed look, he hurried to add. "She means more to me than my own life. She is brilliant and must be given a chance to live and thrive, to rule her slice of this world."

Jozef thought for a moment, then asked, *what will it take to convince you she will come to no harm?*

Vasiliy looked at him quizzically. "Will you promise not to hurt my daughter?"

Jozef thought about lying, but decided the truth was better in this instance. Vasiliy was being unexpectedly honest, Jozef could give him the same. *I can't make that promise.*

Vasiliy smiled broadly. "I knew I could trust you. It's why I've been waiting years for you to come find me."

Jozef was deeply confused. Years? Vasiliy hadn't even been on Jozef's radar until Krystoff's abduction.

As if reading him, Vasiliy clarified. "I knew eventually she would do something to bring your attention down on my family. I wish it hadn't taken maiming your uncle to get you here, but I'm not sorry to finally be speaking with you. I have heard many good things about your loyalty and determination."

Jozef had so many questions, he didn't know where to start, but was interrupted by several sharp taps on his headset. Terek was telling him that Krystoff wanted a mission update. It was time to finish this and go home.

Vasiliy's sharp eyes followed Jozef's movements. "You have to leave." He sounded almost disappointed, like he wanted to hang out a little longer with his soon-to-be murderer. Jozef didn't know who this guy's daughter was, but she was probably just as crazy.

Jozef lifted his gun.

"May I give you a gift first?" Vasiliy asked quietly.

Jozef tensed as Vasiliy reached for the work bench he'd been painting at when they arrived, but he only picked up a doll. It was about the length of Jozef's forearm, with a chubby body that would fit other dolls inside. It was female, with long dark brown hair painted over the head and shoulders, a red and white patterned dress and a face that was both sweet and haunting.

Jozef held the doll in one arm and lifted his gun in the other, setting it against Vasiliy's head.

"When you meet her, give her the doll. I made it in her likeness." Vasiliy closed his eyes and whispered a prayer.

CHAPTER FORTY

"Dr. Patterson, if you'll just hold your head still for me."

Shaun wanted to growl her annoyance as the person doing her hair straightened her head by pushing her chin forward. The man was fingers deep in Shaun's tight curls, trying his best to straighten them. She could tell he wasn't used to working with hair like hers. Her tight curls were usually pulled back in a ponytail or left in an afro that framed her head. Sometimes when she was travelling, depending on the country and her access to clean hygiene, she would have her hair braided into tight rows to keep maintenance down.

Shaun was being, poked, prodded, measured, plucked and made-up for the engagement party due to start in just over two hours. Dasha had sent her beauty team to Jozef's suite to help Shaun prepare. She felt like an expensive, very useless doll.

Shaun hadn't noticed Jozef enter the room until he stepped up to the man who was working on Shaun's hair, giving him a glare that had the man's hands freezing on Shaun's head. She smiled at Jozef in the mirror, her eyes meeting his.

He'd arrived back at the house in the very early morning and, after kissing her awake, made exquisite, leisurely love to her warm, sleepy body. He'd told her he missed her while he was gone. He hadn't given Shaun any details and she hadn't asked, but she'd spent half the night awake and worrying about him.

Jozef's gaze met Shaun's in the mirror. *What is he doing to your hair?*

I don't know, Shaun signed back, much to the bewilderment of her hair stylist. *I think he's trying to straighten it.* She snickered and shook her head. Straightening her hair would absolutely not happen unless the man had some very specific products.

Still standing behind her, Jozef brushed his fingers over her jaw then sank them into the springy curls around the base of her head. He freed his fingers and signed, *how do you want it to look?*

Shaun shrugged, *I guess I like it the way I usually have it.*
Then that's how it should look, Jozef agreed.

He turned his freezing stare to the hapless man attempting to painfully comb out Shaun's hair. Somehow the guy knew exactly what Jozef was saying, though not a word was spoken. The others in the room, two dressmakers, a jeweler, and a makeup artist watched the encounter with curiosity until Jozef turned the heat of his glare on them.

He snapped his fingers and pointed at the door. There was a moment of hesitation and then one very brave dressmaker stepped up. "But Mrs. Koba insisted we attend to Dr. Patterson. How will she get ready for the party?"

Jozef let out a ferocious growl that had the stylists running for the door while Shaun covered a fit of giggles with her hand. Jozef closed and locked the door once the last person was out of their suite, leaving him alone with Shaun.

He met her shining eyes in the mirror and smiled, a genuine smile, for her alone.

Shaun felt it right down to her toes.

I will help you prepare, Jozef signed as he approached her.

She turned in her seat and smiled up at him. "Thank you."

He stood staring at her, the tension building between them until the rest of the world faded. It was just the two of them in a bubble of their own making. No gangsters, no forced engagement, no death, no family intrigue. Just them.

Shaun broke the moment by asking bluntly, "Did you take my phone? I couldn't find it."

Jozef's gaze dimmed a little and he nodded. *I had to know if my uncle set you up.*

Shaun's eyes widened. "He can't have, I didn't get the phone from him."

Who did you get it from? Jozef asked.

Shaun sat silently, wondering what to do. She had to decide if she was going to trust Jozef with the information. Trust that he wouldn't do anything to Saskia. Trust that he was telling Shaun the truth when he said his uncle set the whole thing up and that he wasn't just trying to get the name of her ally. Then Shaun realized she'd already made her choice to trust Jozef when she'd told him about the phone call.

"I got it from Saskia," she whispered, her eyes pleading. "But I know she wasn't a part of any conspiracy to trap me. She's too honest with her emotions."

Jozef's lips twisted in a grim smile. *Yes, I agree. And it pleases me that you would protect the youngest member of my family. I believe my uncle found a way to get the phone to my cousin without her realizing he was manipulating the situation.*

Shaun nodded her agreement. Then it struck her. Jozef didn't need to tell her the truth of his uncle's machinations. He could have left her in the dark. Instead he was trusting her with the information, firmly pitting them together against his uncle in this situation. They were inside the bubble, just the two of them.

Jozef rotated the chair away from the mirror until she was facing him, then he sank onto his knee in front of her. Shaun's eyes widened and the breath caught in her chest as Jozef reached into his leather jacket and pulled out a box. This one was different from the one he'd shown her on the bridge. This one was a plain old-fashioned blue velvet box with faded gold trimming.

He opened the box and held it up for her to see. Nestled in the creamy satin folds of the box was a gold band with a single solitary diamond. The ring wasn't new, though it looked like it had been refurbished. She sensed that there was a sentimental value to this ring that hadn't belonged to the one on the bridge.

"It's beautiful," she whispered, touching the ring with her fingertip.

Encouraged by her lack of immediate refusal, Jozef pulled the ring from the box and gently slipped it on the third finger of her left hand. After Jozef had forced the other ring on her finger, after their botched date night, she'd taken it off and shoved it in a dresser drawer. When she'd gone back to look a few days later, it was gone.

Shaun stared down at the beautiful ring he'd placed on her finger, trying to remind herself of all the reasons she couldn't accept it. Yet, none of the reasons would surface. They were all still there, but all she could concentrate on was the darkly handsome man on his knee, making her feel as though she was the only woman in the world.

He squeezed her fingers, bringing them to his lips for a lingering kiss that sent her heart racing.

He dropped her hand so he could sign. *It was my mother's ring.*

Shaun nodded and blinked back tears at the thoughtful

gift. Not knowing what to say, she repeated, "It's beautiful, Jozef."

One day I will ask you to marry me properly.

"Not today?" she whispered, bewildered. Why was he on his knees if he wasn't proposing?

He shook his head. *No, I won't propose to you again until I know you will give me the answer I want to hear.* He stared at her with his steady lake-blue gaze. *Is today that day?*

Shaun thought about his question and then shook her head, dejected that she couldn't give him what he wanted. She wasn't ready to give herself up wholeheartedly to her situation. There was too much about it that was wrong. She was a captive with no real free will. She had been torn from her family and forced to put her career on hold. She couldn't reconcile herself to a life where so many of the things she loved and had worked hard for were being taken from her.

"I'm sorry," she whispered.

She was afraid she'd ruined the moment with her refusal, that Jozef would grow cold again, but he didn't. He looked at her with understanding and dipped his head in a brief nod.

I will not ask you to marry me then, he signed. *But I will ask you to wear my ring, in whatever form of commitment you are able to give at this moment.*

Commitment. Was she ready to wear a symbol of Jozef's ownership? She knew the Koba family and their elite friends would see it that way. She was property of the Koba family, and the ring sealed that fate. Shaun preferred to look at the ring in the spirit in which it was being given, a sign of Jozef's commitment to her. A request that she consider one day giving him more when she was ready.

It amazed her how far Jozef had come from the brutal killer who'd kidnapped her. She wasn't fooling herself into believing that he was no longer dangerous. All she had to do was remember the men who'd attacked her in the alley. He'd dealt with them with brutal efficiency and then walked away with Shaun as though he hadn't a moment's remorse for the lives he'd just taken. And though he'd admitted to her that he could remember the face of every person he killed, he still committed the act. He'd been raised a killer and he would die a killer.

Yet, the feral dog of the Koba family was softening for her, and even though she didn't agree with his line of work, it was impossible to resist the raw romance Jozef was determined to show her.

"Thank you." She curled her fingers into her palm, feeling the press of her new ring. "I'll treasure it."

Jozef reached up and, gripping her head in his palms, dragged her into his body for a kiss. She fell out of her chair, but he caught her before she could hit the floor and cradled her against his chest while deepening the kiss. Shaun clung to him, feeling the intense emotion of the moment mixing with the rising lust that seemed to always swirl around them.

Finally, he broke the kiss, touched his lips to her nose, then set her back in her chair. Standing up, he signed, *let's finish getting ready. I want this party done so I can get you to myself.*

He gave Shaun a distinctly lascivious look, telling her exactly why he wanted to get her alone.

Shaun laughed and turned her chair back to the mirror, picking up a nearby comb. She was relieved Jozef had sent the hair stylist away. She much preferred her own style over the smooth and straight version the man was trying to give her. She teased her hair until she got it exactly right. When she finished, it stood several inches out from her head in perfect symmetry all the way around.

Jozef sent a servant to the ballroom for a single gold-dipped black rose. Using his switchblade, he cut the stem off and tucked the rose into Shaun's hair, just above her ear. She touched her fingers to the rose, marveling at the unique beauty, then she used pins to secure it. She sprayed her hair into place and then turned away from the mirror.

Together they got ready for the party, signing to each other and laughing. It was the most relaxed Shaun had been in that house and she found herself wishing she was getting ready for an evening out with Jozef, rather than a big fancy engagement party.

Can you please zip me? Shaun signed, turning her back to Jozef, who was standing in only his suit pants and a belt. She found his bare feet unbearably sexy, especially when paired with his bare chest, which was truly a beautiful sight with its wealth of tattoos. Shaun held her breath as he stepped up to her, the heat of his body caressing her. He took the zipper of her dress and pulled it up from her butt to halfway up her back, his knuckles deliberately touching the skin of her back.

She tried to step away, but he took her shoulders and turned her until she was facing him. His eyes drank her in, from the top of her afro to the dip in her cleavage, all the way down the slinky floor length gold silk gown to her bare toes peeking out from the hem. When he lifted his eyes to hers, his gaze held fire and admiration. He was telling her she was beautiful; she didn't need to hear the words to know.

"Thank you," she said with a smile.

Jozef stepped away from Shaun and reached for his white button up shirt. His aunt had sent a tuxedo for him to wear, but Jozef had chosen one of his finer suits instead. He told Shaun that he would wear the tux if she wanted, but he hated feeling confined. Shaun replied that she didn't have an opinion. She didn't say out loud that it didn't matter what Jozef wore, he would be the sexiest man in the room. There was something magnetically appealing about his darkly intense demeaner. As if he hid a wealth of secrets and the only way he would give them up was if he was either fucking or killing.

Finally, they were ready.

Shaun added a hint of shiny lip gloss to her nude lips, otherwise she wore little makeup, allowing the shimmery golden dress to speak for itself. Leeza had given Shaun a pair of strappy satin sandals to match the dress. Shaun was grateful as the straps helped her feel more secure in the three-inch heels.

Jozef held her arm while she bent to slide each shoe on. He then bent down, kneeling at her feet, and buckled them for her. When he stood, he didn't move away, instead taking her shoulders in his hands and rubbing his thumbs over her skin. In her shoes, Shaun was nearly the same height as Jozef. They would make an imposing pair.

He continued to stare at her as the air heated around them, charged with their chemistry. Jozef was a tactile person, always touching her when he got the chance. At first, Shaun thought it was his way of controlling her, but she quickly realized it was his love language. He was always touching her, whether they were having sex or not. He didn't get anything out of it, except for basic human contact. He wanted to touch her and truly enjoyed it.

Shaun wished she felt more comfortable touching him back. Though her family was a loving one, they hadn't been demonstrative. They didn't often hug unless one of them had been absent for an extended period of time, and none of Shaun's previous boyfriends had been particularly touchy with her. Shaun hadn't realized she was missing anything until Jozef touched her, his magical fingers working to almost instantly relax her.

He turned away and Shaun thought they were going to leave to go to the ballroom, but he caught her arm and held her still. He pulled open the drawer to his desk and picked something up. As he turned back to Shaun, she caught a flash of something shiny. Curious, she watched as he opened his palm, showing her a delicate chain with a tiny heart.

She hadn't expected anything else from him, but if she had, she would have thought a family of the obvious wealth the Kobas had would give huge, shiny, opulent jewelry. In fact, Shaun was positive none of the women of the family would show up at the party less than fully decked out in their icing. Yet, this simple and delicate chain meant so much more to Shaun because she knew it had come from Jozef alone.

He took her shoulders in his hands and turned her until her back was to him, then he placed the tiny heart against the dip in her throat, linking the chain at the back of her neck. Shaun lifted a hand to touch the precious metal as Jozef kissed the back of her neck.

He stepped away from her and, as she turned, held a hand out to her. She slid her fingers into his palm and looked at him, her vulnerability shining bright in her eyes. She didn't think she was imagining the same look in his velvet blue eyes.

CHAPTER FORTY-ONE

Every head in the room turned and the orchestra fell silent as Jozef led Shaun into the ballroom, pausing in the doorway for the occupants to look their fill. Shaun clung tighter to Jozef's arm, while he squeezed her hand reassuringly. Being the object of such focused attention made her nervous and reminded her all over again of how different she was from these people.

Though Shaun had helped prepare the house for the party, she was still shocked by the transformation of the ballroom. It was dripping in glittering crystal, gold and black accents and the most expensive settings money could buy. Shaun stared at the tablecloths covering the buffet tables. If she wasn't mistaken, they were the exact same shade as her gown. She stared open-mouthed at Dasha, who was standing near the front of the crowd with her hand on Krystoff's arm. The woman had outdone herself. When Shaun caught Dasha's eye, the older woman lifted her champagne glass in salute. Shaun was truly impressed.

Dasha and Krystoff approached Jozef and Shaun, and in a moment of choreographed harmony, the matriarch and patriarch of the Koba crime family each took Shaun in their arms and kissed her cheeks. They were showing their assembled guests that they wholeheartedly accepted and endorsed Jozef's choice for wife. It was a fraught moment as the guests whispered and Leeza and Saskia approached to follow suit.

When it was Leeza's turn, Shaun was surprised to see the other woman's husband reach for her hand, then felt guilty for forgetting the man existed. He was a quiet non-entity in the family. He'd been introduced as an accountant, but Shaun had since learned he was actually *the* accountant for the entire organization; the same man who blew the whistle on Jozef's childhood friend.

He looked like every stereotype of a mafia accountant that Shaun might have imagined; short, or at least shorter than Shaun, balding, thick glasses with a slight paunch around his middle. Shaun suspected he might be pre-diabetic based on the slight shake to his hands as he touched her, a pale fatigue to his features and dry skin with some dark patches that shouldn't be there for his age. Shaun would talk to him about it later, at a more appropriate time, maybe suggest some treatments.

Leeza stepped up and hugged Shaun warmly, kissing her cheeks. "Welcome to our family."

"Thank you."

Shaun watched as Leeza and her husband walked away, his hand hovering over her waist but not touching her. It was odd, but Shaun couldn't detect even a hint of warmth in their marriage. She wondered how they got together in the first place. Leeza couldn't be more than 28 years old, while her husband was significantly older. They shared a five-year-old son, which made Shaun suspect they'd gotten together while she was still quite young.

Saskia hugged Shaun next. "Can't wait for you to join our shitshow of a family."

Shaun laughed and shook her head. Instead of leaving to mingle among the guests, as the others had done, Saskia glued herself to Shaun's side. She made it her personal responsibility to impart every piece of gossip she had on the assembled guests. Shaun laughed at Saskia's unabashedly disrespectful opinions.

"See that guy over there in that seriously out of date cravat?" Saskia pointed at a man, drawing the attention of several people surrounding them.

Shaun laughed and pushed Saskia's arm down.

"He's a prince, but he's living in exile now. He became embroiled in a political shitstorm in his home country and the parliament asked him to leave. That woman standing next to him is his number one whore. He leaves his wife at home and brings his bimbos out to these things."

Shaun tried to stifle her peals of laughter, but it was useless. Saskia was the only true friend she had in the room. The younger woman was an unrepentant gossip, and even though she shouldn't, Shaun ate it up with glee. Knowing the foibles of the super-rich people surrounding her made her feel more comfortable in their presence. She suspected Saskia knew it and that was why she was chattering nonstop in Shaun's ear while Jozef looked on with amusement.

After a few minutes, guests started to make their way over to congratulate the couple. Saskia maintained her position at Shaun's side, continuing to whisper her judgments in Shaun's ear. It was funny, but Shaun was getting the distinct impression that Saskia was trying to protect her. Shaun decided the younger woman acted just as much a guard dog as her older cousin.

"Jozef, I've been dying to see you again!"

Shaun turned in time to see Giselle from the club throw herself into Jozef's arms. Apparently her near death experience at Jozef's hand hadn't had much of an effect. The look of disgust on Jozef's face while he tried to disengage the heavily perfumed, scantily clad woman was enough to calm any jealousy Shaun might have felt. She knew the two had a past, but it was clear that Jozef felt nothing for Giselle now, except maybe annoyance.

Despite his obvious rejection, Giselle wrapped her arm around his and wedged herself between Shaun and Jozef. Shaun stifled a laugh at the blatant desperation of the other woman. Saskia was less diplomatic.

"Bitch... gross," she drawled, wrinkling her nose at Giselle. "Why don't you go hump something a little closer to your league."

Shaun choked on her laughter while Giselle looked like she was about to launch herself at them, claws out. Shaun decided to salvage the situation before they ruined Dasha's fancy party by brawling next to the champagne fountain.

"I need to have a private talk with Saskia," she said, her gaze caressing Jozef. "Will you get me a drink?"

Jozef dipped his head, his blue eyes sliding from Shaun to Saskia. He knew what she was up to. Shaun was worried he would try to stop them, but he simply watching as Shaun and Saskia slipped from the room together. Shaun looked around and caught sight of a storage closet.

"In here."

"Ohhh.... I'm intrigued," Saskia said with a laugh, following Shaun.

The 'closet' was more of a utility room, stretching so far back that Shaun wondered where it ended. It was filled with spare furniture in a wide variety of colours and materials. Clearly Dasha's party reject closet.

Saskia hopped up on a pile of chairs and crossed her legs, showing Shaun that she was wearing a pair of knee length tights beneath her tulle-heavy pink ball gown.

"What's up, doc?" Saskia asked, then burst into a fit of giggles.

Shaun raised an eyebrow in amusement. "Have you been waiting long with that one?"

"Pretty much since the moment you arrived."

Shaun smiled at the joke, then grew serious. "I need to know where you got that burner phone from."

Saskia's face straightened as well. "I told you, I can't say."

"I know you did, and I hate to ask. I know how much of a risk you took getting me the phone." Shaun paced the room, wondering how to get the information she needed without pushing Saskia into disclosing something she didn't want to. "Okay, let's try this another way. You don't have to tell me who gave you the phone, but can you tell me, is it someone who works here?"

Saskia chewed her lip, thinking about Shaun's question. She must have decided it wouldn't hurt to give Shaun what she was asking. "Yeah, I have a friend who works here, for my father. He'd be in really big trouble if it got out that he gave me a burner phone, so I won't say who he is."

"I understand," Shaun reassured her. "You don't need to say anything else."

Saskia tilted her head, her sharp gaze on Shaun's face. "Why are you asking me? Did something happen?"

Now it was Shaun's turn to decide how much to give the younger woman. She didn't want Saskia to be left in the dark when she'd gone out on a limb to help Shaun, but she also didn't want to pull Saskia further into her mess. Finally, Shaun decided that Saskia should be warned.

"Jozef knows about the phone." When Saskia gasped and looked alarmed, Shaun rushed to reassure the young woman. "He's not angry, but he did talk to your father and found out the phone was a plant. Krystoff was trying to trap me with that phone call I made."

Saskia jumped down from the chairs and grabbed Shaun by the arms. "Did you say anything incriminating during the call?"

The line could've been part of a bad detective film, yet it was directed at Shaun in earnest because both women knew if Shaun had taken a misstep in her recorded conversation she would be in big trouble. They likely wouldn't be chatting cozily in a closet together.

Shaun shook her head.

"Thank god." Saskia released Shaun. She frowned and paced up and down the storage room, her arms crossed over her chest. "It doesn't make any sense though. The guy who gave me the phone wouldn't betray me." Her eyes lifted guiltily to Shaun. She'd said more than she intended to. "He... he cares about me."

Shaun's understanding of the situation grew. Saskia had gotten the phone from an admirer, a man she trusted, but Shaun wasn't so sure the young woman should trust a man under her father's employ. She didn't want to scare Saskia, but she wanted her to be careful around the person willing to give her a burner phone. A man who may or may not have manipulated her.

"Saskia..." She wasn't sure what she wanted to say, and finally settled on, "if you ever need anything, please come to me. I'll do whatever I can to help you."

It was a weak promise, considering she held no real power within the household, but she was intelligent and resourceful. If Saskia needed her, she'd find a way to protect her.

"Should we go back to the party?" Shaun asked, reaching for the door. "Considering I'm the guest of honour, I should probably attend for at least a few minutes."

They were halfway out of the closet when Shaun found herself pushed back inside.

"Hey!" She twisted around to look at her attacker and

found herself face-to-face with Jozef. He winked at his cousin and slammed the door in her face.

When he turned back to Shaun, his gaze was distinctly predatory.

"What?" she asked, backing away from him.

You left me alone with that soul-sucking witch. His eyes were gleaming with lust and mischief as he stalked her into the far reaches of the closet.

"I figured you'd be okay in the claws... I mean hands of an old girlfriend," Shaun said casually, feeling anything but casual. Sexual tension filled the closet, sizzling and snapping around them like a live wire, heating the air with their energy.

She continued to back away from him, into the shadowy depths of the closet until her back hit something hard. Glancing over her shoulder she realized she was pressed up against a stack of tables. Jozef gave her a another charged look as he reached for her, dragging her into his embrace, his intentions clear.

"Don't rip my new dress," she told him breathlessly, right before his lips met hers.

His kiss was seductive, immediately pulling her into the wild vortex of sizzling sensuality that constantly surrounded them. She never knew a man could taste so good, like heat, smoke and the forbidden. Jozef was every female fantasy come to life, impossible to resist for a mere mortal. Shaun didn't even try. She wrapped her arms around his neck as he dragged her more fully into his embrace.

They kissed as if time didn't matter, as if the engagement party of the season wasn't on the other side of the door, the orchestra now in full swing. Shaun realized the orchestra was playing a rendition of Don't Fear the Reaper by Blue Oyster Cult. The wild, heart pumping music entwined them as they clung to each other, kissing as though they would never get another chance. Shaun's heart beat with the music, with the sweep of Jozef's hands, with the beat of his heart against her chest.

She gasped into his mouth as he lifted her off the ground and set her ass on the table behind her. It rocked under her, but she trusted him to keep her safe. His skilled hands swept her body, caressing, touching, memorizing. He bunched her skirt in his fist and yanked it up past her hips. Shaun spread her legs and wrapped them around his waist, dragging him closer.

Jozef reached between them, gripped the soaking crotch of her delicate lace panties and tore. She moaned into his mouth, the sting of the tearing fabric on her thighs driving her higher into exhilarating passion. He sank his fingers into her needy pussy, stroking her until she was so turned on she was riding his hand, thrusting her hips against him.

"Please, Jozef, please...." Whimpers spilled from her lips, igniting the simmering blaze of his answering desire.

He freed his cock from the confines of his pants, pressed the crown against her and thrust home. Their eyes met, soul-searing blue clashing with golden brown in a moment of total unity. Shaun had never felt such intense attraction before, and it was unlikely she would find it again with anyone else. They were a perfectly imperfect match.

He hugged her to him and fucked her, at first slow and gentle, but soon his thrusts became ferocious. His hips slammed into the cradle of her thighs, bruising the tender flesh, the tiny bite of pain that sent her higher and higher. She tried to bite back the screams that threatened to erupt, but his wild lovemaking took her over completely.

Shaun screamed as her orgasm hit with the force of a lightning bolt, slamming through her body and sending her into the stratosphere. He continued fucking his way into her as she tightened around him, strangling his cock with the force of her orgasm. He grunted against her throat and bit her neck, taking the delicate necklace into his mouth for a moment. She thought he might break it, but he used it to tantalize her, dragging the metal along her skin as he licked and nipped.

As she floated down, surrounded by a cloud of utter bliss, Jozef reached his own peak. He thrust his tongue into her ear as he came inside her, his cock growing unbearably large. The sensation of his tongue in her ear and his cock slamming against her cervix sent Shaun spiralling over the edge once more.

As they both drifted back to the present, Jozef pressed his forehead to hers, their breaths mingling in unison. Finally, he pulled out of her. Instead of stepping away, he ran his fingers through her folds, gathering their combined fluids. He brought his fingers up to her mouth, the scent of them reaching out to her in an erotic embrace.

He held still, waiting for her. She leaned forward and sucked his fingers into her mouth, swirling her tongue around the roughened digits. He growled, the sound sending pleasurable shivers down her spine. Then he took it one step further and leaned in to take her lips, thrusting his tongue past his own fingers into the depths of her mouth, then finishing by sucking his own finger.

Shaun was breathless and brainless by the time he stepped away from her. She was so fuck-drunk, the mansion could've caught on fire and she wouldn't have noticed.

"I'm a mess," she said, with a breathless laugh. She was giddy from the endorphins rushing through her.

You will not clean up; you will wear our love proudly on your thighs.

She stared at him in shock. Not because he was asking her to walk around a room full of people with his cum dripping down her legs. He'd used the wrong sign for love. Instead of tapping his fist against his palm as if to say something was a symbol of love, such as their combined fluids, he used the crossed fists. Romantic love. Unless her sign language lessons were completely failing her, his words roughly translated to, "I love you and want the world to know."

He helped her off the table, lowered her skirt and took her hand, leading her from the closet.

CHAPTER FORTY-TWO

"There you two are," Dasha scolded, though her tone was jovial. The party was turning into a spectacular success and it was clear she couldn't be happier. "Come meet the Croziers, they flew in from New York just to be here for your special day."

Shaun and Jozef linked fingers, a united force, as they were paraded around the ballroom and introduced to a dizzying number of people. Shaun accepted a champagne glass somewhere along the way, and another as her empty one was replaced the instant the last drop slipped down her throat. She didn't drink often and was beginning to feel the effects of the champagne. She became more relaxed, her responses to whatever inquiries came her way far more candid than they would have been if she'd been sober.

For a shining moment, Shaun felt as if she belonged to this glamorous and wealthy family. She was one of them. She was able to talk about her career with their guests as if it were simply on hold while she and Jozef figured out their future together. No longer the kidnap victim, she could pretend that she and the man by her side were deeply in love.

Dasha explained to Princess Amelia of Andorra that Jozef and Shaun had met in a hospital in Ukraine while she was treating him for concussion. Shaun laughed in all the right places as doctor-patient jokes became the norm for the evening. She smiled and faked her way through everything, pretending she was nothing more than a soon-to-be happy bride, while the slippery sensation between her thighs reminded her of her closet tryst.

It wasn't until she looked at her fiancé that she saw the truth in the shutter that had dropped over his face as she was paraded in front of dozens of crime families. It didn't take Shaun long to realize that she was being shown off to all these people, not as a way to introduce her to the world, but to tie her more firmly to the family. Being known by everyone who associated with the Kobas would make escape that much more impossible. She was well and truly caught in their trap. Her introduction also had the added bonus of ensuring she looked like a happy, healthy and very willing soon-to-be bride if anyone recognized her as the missing doctor from Luhansk.

Desperation rose up inside her, threatening to choke her. She felt suddenly hot and a little sick. She looked around for Jozef, finding him deep in conversation with Havel. He frowned as he caught sight of her expression and immediately made his way to her side, sliding his arm along her back. His warmth helped to steady her, but she still didn't feel well.

By the time a third glass of champagne was pressed into her hand, Shaun was done. She didn't want to be there anymore. She looked up at Jozef, who was studying her with concern. "I... I..." She didn't know what she wanted. She took a long sip of her drink to clear the cobwebs. "I think I'm done pretending."

Jozef didn't ask her what she meant by 'pretending', he simply nodded. *Do you want to leave?*

"Yes."

He took her arm and led her deeper into the room. At first Shaun held back, unsure why he'd be taking her further into the throng of guests when he was supposed to be getting her out of there. Then she realized he was guiding her toward the doors, which were opened into the rose garden. Relief rushed through her as the fresh air hit her heated skin.

Giselle stepped in front of them before they could reach the door, cutting them off. Shaun was so annoyed at the other woman, that she stepped in front of Jozef to confront her. This was one situation where verbal communication was needed. Bitch just wasn't smart enough to understand Jozef's less than subtle fuck off when he threw her into a wall at the club.

"Leave," Shaun said coldly.

She was standing in front of Jozef so she couldn't see his expression, but assumed it was something that would back her up.

"Do you have any idea who I am?" Giselle hissed.

"No," Shaun admitted. "Do you have any idea who I am?"

Giselle looked shocked, clearly having assumed Shaun was a nobody. Which of course she was when it came to the circles these people inhabited. Thank god for that. So far at the hands of their party guests she'd experienced a boatload of fake congratulations, some jealousy and a whole lot of speculation. She was pretty sure she didn't want to be friends with a single one of them.

"And who exactly are you?" Giselle eyed Shaun as if she might've missed something in her previous assessments. Maybe Shaun was the American heiress to a perfume fortune? Or maybe she was the illegitimate love child of a king.

"I am Dr. Shaun Patterson of Montréal, Canada," Shaun told the other woman, her voice strong as she defended her right to be there. "Six weeks ago, I reached into an open chest cavity and pumped a heart with my bare hands, the blood of my patient slipping through my fingers. I saved that man's life. What have you done lately?"

Giselle stared with her mouth open. She suddenly looked less glamorous in her low-cut black evening gown, her neck and wrists dripping in Cartier diamonds. Her eyes moved over Shaun's shoulder; Shaun assumed to meet Jozef's gaze. Whatever Giselle saw there crushed any last hope the tenacious woman might have had.

Shaun was suddenly seized by a painful cramp in her stomach. It was everything she could do to remain upright and not ruin her grand moment. Eyes bright with tears, Giselle drifted away without saying another word.

Shaun moaned and doubled over, clutching her middle.

"Jozef!" she gasped.

Something was wrong with her, but she didn't know what. She'd barely eaten that day, only snacks from a tray in her room sent up from the kitchen. Multiple people, including Jozef, Dasha and Saskia had shared the food she'd eaten and no one else looked sick.

Jozef's arms wrapped around her from behind as her knees buckled. Together they stumbled through the door onto the garden patio. Shaun collapsed to the ground, the scent of roses rising up as they entered the garden area. She blinked as Jozef's face floated in front of her face. She reached up to touch him, but missed, her arm falling uselessly to her side.

She let out a soft scream as her stomach cramped again. She tried to roll onto her side, her arms wrapped around herself, but Jozef held her in place, his frantic face swimming in and out of her vision.

Suddenly the orchestra seemed louder. They were playing an instrumental version of 'The Sound of Silence'. Tears gathered in her eyes as she realized how perfect the song was. With Jozef she was surrounded by silence, and like the lyrics of the song, the silence had become an old friend. Without the constant chatter of voices, she could hear the beat of her own heart, see the expressions on her lover's face as they sat together speaking their silence.

Shaun knew she was slipping away. Her thoughts were fragmented, and her body was no longer obeying her commands. Her limbs refused to move as dizziness engulfed her, each wave lasting longer than the one before until she knew that soon she would close her eyes and allow the darkness to take hold.

She wanted to call to Jozef, but she didn't want to use her voice. It wasn't how they communicated. He preferred when she used sign language and she preferred it too. In one last burst of energy she lifted her arms and crossed her fists over her chest. Vomit rushed up her throat and she turned her head to throw up, champagne searing her throat as she emptied her stomach.

Her lips felt foamy and she knew something terrible was happening. She shouldn't be foaming at the mouth. She tried to force her doctor's brain to rapidly diagnose, but the darkness was taking her.

She heard a muffled shout and thought it was her own voice calling out for help. Someone dropped to her other side and she felt hands on her face. Voices rose up around her, but she couldn't concentrate. She wished she could help the frantic voices, but she had to go.

As the shadows took her, she thought she heard a growl so ferocious it shook the windows next to them. Then she was gone, her world fading to nothing.

CHAPTER FORTY-THREE

Jozef's arms wrapped around Shaun as she fell to the patio deck, her body going limp against him. He kneeled with her, setting her gently on the ground. He couldn't tell what was wrong and her eyes were closed so he couldn't ask her. He'd never been so frustrated at his lack of voice before. Shaun moaned and a trickle of white foam spilled from her lips. An unfamiliar sensation hit Jozef at the sight. Burning fear.

He glanced frantically around and, spotting Havel striding toward them, quickly signed, *help her.*

Havel dropped to his knees on Shaun's other side, his concerned gaze running down her prone body. He lifted her wrist and felt for a pulse. Havel was the only man on his team with more than basic First Aid knowledge. He'd been forced to patch up their men on several occasions.

"Got it. Steady but slowing down." He touched her face, leaning in for a closer look. "Poison, I think."

Their eyes met in a moment of mutual understanding. It made sense: the sudden attack, the foaming around her lips, her garbled speech as she fell. Jozef looked around and seeing

Shaun's champagne glass, now on its side, the contents spilling out, grabbed a napkin and soaked up what he could. He shoved the napkin into his suit jacket pocket. Even while his frantic brain was completely focused on his ailing fiancé, he knew that identifying the poison would be imperative to her survival.

Call an ambulance, Jozef told Havel.

To his credit, Havel didn't hesitate, though he knew better than any of them the consequences of calling for help. Havel nodded and pulled his phone out of his pocket. He was about to dial 112 for emergency services, when a hand came down on top of his. Havel reacted instantly by lifting his fist to hit the person touching him but lowered it once he recognized Dasha's stony features.

"No," she said firmly, turning her gaze on Jozef who knelt at her feet. Dasha spoke quickly. "If we call an ambulance the police will come too. Shaun is too recognizable. They'll know her as the doctor who went missing from Luhansk."

Krystoff walked up behind his wife and quickly took stock of the situation. He took her by the shoulders and gently pulled her back. "Dasha, love, she could die without immediate intervention."

She looked startled as she stared up at her husband. "I know, but we never call the authorities, no matter what."

Krystoff looked down at Shaun who was beginning to convulse, Jozef's frantic hands on her face. "This is different." He turned his gaze to Havel. "Make the call, tell them to drive through the garden entrance. We'll meet them at the gate."

Guests were starting to look curiously through the patio doors. Seeing what was going on outside, Leeza grabbed the nearest servant and snapped at them to close the patio doors and draw the curtains. She told another to ask the orchestra to play a livelier tune. Her concerned gaze met Jozef's as the doors were closed and the curtains drawn, leaving Jozef, Dasha, Krystoff and Havel outside with Shaun.

Jozef touched her face, but she'd passed out. Her cheeks felt like fire and her skin was ashen beneath the rich brown tone. He could feel her life slipping away beneath his fingertips and he was helpless to stop it. Their entire relationship flashed in front of him: the moment he took her, put a gun to her head, the feeling he had when she communicated in his language, the incredible mind-blowing sex, getting to know the kindness and compassion in her heart.

He could not allow her to die. She was a true innocent, too delicate for their world, but too entwined in their lives to set free. And then it hit him. Someone in his own organization had poisoned her. It was the only explanation. She was a threat to everything they stood for. If she somehow managed to escape and give her story to the authorities, she could bring down a multi-generational crime family like they were a house of cards.

Jozef stared at his aunt, anger building in his heart as she dropped next to him and touched his arm. He thought it was for comfort, but then she spoke. "There will be only one end to this evening, Jozef. She will be recognized at the hospital; the authorities will be called in and an arrest will have to be made." When Jozef didn't react, she dug her nails into his sleeve. "Don't you see, they'll have to take someone into custody."

Jozef shook her hand away with a growl but didn't lift his gaze from Shaun's face. If he did, she might die while he wasn't looking and he wanted to be with her to the end, if the end was coming. He didn't care what happened when the ambulance came, didn't care about the authorities. If there was any chance of saving Shaun then he was taking it, no matter the consequences.

Later, he would do some digging. Find out who had

poisoned his beautiful fiancé. If someone on the inside had betrayed him, then he would take down the house of cards himself one card at a time until their entire legacy was dismantled.

The ambulance arrived less than five minutes later, waved onto the garden terrace by Krystoff himself, who'd discarded his jacket and opened the gates. Jozef refused to move back for the paramedics until Havel gripped his shoulder and pulled him away. He understood on one level that the two medics needed to stabilize Shaun so she could be moved, but he had this terrible feeling if he stopped touching her, took his eyes off her, she would disappear.

As he moved back, his hand landed on something. He picked it up and looked down. It was the delicate necklace he'd given Shaun, the delicate chain likely broken in the panic. Jozef shoved it in his pocket.

A few minutes later Shaun was loaded onto the ambulance, Jozef climbing in behind her. Havel followed Jozef and when the paramedic told him he'd have to leave, Havel set him straight. "I go where he goes and he's not leaving her side." When it looked like the man would continue to argue, Havel interrupted. "Besides, he needs an interpreter."

Not wanting to waste another second of the critically ill woman's life, the medic simply nodded and slammed the door shut between the two men.

Without looking up, Jozef signed, *thank you*.

Havel squeezed his shoulder and nodded.

The two men tried to stay out of the way as much as they could but Jozef refused to stop touching Shaun. He held her limp, clammy hand during the entire harrowing trip to the hospital. The paramedic ignored them, focusing entirely on Shaun while the other drove. Jozef's heart pounded in fear as the man's hands flew over Shaun.

When they arrived, Havel jumped out of the ambulance

and reached for the stretcher. The paramedics looked concerned and tried to argue about protocol, but it was hard to argue with a man of Havel's size and unmistakable air of deadliness. As Shaun was rushed through the bright front doors of the hospital, more personnel tried to stop the two gangsters from following Shaun's stretcher down the hall. Jozef was about two seconds from shooting the next person who tried to limit his access to his fiancé, but Havel hung back, smoothing over the ruffled feathers they left in their wake.

Jozef could do nothing but watch helplessly as Shaun was transferred onto another bed and surrounded by doctors and nurses. The screaming in his head got so loud he barely noticed when a young nurse put her hand on his arm.

"Are you a member of her family?"

Jozef looked down sharply, about to shove her away, then looked at her face. The seriousness, the compassion, the kindness reflected there reminded him so much of Shaun he didn't have the heart to reject the woman. He nodded, his gaze fixating on the bed once more.

"Can you tell us what happened?" she asked kindly.

Jozef shook his head and, without taking his eyes off Shaun, signed that he was nonverbal. The likelihood of this nurse understanding the language was slim, but she would recognize the form of communication and hopefully realize that they wouldn't be having any in depth conversations without an interpreter.

"Oh, you're nonverbal?" she asked.

He jerked his head in a nod but was saved from having to make further efforts at communication when Havel finally made his way into the room. Clearly, he'd run into his share of obstructions, because the first thing out of his mouth when he arrived was, "I'm family." When the nurse looked skeptical, he added, "Her brother."

If Jozef hadn't been so terrified for Shaun, he might have laughed. Havel was a big, ugly, broad, bald-headed Caucasian gangster while Shaun was a beautiful, delicate-featured black woman. They were so far from siblings even adoption was a leap.

"Uhh... and he is?" She gestured to Jozef.

"Her husband," Havel grunted, standing next to Jozef with his bulging arms crossed over his chest.

"Can you tell me what happened? The more information we have, the better able we'll be to treat her."

"Poison," Havel said steadily, his disturbed gaze sweeping Shaun's bed.

The nurse looked alarmed, her gaze swinging to Jozef for confirmation.

Jozef nodded his agreement and reached into his pocket for the napkin. *She was fine one minute, then after drinking some of her champagne she collapsed.*

Havel interpreted what Jozef was saying to the nurse. "He says she was fine and then she had a drink and collapsed. When I arrived, she was already down, spitting up and convulsing." He nodded his head to the napkin Jozef was holding. "He wiped up the leftover champagne with the napkin and brought it in case you need to identify the poison."

The nurse rushed to the attending physician, speaking to him in rapid sentences. He nodded and replied, which sent her rushing back to their side. She pulled gloves from her pocket, put them on and reached for the napkin. "I'll get this to the lab right away."

As she left, Havel turned to Jozef, his back to the room so no one could see his lips as he spoke. "Who would poison her? There were dozens of people there, but they don't know her well enough to want her dead." He thought about it for a few seconds, then asked, "Giselle?"

Jozef shook his head. Eyes still on the glimpses he could get of Shaun as the hospital staff moved around her bed. *Not her style.*

"Then who?"

Jozef finally shifted his gaze to his second-in-command, but he didn't speak.

Havel nodded his understanding. The only people who might gain from Shaun's death all lived under the Koba roof. There was an enemy in their home. Havel placed his hand on Jozef's shoulder and squeezed. "I'll go hunting. You worry about your girl."

Jozef hoped Havel could read the gratitude on his face. He didn't doubt Havel for a second, and hearing the other man pledge his loyalty once more was exactly what he needed. He was too terrified for Shaun to think straight. He needed his men now more than ever. Needed them to have his back while he took care of his woman.

It was a strange sensation. For the first time in his life he was putting someone else first, someone other than his aunt, uncle and cousins. His entire life had been devoted to the Koba clan, yet in the course of a few short weeks, Shaun had come to mean everything to him. If his family had tried to have Shaun killed, he would destroy them.

A terrible beeping sound filled the room as Shaun stopped breathing and her heart rate began to plummet. Jozef and Havel were forcibly shoved from the room as Shaun was being intubated. The last glimpse Jozef was able to get was of her face, ashen and angelic in repose before the doors were slammed shut.

CHAPTER FORTY-FOUR

Jozef did not get to see Shaun again before he was arrested for murder and kidnapping. True to Dasha's words, the police arrived shortly after a relieved doctor came into the waiting room to reassure Jozef and Havel that Shaun had pulled through and was currently in a medically induced coma while they assessed her condition and researched the poison.

Jozef's relief was such that he barely noticed as several police officers stormed through the hospital corridors, clearing them as they made their way to Jozef's waiting room. Jozef received a message from Halil, who was watching the hospital for activity, warning them that the police were on their way.

Jozef jerked his head toward the door, indicating Havel should leave. *I need you on the outside acting as my eyes and ears.*

Havel shook his head, but backed toward the door, knowing Jozef was right. "I can't leave you, brother."

Jozef gave him a grim look. *It's my time to take this fall. We both knew this was coming the second you called emergency services.*

"I'm sorry." Havel's eyes were troubled. He hated that Jozef was about to take the fall for the rescue of his uncle.

Go, they'll be here soon.

Havel nodded and opened the door, glancing down the deserted hallway. Still he hesitated, then his expression grew angry and he pointed at Jozef, stabbing at the air. "I'll get you out," he growled. "No matter what happens, I'm coming for you."

Jozef wasn't given an opportunity to answer. Havel took off down a side hall, heading toward an exit door. He wasn't the one the cops were looking for so he shouldn't have any problems leaving the hospital. He was a known associate of Jozef's, but Jozef didn't think the police would grab Havel. They were here for him and he was going to make it easy for them. He would do it for Shaun. He wouldn't shoot up the hospital that was dedicating itself to saving her life.

Jozef sank to his knees on the cool ugly tiles of the hospital floor and reached into his pocket, pulling out the heart necklace. He held it in between his laced fingers as he placed his hands behind his head. He had to wait about two minutes before the door was flung open and police officers filled the room, shouting at him to get down and stay down. He was roughly shoved to the floor and handcuffed while an officer read him his rights.

To be continued...

I hope you loved Sin of Silence. I'm working hard on the next book! Grab your preorder for the next book in Shaun's and Jozef's story, A Silent Reckoning (Sinner's Empire Book 2). Available February 27th, 2021.

NIKITA'S NEWSLETTER!

Sign up today for Nikita's newsletter and receive a FREE copy of Nikita's bestselling dark romance novella, Stalked!

www.authornikitaslater.com

EXCERPT: SCARRED QUEEN

Ignacio Hernandez had never before brought a woman to a meet. Then, they'd never met at a club before. The entire scene was unprecedented. Reyes didn't do unprecedented, but he was willing to make an exception because he was curious. He could sever the Miami connection if he had to. It would cause some shockwaves, but it wasn't out of the question. Ignacio was beginning to annoy him anyway. His poor decisions were beginning to affect the Bolivian. Such as bringing a woman like *her* to a meet with a man like *him*. Something that was meant to show off Ignacio's power and wealth would become a big mistake.

His gaze flickered over the woman, calmly drinking her champagne and orange juice as though she weren't sitting at a table with four of the most dangerous men on the continental East coast. Two kingpins and their right hands. Only Reyes didn't think she was as calm as she appeared. Her wrist trembled slightly, giving her away. She had enough presence to make sure that tiny shake ceased by the time it got to her slim fingers where they clenched the crystal of her glass. It wasn't the fingers or her ability to remain coolly poised while the men around her talked business that captured his curiosity. It was the mark on the back of her delicate hand, permanent slash lines, viciously marring her porcelain skin.

Anger burned deep in his gut, surprising him. Reyes rarely felt anything. Ever. Certainly not for a woman. This was how he made effective decisions. How he moved trade across borders with ease and cool logic. Emotion had been removed from him. First by a ruthless father, then by a vicious military stint in his home country and finally by an unrelenting, merciless prison sentence that had systematically broken him before he had, in turn, broken down the prison itself and owned it from the inside out. By the time he was released it was into a world of his own making; a world shaped by him on the inside and ruled by him on the outside.

Yet the sight of this cool, blond beauty, so broken yet utterly resilient was doing something to him, forcing him to *feel*. He shifted in his seat, sliding his arm across the back of the leather, his eyes never leaving her while he listened to the other men speak. Negotiate terms. He didn't need to add his voice. Alejandro, his right hand, knew the terms. Knew not to fuck up while in pursuit of new deals for the boss.

Reyes wanted her. The electrifying anger he felt when his eyes caressed that mark assured him he would take the woman and make her his. Not because it infuriated him that she had been abused. No, he was not a good enough man to care about that. He was under no illusions he would treat her any better than Ignacio. Hell, he'd probably treat her much worse. Because Ignacio undoubtedly set her up like a trophy in his great mausoleum of a house and then ignored the unapproachable beauty.

Reyes had no intention of ignoring her. He was going to take her and fuck every inch of her, just the way he wanted. Hard, brutal, mean. Exactly how he was. Exactly how this world had shaped him. Because he could. She was about to become spoils of war.

No, he wasn't angry about the mark on her hand at all. He was pissed that the mark was twisted into the shape of an "H" and not an "R." He wanted her to belong to him, to the King. When he got his hands on the woman, that would be the first thing he changed.

Finally, after nearly an hour of sitting in the booth together, his eyes rarely leaving her face, she lifted hers to meet his uncompromising gaze. And for the first time in his life, he felt his heart stop in his chest. He was unprepared for the impact. Her eyes – one startling green and the other amber brown – were vivid, stunning and unrelenting. Though her expression didn't flicker once from the blank mask of icy beauty, he saw the burning disdain, the heated fury buried deep within those fiery orbs for the men that surrounded her. She despised all of them.

His lip lifted in an answering sneer. She refused to drop her eyes from his challenge, despite her husband sitting at the same table. He wanted nothing more, in that moment, than to take this scarred Queen from her throne and tame her. He vowed, then and there, that he would eventually have her.

Now available for purchase!

"How long are you going to keep me here?" Allie finally decided to brave the questions she knew needed asking.

His eyes sharpened on her face. "You're here to stay, Allison," he said implacably using her full name, which he did when he wanted her to know he meant what he was saying.

She shook her head. "No, I'm not."

"This isn't a negotiation." His voice was hard, his eyes harder.

Anger and a dose of panic rose up in Allie. She knew when Jay decided something he was immovable. "Jay, I can't stay here with you. I'm still married to Derrick. I still have a job. I have to go home. I can see exactly what you've done. You've built this beautiful home and filled it with things that you know I love. But its too late for us, Jay. Even a beautiful prison is still a prison. You can't just keep me here forever!"

Something frightening flared in Jay's eyes, stopping the flow of Allie's words. He stepped toward her. Allie stepped back. He stalked toward her until only inches separated them. She felt the electric attraction jump between them, stronger than ever, and gasped. He didn't touch her, yet every part of her felt alive from his nearness. It had always been there, the thing that lay between them, but Jay had suppressed it before, sending her away. He was doing nothing to hold himself back from her now. Her head spun from the knowledge that he was done hiding his attraction.

"You've always belonged to me, Allison," his quiet voice sounded guttural with need. "I should have taken you when you were eighteen, but I didn't. For better or worse, I sent you away instead."

She nodded mutely, eyes wide on his face.

"I let you go once."

Her lips parted and her breath escaped in a shudder.

"It'll never happen again."

Allie whimpered, half in fear and half in arousal, as he pinned her with his possessive grey eyes. He looked as though he wanted to reach for her, but was ruthlessly holding himself back so he wouldn't hurt her. His long fingers curled into fists and his cruel lips compressed into a line. Allie shivered as he stepped away from her. Some of the tension diffused.

"Get some rest," he said.

He turned and left the room, locking the door behind him.

Keep reading. Download this title now!

ALSO BY NIKITA SLATER

If you enjoyed this book, check out some other works by #1 International Bestselling Author, Nikita Slater. More titles are always in progress, so check back often to see what's new!

SINNER'S EMPIRE

Book 1 - Sin of Silence - Preorder

Book 2 - A Silent Reckoning - Coming Soon!

Book 3 - Goodnight, Sinners - Coming Soon!

THE QUEENS SERIES

Book One – Scarred Queen

Book Two - Queen's Move

Book Three - Born a Queen

Book Four - The Red Queen (Coming 2021)

Alejandro's Prey (a novella)

The Queens 4 Book Box Set

FIRE & VICE SERIES

Book One – Prisoner of Fortune

Book Two – Fight or Flight

Book Three – King's Command

Book Four – Savage Vendetta

Savage Boss (a novella)

Book Five – Fear in Her Eyes

Book Six – Bound by Blood

Book Seven – In His Sights

Book Eight - Burning Beauty

Book Nine - Chasing Ecstasy (Coming soon!)

Fire & Vice 6 Book Box Set

THE DRIVEN HEARTS SERIES

Book One - Driven by Desire

Book Two - Thieving Hearts

Book Three - Capturing Victory

Novella - The Princess and Her Mercenary

Driven Hearts 4 Book Box Set

THE SANCTUARY SERIES

Book One - Sanctuary's Warlord

Book Two - Sanctuary on Fire

Book Three - The Last Sanctuary

Book Four - The Road to Wolfe

Book Five - Skye's Sanctuary (Coming soon!)

The Sanctuary Series 3 Book Box Set

LOVING THE BAD BOY SERIES

Loving Vincent

Loving Jared

Loving Rico (Coming Soon!)

STANDALONE BOOKS

The Assassin's Wife

Because You're Mine

Mine to Keep (a novella)

Luna & Andres

Kiss of the Cartel

Stalked

AFTER DARK

In collaboration with Jasmin Quinn

Collared: A Dark Captive Romance

Safeword: A Dark Romance

Chained: A Mafia Marriage Romance

Good Girl: A Captive BDSM Romance

Hostile Takeover: An Enemies to Lovers Romance

The After Dark Box Set

Visit **nikitaslater.com** for more information

and the latest updates!

Nikita Slater is the International Bestselling dark romance author of the Fire & Vice series, Angels & Assassins series, The Queens series and several standalone novels. Her favourite genre is mafia romance, the bloodier the better, though she loves to write about every subject under the sun. She lives on the beautiful Canadian prairies with her son and crazy awesome dog. She has an unholy affinity for books (especially erotic romance), wine, pets and anything choco-late. Despite some of the darker themes in her books (which are pure fun and fantasy), Nikita is a staunch feminist and advocate of equal rights for all races, genders and non-gender specific persons. When she isn't writing, dreaming about writing or talking about writing, she helps others discover a love of reading and writing through literacy and social work.